RAZORED SADDLES

RAZORED SADDLES

— Edited By —

Joe R. Lansdale and Pat LoBrutto

Robert R. McCammon
Joe R. Lansdale
Al Sarrantonio
Richard Laymon
Scott Cupp
Neal Barrett, Jr.
Ardath Mayhar
Chet Williamson

F. Paul Wilson
David J. Schow
Howard Waldrop
Lewis Shiner
Richard Christian Matheson
Gary Raisor
Lenore Carroll
Melissa Mia Hall
Robert Petitt

— Illustrated by —

Rick Araluce

DARK HARVEST
Arlington Hts., Illinois · 1989

— TABLE OF CONTENTS —

The Publishers would like to express their gratitude to the following people. Thank you: Pat LoBrutto, Kathy Jo Camacho, Stan and Phyllis Mikol, Dawn Austin, Wayne Sommers, Luis Trevino, Dr. Stan Gurnick PhD, Bertha Curl, Kurt Scharrer, Gary Front, Linda Solar, Ken Morris, Raymond, Teresa and Mark Stadalsky, Tom Pas, Tony Hodes, Lynda and Ken Fotos, and Ann Cameron Williams.

And, for all that extra help, special thanks go to Joe R. Lansdale and Rick Araluce.

INTRODUCTION

The Cowpunk Anthology

This is a book of offbeat stories with a Western theme. In some cases, it might be fairer to say that the writers started with a Western element and let the story run from there, and the faster it ran, the more the Western element was left behind.

That's okay.

Western was meant as a starting point, and not necessarily anything more. If something new and unique could be done with a Western theme, and still obviously be Western in nature, then, yippie ki yea. And if it served merely as a catalyst and mutated, into something else, well, that was all right too.

Some stories are serious, some powerful, some light and frothy, some a mixture of many things, but all are fun and audacious.

We your erstwhile editors, jokingly refer to this book as The Cowpunk anthology. It's our chance to breathe life into a genre (the Western) that has suffered much complacency over the years. This is not to say we're against the traditional. We love it. There is much good to be said for it, but so many writers confuse traditional with familiar. The same is true of other genres. For that reason, we thought it might be fun, and even impish (doesn't that word sound both naughty and petite?) to stir things up a bit, and to do this, why not pick on one of our favorite genres, the Western. Give writers of different persuasions, horror, s.f., literary, etc., a chance to try something different. In other words, let them do as they willed with the Western. Let them feel no boundaries beyond the use of, or the abuse of, or the mutation of, the American Myth of the West.

And we didn't leave it to "outsiders" alone. We also invited Western writers in. Lenore Carroll comes immediately to mind.

But, the term Cowpunk is a joke, nothing more. It is not the beginning of a movement. No secret handshakes or code rings here. It is as much a playful poke at such "movements" as Cyberpunk and Splatterpunk as it is anything.

I do however think there is a broader, unnamed movement in the air, and it's one that combines genres, both those commonly considered, and the genres of the literary and the mainstream—yes, they are genres too. So if we're part of any movement, it's one that wants to see more unique stories. Stories that do not feel bound and gagged to any tradition, and the best way to do this is to assault a tradition. Tomorrow we may feel better and take a Louis Lamour book to lunch.

Let me say this about movements. Much has been written about Cyberpunk and Splatterpunk, and what have you, and the response has been that there is nothing new under the sun.

True.

Also stupid.

There is nothing new in the sense that human emotions and needs are basically the same, and therefore will surface repeatedly in fiction. Certain techniques that many writers feel are new, or they discovered, have been used many times in the past, and their lack of awareness concerning this merely shows how limited their reading is.

The soft approach has been done, the quiet approach has been done, the hard approach has been done, and so has the graphic. But any writer who thinks nothing new *can* be done should quit.

About to get opinionated here. Got to. If we don't, then we're shuffling our feet. If we do, then it's "who the fuck are these guys?" So there's no way we can win, and we won't try. All we can say in our defense is that what we're about to say needs to be said, and that we as much as anyone need to listen. Let he who is without sin cast the first stone. And though we are not without sin, we're going to pick up some rocks and throw them anyway. We're going to throw them mostly at writers, and a few at readers, and in a left handed way at editors, and of course, a rock or two at publishers and ourselves.

What's new about anything is the ability to find that individual voice inside you and transmit it to paper. A writer starts off a little like a ventriloquist, talking through the styles of others, and finally those styles blend, and if the writer is good, and most of us aren't, he

12

INTRODUCTION

or she finds that they see things a little differently. That Chandler or Bradbury or Haycox or King or Goldman or Hemingway or Updike, or whoever, were merely sign posts on the horizon. To be good, to be original, you have to blaze your own path, and sometimes it's a hard work and it feels as if you're doing your blazing with a dull axe and no clothes against the weather.

The results may not be as good as the names on the sign posts. You may never give back all the writer tricks you've stolen, but by the time you've worked over your theft with the sandblaster and paint gun of your own voice and imagination, you just might have something. It might even be as good as those folks named on the sign posts. It might be better. At its worse, it will be yours.

So in that way, this sad old refrain of there's nothing new out there, it's all been done before, is just so much stringy, fly-infested dog shit. Long as you think that way, long as you try to guess what the reader likes or expects, chances are you'll come up with the same combinations written in the borrowed voices of others. It's like tv. It tries to please everyone, offend no one, and it's crap.

Fuck this imaginary reader.

Once you realize you can't second guess this mythical reader, because in the same way that we all have individual personalities, we all have individual taste as readers, you'll be a happier writer. And once you as a reader disregard set expectations of what a story should do, the sooner the boredom of the last paint by numbers books will fade. You'll seek out stories and books that piss on the old comfortable fires. You'll find scorpions in your boots and sugar in your coffee, a razor blade in your toothbrush and a blond (male or female, make your choice) in your bed.

Surprises, goddamnit, surprises.

What we're saying is this: by not catering to the reader, a writer is much more likely to produce something interesting, something truely unique.

Readers may never respond to it as well as the writer would like. Ain't gonna lie to you. You writes your stories, you takes your chances. But odds are, and it may take some time, they will eventually respond with greater enthusiasm than they would have to your clones of other writer's work. Historically it has been the trail blazers who have made their mark, not the petty thieves of voice and style and idea.

Thus, the purpose of anthologies like this.

RAZORED SADDLES

If you want a standard Western, they're out there. Get one off the rack and read comfortably of the school marm and the fast gun and know how it's all going to end.

And many of these "standard" books may in fact be more than that. There's always someone who deals in the old with such a fresh eye it's as if they invented the cliches. (LONESOME DOVE by McMurtry comes immediately to mind.)

But most books of this sort will be the shoot-em-up-of-the-month club. You know the type.

If you want that, hop to it, babe.

If you want horror that's the boo-of-the-month club, spring for it. It's out there, thick as ticks on a hound's nuts. The original stuff, the good stuff that uses the traditional form, is a little harder to find. When you look for it, you might have to take a lunch with you, maybe some camping supplies. You might even have to avoid the labels of horror and science fiction and the like.

But the good stuff's there. And it's worth the search.

There is new under the sun, folks. There is gold in them thar hills, but you got to prospect a little. That's what we did when we put this book together. We got out the pick and the shovel and started looking for gold. Maybe we got silver and copper in a few cases, some ores with traces of gold and the rest iron pyrite, but that beats the same old caly and sandstone. It's still precious metal.

Not all classics, but written from the heart with original voice and enthusiasm. Special stuff.

But enough. We end now with this: we tried to accomplish what those old movies of the 30's or maybe it was the 40's (maybe both) tried to do. The movies that had drama, comedy, dancing, action, adventure and maybe a little mystery and social commentary thrown in for good measure. In other words, we've tried to give you all out entertainment. And please do not confuse entertainment with tap dancing and yodeling. Entertaining enough, I guess, but entertainment can not only be light (and we got the light stuff here too), it can be sad and thoughtful and down right maddening. It can work like flint and steel and throw sparks into the tender of the brain and maybe cause a fire there. Sometimes just a flash, sometimes a thing that rages strong enough to bring in the smoke jumpers.

So read.

Enjoy.

And Happy Trails to you.

Robert R. McCammon may be the hottest new horror writer working today. He's the author of numerous popular horror novels, my favorite among them being the wonderfully gaudy THEY THIRST, a vampire novel that takes the vampire story to the edge of the cliff and throws it off. That one has everything. It's like the greatest B-movie ever made. But his short stories are even better. "Nightcrawlers" being the most famous of the bunch. It was filmed for the revived TWILIGHT ZONE television show. Come to think of it, the following story would also make a nice episode.

BLACK BOOTS

by Robert R. McCammon

Under the hard green sky, Davy Slaughter ran from Black Boots.

He glanced back over his shoulder, his face shadowed by the brim of his sweat-stained hat. Gritty sand and stones shifted underfoot, and his horse nickered with thirst. He had been leading the roan for the better part of an hour, across the no-man's land between Jalupa and Zionville. The sun, white as a pearl in the emerald air, was burning the moisture out of both man and beast. Davy thought he could hear his skin frying. He reached for his canteen, slung around his shoulder, uncapped it and took a drink. Then he poured a little in his hand and gave it to the horse. The roan's tongue scraped his palm. Davy swigged once more from the precious canteen, and something writhing oozed into his mouth.

Davy gagged and spat. White worms trailed from his lips, and fell to the sand. He watched, with almost a bland curiosity, as they squirmed around to his feet. One was caught between his cheek and gum, like a little plug of tobacco. He picked it out and let it fall.

15

The worms were bleeding into the sand. They were becoming less solid and more liquid with each passing second. And then they were gone, just a wet blotch where they'd been. That was a new one, Davy thought. His tongue roamed his mouth, but found no more invaders. He shook the canteen, and a measly amount of remaining water sloshed faintly inside it. He capped the canteen, wiped his mouth with the back of his sweating hand, and looked toward the shimmering horizon in the direction of Jalupa.

Scraggly cacti, as purple as bullet holes on the body of a dead man, stood on the desert's floor. Furnace heat undulated before him like banners of misery. But of Black Boots there was no sign. That didn't matter, Davy knew. Black Boots was back there, somewhere. Black Boots was always back there, coming after him. Getting closer and closer, as the white sun beat down and the desert was hot enough to cook lizards in their skins. Black Boots was always back there.

Davy should know. He'd killed Black Boots yesterday afternoon, at just after four o'clock, in a barroom in Cozamezas. Two bullets had done the job: one to the chest, one to the skull. Black Boots had gone down, spewing blood onto the dirty boards.

But Black Boots—the crafty bastard—had gotten off a single shot. Davy looked at the back of his gunhand, where the slug had left a burned streak. His fingers were still stiff from the shock. Crafty bastard, Davy thought. Softening me up, for the next time. Used to be I could cut him down before he drew his pistol. Used to be I could send him to Hell in an eyeblink. But Hell couldn't hold Black Boots. He was back there, crossing the no-man's land, getting closer all the time.

Davy worked his fingers, his eyes scanning the horizon. No sign of Black Boots. There never was, until it happened. He turned away from Jalupa and, holding the horse's reins, continued walking toward Zionville. His stride was a little faster than before. He glanced at his gunbelt, fastened around the roan's saddlehorn. His Colt pistol had a handle of yellow ivory, and in that ivory were twenty-two notches. He'd stopped notching it, the fifth time he'd killed Black Boots.

The horse made a nervous, rumbling noise. Davy saw a vulture, circling overhead. It swooped down low, smelling him. And then it climbed again into the green sky, and as it flapped its wings it began to fall to pieces, drifting apart like dark whorls of smoke. Davy looked away from it, and went on.

16

BLACK BOOTS

His real name was not Slaughter. It was Gartwood. He was twenty-four years old, and he had been born with the eyes of a rattlesnake. Speed was his mistress, and gunsmoke his god. When he'd run with the Bryce Gang three years ago, they'd called him "Slaughter' after the bank job in Abilene. That had a better ring than Gartwood. Gartwood was the name of a grocer, or a shoe salesman. Slaughter was his name now, and he was proud of it. He'd shot down four people in a two minute gun battle in Abilene. So Slaughter it was.

A sidewinder moved across his path, leaving a trail of fire that dwindled to cinders as he passed. He stared straight ahead, toward unseen Zionville. He knew this country, with the true knowledge of a predator. Another glance over his shoulder; Black Boots was still not in sight. Davy felt tight inside, full of rusted springs. His bones were melting, under this terrible heat. He touched his Colt, to make sure it was still real. It was, mercifully. In this day and age, a friend was hard to find.

How Black Boots had gotten onto his trail, he didn't know. The Wanted Dead Or Alive posters were up all over Texas and Oklahoma. Maybe that was it. Black Boots had seen the posters, and he wanted the fifty dollar bounty. A man who could get killed so many times and come back again with a cold hand must need money mighty bad, Davy figured. Hell, if I had fifty dollars I'd give it to him, just to let me be. But Black Boots wanted to earn his money, that much was crystal clear.

Davy started to look back again, but he checked himself. I don't need to, he told himself. "I ain't scared of him," he said, aloud. The roan's ears twitched. "I've killed him eight damn times. I can kill him again. I ain't scared of him, no sir."

A half-dozen more steps, and his head swivelled back over his shoulder.

Davy Slaughter stopped in his tracks.

There was a figure on the horizon. A man on horseback? Maybe. It was hard to tell, because the heatwaves were tricky. They made you see things that weren't there. Davy reached for his Colt, twisted his stiff fingers around the notched handle, and lifted the gun from the supple leather. Davy's heart was beating harder, and his throat was dry. His mouth tasted of white worms, and there was a hurting in his skull. He eased the Colt's hammer back, then he stood and watched the faraway figure coming as drops of sweat trickled through his beard.

17

The figure had stopped too. Whoever it was, they were a long ways off. Davy squinted in the green glare. The figure was just sitting there, watching him. Davy felt one of the rusted springs inside him break, and his mouth opened. "You after me?" he shouted. The roan jumped, startled. "You after me, you sonofabitch?" He took aim, his gunhand trembling. Green fire glinted off the barrel. Steady! he told himself. Damn it, *steady!* He let go of the horse's reins, and grasped his wrist with his other hand.

Behind a haze of rising heat, the figure neither retreated nor advanced.

"How many times do I have to kill you?" Davy shouted. "You want another bullet in your damned head?" The calmness of the figure enraged him. If there was anything he couldn't stand, it was when somebody had no fear of him. "All right!" he said. "All right, then!" He squeezed the trigger, a motion he'd performed so many times that it was as instinctive as breathing and just as sweet. The solid, balanced weapon gave a little kick, but it was a tame beast. The noise of the shot made his eardrums crack. "All right, have another one!" he cried out, his voice getting ragged. A second, almost loving squeeze of the trigger, and another bullet left the Colt's barrel.

He was about to fire off a third shot when it came to him, quite clearly. He was shooting at a cactus.

Davy blinked into the distance. He laughed, a croaking sound. It wasn't Black Boots after all, was it? Hell, no! He rubbed his eyes with grimy fingers, and looked again. The cactus was still there, and Black Boots was nowhere in sight. "Wasn't him," Davy said to the roan. "Oh, he's scared of me, is what he is. Keepin' his distance. He knows I'll kill him again, stiff hand or not. Hell, I'll drill him right straight through the eye next time." He returned the hot Colt to the gunbelt, and grasped the horse's reins again. He began walking, leading the roan across the tortured land to Zionville. Davy looked back a few times, but Black Boots wasn't there. Not yet, anyway. It occurred to Davy that this was the type of day his father would've liked. The elder Gartwood, in his last years, used to like to strip naked and lie out in the sun, reading his Bible. The elder Gartwood burned raw, was covered with blisters and boils, and he read the Good Book aloud as the sun ate him alive. Not Davy nor his mother nor his sister could get the elder Gartwood to find some shade. He wants to die, Davy remembered his Ma saying. And something else, too, she used to proclaim in her righteous voice: Those whom the Lord would destroy, He first makes insane.

Davy's gunhand was aching. He worked the fingers. The knuckles felt bruised. He gazed at the burned streak of the bullet's kiss, and he recalled that the first time he'd killed Black Boots the sonofabitch hadn't even been fast enough to clear leather. The second time, Black Boots had died with his gun just barely out of the holster. In their third encounter, Black Boots had fired into the ground as he'd stumbled backward with a Colt slug in his throat. Davy licked along the bullet's track, tasting the salt of his sweat.

No doubt about it, Davy thought. No doubt at all. Black Boots was getting faster.

It stood to reason. A man couldn't die eight times without learning something.

Davy was thirsty again. He uncapped the canteen, opened his mouth, and drank.

Warm liquid trickled over his tongue. It tasted coppery. Water's gone bad, he thought. He spat it out in his palm, and watched as the crimson blood oozed through his fingers and dripped to the sand.

Davy walked on, leading the roan, as the white sun burned down from an emerald sky and blood dribbled over his chin. Black Boots was on his mind.

Zionville wasn't much. There was a stable, a general goods store, a saloon, a church and graveyard and a few ramshackle houses, all bleached white as old bones. A red dog with two heads ran circles around Davy and the roan, both mouths yapping, but a kick to its ribs taught it some respect. In front of the goods store, a gawky kid with a bowl-haircut was sweeping off the boards, and he stopped his work to watch Davy pass. Two elderly women stood in a slice of shade, speaking in whispers. Davy noticed a little stucco structure with SHERIFF'S OFFICE painted on the door, but the windows were boarded up and the way the sand had drifted against the bottom of that door told him Zionville's sheriff was long gone. That suited him just fine. He tied the roan to the hitch in front of the saloon, which had no name, and then he took his gunbelt off the saddlehorn and buckled it on. As he laced the holster down against his thigh, he felt himself being watched. He glanced around, his eyes narrowed in the glare, and saw a thin man wearing dungarees and a sodbuster's shapeless hat sitting on a bench in front of a small wooden building. A weatherbeaten sign identified the place as a Wells Fargo Bank. Rathole wasn't worth robbing, Davy decided. Probably didn't have anything in there but a few sacks of change. Still, it might be nice to hear his pockets jingle when he left town.

He saw the kid in front of the goods store staring at him, leaning on his broom. The door opened with the clang of a cowbell, and a brown-haired woman in an apron peered out. She followed the kid's line of sight and saw Davy. "Joseph!" she said. "Come inside!"

"In a minute, Ma," the kid answered.

"Joseph, I said *now!*" The woman caught his sleeve and tugged at him, and the kid was reeled inside like a hooked fish. The door was firmly shut.

"Yeah, Joseph," Davy said under his breath. "You mind your momma." He gazed along the length of the street, saw a few more faces watching him through windows. Nobody was going to give him any trouble here. He walked into the saloon, his boots clumping on the boards. One drink of whiskey and a mulling over of whether to take the bank or not, and then he was going to be on his way.

Stale heat hung in the saloon. Sawdust had been scattered on the floor, and the light was gray through dirty windows. The bartender was a fleshy man with slicked-back black hair and a bovine face. He was swatting flies with a rolled up newspaper when he looked into the cracked mirror behind the bar and saw Davy approaching. "Afternoon," he said, to the mirror image.

Davy nodded. He leaned against the bar and propped one foot up on the bar rail. "Somethin' wet," he said, and the bartender pulled the cork from a brown bottle and poured him a shot. Davy had already seen the two middle-aged men who were playing cards at the back of the saloon. They'd paused only briefly, to note his laced-down holster, before they returned to their game. Over by a battered old piano, an elderly man slept in his chair as a fly buzzed his head. Davy accepted the shotglass, and sipped fire.

"Hot day," the bartender said.

"Sure is." Davy scanned the shelves behind the bar. "Got any cold beer?"

"Got beer. No ice, though."

Davy shrugged and sipped at the whiskey again. There was more water in it than liquor, but that was all right with him. He'd killed a man for watering his whiskey once, when he was younger. Today it didn't matter so much. "Quiet town you got here."

"Oh, yeah. Zionville's real quiet." The bartender swatted another fly. "Where you goin'?"

"Me? From here to there, I reckon." Davy watched the man's thick hands as they scraped the smashed fly off the bartop. "I just stopped to rest for a little while."

"You picked the right place. What's your name?"

Davy looked into the bartender's face. It was a mass of green flies, only the small dark eyes showing. Flies were crawling merrily in and out of the man's nostrils and they covered his lips. "Ain't that kinda uncomfortable?" Davy asked.

"Huh? What's uncomfortable?" The bartender's face was clear again, not a single fly on it.

"Nothin'," Davy said. He stared at the bullet crease on the back of his hand. "My name's Davy. What's yours?"

"Carl Haines. This is my place." The man said it proudly, as if talking about his child.

"I pity you," Davy told him, and Carl looked stung for a few seconds but then he laughed. It was a nervous laugh. Davy had heard that kind of laugh before, and it pleased him. "You got a sheriff in this town?"

Carl's laugh stopped. He blinked. "Why?"

"Just curious. I saw the sheriff's office, but I didn't see no sheriff." He took another taste of the watered-down whiskey. "I'd like to know. Do you have a sheriff?"

"No," Carl said warily. "I mean . . . there's one on the way. He'll be here directly. Comin' from El Paso."

"Well, that's a far piece from here, ain't it?" Davy turned the shotglass between his fingers. "An awful far piece."

"Ain't so far," Carl said, but his voice was weak. He cleared his throat, glanced at the card players and then back to Davy. "Uh . . . you wouldn't want to cause any trouble now, would you?"

"Do I look like the kind of fella who'd want to cause—" Davy stopped speaking. He noticed that Carl Haines had only one eye. There was a black, empty socket in the bartender's face. And from that socket began to slide the snout of a rattlesnake, forked tongue flicking out to taste the air.

"We're peaceful folks here," Carl said, as the rattler slowly emerged from his eyehole. "We don't quarrel with nobody. Honest to God."

Davy just stared, fascinated. The rattler's wedge-shaped head was all the way out now, and its eyes were bright amber. Davy's skull hurt. It felt about to burst open, and the thought of what might

21

spew out terrified him. He had an image of a withered skeleton lying in the burning sun, reading aloud from the Book of Job.

"Nothin' around here worth takin'," Carl went on. "Zionville's about dried up."

The bartender had two eyes again. The rattlesnake was gone. Davy set the shotglass down and pushed it aside with trembling fingers. Something wanted to scream inside him; he almost released it, but then he smashed it down and it shrank to its dark place.

"What's wrong?" Carl asked. "How come you're lookin' at me like that?"

"My last name," Davy said, his voice husky, "is Slaughter. Do you know that name?"

Carl shook his head.

"Anybody been around here, askin' for me?"

Again, a shake of the head.

"You ever see a man," Davy said, "who wears black boots?"

"I don't know. Hell, a lot of drifters pass through. I can't remem—"

"You'd remember him, if you saw him." Davy leaned forward slightly, staring into the bartender's eyes. He was looking for the rattlesnake again. It was hiding inside Carl's head. Hiding there, coiled up and waiting. "This man who wears black boots is tall and skinny. He looks like he ain't had a good meal in a long time. He looks hungry. His face is dusty-white, but you can't set eyes on him very long because you feel cold inside, like your bones are freezin' up. Sometimes he'd dressed like a dandy. Sometimes he's ragged. Have you ever seen a man like that?"

"No." The word was soft and strained. "Never."

"I have." Davy's fingers played on the handle of his Colt, where the notches were. "I've killed him eight times. The same man. Ol' Black Boots. See, he's stalkin' me. He figures he can catch me when I'm not ready for him. But I was born ready, Carl. You believe that?"

Carl made a choking sound, and a bead of sweat ran along his hooked nose.

"He's got nerve, I'll say that for him," Davy continued. "Not many men would face me down eight damned times, would they? No sir." He smiled faintly, watching a nerve tick at the corner of Carl's mouth. "Oh, he won't give up. Nope. But I won't give up neither." He took his hand off his gun, and worked his fingers. "He's gettin' faster, Carl. Everytime I kill him, he gets a little faster." Davy heard the soft crackling of flames. He looked toward the piano, and saw the old sleeping man ablaze with blue fire. In the old man's lap was an open Bible, and black pages were whirling out of it like bats at twilight.

"I swear," Carl managed to say, "I . . . ain't seen nobody like that."

There was the scrape of a boot on timbers. Davy saw Carl glance quickly toward the saloon's swinging doors. Davy felt the presence behind him, and fear like a streak of lightning shot through his bones. As he twisted toward the door, he had his hand on the Colt and had drawn and cocked it before the movement was complete. He brought the gun up to fire at chest-level, his finger tightening on the trigger.

"No!" Carl shouted. "Don't!"

Davy hesitated, ready to blast Black Boots to Hell again. But it wasn't Black Boots. It was the lanky kid who'd been sweeping in front of the goods store, his eyes wide as he peered over the doors at the gunfighter. The seconds stretched, Davy's finger touching the trigger. The kid lifted his hands. "I ain't got a gun, mister," he said in a reedy voice. "See? I'm just lookin'."

Davy scanned the other men in the bar. The card players had stopped their game, and the old man by the piano was awake and had ceased burning. Carl said, "It's just Joey McGuire. He don't mean no harm. Joey, get on away from here! You know your Ma don't like you hangin' around!"

The kid stared at the Colt in Davy's hand. "You ain't gonna shoot me, are you?"

Davy thought about it. Once his blood was stirred, it was hard to cool it down. But then he eased the trigger forward. "You came mighty close to playin' a harp, boy."

"Go on home, Joey!" Carl urged. "This ain't no place for you!"

"Do like he says," Davy told him. He returned to Colt to his holster. "This is a man's place."

"Hell, *I'm* a man!" Joey had pushed one of the doors partway open. "I can come in if I want to!"

The kid was fifteen or sixteen, Davy figured. Eager to set foot where it didn't belong. Eager to grow up, too. Like I was, Davy thought. He turned his back on the kid and finished off his shot of whiskey. It was time to be on his way, before Black Boots got here. He looked at Carl. There was a red-edged, jagged fissure across the bartender's forehead, and something gray was oozing out. "How much I owe you?"

"Nothin'," Carl said quickly, slime trickling down his face. "It's on the house. Okay?"

"Mister?" Joey had put a foot into the saloon. "You from around here?"

"Nope." Davy watched the fissure in Carl's head writhe. It was splitting open some more, and the brains were swelling out. "I ain't from nowhere."

"You know how to use that gun?"

"Maybe." Davy heard the kid's mother calling. Her voice echoed up the street: "Joseph! Joseph, come back here!" Twisted gray tissue was squeezing through the wound in Carl's forehead. Davy thought it was an interesting sight.

"I can come in if I want to," Joey said adamantly, turning a deaf ear to his mother. "Ain't no place I can't go, if it suits me."

"Your Ma's callin' you, Joey," Carl told him. "She'll raise hell at me again."

"I'm comin' in," the boy decided, and he pushed through the saloon doors. His boots clomped on the sawdusty boards.

"Don't that hurt?" Davy asked, and started to poke a finger at the oozing wound. Before his finger got there, he glanced up into the mirror behind the bar.

The kid who'd been sweeping in front of the goods store was not reflected there. The mirror told Davy Slaughter that someone else had entered the saloon.

The man was tall and skinny. He looked hungry, and his face had never seen the sun. Davy heard the black boots on the floor, saw the gunfighter who would not die reaching in a blur of motion toward the pistol slung low on his hip.

Black Boots, that crafty bastard, had gotten in wearing a kid's skin.

A surge of cold terror gripped at Davy's throat. He saw the shine of the man's black, fathomless eyes in the mirror, and then Davy shouted, "Damn you!" and was whirling as he shouted it, his stiff hand going for his Colt. Black Boots was drawing his own pistol out, was just about to clear leather. Davy's Colt slid out, quicker by far. He heard Carl shout something, but Davy was already lifting his gun. He thrust it toward Black Boots, and squeezed the trigger.

Black Boots was knocked backward, a hole appearing in his

chest. He gripped his pistol, but hadn't been fast enough to take aim. Black Boots staggered back, through the saloon doors with blood all over his chest.

"Are you crazy?" Carl screamed. "Are you crazy?"

"I got you, didn't I?" Davy jeered. His voice cracked. "I got you again, you bastard!" He strode to the swinging doors, his heart hammering but his mind clear and calm, and he stood there watching as Black Boots fell to the dust on his knees. A woman screamed. Davy saw the kid's mother about twenty feet away. She retreated a drunken step, her face bleached white and her hand pressed to her mouth. Her shocked eyes found Davy, and seized on him. Black Boots was trying to get up, trying to aim his gun. "You sonofabitch," Davy said, and fired a shot into Black Boots' forehead. The woman screamed again, a nettlesome sound. Black Boots pitched over on his side, the back of his head burst open. "I got you," Davy told him. "Serves you right, sneakin' up on me like—"

Black Boots was no longer lying in the dust. Where Black Boots had been was a kid, maybe fifteen or sixteen. His face and chest were all bloody. The woman made a groaning sound, turned and ran toward the goods store with dust whirling up beneath her shoes. Davy's head was hurting something awful. He looked up at the green sky, and his eyes stung. Then he returned his gaze to the dead boy. What had happened to Black Boots? He was there just a minute ago. Wasn't he? Davy backed away from the corpse. Somebody else was shouting in the distance: "Get off the street! Get off the street!" Davy kept backing away, and he retreated through the swinging doors into the saloon, away from the blinding light and that dead boy somebody had shot.

He heard the click of a trigger being cocked.

He spun around, cocking his Colt at the same time, and that was when Black Boots rose up from behind the bar. Black Boots had a rifle this time, and as its barrel swung upon him Davy shouted with rage and fired his pistol.

The Colt and the rifle spoke at the same instant. Davy was suddenly on the floor, though he had no recollection of how he'd gotten there. His left shoulder was wet and numb. Black Boots was chambering another slug, and behind him the mirror had been shattered to pieces. "Get him!" one of the card players hollered. The rifle took aim, but Davy had already found his mark and he shot Black Boots in the throat before another heartbeat had passed.

Black Boots slammed back into the shelves of bottles, his throat punctured, and the rifle went off but the bullet whacked into the wall over Davy's head. With a rush of air through the hole in his throat, Black Boots slid down to the floor behind the bar.

Davy got up. He glanced at the old man who'd been over by the piano; the man was hiding under a table, his flesh patterned with gray diamonds like the skin of a sidewinder. Davy walked to the bar, his head pulsing with pain, and he leaned over and shot Black Boots in the face.

Except it was not Black Boots. It was a man with slicked-back black hair, a rifle clenched in his twitching hands. Blood and air bubbled from the ruin of Carl's throat. Davy's legs felt weak. About to pass out, he thought. I'm shot. Sonofabitchin' Black Boots got me, didn't he? He staggered through the swinging door, leaving a trail of crimson, blue smoke wafting from the Colt's barrel.

In the glare of the hard green sky, Davy saw that the horse he'd hitched in front of the saloon no longer had skin. It was a skeleton horse with a saddle and bridle. But it still had four legs, and in its cage of bones its red lungs and heart were still working. Davy pulled the reins free, swung himself up onto the skeleton horse, and turned it toward the way out of Zionville. He dug his heels into the bare ribs. The horse shot forward, but in the next instant Davy realized he was going the wrong way. He was heading back the way he'd come, toward Jalupa again. He tried to get the skeleton horse turned around, but it wheeled and fought him.

He heard the noise of a cowbell.

Black Boots had just emerged from the goods store, a pistol in his hand. Davy lost the reins. He saw Black Boots running toward him, and Davy tried to take aim but the horse wheeled again and then Black Boots was right there and the pistol was thrust out at arm's-length. He thought he saw Black Boots smile.

The first bullet grazed Davy's cheek. The second hit him in the side, and the third caught him in the stomach and knocked him out of the saddle. He fell into the dust, the horse's bony legs thrashing around him. Davy crawled away from the bucking skeleton, and a shadow fell upon him.

His eyes heavy-lidded and blood in his mouth, he looked up at Black Boots. The man was just standing there, dust swirling around him, the gun hanging at his side. Davy coughed up crimson, and he forced a crooked grin. "You . . . never beat me," Davy whispered. "I

was always faster. Always." And then he lifted his own gun, aimed it at Black Boots' chest and squeezed the trigger.

The hammer fell on an empty chamber. Six bullets had been fired: two in the no-man's land, four killing Black Boots.

Davy laughed, a broken sound.

Black Boots shot Davy Slaughter twice, once in the belly and once at close range in the skull. Davy twitched a few times. The Colt fell from his fingers, and he lay staring up at the sky.

Joey's mother stood there a moment longer. She was shaking, and tears had streaked her face. She dropped the pistol, wiped her palm on her apron, and then she began to walk toward her dead son as the people of Zionville emerged from shelter. Burning down from a fierce blue sky, the sun threw long shadows. Not far away, the roan horse had ceased its bucking and stood in the middle of the street waiting for a guiding hand.

No one knew the gunfighter. He was crazy as hell, old Braxton said. Shot Joey down for no reason at all. Crazy as hell, he was.

Pine boxes cost money, and no one came forward to offer any. The gunfighter was wrapped up in a canvas sack, his pallid face showing through, and somebody leaned him up against a wall while a picture was taken. The new marshall from El Paso would want to know about this. Then a hole was dug, way over on the edge of the cemetery away from where Zionville's own lay. The reverend said a few words over the gunfighter, but nobody was there to hear them. Then the corpse was laid down into the hole, the reverend went away, and the man who threw dirt on the gunfighter's face wore black boots.

Scott Cupp lives in Dallas, Texas, and is the author of two other stories. This is his second pro sale. His other, "Jimmy and Me and the Nigger Man", is a cross between Lovecraft, Huckleberry Finn, Frankenstein, the Tar Baby and Disney's Fantasia. After this story appears he may well be forced into becoming a Yankee. If he gets out of Texas alive.

THIRTEEN DAYS OF GLORY

by Scott A. Cupp

December 7, 1835

The call has finally come! Word was delivered today that Houston sees the Texas uprising as being inevitable and all men who support the cause have been requested to rally in San Antonio. They have taken a mission, San Antonio de Valero, as their headquarters and expect that early next year, the actual conflict may begin.

My soul tells me that men such as these must have my support. This nation was founded on the rights of men to be free from persecution regardless of their beliefs. The Mexs must be stopped and I will be there to witness the triumph of the Spirit of Man.

Jamie, on the other hand, does not seem to understand. He stares at me with those deep brown eyes and says, "Don't go." Every fibre of my being wants to turn back and throw my gear in the corner, scooping him up to the bed.

My resolve is firm, however. If I pass and do not fight for the rights of Man. I feel that I would never forgive myself. There will be yelling and crying and quiet love and whispered good-byes tonight. But tomorrow, I depart.

February 4, 1836

San Antonio is a miserable town. It is flat and has few trees. Although it is January there is no snow. Nor are there the mountains that so frame the scenery of my native Tennessee. Instead, there is the wind and the rain and the mud. The things that pass as trees are the cottonwood and the mesquite. Neither is particularly appealing. The cottonwood is the more prevalent, having a white residue that it sheds everywhere. The mission here is called by the Spanish name for cottonwood—Alamo.

The mission itself is rather small and made from a baked mud called adobe. Inside it is relatively cool.

There are maybe 150 men here. All seem dedicated to the cause. There has been no word on the rebellion or the Mexs. Some say that Santa Anna himself may be leading the fight. I hope to show him what Tennessee lead can do to Mexican flesh.

Travis and Bowie are in charge. Neither is exactly as I had envisioned them, but dreams rarely measure up to life. Both have an air of command that is unmistakable. Others who said that they would follow either of them to the ends of the world and both of them further than even that. Having met them, I would probably do the same. Can a cause which enlists such men as these fail? And they say Crockett is soon to arrive with his men!

I still have the dreams of Jamie and there are times when my aching for him is so bad that I look for my horse so that I might leave. I think that it is his beard that I miss most of all. The lust that it arouses as it strokes the small of my back when we make love is almost too much to bear. Most nights I find myself unable to sleep until I have shed silent tears for my true love and I.

THIRTEEN DAYS OF GLORY

February 9, 1836

Crockett arrived yesterday in all of his buckskin glory. He truly measures up to the myths about him. He is a strong burly man with a soft touch and a sense of humor. We're from different areas of Tennessee but he was pleased to see that I had arrived before him and welcomed me as a comrade in arms. He is a man's man, compared to Bowie who is more genteel.

Though he could easily be the leader of the rebellion, he has deferred to Travis and Bowie to prevent dissention. The rebellion couldn't help but succeed now. The Tennessee volunteers are all crack shots and afraid of no man or Mex.

February 20, 1836

Santa Anna is coming! For the last two days we have seen the dust cloud approaching. Travis has not been able to determine the size of the force yet but it must be 4,000 or more. We are less than 200. Men have been coming and going all along, though for the last few days more have left than have arrived.

We are prepared for the fight. Though we have food and ammunition for a long siege, the sight of this large force may be more than many will be able to endure. I am prepared.

I find myself musing on the possibility of Death more frequently now. Perhaps I will die in the forthcoming battle. If it must be so to win freedom for my comrades, then I will gladly go. Men have been persecuted for their beliefs for too long. To the Mexs, the Inquisition still persists. And we are the prime targets for their persecution. They have said that they will never relinguish Texas to us for the homeland we desire, free from the religious persecution that has haunted us through the ages—from Europe, into America, and now into the undeveloped territories.

There is to be a party tonight as it appears that the fighting will soon begin.

February 22, 1836

Their army is spread before us like the sands on a beach. All that you can see for miles and miles are the tents and fires of our foes. DEATH AND DESTRUCTION! WE WILL BE FREE!

From my sleeping place I can hear the sounds of their bands, their women and children (for they often accompany their soldier fathers), and their whores.

Our party last night may have been a mistake. I decided, as did several of the others, to put on my finest. The dress I chose was bright and colorful. My earrings flashed in the firelight. On my face, I put only some rouge and lip colors. I was the desire of every man present.

Unfortunately, I drank too deep, trying to forget the memories of Jamie. A young boy was there. I never learned his name, but the caresses he gave me sent shivers down my spine. He, too, was trying to become lost in the moment. We went to my pallet and made drunken, passionate love. I called him Jamie several times; he called me Charles. The feel of penetrating him was like a long forgotten joy. I had had no man since leaving Jamie and the release of that tension was utterly draining.

Others must have felt the same. The soft moans of men joined in ecstatic love filled the night. The sound of the Mex's whores were wiped from our ears. We were 180 men in love with each other. We would do anything to help one another or we would die trying.

February 23, 1836

The Mexs sent their emissaries out to see us and demand that we surrender. Some of the men still wore the makeup and skirts. Knowing that it would infuriate the Mexs. One of their priests said that we were the Whores of Babylon and an Abomination on the Face of the Earth. Travis, Bowie, and Crockett were all described as the Anti-Christ, which amused them. They had stayed the night together in an erotic tangle and were still in the ecstatic afterglow of love.

Travis told the emissaries to be damned. We were free men trying to find a place to live away from the persecution of unknowing
religious zealots. Texas would be *our* homeland. The archbishop
called him a nasty faggot. Travis was shaken by this. None of us will
ever forget that image, as the Inquisition would take one of our
own, dip him into the tar, and set him afire to the delight of the
crowd.

Travis struck the man across the face. Bowie brandished his
famous knife, slicing the air wickedly, bringing the point up to the
throat of a priest, but Crockett restrained him. The conference was
over. Within 15 minutes, the battle was on. The boy from last night
fought by my side. We were greatly outnumbered and I feared that
we would be overrun quickly. But, the Mexs were unable to co-
ordinate their attack. The size of their force must have made com-
munications difficult. Whatever the reason, we survived that first
day well, none dead and only five wounded. I slept on the wall with
my rifle in my hand.

February 28, 1836

It is day 6 of the siege. I have seen the sea of blue and red
jackets, relentless as the tide, lapping up the sides of the Mission.
They fight doggedly, urged on by their leaders and priests. Each
morning the archbishop arises, leaving a new whore, to speak the
Mass that he hopes will bring about our end and restore order to his
world. Other priests stand in the battlefield giving last rites, swinging censers, and attempting to inspire the troops.

We have lost 25 or 30 men, bringing us to somewhere near 150.
Many of those remaining have injuries of one form or another.
Travis is among these, but he refuses to quit. He is an inspiration to
us all. At night he roams the walls, throwing kisses to the Mexs,
enticing them to join us.

The boy from the party is dead. He took a shot full in the chest
on the second or third day. All days now seem to be the same.
Nonetheless, he held on for another day, wheezing loudly, blood
gurgling in his lungs. At the end, he began crying loudly for Charles.
I came to him and held his hand as he died. We talked and, in his

delirium, I was Charles again and we reminisced.

This has caused me more pain than anything the Mexs could have ever done. Why do young boys such as he have to die to satisfy the prejudices of others? He had harmed no one nor did he hold anyone in contempt. He was, and remains, a good man whose memory will not be forgotten.

March 3, 1836

Will this siege never end? It is ten days now and it appears that the Mexs will never give up or leave. Our forces are dwindling rapidly. Travis sent several couriers to Sam Houston requesting re-inforcements. We all pray for their raucous shouts and laughter to be on the next breeze. Some men are becoming desperate for their lives. And who can blame them? Nearly everyone carries some scar from the battle. Many are dead.

The talk of our homeland is dying. Bowie had been its chief spokesman in Louisiana and had urged Travis and Houston into the rebellion. Travis and Bowie are now wounded and Houston is still missing from the fight. Travis is unable to continue and is confined to his bed with a fever. Bowie is among the wounded and appears to be on his last legs. He keeps his knife close at hand to prevent being killed by a spy. His delirium seems to spread among the troops. It is not right that men of such power should not be able to die in dignity. Crockett is now the leader in the battles.

I saw a sight this morning that I shall never forget. Out among the fields, pocked with cannon holes, a young Mex boy played near the tent of his father. It seemed odd that the young can endure such horrors and still be able to play among the dead.

March 5, 1836

The end is near! Surely the morrow will bring the resolution. The fighting has continued for 12 days. We are exhausted. Our food, which seemed so bountiful, is at an end. The supplies of ammunition are also near the end. Unless Houston shows on the dawn, we will be unable to finish the fight. The walls of the garrison have been breached with cannonfire in several places but we have secured these areas with overturned wagons and furniture. But, we are now unable to guard these areas and also maintain sufficient cover on the walls. Crockett has talked of retreating to the chapel and blowing the magazine, taking as many of them with us as we might. We do not want to have to consider this, but I feel that none will hesitate if it is needed.

My thoughts run continually to Jamie and I hope he will forgive me for leaving him, for it appears that I will be unable to return. Jamie, if for some reason this journal finds its way to you (and I can but hope that it will), do not mourn for me. Rather, continue the fight for the Rights of Man. I am but one small soldier in the bigger fight. Carry that fight on to its conclusion. Show others that we live and die with the same fervor. Remember me—no, rather, remember us and the good times that we have had. Let these memories spur you on. FIGHT . . . and, better yet, win for us that homeland which we desire and bring others safely into it.

Others have approached me with a plan. It is foolhardy and will only hasten the end. But, in a perverse way, it pleases me. We will all face the final day in full feminine garb and makeup. Those who have none will be given items from those with extra. Tomorrow Santa Anna and his Inquisitors will see us as the men we really are. Their rage will be unrelenting. They will never forget our reasons for the fight.

The dawn is soon approaching and I must prepare myself for the battle. The world shall not soon forget what we will do this day. Hail and Farewell!

(for Neal Barrett, Jr.)

Lewis Shiner—Lew to his friends, maybe his enemies too— lives in Austin, Texas, and is justly considered to be one of the best new writers in science ficiton today. He's also striking out in different directions, as with his mainstream novel, SLAM, forthcoming from Doubleday. The following story is beautifully written and never puts a foot wrong. It's kind of a pirate story. Kind of.

GOLD

by Lewis Shiner

Pirate gold. Coins, rings, ingots. Necklaces of emeralds and opals and sapphires. Chalices, bracelets, daggers inlaid with diamonds and lapis and ivory.

Malone rolled over in the soft hotel bed.

Not just the gold but the things it would buy. A two-story house of brick and wrought iron. Greek columns in front and coaches parked in the drive. Built high on the center of Galveston Island, away from the deadly storms of the Gulf, away from the noise and stink of the port. White servants and negro slaves. Fair haired women to sit at the piano in his parlor. Dark skinned women to open their legs to him in the secrecy of the night . . .

He sat up in a sweat. I will think no evil thoughts, he told himself.

Outside, the sun rose over New Orleans. Horse-drawn carts creaked and rattled through the streets, and chickens complained about the light. The smell of the Mississippi, damp and sexual, floated through the open window.

Malone got up and put a robe on over his nightshirt, despite the heat. He turned up the gas lamp over the desk, took out pen, ink and paper, and began to write.

"My dearest Becky . . ."

*   *   *

He smelled the French Market before he saw it, a mixture of decayed fruit, coffee, and leather. He crossed Decatur Street to avoid a side of beef hung over the sidewalk, swarming with flies. Voices shouted in a dozen different languages. All manner of decrepit wooden carts stood on the street, their contents passed from hand to hand until they disappeared under the yellow canvas awnings of the market. Beyond the levee Malone could see the tops of the masts of the tall ships that moved toward the Governor Nicholl's Street Wharf.

The market was crowded with cooks from the town's better families, most of them Negro or Creole. The women wore calico dresses and aprons and kerchiefs, in all shades of reds and yellows and blues. The men wore second-hand suits in ruby or deep green, with no collars or neckties. Like their suits, their hats were battered and several years out of style. They carried shopping baskets on their shoulders or heads because there was no room to carry them at their sides.

Malone let himself be drawn in. He moved slowly past makeshift stands built of crates and loose boards, past heaps of tomatoes and peppers and bananas and field peas, searching the faces of the vendors. His concern turned out to be groundless; he recognized Chighizola immediately.

Nez Coupe, Lafitte had called him. With the end of his nose gone, he looked like a rat that stood on hind legs, sniffing at something foul. The rest of his ancient face was covered with scars as well. One of them, just under his right eye, looked pink and newly healed. He was tiny, well over eighty years old now, his frock coat hanging loose on his shoulders. Still his eyes had a fierce look and he moved with no sign of stiffness. His hands were large and energetic, seeming to carry his arms unwillingly behind them wherever they went.

"Louis Chighizola," Malone called out. The old man turned to look at him. Chighizola's eyes were glittering black. He seemed ready to laugh or fly into a rage at a moment's notice. Malone pushed closer. "I need a word with you."

"What you want, you?"

"I have a proposition. A business proposition."

"This not some damn trash about Lafitte again?" The black eyes had narrowed. Malone took a half step back, colliding with an enormous Negro woman. He no longer doubted that some of Chighizola's scars were fresh.

"This is different, I assure you."

"How you mean different?"

"I have seen him. Alive and well, not two weeks ago."

"I got no time for ghosts. You buy some fruit, or you move along."

"He gave me this," Malone said. He took a flintlock pistol from his coat, holding it by the barrel, and passed it to the old man.

Chighizola looked behind him, took one reluctant step toward Malone. He took the pistol and held it away from him, into the sunlight. "Fucking hell," Chighizola said. He turned back to Malone. "We talk."

*　　*　　*

Chighizola led him east on Chartress Street, then turned into an alley. It opened on a square full of potted palms and flowers and sheets hung out to dry. They climbed a wrought-iron spiral staircase to a balcony cluttered with pots, old newspapers, empty barrels. Chighizola knocked at the third door and a young woman opened it.

She was an octoroon with skin the color of Lafitte's buried gold. She wore a white cotton shift with nothing under it. The cotton had turned translucent where it had drunk the sweat from her skin. Smells of fruit and flowers and musk drifted from the room behind her.

Malone followed the old man into an aging parlor. Dark flowered wallpaper showed stains and loose threads at the seams. A sofa with a splinted leg sat along one wall and a few unmatched chairs stood nearby. An engraving of a sailing ship, unframed, was tacked to one wall. Half a dozen children played on the threadbare carpet, aged from a few months to six or seven years. Chighizola pointed to a chair and Malone sat down.

"So. Where you get this damn pistol?"

"From Lafitte himself."

"Lafitte is dead. He disappears thirty years ago. The Indians down in Yucatan, they cook him and eat him I think."

"Is the pistol Lafitte's, or is it not?"

"You are not Lafitte, yet *you* have his pistol. Any man could."

Malone closed his eyes, fatigue taking the heart out of him. "Perhaps you are right. Perhaps I have only deceived myself." A small child, no more than two years old, crawled into Malone's lap. She had the features of the woman who answered the door, in miniature. Her dress was clean, if too small, and her black hair had been pulled back and neatly tied in red and blue ribbons. She rubbed the wool of Malone's coat, then stuck two fingers in her mouth.

"I do not understand," Chighizola said. "You come to me with this story. Do you not believe it yourself?"

"I wish I knew," Malone said.

* * *

Malone was born poor in Ohio. His parents moved to the Republic of Texas in 1837 to get a new start. Some perverse symbolism made them choose the island of Galveston, recently swept clean by a hurricane. There they helped with the rebuilding, and Malone's father got work as a carpenter. Malone was ten years old at the time, and the memories of the disaster would stay with him the rest of his life. Block-long heaps of shattered lumber, shuffled like cards, the ruin of one house indistinguishable from the next. Stacks of bodies towed out to sea, and those same bodies washing in again days and weeks later. Scuff marks six feet up inside one of the few houses left standing, where floating furniture had knocked against the walls. The poor, Malone saw, would always be victims. For the rich there were options.

One of the richest men on Galveston Island was Samuel May Williams. On New Year's day of 1848 he had opened the doors of the Commercial and Agricultural Bank of Texas, his lifetime dream. It sat on a choice piece of land just two blocks off the Strand Avenue, "the Wall Street of Texas." Williams' fellow Texans hated him for his shrewd land speculation, his introduction of paper money to the state, his participation in the corrupt Monclova legislature of '35. Malone thought them naive. Williams was a survivor, that was all.

Not like his father, who found that a new start did not necessarily mean a new life. Malone's mother died, along with a quarter of Galveston's population, in the yellow fever epidemic of '39. Soon his father was drinking again. Between the liquor and his son's education, there was barely money for food. Malone swore that he would see his father in a fine house in the Silk Stocking district. He never got the chance. Instead he returned from Baylor University in the spring of '48 in time to carry one corner of his father's coffin.

Malone's classes in accounting were enough to land him a position as a clerk in Sam Williams' new bank. Within a year he had married the daughter of one of its board members. His father-in-law made Malone a junior officer and an acceptable member of society. A long, slow climb lay ahead of him, leading to a comfortable income at best. It did not seem enough, somehow.

He had been in Austin on the bank's business. It was a foreclosure, the least pleasant of Malone's duties. The parcel of land was one that Williams had acquired in his early days in Texas, "going halves" with immigrants brought in by the Mexican government.

That night he had stood at the Crystal Saloon on Austin's notorious Congress Avenue, drinking away the sight of the sheriff examining Malone's papers, saying, "Sam Williams, eh?" and spitting in the dirt, the sight of the Mexican family disappearing on a mule cart that held every battered thing they owned.

A tall man in a bright yellow suit had stood at Malone's table, nodded at his satchel, and said, "On the road, are you?" The man spat tobacco onto the floor, the reason Malone had kept his satchel safely out of the way. The habit was so pervasive that Malone took precautions now by instinct. "I travel myself," the man said. "I am in ladies' garments. By trade, that is."

Malone saw that it was meant to be a joke. The drummer's name was O'Roarke, but he constantly referred to himself in the third person as Brimstone Jack, "on account of this head of hair." He lifted his hat to demonstrate. The hair that was visible was somewhere between yellow and red, matching his mustached and extravagant side-whiskers. There was, however, not much of it.

Malone mentioned Galveston. The talk soon turned to Jean Lafitte, the world's last pirate and the first white settler of Galveston Island. That was when O'Roarke offered to produce the genuine article.

41

RAZORED SADDLES

Four glasses of bourbon whiskey had raised Malone's credulity to new heights. He followed O'Roarke to a house on West Avenue, the limits of civilization, and there stepped into a world he had never seen before. Chinese, colored, and white men sat in the same room together, most of them on folding cots along the walls. Heavy, sour smoke hung in the air. The aroma left Malone both nervous and oddly euphoric. "Sir," he said to O'Roarke, "this is an opium den."

A man in the far corner began to laugh. The laugh went on and on, rich, comfortable, full of real pleasure. Malone, his good manners finally giving way to curiosity, turned and stared.

The laughing man had fair skin, a hatchet nose, and piercing black eyes. His black hair fell in curls to the middle of his back. He was in shirt sleeves, leather trousers, and Mexican sandals. There was a power about him. Malone felt a sudden, strong desire for the man's good opinion.

"May I present," O'Roarke said with a small bow, "the pirate Jean Lafitte?"

Malone stared in open disbelief.

"Privateer," the dark-haired man said, still smiling. "Never a pirate."

"Tell him," O'Roarke said to the dark-haired man. "Tell him who you are."

"My name is John Lafflin," the man said.

"Your real name," O'Roarke said, "damn you."

"I have been known by others. You may call me Jean Lafitte, if it pleases you."

"Lafitte's son, perhaps," Malone said. "Lafitte himself would be, what, nearly seventy years old now. If he lived."

The hatchet-faced man laughed again. "You may believe me or not. It makes no difference to me."

*　　*　　*

Sitting there in Chighizola's apartment, watching dust motes in the morning sunlight, Malone found his own story more difficult to believe than ever. From the shadows the woman watched him in silence. He wondered how foolish he must look to her.

"And yet," Chighizola said, "you *did* believe him."

42

"It was something in his bearing," Malone said. "That and the fact that he wanted nothing from me. Not even my belief. I found myself unable to sleep that night. I returned to the house before dawn and searched his belongings for evidence."

"Which is when you stole the pistol. He did not give it to you."

"No. He had no desire to convince me."

"So why does this matter so much to you?"

Malone sighed. Sooner or later it had to come out. "Because of the treasure. If he is truly Lafitte—or even if he is merely Lafitte's son—he could lead us to the treasure."

"Always to the treasure it comes."

"I grew up on Galveston Island. We all live in the shadow of Jean Lafitte. As children we would steal away into the bayous and search for his treasure. Once there we found grown men doing the same thing. And if I feel so personally connected, how can you not feel even more so? It is your treasure as much as Lafitte's. You sailed with him, risked your life for him. And yet look at yourself. In poverty, living by the labor of your hands."

"I have not much time left."

"All the more reason you should want what is yours. You should want the money for your family, for your daughter here, and her children."

Chighizola looked at the woman. "He thinks you are my daughter, him." She came over to kiss his scarred and twisted face. Malone felt his own face go red. "Here is a boy who knows nothing of life."

"I am young," Malone said. "It is true. But so is this nation. Like this nation I am also ambitious. I want more than my own enrichment. I know that it takes money to bring about change, to create the growth that will bring prosperity to everyone."

"You sound like a politician."

"With enough money, I would become one. Perhaps a good one. But without your help it will never happen."

"Why am I so important? This man, Lafitte or not, what does it matter if he can lead you to the treasure?"

"If he is Lafitte, he will listen to you. He cares nothing for me. He will lead me nowhere. I need you to make him care."

"I will think on this."

"I am stopping at the French Market Inn. My ship leaves tomorrow afternoon for Galveston. I must know your answer by then."

"Tell me, you who are in such a hurry. What of ghosts?"

"I do not understand."

"Ghosts. The spirits of the dead."

"Lafitte is alive. That is all that concerns me."

"Ah, but you seek his gold. And where there is gold, there are ghosts. Always."

"Then I leave them to you, old man. I will take my chances with the living."

*　　*　　*

Malone had already packed his trunk and sent for his bill when the woman arrived. He mistook her knock for the bellman and was shocked into silence when he opened the door. Finally he backed away and stammered an apology.

"I bring a message from Chighizola," she said. She pushed the door closed and leaned her weight against it. "We will go with you to see this Lafitte."

"We?'" Malone could not take his eyes away from her.

"He says we are to divide the treasure four ways, equal shares, you, me, Louis, Lafitte."

"Which leaves the two of you with half the treasure. I thought he did not care for money."

"Perhaps not. Perhaps you care too much for it."

"I am not a schoolboy. I have no desire to be taught humility at Chighizola's hands."

"Those are his terms. If they are agreeable, we leave today."

Malone took a step closer to her. Curls of black hair had stuck to the damp flesh of her throat. It was difficult for him to speak. "I do not know your name."

"Fabienne."

"And what is your interest in this?"

"Louis," she said. "He is my only interest." She stepped to one side and pulled the door open. "We will meet you at the wharf in one hour." She closed the door behind her.

*　　*　　*

GOLD

The voyage to Galveston took a day and a half aboard the S.S. Columbia, now-aging stalwart of the Morgan line. Malone saw Chighizola and his woman only once, when the three of them shared a table for dinner. Otherwise Malone remained in his cabin, catching up on accounts and correspondence.

Malone stood on the bow as the ship steamed into Galveston Bay. Even now Sam Williams might have his eye on him. Legend had it that Williams watched incoming ships with a telescope from the cupola of his house, deducing their cargos from their semaphored messages. He would then hurry into town to corner the market on the incoming merchandise. It did not increase his popularity. Then again, Williams had never seen public opinion as a necessary condition for money and power.

Williams had proven what a man of ambition could do. He had arrived in Texas under an assumed name in May of 1822, fleeing debts as so many others had. He had created himself from scratch. Malone knew that he could do the same. It was not proper that a man should live on his wife's fortune and social position. He needed to increase and acquire, to shape the world around him.

Chighizola joined him as they swung in toward the harbor. "Do you never miss the sea?" Malone asked him.

"I had enough of her," Chighizola said. "She care for nobody. You spend your life on top of her, she love you no more than she did the first day. A woman is better." He squinted at the island. The harbor was crowded with sailboats and steamers, and beyond it the two-story frame buildings of the Strand were clearly visible. "Hard to believe that is the same Campeachy." He looked at Malone. "Galveston, you call it now. Are there still the snakes?"

"Not like there used to be."

"Progress. Well, I will be glad to see it. Every new thing, it always is such a surprise for me."

"You will have to see it another time. We must catch a steamer for the mainland this morning, then a coach to Austin."

"Yes, I forget the hurry you are in."

"I have to know. I have to know if it is Lafitte or not."

"It is him."

"How can you be certain without even seeing him? I tell you he looks no more than forty years old."

"And I tell you we buried Lafitte twice, once at the Barataria, once at Campeachy."

45

"Buried him?"

"For being dead. Lafitte, he eats the blowfish, him. You under-stand? Poison fish. In Haiti he learns this. Sometimes he eats it, nothing happens. Sometimes he loses the feeling in his tongue, his mouth. Twice he gets stiff all over and looks dead. Twice we bury him, twice the Haitian spirit man watch the grave and dig him up again. Ten years he eats the blowfish, that I know him. In all that time, he gets no older. But it makes him different, in his head. Money is nothing to him after. Then the second time, he cares about nothing at all. Sets fire to Campeachy, sails off to Yucatan with his brother Pierre."

"I have read the accounts," Malone said. "Lt. Kearny and the *Enterprise* drove him away."

"You think one man, one ship, stand against Lafitte if he wants to fight? He sees the future that night. He sees more and more Lt. Kearnys in their uniforms, with their laws and courts and papers. More civilization, like in Louisiana. More government telling you what you can do. No more room for privateers. No place left to go in this country where a man can stand alone. So he goes to Mexico. But first, before he goes, we burn the whole town to the ground. So Lt. Kearny does not get Lafitte's nice red house."

Malone knew that Lafitte's pirate camp had numbered two thousand souls by the time Kearny arrived in 1821. Lafitte himself ruled from a two-story red house near the port, surrounded by a moat, guarded by his most loyal men. Campeachy had been a den of vice and iniquity: gaming, whores, liquor, gun-fights and duels. There were those in Galveston still that wondered if the island would ever recover from the evil that had been done there.

Malone shook his head. Chighizola had got him thinking of ghosts and now he could not rid himself of them.

"You did not go with him," Malone said. "To Mexico. Why not?"

"I do not like the odds. I think, a man looks at Death so many times, then one day Death looks back. Life always seems good to me. I am not like Lafitte, *moi*. I do not have these ideas and beliefs to keep me awake all night. You are still young, I give you advice. To sleep good at night, this is not such a bad thing."

*   *   *

GOLD

The coach took them from Houston to San Felipe along the Lower Road, then overland to Columbus. From there along the Colorado River to La Grange and Bastrop and Austin. Chighizola was exhausted by the trip, and the woman Fabienne blamed Malone for it. Malone was tired and irritable himself. Still he forced himself out of the hotel that night to search for Lafitte.

The opium house was deserted with no sign left of its former use. He stopped in two or three saloons and left word for O'Roarke, then gave up and retired to the comparative luxury of the Avenue Hotel.

Malone searched all the next day, asking for both O'Roarke and Lafitte by name. The first name met with shrugs, the second with laughter. Malone ordered a cold supper sent to his room, where he ate in silence with Chighizola and the woman.

"It would seem," the woman said, "that we have come a long, painful distance for nothing." She was dressed somewhat more formally than Malone had seen her before, in a low-cut yellow frock and a lace cap. The dangling strings of the cap and her dark, flashing eyes made her seem as wanton as ever.

"I do not believe that," Malone said. "Men have destinies, just as nations do. I cannot believe that my opportunity has passed me by."

There was a knock and Malone stood up. "That may be destiny even now."

It was in fact O'Roarke, with Lafitte in tow. "I heard," O'Roarke said, "you sought for Brimstone Jack. He has answered your summons." He noticed Fabienne, removed his hat, and directed his goblet of tobacco juice at the cuspidor rather than the floor.

Malone turned back to the room. Chighizola was on his feet, one hand to his throat. "Holy Christ," he said, and crossed himself.

Lafitte sank into an armchair. He seemed intoxicated, unable to focus his eyes. "Nez Coupe? Is it really you?"

"Me, I look how I should. You are the one that is not to be believed. Lafitte's son, you could be."

Malone said, "I warned you."

"A test," Chighizola said. "That is what you want, no?"

Malone shrugged. "I feel certain it would reassure us all."

Chighizola rubbed a thick scar that ran along the edge of his jaw. "There is a business with a golden thimble I could ask him about."

Lafitte waved his hand, bored. "Yes, yes, of course I remember the thimble. But I suppose I must tell the story, to satisfy your friends." He shifted in the chair and picked at something on his shirt. "It happened in the Barataria. We had made the division of the spoils from a galleon taken out in the Gulf. There were three gold coins left over. I tried to give them to your wife." His eyes moved to Fabienne, then back. "Your wife of the time, of course. But you were greedy and wanted them for yourself. So I had the smith make them into a thimble for her. I think it ended up in a chest full of things that we buried somewhere."

"It is Lafitte," Chighizola said to Malone. "If you doubted it."

"No," Malone said, "I had no doubt." He turned to O'Roarke. "How can we reward you for bringing him to us?"

"You can cut me in on the treasure," O'Roarke said. Lafitte put back his head and laughed.

"I do not know what you mean," Malone said.

O'Roarke's face became red. "Do not take Brimstone Jack for an idiot. What you want is obvious. You are not the first to try. If you succeed I would ask for only a modest amount. Say, a hundredth share. It would be simpler to cut me in than to do the things you would have to do to lose me."

Malone looked at Chighizola. Chighizola said, "It comes from your share, not from ours." Fabienne smiled her agreement.

"All right, damn it," Malone said. "Done."

Lafitte leaned forward. "You seem to have matters well in hand. Perhaps I should be on my way."

Malone stared at him for a second in shock. "Please. Wait."

"You sir, though I know your face, I do not know your name. I seem to remember you in connection with the disappearance of my pistol."

Malone handed the pistol to Lafitte, butt first. With some embarrassment he said, "The name is Malone."

"Mr. Malone, now that you have divided up my treasure, may I ask a question or two? How do you know the treasure even exists? If it does exist, that I have not long ago spent it? If I have not spent it, that I even recall where it was buried?" Unspoken was the final question: if he recalled it, why should he share?

"Is there a treasure?" Malone asked at last.

Lafitte took out a clay pipe shaped like some Mexican deity and stuffed it with brittle green leaves. He did not offer the odd tobacco to anyone else. When he lit it the fumes were sour and spicy. Lafitte held the smoke in his lungs for several long seconds then exhaled loudly. "Yes, I suppose there is."

"And you could find it again?"

Lafitte shrugged again. "Perhaps."

"You make sport of us, sir. You know our interests, and you seem to take pleasure in encouraging them. But you give us no satisfaction. What are your motives in this? Has money in fact lost all appeal for you?"

"I never cared for it," Lafitte said. "You may believe that or not. I cared for justice and freedom. Spain stood against those principles, and so I carried letters of marque to make war upon her. The riches were incidental, necessary merely to prolong that war. But time has moved on. Justice and freedom are antique concepts, of no importance to our modern world. The world, in the person of Lt. Kearny, made it clear that it had no use for me or my kind. I have learned to return the sentiment. I have no use for the things of this world."

He relighted his pipe and took another lungfull of smoke. "You ask about my appearance. I met a brahman from the Indian continent a few years ago. He explained that it is our connection to worldly things that ages us. *Karma,* he called it. I believe I am living proof of the Brahman's beliefs."

"What of those of us still in the world?" Malone said. "I see in you the signs of a former idealist, now disillusioned. I still have ideals. There are still wars to be fought, against ignorance and disease and natural disaster. Wars your treasure could fight. And what of Chighizola, your shipmate? Is he not entitled to his share?" For some reason the fumes from Lafitte's pipe had left Malone terribly hungry. He cast a sideways glance toward the remains of supper.

"If you sailed with him," O'Roarke said to Chighizola, "you must persuade him."

"I think," Chighizola said, "people try that for years now."

"You never answered my question," Malone said to Lafitte. "Money does not motivate you. Neither, it seems, does idealism. At least not any longer. So what is it you care for? What can we offer you?"

"A trip to Galveston," Lafitte said. "I would like to see my island again. To see how things have changed in thirty years. Then we will talk some more." He set his pipe down. "And for the moment, you could hand me the remains of that loaf of bread. I find myself suddenly famished."

49

RAZORED SADDLES

They occupied an entire coach on the return trip. Between
O'Roarke's spitting and Lafitte's pipe, it was even less pleasant than
the outbound journey. They got off the steamer in Galveston late in
the evening of a Sunday. The wharf was crowded nonetheless.
Several freighters were being filled with cotton, the bales crammed
into place with mechanical jackscrews to allow larger loads. The
screwmen were the kings of the dock and shouldered their way
contemptuously through the newly-arrived passengers, carrying
huge bales of cotton on their backs.

Malone led his party, now including a couple of Negro porters,
past Water Street to the Strand. It felt good to have the familiar
sand and crushed shells under his feet again. "The Tremont Hotel is
just over there, on 23rd Street," he said. "If there's any problem with
your rooms, just mention the Commercial and Agricultural Bank.
Mr. Williams, my employer, is part owner of the hotel."

"And where do *you* live?" Lafitte asked. He had not ceased to
smile in the entire time Malone had known him.

"About a mile from here. On 22nd Street. With my wife and her
family."

"Do they not have guest rooms?"

"Yes, of course, but it would be awkward . . ."

"In other words, since this is a purely business venture, you
would prefer to put us up like strangers, well away from the sanctity
of your home."

"That was never my intent. My wife, you see, is . . . highly
strung. I try not to impose on her, if at all possible."

"We are in imposition, then," Lafitte said. "I see."

"Very well! Enough! You shall stop at our house then. We will
manage somehow."

"That is gracious of you," Lafitte said. "I should be delighted."

※　　※　　※

There was no time, of course, to warn Becky. Thus Malone
arrived on his wife's doorstep with four strangers. He had the porters
bring the luggage up the long flight of steps to the porch; like most

Galveston houses, it was supported by eight-foot columns of brick.

Jefferson, the Negro butler, answered the door. "Please get the guest room ready," Malone told him. "I shall put a pair of cots in the study as well, I suppose. And tell Mrs. Malone that I have returned."

"Sir."

Chighizola and his woman left with Jefferson. Malone paid the porters and took Lafitte and O'Roarke into the study.

"Nice place," O'Roarke said.

"Thank you," Malone said, painfully pinching a finger as he set up the cots. "Use the cuspidor while in the house, if you do not mind."

Becky appeared in the doorway. "How nice to see you again," she said to Malone, without sincerity. "It would appear your expedition was more successful than you expected."

"This is Mr. O'Roarke and Mr. . . . Lafflin," he said. Lafitte smiled at the name. "This is my wife, Becky."

She sketched a curtsy. "How do you do."

"They are business associates of mine. I regret not letting you know they would be stopping here. It came up rather suddenly."

"I trust you will find a way to explain this to my father. I know it is hopeless to expect you to offer any explanation to me." She turned and disappeared.

"When I lived on the island," Lafitte said, "we had a whorehouse on this very spot."

"Thank you for that bit of history," Malone said. "My night is now complete."

"Is there anything to eat?" O'Roarke asked.

"If you cannot wait until morning, you are welcome to go down to the kitchen and see what you can find. Please do not disturb Jefferson unless you have to." Malone felt sorry for the old Negro. In keeping with current abolitionist sentiment in Texas he had been freed, but his wages consisted of his room and board only. "And now, if you have no objections, I shall withdraw. It is late, and we can resume our business in the morning."

*　　*　　*

The house was brutally hot, even with the doors and windows open. There had been a southeast breeze when it was first built; the city's growth had long since diverted it. Malone put on his nightshirt and crawled under the mosquito net. He arranged the big square pillow under his shoulders so that night-borne fevers would not settle in his lungs. Becky lay under the covers, arms pressed against her sides, feigning sleep.

"Good night," he said. She made no answer. He knew that he would be within his rights to pull the covers off and take her, willing or not. She had made it clear she would not resist him. No, she would lie there, eyes closed, soundless, like a corpse. He was almost tempted. The days of confinement with Fabienne had taken their toll.

He could recall the flush of Fabienne's golden skin, her scent, her cascading hair. She would not receive a man so passively, he thought. She could, he imagined, break a man's ribs with the heat of her passion.

Malone got up and drank a small glass of whisky. Imagination had always been his curse. Lately it kept him from sleep and interfered with his accounts. Enough gold, he thought, would cure that. The rich needed no imagination.

*   *   *

Malone rose before his guests, eyes bloodshot and head aching. He scrubbed his face at the basin, dressed, and went downstairs. He found his father-in-law in the breakfast room and quickly put his lies in order. He explained Lafitte and the others as investors, wealthy but eccentric, here to look at the possibility of a railroad causeway to the mainland. Becky's father was mad for progress, in love with the idea of the railroad. He smiled and shook Malone's hand.

"Good work, son," he said. "I knew you would make your mark. Eventually."

Chighizola and Fabienne came down for breakfast at eight. Becky had left word for Cook and there were chafing dishes on the sideboard filled with poached eggs, liver, flounder, sausage, broiled tomatoes, and steak. There was a toast rack, a coffee service, a jug of orange juice, a tray of biscuits, and a large selection of jams in small porcelain pots. O'Roarke joined them shortly before nine. He seemed rather sullen, though he consumed two large plates full of food. He ate in silence, tugging on his orange side whiskers with his left hand.

Lafitte, in contrast, was cheerful when he finally arrived. He was unshaven, without collar, braces, or waistcoat, and his long hair was in disarray. He ate only fish and vegetables and refused Malone's offer of coffee.

When Jefferson came to clear away the dishes Malone asked, "Where is Mrs. Malone this morning?"

"In her room, sir. She said to tell you she had letter writing to see to."

She might come down for supper, then. Unless, of course, she suddenly felt unwell, a condition he could predict with some confidence. "If she asks, you may tell her I have taken our visitors for a walk."

First he showed them St. Mary's cathedral, at 21st Street and Avenue F, with its twin Gothic towers on either side of the arched entranceway. It was barely two years old, the first church on the island and the first cathedral in Texas. To Malone it was a symbol. Virtually the entire city had been rebuilt since 1837 and structures like St. Mary's showed a fresh determination, a resolution to stay no matter what the odds.

He pointed out the purple blossoms of the oleanders that now grew wild all over the city, brought originally from Jamaica in wooden tubs. He led them west to 23rd Street, past Sam William's bank. Then he brought them down the Strand, with its commission houses and government offices.

"The similarities to Manhattan Island are clear," Malone said. "Galveston stands as the gateway to Texas, a perfect natural harbor, ideally situated on the Gulf."

"Except for the storms," Lafitte said.

"Man's ingenuity will find a way to rob them of their power. Look around you. This is already the largest city in Texas. And everything you see was brought about by human industry. Nature withheld her hand from this place."

"You need hardly remind me," Lafitte said. "When we first came here there were salt cedars and scrub oaks, poisonous snakes, and man-eating Indians. And nothing else. Am I right, Nez Coupe?"

Chighizola said, "You leave out the malaria and the infernal gulls."

"You can see that things have greatly improved," Malone said.

"Improved? Hardly. I see churches and banks, custom houses and shops, all the fetters and irons of civilization."

"Shops?" O'Roarke said. "Against shops as well, are you? What would you have?"

"No one owned the land when we lived here. Everything was held in common. The prizes we took were divided according to agreed-upon shares. No one went hungry for lack of money."

"Communism," Malone said. "I have heard of it. That German, Karl Marx, has written about it."

"He was hardly the first," Lafitte said. "Bonaparte urged many of the same reforms. As did Rousseau, for that matter."

They had turned east on Water Avenue. At 14th Street Lafitte stopped. He turned back, with one hand shading his eyes, then smiled. "Here," he said.

"Pardon?" Malone asked.

"La Maison Rouge. This is where my house was. Look, you can see where the ground is sunken. This is where I had my moat. Inland stood the gallows. Rebels and mutineers, those who raided any but Spanish ships, died there."

Now there was only an abandoned shack, with wide spaces between the boards where the green wood had shrunk. Malone stepped into its shade for a moment to escape the relentless sun. "Truly?" he said. "Truly, you never attacked an American ship?"

"Truly," Chighizola said. "The Spanish only. He was obsessed."

"Why?"

Chighizola shook his head.

"A private matter," Lafitte said. "I was angry then. Angry enough to burn La Maison Rouge and all the rest of it when I left, burn the entire city to the ground."

"Your anger," Malone said, "is legendary."

"No more," Lafitte said. "To have that much anger, you have to care deeply. To be attached to the world."

"And you care for nothing?" O'Roarke said. "Nothing at all?"

Lafitte shrugged. "Nothing comes to mind."

* * *

Dinner was long and arduous. Lafitte seemed willing enough to play along with Malone's railroad charade. However his lack of seriousness, bordering on contempt, left Becky's father deeply suspicious. O'Roarke's crude speech and spitting would have maddened Becky had she not been upstairs, "feeling poorly," in the words of her maid. As for Chighizola and Fabienne, they were simply ignored.

Afterwards O'Roarke stopped him in the hall. "How much longer? By thunder, Brimstone Jack is not for waiting around. We should be after the treasure."

"If it is any consolation," Malone said, "I am enjoying this no more than you."

Malone retired, but was unable to sleep. Exhausted, yet with his nerves wound tight, he lay propped up in bed and listened to the clock on the dresser loudly tick away the seconds. He finally reached the verge of sleep, only to come awake again at the sound of someone moving in the hallway.

He dressed hastily and went downstairs. He found Lafitte in the porch glider, smoking his hemp tobacco.

"Might I join you?" Malone asked.

"It is your house."

"No," Malone said, sitting on the porch rail. "It is my wife's house. It is a difference that has plagued me for some time. I crave my independence."

"And you think my treasure will buy that for you."

"That and more. Political power. The ability to change things. To bring real civilization to Galveston, and all of Texas."

"I am no admirer of civilization."

"Yet you fought for this country against the British. You were the hero of New Orleans."

"Yes, I fought for your Union. I was young and foolish, not much older than you. I believed the Union would mean freedom for me and all my men. Instead they pardoned us for crimes we had not committed, then refused to let us make a living. When we removed ourselves to this island of snakes, your Lt. Kearney found us. He came with his laws based on wealth and social position, to tell us we were not to live equally, as brothers. Is this civilization?"

"You cannot judge a country by its frontier. It is always the worst of the old and the new."

"Perhaps. But I have seen New York and Washington, and there the poor are more oppressed than anywhere else. But I shall not convince you of this. You shall have to see it for yourself."

They sat for a few moments in silence. A ship's horn sounded faintly in the distance. "What of your wife?" Lafitte asked. "Do you not love her?"

"Certainly," Malone said. "Why do you ask that?"

"You seem to blame her for your lack of independence."

"Rather she seems to blame me, for my lack of a fortune. It is the same fortune I lacked when she married me."

"She is a lovely woman. I wish there were more happiness between you."

"What of you? Did you ever marry?"

"Once. Long ago."

"Was this in France?"

"I never lived in France. I was born and raised in Santo Domingo. My parents were French." He stopped to relight his pipe. Malone could see him consider whether he would go on or not. At last he said, "They came to the New World to avoid the guillotine. Trouble always found them, just the same. Haiti and Santo Domingo have been fighting since Columbus, two little countries on one island, back and forth, the French against the Spanish, the peasants against the aristocracy."

"And your wife?"

"She was fourteen when we married. I was twenty. She was pledged to a Spanish aristocrat. We eloped. He took her from me by force. She killed herself."

"I—"

Lafitte waved away his apologies. "It was long ago. I took my revenge against Spain, many times over. It proved nothing. I always hoped I would find him on one of the ships we captured. Of course I never did. But as I have said, that was long ago. When my anger, as you say, was legend."

"I do not believe you," Malone said.

Lafitte raised one eyebrow.

"You have told me again and again how you care nothing for things of this world. Yet you nearly destroyed Spanish shipping in the gulf of the sake of a woman, and that pain eats at you still. As does your hatred of Lt. Kearny and everything he stood for. As does your belief in liberty, equality, fraternity. Perhaps I am young, but I have seen men like you, men who numb themselves with alcohol or other substances to convince themselves they have no feelings. My father was one of them. It is not your lack of feeling that has preserved you. It is your passion and committment that has kept you going. Whether you have the courage to admit that or not."

Lafitte sat for at least a minute without moving. Then, slowly, he tapped the ash out of his clay pipe and put it in his coat pocket. He stood up. "Perhaps you are right, perhaps not. But I find myself too weary for argument." He began to descend the stairs to the street.

"Where are you going?"

"Mexico, perhaps. I should thank you for your hospitality."

"What, you mean to simply walk away? With no farewell to Chighizola or the others? All this simply to prove to yourself how unfeeling you are?"

Lafitte shrugged.

"Wait," Malone said. "You are the only hope I have."

"Then you have no hope," Lafitte said, but he paused at the bottom of the steps. Finally he said, "Suppose I took you to the treasure. Tonight. Right now. Would that satisfy you?"

"Are you serious?"

"I do not know. Perhaps."

"Yes, then. Yes, it would satisfy me."

He took another half dozen paces, then turned back. "Well?"

"Am I not to wake the others? To fetch tools? To tell anyone where I am bound?"

"If we are meant to succeed, fate will provide. That is my whim. Come now or lose your chance."

Malone stood, looked uncertainly toward the house. "I will share it with the others," he said. "Just as we agreed. I swear."

"That is your concern, not mine. If you are coming, then come now."

*   *   *

Lafitte led him to the harbor at a pace too rapid for conversation. The docks still swarmed with activity. With no attempt at stealth Lafitte stepped into a small sailboat. He motioned Malone to silence and gestured for him to get aboard. Malone saw a shovel, a machete, and several gunny sacks on the floor of the boat.

"But . . ." he said.

Lafitte held a finger to his lips and then pointed it angrily at Malone. Malone untied the stern line and got in. Lafitte rowed them out into the channel. Once they were well away from land Malone whispered, "This is not your boat!"

Lafitte smiled. There was little humor in it. "Do you accuse me of piracy, sir? I warn you I am not fond of the term."

"Is this not theft, at least?"

"Reparations. Owed me by the Republic of Texas and the United States of America. Besides which, you shall have it back before dawn."

Once into Galveston Bay the wind picked up. A chill came off the water and Malone was glad for his coat. In the moonlight the Texas coast was clearly visible, a gray expanse dotted with darker patches of brush. Malone counted at least another dozen sails on the water. Shrimpers, probably, though smuggling was still common. As they passed Jones Point the mainland receded again.

Lafitte was a mediocre sailor at best. He steered them inside South Deer Island, barely avoiding the sandbars. At one point they had to wait for a swell to lift them free. Then, a few minutes later, they rounded a spit of land and headed into Gang's Bayou. It was little better than a swamp, full of marsh grass and sucking mud. Mesquite bushes, with their thorns and spindly branches, grew along the banks around an occasional salt cedar or dwarf willow. It seemed unlikely that Lafitte could hope to find anything in this shifting landscape. Malone began to fear for his life. He should not, he thought, have challenged Lafitte on his lack of feeling.

Lafitte passed one paddle to Malone and kept the other for himself. He lowered the sail and together they pulled the boat into the bayou. The inlet turned quickly around a U-shaped intrusion of land. At the base of it, out of sight of the bay, Lafitte tied up to a squat, massive old oak.

"Bring the shovel," Lafitte said. Malone gathered it up with the gunny sacks. He brought the machete as well, though the thought of violence appalled him. Lafitte took his bearings from the low, marshy ground around them, then drew an X with his boot near the base of the tree. "Dig here," he said.

"How far?"

"Until you strike the chest."

Malone removed his coat and waistcoat and began to dig. He soon lost his chill. Sweat ran into his eyes and his hands began to blister. Lafitte sat a few yards away, uphill on a hummock of grass, smoking his pipe again. The swamp dirt was fine-grained and damp and had a cloying smell of decay. Malone managed a hole three feet around and at least that deep before giving out. It was as if the evil air that came up from the earth had robbed him of his strength.

"I must rest," he said. He laid the shovel by the hole and then crawled over to the trunk of the tree.

"Rest, then," Lafitte said. "I will take a turn."

*   *   *

Malone fell into a trance between waking and sleep. He knew he was on Gangs Bayou, on the north shore of Galveston Island. He had lost track of the year. From where he sat it seemed he could see the entire city of Galveston. The streets of the city began to pulse and swell, like an animate creature. Bricks and blocks of quarried stone floated in the air overhead, then alighted on the ground. They formed themselves into towering heaps, not in the shape of houses and churches and schools, but rather in chaotic columns that swayed to impossible heights, blocking the sun. They filled nearly every inch of the island.

Then Malone noticed bits of paper floating in the air between the towers. They seemed to guide the shape of the buildings as they grew. There was printing on the bits of paper and Malone suddenly recognized them. They were paper notes from Sam Williams' C&A Bank. As he watched they folded themselves into halves and quarters and diagonals. He had once seen a Japanese sailor fold paper that way. They made themselves into people and dogs and birds, and they crawled over the crevices between the bricks, as if looking for shelter. Then, slowly, their edges turned brittle and brown. They began to burn. As they burned the wind carried them toward Malone, who huddled in terror as they began to fall on him.

"Wake up," Lafitte said. "I need your help."

Malone lurched forward, grabbing at nothing. It took him a moment to remember himself. "Forgive me," he said. "I have had the strangest dream. Less a dream than some sort of vision." His head hurt from it, a dull ache that went all the way down his neck.

"Ghosts, most likely," Lafitte said. "They favor treasure. Now come help me get it out of the hole."

"The gold?" Malone said. "You have found it?" It seemed beyond belief.

"See for yourself."

Malone got up and peered into the hole. There did seem to be some sort of trunk there, though mud obscured its details. The top of it was more than four feet down, one end higher than the other. The hole around it, seeping water, was another two feet deep. The thing seemed to have fetched up against the roots of the tree, else it might have sunk to the center of the earth. Malone climbed into the hole and found a handle on one end. Lafitte joined him at the other and together they wrestled the box up onto solid ground.

"Have you the key?" Malone asked, his voice unsteady.

"It is not locked."

Malone used the machete to pry open the lid. Inside he found a greasy bundle of oilcloth. He tugged at it until it unfolded before him.

Even in the moonlight its contents glowed. Gold, silver, precious gems. Malone knelt before it. He took out a golden demitasse and rubbed it against a clean spot on his sleeve. It gleamed like a lantern.

A voice behind him said, "So. This is what you made off to do."

It was O'Roarke. Malone got up to face him. Behind O'Roarke stood Chighizola and the woman. O'Roarke kept walking, right up to Malone. He took the demitasse from Malone's left hand, looked it over, then threw it in the chest. "We thought as long as you were determined to cross us, we would let you do the work. I see now what your promises are worth. You never intended me to gain from all my efforts on your behalf. You merely waited for me to turn my back."

"I swore I would share this with you," Malone stammered, knowing how weak it sounded. "Lafitte witnessed my vow."

"Liar," O'Roarke said. He turned to Lafitte, looming half a foot over him. "And as for you. I should have expected no less from your kind. Once a pirate, always a pirate."

Lafitte slapped him, hard enough to send O'Roarke staggering backward. Malone was suddenly aware of the machete, still in his hand. He wished he were rid of it but was afraid to let it go, afraid to do anything to call attention to himself.

O'Roarke's hand went to his waist. It came up with a pistol, a two-shot derringer. "Die here, then," he said to Lafitte. "Treacherous bastard."

GOLD

Malone knew he had to act. This was neither dream nor vision, and in a second Lafitte would die. He took a single step forward and swung the machete blindly at O'Roarke's head. O'Roarke's eyes moved to follow the blade and Malone realized, too late, how terribly slow it moved. But O'Roarke turned into the blow and the machete buried itself two inches into his neck.

O'Roarke dropped to his knees. The blade came free, bringing a geyser of blood from the wound. O'Roarke's eyes lost focus and his arms began to jerk. A stain appeared on his trousers and Malone smelled feces, almost indistinguishable from the odor of the swamp. O'Roarke slowly tumbled onto his back, arms and legs quivering like a dreaming dog's.

"Christ," Fabienne said, turning away.

"Finish him, for God's sake," Lafitte said.

Malone was unable to move, unable to look away. He had witnessed violence all his life: the drowned, the mangled, the amputated. But never before had he been the cause.

Chighizola grabbed Malone's arm. "Kill him, you stinking coward, eh? Or I do it myself." The old man jerked the machete from Malone's hand and brought it down swiftly on O'Roarke's neck. It made the same noise as the shovel going into the mud. The head rolled sideways, connected only by a thin strip of skin and muscle, and the hideous tremors stopped.

"So, Lafitte, what you up to here, eh? What tricks you pull now?"

"Whim," Lafitte said. "I thought you did not care for this treasure."

"I do not care to play the fool." He threw the machete toward the hillock and it buried itself in the ground. The man's scars were monstrous, inhuman, in the moonlight. Malone could barely stand to look at them, barely get breath into his lungs. "It makes no difference now," Chighizola said. "The deed is done. Help me put this dead one in the ground."

They dragged O'Roarke's corpse to the hole and threw it in. The head came loose in the process and Chighizola sent it tumbling after the body with a short kick. "So much," he said, "for Brimstone Jack." Malone shoveled mud onto the corpse, eager to see it disappear, to give his shaking hands something to do.

"You have your own boat, I trust," Lafitte said.

Chighizola nodded, then was taken with a bout of coughing.

61

"By Christ, this air is foul. Yes, we . . . borrowed a felucca from the dock." Chighizola seemed exhausted. Fabienne took him by the arm. When she looked away from him, at either Lafitte or Malone, her face filled with contempt.

"The three of you can take the treasure back in your boat then," Lafitte said. "I shall keep this one for myself."

"You will take none of the gold?" Malone asked.

Lafitte shook his head. "It would only be extra weight."

Fabienne said, "I will help Louis back to the boat. The two of you can manage the trunk."

Malone watched her help Chighizola up the hillock. "This is the end, then. You will simply disappear again into Mexico. To hide in a drunken stupor from a world you have not the courage to change."

Lafitte smiled. "Courage is certainly not something you lack. Not for you to speak to me this way."

"I have come to respect you," Malone said. "I had hoped for better from you."

"Would it please you to know that I have given much thought to your words? All that thought, and now the sight of your gold and the things it has already brought you. Quarrels and deceit and death. For one who is wrong in so many, many ways, you are right in at least one small one. Perhaps it is time to take the lessons of Campeachy to the world. To Europe. Perhaps to this German, Marx. I think we might have much in common."

Malone held out his hand. "I wish you luck."

Lafitte took it. "And I you. I fear you will need it far more than I."

Lafitte got in the boat. "How will you get to Europe without gold?" Malone asked. "What will you have to offer this Marx?"

Lafitte took up the oars, then looked back at Malone. "Life is simpler than you believe it. I hope some day you will see that." He raised one hand and then pushed away from the bank, into darkness.

*   *   *

Malone divided the treasure between the two gunny sacks and carried them to the other boat. The sacks must have weighed thirty pounds each. That much gold alone was worth a fortune, even before including the value of the jewels.

Chighizola did not look well. He lay with his head in Fabienne's lap, pale and sweating. Malone rowed them out into the bay, then Fabienne raised the sail. She was far more skillful than Lafitte had been. She took them through the Deer Island sandbars without incident, the water hissing smoothly past the hull.

There was no sign of Lafitte or his boat. He had utterly disappeared.

As the lights of the harbor grew close, Fabienne said, "We shall not return to your house, I think. Louis is very sick. We shall find the first boat headed for New Orleans and be gone this morning."

"I will not argue with you," Malone said. "No more than I would with Lafitte. The agreement was equal shares. You must help me divide it."

She looked at the two sacks. "We will take this one," she said. "You keep the rest."

"As you wish. I shall forward your luggage to you in New Orleans." She had picked, Malone was sure, the smaller of the sacks. His heart filled with joy.

*   *   *

He took the burlap sack to the carriage house. There he transferred the treasure to a steamer trunk, piece by piece. At the bottom of the sack was a golden thimble. Malone held it up to the lantern. The words CHARITY & HUMILITY were engraved around the inner lip. He placed the thimble in his waistcoat pocket, locked the trunk, and put it safely away.

He was clean, with his muddy pants and shirt hidden away, by sunrise.

*   *   *

Discreet inquiries provided Malone with a man in San Felipe willing to dispose of "antiquities" with no questions asked. Malone began to carefully convert the treasure to gold specie, a piece at a time, whenever he travelled north on bank business.

In the fall of 1851 he arranged an invitation to dinner at Sam

Williams' house, set on a twenty-acre tract west of the city. Williams was in his mid-fifties now, his hair completely white and parted high on the left side. He was short and heavyset, with a broad forehead and deep lines at the corners of his mouth. He took Malone up to his cupola, where they stood on the narrow walkway and watched for ships in the Gulf. They could hear Williams' daughter Caddy, aged nine, as she played the piano downstairs.

"I understand you have come into some money," Williams said.

"Yes, sir. An inheritance from a long-lost uncle."

"And you are interested in politics."

"Yes, sir."

"There is a good deal an able politician could accomplish these days. I regret I had no knack for it. People found me cold. I do not know why that is." After a moment he said, "You know they are determined to destroy my bank."

"There is a faction, of course, sir, but . . ."

"Make no mistake, they are out to finish me. They consider me a criminal because I made a profit while I worked for the public good. Why, profit is the heart of this country. It is the very thing that makes us grow. And paper money is essential to that growth. Paper money and venture capitalism. Mark my words. That is where the future lies. You're married to—"

"Becky Kinkaid, sir. John Kinkaid's daughter."

"Yes, a good man. And an important connection. You will want to hold on to her, son, believe me. That name can take you a long way."

"Yes, sir."

"Well, let us see. We can start you out on the city council. It will not be cheap, of course, but then you understand that already."

"Yes, sir."

"Good lad. Nothing like a realistic attitude. You will have need of that."

*   *   *

There was nearly a run on the C&A the following January when a rival bank folded. But Galveston merchants exchanged Robert Mills' paper at par and disaster was narrowly averted. In

March the Supreme Court upheld Sam Williams' charter. The anti-bank faction replied with yet another suit, this one based on the illegality of paper money. In April Malone took his seat on the city council and bought his first block of shares in the Commercial and Agricultural Bank.

He found himself with many new friends. They wore tight-fitting suits and brightly colored waistcoats and smoked Cuban cigars. Their opinions became Malone's own by a process he did not entirely understand. But he learned how things were done. A divorce, for example, or even a separation, was not to be considered. Instead he kept a succession of mulatto girls in apartments on the Gulf side of the island, girls with long, curling black hair and unguessable thoughts behind their dark eyes. In time he found that he and Becky could live together with a certain affection and consideration, and it was quite nearly enough. Except for certain hot, muggy nights in the summer when his dreams were haunted by Fabienne.

Still, they were preferable to the nights when he dreamed of towers of stone and folded bank notes and Brimstone Jack O'Roarke with a machete buried in his neck. On those nights he awoke with his hands clutched in the air, on the verge of a scream.

In the next five years he moved from the city council to the Railroad Commission. The next step was the state legislature, via the election in February of 1857. Malone had thought himself a Democrat, but Williams' power lay with the Whigs. The Whigs were traditionally the money party in Texas, and so Malone became a Whig. The campaign was expensive, and took a firm pro-banking stance. On January 19th, banker Robert Mills was fined $100,000 for issuing paper money. Two days later Williams settled out of court on similar charges, paying a token $2,000 fine. Editorials condeming banks and paper money appeared throughout the state.

The Democrats carried the election. The week after his defeat, Malone accepted a position on the board of directors of the C&A.

In August the Panic of '57 brought the closure of one bank after another, all across the country. Tales of bank failures in New Orleans arrived via steamer on October 16. There was a run on the C&A. Williams exchanged specie for his own notes, but refused to cash depositor checks. Malone sat through the night with him, drinking brandy, waiting to see if the bank would open the next day. They did open, and Malone brought in the last of the gold coins from his safe deposit boxes to make sure there would be enough.

That afternoon the bank closed early. Malone stopped for a whiskey on the way home and found the bartender honoring paper money at 75 cents on the dollar. Malone saw only fear and resignation in his eyes. "I got kids, mister," he said. "What can I do? Blame the bankers."

Williams continued to pay gold the next day. The police came to keep lines orderly. By noon the fear had gone out of the customer's eyes. By the end of the month the crisis had passed, only to make way for a new one: counterfeit C&A notes.

The weeks began to blur. In December, Sam Williams' eldest son died. In January the Supreme Court postponed another anti-banking suit, and Williams lawyers fought delaying actions through the spring and summer. In the first days of September the yellow fever came again.

Malone watched the fever take Becky, watched her skin jaundice and her flesh melt away. Williams' wife Sarah, ever thoughtful, sent servents with ice to soothe Becky's fever. It was no more use than Jefferson's herbs. She died on September 7th, a Tuesday.

That Friday Samuel May Williams succumbed to old age and general debility. He was 62.

It was the end of an era. Malone moved out of Becky's parents' house and took a suite of rooms on Water Street. The building was not far from where Lafitte's Maison Rouge had stood. Nothing remained of the treasure but the golden thimble, which Malone still carried in the watch pocket of his waistcoat. He sat at his window and studied the workmen as they built the trestle for the first train from Houston, due to arrive in a little over a year.

He still attended board meetings, though there was little hope the bank could survive. Malone watched with detachment. He saw now how money had a life of its own. For a while he had lived the life of his money, but that life was drawing to a close. The money would go on without him. It was money that had brought the future to Galveston, not Malone. The future would have come without him, in spite of anything he might have done to stop it, had he wanted to. Lafitte had learned that lesson long ago.

He gave up the last of his string of mistresses. The sight of her parents, living on fish head and stale bread, was more than he could bear. He mounted one final campaign for mayor. His platform advocated better schools, better medicine, a better standard of living. But he was unable to explain where the money would come from. He lost by a landslide. 59

On February 28, 1887, the Texas Supreme Court ruled that the Commercial and Agricultural Bank of Texas was illegal. Its doors were closed, its assets liquidated. The last of Malone's money was gone.

*   *   *

He arrived in New Orleans early in the morning. The city had grown as much as Galveston had. The changes were even more obvious to his stranger's eye. The old quarter was bordered now by a new business district, with bigger buildings growing up every day.

They still knew Chighizola's name at the market. Many of them had been at his funeral, years before. They knew his children and they remembered the beautiful octoroon with the French name. Malone followed their directions through crowded streets and stopped at an iron gate set into a brick wall. Through the arch he could see a shaded patio, broadleafed plants, small children.

Fabienne answered the bell herself. She was older, her skin a dusty tan instead of gold. Strands of gray showed in her hair. "I know you," she said. "Malone. The hunter of treasure. What do you want here?"

"To give you this," Malone said. He handed her the golden thimble.

She took it and turned it over in her hands. "Why?"

"I am not sure. Perhaps as an apology."

She held it out to him. "I do not care for your apology. I do not want anything of yours."

"It is not mine," Malone said. He closed her hand over it and pushed it back toward her. "It never was."

He turned away. A sudden movement in the crowd caught his attention and, for a moment, he thought he looked into the sparkling black eyes of Jean Lafitte, unchanged, despite the years. Malone blinked and the man was gone. It was merely, he thought, another ghost. He took a step, then another, toward the river and the ships. He had enough left for a passage somewhere. He had only to decide where to go.

"Wait," Fabienne said.

Malone paused.

"You have come this far," she said. "The least I can do is offer you a cup of coffee."

"Thank you," Malone said. "I should like a cup of coffee very much."

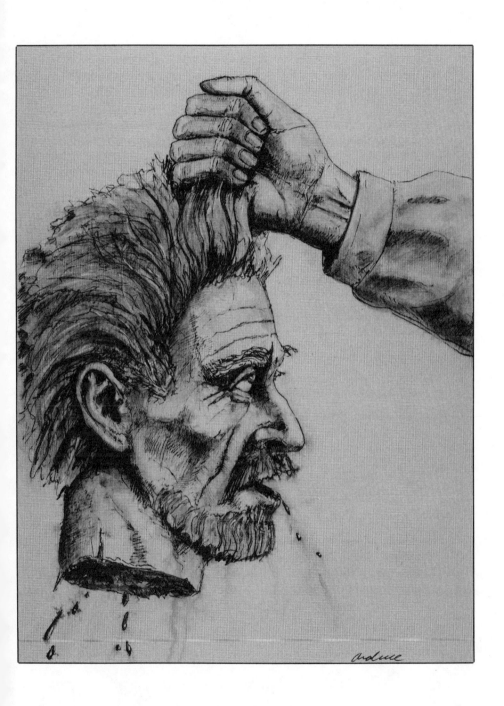

F. Paul Wilson is the author of several highly acclaimed novels, among them THE KEEP, which was filmed with all the love and consideration a hound dog gives a rabbit it's mangling. Looked like a series of hair commercials. Among his other popular books are THE TOUCH and BLACK WIND. What follows is a narrative by Doc Holliday, recorded by Mr. Wilson.

THE TENTH TOE
(or: The Beginning of My End)

by Doc Holliday
(transcribed by F. Paul Wilson)

I am thirty-five years old and will not see thirty-six.

I was not always the weak, wheezing, crumbling sack of bones you see before you, a man whose days can be numbered on the fingers of one hand. Nor was I always the hard drinking gambler and shootist you read of in the penny dreadfuls. I started out a much more genteel man, a professional man, even a bit of a milquetoast.

I attended medical school but did not succeed there, so I became a matriculant at a nearby dental school, from which I managed to graduate. I was then a professional man, and proud of it. But I remained flawed—cursed with a larcenous heart. No amount of schooling, be it of the medical, dental, or (I dare say) divinity sort, can extract that stubborn worm. You are born with it, and you die with it, if not from it.

I am dying from it. It was that young professional man with the larcenous heart who led me to notoriety, and to this premature death from consumption.

Allow me to explain . . .

71

*   *   *

The first inkling I had of the curse was in the spring of 1878 while I was examining Mrs. Duluth.

Mrs. Duluth's husband owned the Dodge City General Store and it was obvious (at least to me) that food was not in short supply on her supper table. She was fat. Truthfully, I have been in out houses smaller than this woman. Everything about her was fat. Her face was fat and round like a huge honeydew melon. Her lips were thick and fat. Even her nose and ears were fat.

"Will this hurt?" she said as she lay back, overflowing my relatively new reclining dental chair. I hoped she wouldn't break its lift mechanism.

"Not a bit," I told her. "After all, this is 1878, not the Dark Ages. We are now blessed with the modern methods of painless dentistry."

"What do you plan to do?"

"I'm going to administer some sulfuric ether," I heard myself say. "And when you're unconscious, I'm going to rob you."

I saw her eyes widen and she must have seen mine do the same. I hadn't meant to say that. True, I had been thinking it, but I'd had no intention of verbalizing it.

"What . . . what did you say, Doctor Holliday?"

"I said I'm going to rob you. Just a little. I'll go through your purse and take some of your money. Not all of it. Just enough to make this exercise worth my while."

"I really don't think that's very funny, Doctor," she said.

I gulped and steadied myself with an effort. "Neither do I, Mrs. Duluth." And I meant it. What was coming over me? Why was I saying these things? "A joke. A dentist's joke. Sorry."

"I should hope so." She seemed somewhat mollified. "Now, about this tooth—"

"Who cares about that tooth. I'm interested in the third molar there with the big gold filling. I'm going to pop that beauty out and replace it with some garbage metal that looks like gold."

(What was I *saying*?)

"That is quite enough!" she said, rolling out of the chair. She straightened her enormous gingham dress and headed for the door.

"Mrs. Duluth! Wait! I—"

"Never mind! I'll find myself another dentist! One I can trust.

Like that new fellow across the street!"

As she went down the steps, she slapped at my shingle, knocking it off one of its hooks. It swung and twisted at a crazy angle until I stepped out and rehung it.

JOHN HENRY HOLLIDAY, DDS
Painless Dentistry

I loved that sign. It was making me rich. I could have made a good living just from the usual drilling, filling, and pulling of my patient's teeth, but that was not enough for my larcenous heart. I had to be *rich*! And I was getting rich quickly from the gold I was mining—literally—from my patient's teeth. I'd found an excellent gold-like compound that I substituted for the real thing while they were out cold in the chair. It was nowhere near as good as gold, but no one had caught on yet. I had another couple of years before the replacement fillings started to fall apart.

Of course, my practice wouldn't last a couple of years if I treated all my patients like Mrs. Duluth. Luckily the waiting room had been empty. I closed the door behind her and stood there thinking. I admit I was somewhat shaken. What was wrong with me? I hadn't meant to say any of those things.

A short while later the widow Porter arrived with her daughter, Bonnie, who had a toothache.

Bonnie was sixteen and extremely buxom for her age. Her busom was apparently growing at such a rate that the bodice of her dress could not keep pace. She was fairly bursting from it. The tortured seams appeared ready to split. From the way she carried herself, proudly erect with her bust thrust out at the world, I assumed that she was well aware of (and revelled in) the male gender's reaction to her proportions.

Bonnie had a cavity in her second lower left molar. As I leaned over her to examine the tooth more closely, she arched her back so that her breasts brushed against my arm. I straightened and looked at her. She stared back and smiled boldly. This was one of the most brazen young females I'd ever met! I was becoming (I hesitate to say it) aroused.

Teenaged girls were never my style. They tend to fall in love, which can be most inconvenient. But for a young thing of Bonnie's proportions, I realized that I might make an exception.

73

"She'll need a filling," I told her mother.

"Oh, dear!" the widow Porter said. "You mean you'll have to use the drill?"

"The drill?" Bonnie said, the simper suddenly gone out of her. "The *drill?*"

"Yes." I lifted the instrument from its hook and pumped the pedal to show her how the bit spun.

Her expression was horrified. "You're going to put *that* in my mouth?"

"Yes. But I'd really—"

I could feel my tongue starting to run off without me, but I refused to let it get away this time. I bit down to hold it in place but it broke free.

"—like to put something else in your mouth, if you know what I mean."

Not again! I seemed utterly helpless against this!

"Really?" Bonnie said, smiling again and thrusting her breasts out even further. "Like what?"

I wanted to shove my fist down my throat. Bonnie's mother, I could see, was thinking along similar lines.

The widow Porter shot to her feet and thrust her face to within an inch of mine.

"*What* did you say?"

I tried to pacify her.

"I'm sorry, Mrs. Porter. Perhaps you misunderstood me. Sometimes I don't make myself clear."

She backed off a little. Good. She was listening—even better. I knew I could smooth this over if my mouth would only let me. Just as her face began to soften, I felt my lips begin to move. I could do nothing but listen.

"What I really meant to say was that I'd like to drill her with a special tool I keep buttoned in my pants. As a matter of fact, I'd like to use it on both of you."

"Scoundrel!" she cried, and swung her heavy purse at me, missing my face by a fraction of an inch. "Bounder!"

She grabbed Bonnie by the hand and yanked her from the room. The girl flashed me a smile and a lascivious wink on the way out.

Sweating and gasping, I slumped against the door. I had lost control of my voice! Every thought that flashed into my brain was going straight out my mouth! What was wrong with me?

I was glad it was a slow day. I went to my office and poured two fingers of bourbon from the bottle I kept in the bottom drawer. I downed it in a single swallow. I looked at my framed degree from dental school hanging on the wall. I had counted on becoming wealthy here in Dodge. Now I was ruining it.

When I heard the front door open, I hesitated going out. It was frightening not to be able to control your words. But I had to defeat this malady. I had to overcome it by sheer force of will. I forced myself into the anteroom.

It was empty. I went into the drilling room and I found a familiar figure sitting in the chair. We played draw poker most nights over at the Forty-Niner Saloon. I wouldn't say we were friends in the truest sense of the word, but I was the closest thing he had to a friend besides his brother.

Wyatt Earp slouched in the chair, helping himself to my nitrous oxide.

Wyatt giggled. "Got a toothache, Doc!"

"Don't overdue that sweet air, Wyatt," I said. "I have to send all the way to Chicago for more."

The smile wavered off and on again. "You'll be going to Chicago and staying there if you try anymore funny business with Miss Bonnie Porter."

I remembered then that Wyatt had been keeping company with the Widow Porter lately.

"I never touched her!"

"But you said some lewd and obscene things that I'd jail you for if you weren't a friend. She's a fine example of young Kansas womanhood and should not be exposed to such behavior."

"She's a tease waiting to blossom into a tart," I said.

Wyatt looked at me with a strange expression. He wanted to frown but the nitrous oxide wouldn't let him.

"I won't have you speak that way about the daughter of a woman for whom I harbor deep feelings."

"You harbor deep feelings for her daughter and you don't want anyone to get to Bonnie before you! And as for the widow Porter, your only deep feelings are for her bank account!"

His half-smile finally disappeared. "Hey, now wait a minute, Doc. I really love that woman!"

I laughed. "You must think I'm as stupid as you are!"

(What was I *saying?* Wyatt had four inches and a good hundred pounds over me! I wanted to vomit!)

"I think you might be a stupid dead man, Doc, if you don't watch what you're saying," he said menacingly as he straightened up from the chair.

I tried to stop myself but couldn't. My mouth ran on.

"Come on, Wyatt. You're fleecing her."

"It's true that I'm allowing her to invest in a couple of the mines that I own, but as a peace officer, I resent your implication that I'm involved in anything illegal."

"You're a disgrace to the badge, Wyatt. People laugh at you— behind your back, of course, because they know if they get on your wrong side they'll wind up in jail on some trumped up charge, or backshot by your brother Virgil!"

He was stepping toward me, his right hand balled into a fist. I broke out in a cold sweat and felt my bladder try to empty. I probably could have stopped him there with a few rational words, or even a quick confession of abject fear. I actually felt the words forming in my mouth as he raised his arm to punch me—

—and that was when the odor hit me.

Standing helpless before him as he loomed over me, I listened in horror as my voice said:

"God! You smell, too! Did it ever occur to you to take a bath before—"

When I woke up on the floor, Wyatt was gone. I staggered to my feet. My jaw ached and my upper lip was swelling. When the room stopped tilting back and forth, I stumbled into the waiting room.

This was a nightmare! If I kept insulting everyone who came to my office, I'd have to close my practice. What would I do? I was already twenty-six and not good for much else besides gambling and shooting. I wasn't a bad shot. Maybe I could take over Earp's job when he left for Tombstone next year.

An odd-looking figure entered then. A skinny old squaw with a hooked nose and dark, piercing eyes set in a face wrinkled like a raisin. That was all I could see of her. The rest of her was swathed in a dusty serape. There was a small red kerchief around her head.

I knew her. Everybody in town knew her: Squaw Jones. She'd been married to an old white man, Aaron Jones, until he got drunk and trampled by a stagecoach a few years ago. Now she wandered in and out of town, selling charms and potions.

"I see Doctor Holliday has bad times," Squaw Jones said. "What is problem?"

"That's what *I'm* supposed to say!" I shouted. *"I'm* the doctor here!"

"Is your words? You say what wish to hide inside?"

I was shocked. "Yes! How did you know?"

"Squaw smell bad medicine when she pass."

"Bad medicine?"

"You have curse."

"I am well aware of that!"

"Squaw Jones can help. Know of these things. You victim of curse of Untethered Tongue. Very bad medicine."

"You're serious? You're talking about a *curse*, like the evil eye or something like that?"

"Much worse."

"I feel bad enough already. Don't try to make me feel stupid, too!"

"You will see, Dr. Holliday," she said, reaching for the door handle. "You will see. And then you will come to Squaw Jones."

"I sincerely doubt it."

"Remember these words. When find man with missing piece, you find enemy."

"I haven't *got* any enemies!"

"It could be friend."

"I haven't got many of those, either! At least not after this morning!"

"Remember Squaw Jones," she said as she shuffled out the door. "You will need her."

That'll be the day, I thought. I didn't need an Indian. I needed another drink.

* * *

The next few days recapitulated the events of that morning: I insulted and alienated each member of a steadily dwindling flow of patients. But at least no one punched me.

As I sat and looked out the front window of my empty waiting room, I noticed Mrs. Duluth waddling along the boardwalk. She turned into the doorway of the new dentist who had come into town a few months ago. Dr. James Elliot. He had been starving. Now he had Mrs. Duluth. Glumly, I wondered how many other patients I was driving to him.

The waiting room door opened and there was Squaw Jones again.

"Squaw can come in?"

I motioned her forward. Why not? I had plenty of time on my hands.

Squaw Jones looked the same as she had days ago—a stick figure swathed in a dirty serape. Her bright, beady eyes swept the barren waiting room. I thought I detected a hint of a smile at the corners of her mouth, but it was hard to be sure amid all her wrinkles.

"Curse of Untethered Tongue continue, yes?"

"It's not a curse," I said. "Just a little problem I have to resolve. I don't believe in curses."

She looked me in the eye. There was no doubt about the smile now.

"You could have sent squaw away," she said. "But you chose to see her."

I knew right then I was dealing with a sly old squaw.

"I'm a man of science," I told her. "A dentist. What do you want from me?"

"Squaw wants only to help."

"For a price, I'm sure."

Her shrug was elaborate. "Must clothe this body. Must eat."

"This wouldn't be blackmail, would it?"

"Doctor Holliday!" she said, puffing herself up. "Squaw is like you. Have medicine to sell—like you. Have honor."

"That's not the point. Even granting the existence of such a thing as a curse, I can't imagine anyone who dislikes me enough— before this week, that is—to place a curse on me."

"Unhappy patient, maybe?"

That was all too possible, what with all the gold fillings I'd yanked from people's mouths while they were unconscious in the chair. But someone like that would go to Wyaat first.

"I can't imagine what complaint a patient of mine could have." (I almost choked on that one.)

"Enemy?"

"None whatsoever."

"Someone want to steal your medicine?"

78

"You mean a competitor? Well, there is one of those. There seems to be an increasing flow of new dentists from the East."

"Who win from Doctor Holliday bad medicine?"

"Well, Dr. Elliot is benefiting now, but . . ." I laughed. "No. It's too absurd!"

"May be him."

"Jim Elliot? Putting a curse on me so I'll say things I don't want to? Ridiculous!"

"Curse of Untethered Tongue say what in heart. Perhaps Doctor Holliday not like his patients."

I said, "Look, I'm very busy right now—"

"Bad medicine always help someone."

I felt the first twinges of uneasiness. This whole idea was absurd! And yet . . .

I turned and found Squaw Jones grinning at me with crooked yellow teeth. She said, "Find man with missing piece."

"You could use a good dentist," I said.

*   *   *

Around supper time, I was at my usual table in the Forty-Niner, alone, nursing a whiskey, shuffling a deck of cards. I dared not play for fear that I would tell everyone what was in my hand at any moment. My fingers froze in mid-shuffle when Dr. Elliot walked in.

I watched him for a few moments. As much as my mind rebelled against the concept of such a thing as a curse, I couldn't get the thought out of my head. Could this mild-looking fellow dentist have actually placed a curse on my practice? The more I thought about it here amid the smells and laughter of the cow hands, the stage drivers, the gamblers, and the plain old riffraff, the more laughable it became.

I wandered over to where he stood. He had a round face made wider by bushy sideburns. He looked tired. Why not? He had been drilling the teeth of my former patients all day.

I was about to say hello when I noticed that he was missing a part of his left fifth digit—the terminal phalanx was gone! As I gaped at the shiny pink dome of fresh scar tissue where his first knuckle should have been, I heard Squaw Jones's voice in my head:

. . . *Find man with missing piece* . . .

I was too shocked for subtlety.

"Your finger! What happened to it?"

He jumped at the sound of my voice and his complexion faded a couple of shades as he looked at me.

"Hello, John. My finger? Why . . . why nothing happened to it. Why do you ask?"

"I never noticed that you had a . . . piece missing before now. When did it happen?"

He smiled, regaining his composure. "Oh, that. An old accident when I was in school back east. An industrial accident, you might say. I caught it in a defective drilling machine."

I couldn't take my eyes from that foreshortened digit. "The scar tissue doesn't look that old."

"An old injury, do you hear?" He was becoming agitated. "Very old. Very, *very* old!"

The obvious freshness of the scar and Dr. Elliot's overwrought behavior sent a stream of ice water running through my arteries.

. . . When find man with missing piece, you find enemy . . .

"Yes, of course," I said. "Very old. Of course."

He thrust his hand into his pocket.

I fled the saloon and ran to the stable. I saddled my horse and rode out to where Squaw Jones made her camp.

*   *   *

"So now Doctor Holliday believe in curse of Untethered Tongue," she said, nodding and smiling with smug satisfaction.

"Not completely," I said. "Let's just say I disbelieve in it less than I did this afternoon."

Her tent was dim, the air inside steamy and layered with reminders of past meals, strangely spiced.

"But I just can't believe," I said, "that one of my colleagues, a fellow dental practitioner, would be so unethical as to use such scurrilous means to build his practice at my expense!"

"You would never do such thing?"

"Never! I am an ethical practitioner!"

"And what is your wish, Dr. Holliday?"

"To have the curse—if that's what it is—lifted."

"By this squaw?"

80

"Of course. That's why I'm here."

"Want thirteen ounces gold for ending Untethered Tongue."

"Thirteen oun—?"

"This squaw know it very small price for saving Doctor Holliday's honor, but her heart is touched by his misfortune." She cleared her throat. "Please pay in metal, not bills."

I'd hidden away significantly more than that amount of gold from the fillings I'd removed over the years. But thirteen ounces!

"I'd want a guarantee."

"Nothing sure in magic, Doctor Holliday."

I rose from my seat and started for the door. "I'm sorry. I can't allow myself to be made into a fool." I was bluffing. I bluffed well in poker, even back then, and had little doubt I could get her to back down. But she kept quiet, waiting until my hand closed on the door-knob before she spoke. She did not, however, say the words I was hoping for.

"For three more ounces, maybe this squaw can turn bad medicine back on one who start it."

As I said before: A sly old bird. I had taken the bait, now she set the hook. A gamble of sixteen ounces, but suddenly I didn't care. I wanted to get even.

I returned to my chair.

"Can you really do that?"

She nodded. "If Doctor Holliday make sacrifice.

"Sacrifice? Wait a second here. I—"

"Must have no fear."

"I'll have no fear as long as I have my revenge."

She smiled and rubbed her hands together. "This is good."

"What do I have to do?"

"Doctor Holliday must give three things. First thing closely touches maker of Untethered Tongue. You know who he is?"

"Dr. Elliot," I said. "No doubt about it. But just how 'closely' must this thing touch?"

"Very close. Underclothes. Pen."

I considered that for a moment. How on Earth was I going to handle that? How was I going to get a hold of a pair of Elliot's under-wear? Maybe a sock would do

No matter. I'd find a way.

"What else do you need?"

"Need small amount of Doctor Holliday's liquid."

81

"Liquid?" This was getting more cliched by the minute. "You mean blood?"

She shook her head. She seemed embarrassed. "Fluid that only man can give."

"I don't understand—" I began. And then I did. "What kind of magic is this?"

"Very, very old."

"Really. And what if I were a woman?"

"We wait for your time of month."

"I see." I found it difficult to believe that I was sitting here having a serious conversation about this.

She cleared her throat again. "The sample—you can give soon?"

I squared my shoulders. "Of couse. And the third thing?"

"This squaw will tell when you bring first two."

I wasn't sure I liked the sound of that, but I couldn't turn back now. I had stepped over the edge and had left the safe and sane world behind; I was now adrift in the world of the magical and the irrational. Squaw Jones's world. I had to trust her as a guide.

*　　*　　*

Early the next morning I was at the hotel next to my office eating eggs and potatoes. I've never liked eggs and potatoes, but I was there because Elliot was there. I raged silently as I watched him storing up on his nourishment before a busy day of drilling the teeth of my patients.

I was in a black mood. I had been by his rooming house earlier but had found none of his laundry around. I'd been tempted to break into his quarters but was afraid I'd get caught. I couldn't risk that, not with Wyatt still mad at me.

As I watched him, he stirred his coffee and licked the spoon dry before placing it on the tablecloth. A neat man. A fastidious man. I felt like running over and wringing his—

The spoon.

I almost shouted out loud. *That's it!* The spoon! It had been in his mouth! What contact could be more "close" than being in some-one's mouth?

I waited until he finished his meal and departed, then hurried over to his table, just beating the serving girl to it. She gave me a strange look as I darted in front of her and grabbed his spoon off the tray, but I simply continued on my way without a backward glance, as if this were the most natural thing in the world.

The hard part was over. I headed across the street to the back rooms at the Forty-Niner. Miss Lily would be waking up just about now. For a nominal fee, she'd help me obtain the second ingredient. This was the easy part.

*   *   *

"Now what?" I said as I held out the spoon and a small cup of cloudy liquid to Squaw Jones.

She made no move to take them from me. "You have gold?"

"Yes." I pulled a leather pouch from my coat pocket. "Sixteen ounces, as agreed."

I held my breath as she loosened the draw string and looked inside. My larcenous heart had prevailed on me to cheat her of her payment. No gold for Squaw Jones. Instead I'd made nuggets of lead and coated them with the gold colored material I used for my fake gold fillings. They wouldn't stand close inspection.

She looked inside, gauged the weight of the bag in her hand, then nodded.

"Is good." The pouch disappeared inside her serape and then she took the two ingredients from me. "Now this squaw make mix. Doctor Holliday wait outside."

"What about the third ingredient?"

She smiled. "Soon, Doctor Holliday. Must be patient."

I stepped outside her tent. It was difficult to be patient knowing that Dr. Elliot was busy in his office working on my patients while my office door was locked.

After what seemed like hours, Squaw Jones called me back in. I found her sitting there with a cup of steaming liquid.

"Now time for third ingredient. The sacrifice."

"What sort of sacrifice?" I didn't like the sound of this one bit.

"Small part of you. Something Doctor Holliday will not miss, but something that will not grow back."

"Wait just a minute!" I said. I'd heard about deals like this where you make a trade for "something you'll never miss" and I didn't want to fall into *that* trap! "We're not talking about my soul, are we?"

She laughed. "No! Only small piece of flesh. Token for gods. Dr. Elliot gave finger."

"How did you know that?"

"You told this squaw last night."

"Did I? I don't remember."

"You did. Doctor Holliday must make same sacrifice if he wish bad medicne go away."

Something that won't grow back. That left out hair and finger-nail clippings. I certainly didn't want to lose a part of a finger—I didn't approve of public deformity.

"Maybe this isn't such a good idea."

She shrugged. "Without sacrifice, Dr. Elliot will not feel curse of Unhindered Hands."

"'Unhindered Hands'? Just what is that?"

"Like Untethered Tongue. As Doctor Holliday's lips now speak what he wish kept hidden in heart, Doctor Elliot's hands will do things he only wish to do."

The thought of Dr. Elliot's hands acting upon whatever phys-ical desires occurred to him, to be no more able to restrain his hands than I had been able to restrain my tongue delighted me.

Then I thought of something neither I nor anyone else would miss—

"How about my little toe?"

"It is good," she said.

"How do we do this?"

Following her directions, I removed the boot and sock from my left foot and held it over the steaming liquid.

"Dip toe."

Feeling like a fool for going through this hocus pocus, yet hating myself for not having the nerve to call the whole thing off and take my chances with my unruly tongue, I dipped my little toe into the cup.

"Enough," she said after a moment. She withdrew the cup and handed me a dirty cloth. "Dry toe."

I scrutinized my left fifth toe. It looked just like the others, only wet.

"Something's wrong!" I said. "I thought I was supposed to 'sacri-fice' this toe! Nothing happened!"

"Patience, Doctor Holliday. Patience."

I was convinced now that I was being hoodwinked. I quickly

rubbed my toe dry and rose to my feet.

"This is a farce! I'm glad I didn't give you any real gold!"

Her head snapped around. She stared at me. "Gold not real?"

"No. So you can call off this whole charade."

"Too late. Medicine is made. Curse begins."

"But my toe—"

I looked down at my left foot. There were only four toes. All that remained of my tenth toe was a small pink bulge of fresh scar tissue.

"Where—?"

I opened the cloth and there was my toe. As I watched, it fumed and melted into a pink fluid that was absorbed by the cloth. The odor made me want to gag.

Squaw Jones was pawing through the bag of fake gold nuggets. "Doctor Holliday trick this squaw?"

"Why not? You're probably the one who got me in this fix in the first place. You're playing both sides of street."

She approached me, menace in her eyes. I kept watch on her hands, making sure both were in sight. They were: clutching the pouch of fake gold. Her face came within inches of mine. She stared at me.

Then she coughed. Once.

"Return to your office, Doctor Holliday. Curse of Untethered Tongue is broken; curse of Unhampered Hands begin. Squaw Jones cannot change that now."

I glanced down at my four-toed foot again and realzied I was rapidly becoming a believer. With boot and sock in hand, I hurried from Squaw Jones's tent.

"But you will pay another way!" she called after me.

* * *

The first patient to show up was Mr. O'Toole. My private name for him was "Mr. O'Stool"—he had a bowel fixation which he blamed on his bad teeth. He spent most office visits describing his movements. He was a bore but he came every two weeks for a new filling.

But I got through the visit with no problem. I'd had an urge to tell him that I thought he was suffering from a fecal impaction that had backed up to his brain but the remark remained within my mind while my mouth offered bland reassurances.

I drilled his latest imaginary cavity and fairly danced out of the examining room.

I've done it! I've broken the curse!

I went to the front window in my waiting room and looked across the street at Dr. Elliot's office. I whispered:

"I've beaten you, Elliot! Beaten you at your own game!"

As I watched, I saw Bonnie Porter come racing out of Dr. Elliot's office, trying to cover her bobbing, exposed breasts with one hand while holding up her ripped skirt with the other. In close pursuit, with a piece of Bonnie's torn bodice clutched in his teeth, was Dr. Elliot. And right behind the two of them was the widow Porter, swinging her handbag. She caught Dr. Elliot full force in the back of the head with a swing and he went down. Then she stood over him and began pounding him with the bag.

I watched until Wyatt ran up. He pulled his pistol and just stood there, his eyes captured by the pink-tipped whiteness of Bonnie's breasts. I knew though that as soon as she covered herself, Wyatt would be on Dr. Elliot like a lynch mob. He wasn't going to take at all kindly to someone going after Bonnie Porter before he'd had firsts.

Poor Dr. Elliot. Couldn't control his hands. Such a shame.

As I turned away I felt a twinge behind my sternum. I began to cough. I'd never coughed like this before in my life. Spasms racked my chest. I pulled out my handkerchief and buried my face in it, trying to muffle the coughs, perhaps supress them by trapping them inside. Suddenly I felt something tear free in my chest and fill my throat. I gagged it out.

Blood stained my handkerchief.

Hemoptysis—a bloody cough. A sure sign of consumption, or what they were now calling tuberculosis.

But how could I have tuberculosis? I hadn't been visiting anyone in a sanitarium, and the only people in these parts who had any tuberculosis were . . .

. . . Indians.

Squaw Jones had coughed in my face, but only once, and that had been just a few hours ago. I couldn't have developed tuberculosis in that short of time. It was impossible.

I glanced out the window again. Wyatt was leading Dr. Elliot off toward the jail, and being none too gentle about it. In the crowd that had gathered, all heads were turned to watch them go. All except one. Squaw Jones was there, staring directly at me.

I coughed again.

David Schow lives in L.A., has a ponytail, and a better relationship with my Siberian Husky than I do. Nothing sexual mind you, they just love one another. He's a novelist, short-story writer, screenplay writer and editor. I think short story writer may be his best thing, as evidenced by the off-beat tale that follows.

SEDALIA

by David J. Schow

Due east of Nalgadas Butte, Case could see dinosaurs silhouetted against a sunset the tint of a bruise. He snubbed his filterless Camel against the instep of one boot and dropped it amid the scatter of dead butts at his feet. It smoldered cantankerously. He'd been standing for a long time, just watching.

As he watched, a Mamenchisaurus the length of two tractor trailer trucks eased up from relieving itself on the alkalai hardpan. It switched a thirty-foot neck around to check its business, then promptly faded from view like a fuzzy TV image dissolving into static. The loose pyramid of million-years-old dinosaur shit remained completely corporeal. It was so real heat shimmer curled up from it. Case was accustomed to the stench. A professional, was Whitman Case.

While the big 'dine frizzed into vapor, a bugeyed Coelophysis materialized not ten feet from where Case was loitering. The ostrich throat gulped in surprise as it attained solidity. It spotted Case, did a double-take like a cartoon character, and scampered away on spindly bird legs. It was the riotous color of an amoebic slide at an Iron

89

Butterfly concert. It would be hungry for eggs or perhaps a bite-sized salamander, if it lasted long.

Good hunting, Case thought. He would not have tipped his hat even if he had been wearing one. Too damned hot.

If Whit Case resembled a Marlboro Man it was purely by accident; he felt as incongruous as the notion of a herd of ghost dinosaurs might have been, two years back. Nowadays people accepted the 'dines as part of the same world of betrayal, death and taxes as the one upon which they treadmilled the ole nine-to-fiver. Explanations for the phenomenon had not been instantly apparent, although a corral of academics fell all over themselves proposing theories. The sole halfway sensible explanation had been posited by a man named Seward, and he hadn't even been accredited. He told people why the 'dines had come back in simple language. All the rest had gone crazy with tabloid fever: Dinosaurs were skinks mutated by atomic radiation. From UFOs. From Russia. From Russian UFOs. They were automatons manufactured by corporations hungry to profit from mass panic. They were military biowar accidents.

They were almost overlooked in the mad dash for publicity. Case thought all the scholars and profs and degree chimps suffered from terminal vapor lock of the sphincter. Unlike the big momma 'dine that had just unleashed a megaton of extremely real—though antediluvian—reptile poop to the east of Nalgadas Butte. A *bilingual pun,* thought Case. *Christ, we've been hanging fire in one place so goddamn long the convolutions in my fucking brain are smoothing out.*

He wished he could be as smart as that Seward fella. Intelligent people probably weren't so bored all the time. He tapped out his next Camel. Nothing to do out here except wait, smoke, watch the sun ebb. Sentry the 'dines as they winked in and out, keep them grouped. Wait, smoke some more, cough, ask the drive mojo if they could press forward, onward with the dawn, and if the mojo said no again today, then wait some more, fuck your hand and try to make the day pass quickly so you could ask the mojo again tomorrow.

Aguilar had humped it up the geologic formation the drovers had named the Stirrup. Said he was searching for the limestone plateau where legend had it that a 'dine drover had scattered his mental marbles permanently by playing endless hands of twenty-one with the shade of Jack the Ripper, betting his soul or his life,

SEDALIA

Case has forgotten which. Aguilar had not stuck around camp, knowing that the mojo, whose name was Ernest "Shack" Cocoberra, would just say no again today. So off he rode, without even asking.

Maybe Aguilar was going crazy waiting, too.

Droving had been a lost American craft until the 'dines had resurged. Who cared if they were totally real or not, so long as a profit might be turned from herding them?

The big beasts had rescued Case from the fallout of his third firebombed marriage and a coke habit which, fiscally speaking, had begun to resemble the jackpot of the state lottery on one of those days when nobody had picked the right numbers for awhile. He had not known how appealing a cold-turkey switchoff could be until his droving contract had been bonded. He'd been required to pass urine and blood tests, and had skinned past. Only just.

He had replaced the whoopee dust with Camels and contemplation. The hole left in him by Pearl never closed.

The hornet buzz of Aguilar's trailbike came razzing across the flats. Like Moses, he had come on down. Probably with no news of spirits. And at dawn Shack would gravely inform all hands that they had to stay right where they were for one more thrilling day.

If your honor was intact, the waiting wasn't so bad.

Case waited to swap the usual words with Aguilar. In about an hour there would be microwave chili and seven card stud, and a fire around which the oldest stories would be repeated one more time.

With a wet water balloon squeegee noise, a Triceratops pressed through into the real world, its golden disc eyes glazed from the transfer. It pawed dust and wandered off, making the earth tremble. Case sniffed the languid air. Nothing like fresh dino waft to hand-cancel your appetite.

Below, in the bowl of the valley, a thousand or so dinosaurs milled around in varying states of corporeality. Execreting. Mating. Waiting, like Case.

What started out as a *Time* Magazine cover screamer had become a growth industry. Case's current profession was a by-product of the Sherlockian equations that had come out of that fella Seward's mind. And the happanstance that first set Seward to his brainwork had occurred at a rundown Texaco station in the middle of Riverside, California.

* * *

91

RAZORED SADDLES

The best thing about Lloyd Larned's antique pop machine was that it really kept the bottled soft drinks ice-cold. Lloyd had just taken a good swig off of his Dr Pepper when the Tyrannosaurus Rex crushed his Texaco station. It jammed its grinning, leathery skull through the roof of the garage, nearly uprooting the entire building, and its confined thrashing took out louvered metal doors and cinderblock walls like toothpicks and cardboard. It kicked down the office. It wiped out the Ladies Room with its fat cable of tail.

Lloyd took three staggering backward steps away from the demolition, his dropped pop bottle disintegrating on the hot-topped drive. He never saw the pumps blow up because the devilish reptile snatched him high and segmented him with six-inch teeth. One swallow and most of Lloyd was gone. The fireball born of the exploding service station—two bays, four pumps and one hellacious overhead—billowed skyward, shoving the animal forward on a warm, concussive cushion. Its tail sent a fire hydrant spinning across the residential street. As it recoiled from the heat blast, it stomped on a canary yellow Corvette T-top parked at the curb, reducing it to a mashed tinfoil joke. A plume of water spewed twenty feet into the afternoon air. It bent over in a fashion never depicted in children's books and drank from the flow with a mottled crimson tongue.

Howie Raper, who had been larking on the crapper while Lloyd was stealing the Dr Pepper from his own machine (Lloyd never paid and always used his key), lay buried from the waist down in a fall of shattered concrete, his left eye blinded by the flow of blood from his scalp. He was dying with his pants around his ankles. The vision flickered in his good eye long enough for him to witness the Rex's departure. It rampaged down the side street and into the twilight, away from the blaze, moving with huge, loping strides. Howie made one peculiar observation before he succumbed to smoke inhalation.

Jesus God, a purple dinosaur . . .

*   *   *

Here's Cal Worthington and his dog, Spot!

Seward's subconscious was obstinate. For some reason it kept repeating the seance. It was like a ride in Disneyland where each diorama of pirates or ghosts or whatever had its own tape loop, so as

92

you rode past them in your little car you got an entire canned spiel in sequence. But if the ride broke down and you got stuck in one place, you'd keep hearing the same snippet over and over and . . .

"We call out to you now, Uncle Isaias, from our side of the veil. We are calling to you so that you may help us to contact the spirit of Murial MacKenna, dear, dear departed sister. Oh, Uncle Isaias, do you cleave with us this night? Can you heeeaaar me—?"

When Seward thought of the robot playground that was Disneyland, he was able to fixate on the scam being perpetrated by the woman calling herself Madame Bathsheba Tyndall-Smyth. From behind draperies, an operative of Bathsheba's manned a video projector. Slanted beams bounced from mirror to mirror and recorded images manifested in the Madame's parlor as she held seance. It was taboo for her marks to leave the table. Breaking the circle of hands, she explained, would compel the visiting spirits to instantly depart. They sure as hell would, Seward thought. Worse, they might jump into fast-forward mode and embarrass the bereaved survivors.

Madame Bathsheba employed a Nubian to prevent customers from dashing through the key curtain in their grief. Seward employed a get-around he'd learned from a college pal who had been an All Star linebacker. As he liked to say, he "executed the reveal." The Nubian had almost executed Seward, trapping him inside a particularly stressful bear hug. But the hoax had been exposed.

The mirror gimmick was similar to an illusion Seward had seen in the late Unca Walt's Magic Kingdom. Actually, Unca Walt was supposedly freeze-dried in a cryonic fishtank somewhere, so he wasn't late, just postponed. Even after centuries of fakery, the best tricks were still done with mirrors. The glowering, turbaned sentry had turned out not to be a bonafide Nubian, either.

When Seward managed to slit his eyes, light, and inexplicably, sound flooded his head in a torrent. Fluorescent tubing, miles long and too brilliant. Linens so sterile they whisked away your breath. A mummy. A whipcord dude in a Stetson, stroking an American eagle. Banjo music going a few hundred RPMs too speedy. Seward lost his mental grip and tumbled back down to where the seance was still repeating. A woman's voice, soft and lugubrious, said *oh I AMsorry mister (Seward didn't catch a name), but he's not out of it yet, poor man. Hm? It's major. Sorry.*

Mediums and necromancers of previous centuries had missed

out on the advantages of video technology. Science, the so-called converse of the occult, had kept magic thriving by providing unscrupulous phonies with more efficient ways to bilk the gullible, almost as if some sort of gentleman's agreement existed between the fields of fraud and sorcery. The public was so eager to believe in the spiritual. They required very little prompting.

Well, now they'd *better* believe, Seward thought. Even if it puts me out of a job.

The good Dr. Falkenberg had taped up the damage done to Seward's ribs by the ersatz Nubian, and Seward got the usual admonishment on the physical hazards attendant to the profession of occult debunker. Falkenberg himself had begun to sound like a tape at Disneyland. Seward deposited the good faith check from Eloise MacKenna, sister of the dear, departed Muriel.

Next had come Marybeth's front porch.

He used his own set of keys to get in. The first thing she said to him had been: "Damn you, David Seward." It was her you-always-show-up-when-I'm-a-mess tone, which meant he could get his *own* drink while she polished off her after work shower. He knew his way around her five-room place. He poured a neat scotch and smiled at the thought of Marybeth in her terrycloth bathrobe. Her TV was on, playing to an empty room. As he merged from the kitchen he caught the tail end of a very weird bulletin indeed.

Seward did not believe what he saw. It wasn't the first time.

He had abandoned Marybeth in the shower and run half a block toward Fareholm Drive when he realized he would need a car. He hurried back, scooped up his keys, and forced his aging radials to kiss the pavement with black stripes. Marybeth was still rinsing.

Just south of Sunset Boulevard the traffic had snarled on Fairfax. By then, he could see too well. He clambered onto the roof of his car to see better. He was so stunned by what he saw that he felt his body galvanized by an urban need long unexperienced: The need to have somebody in authority explain just what the hell was going on here.

Incoming automobiles had already closed off escape to the rear, the way litter piles up in a drainage grate after a storm. Seward leapt ungracefully from hood to trunk across a chaos of gridlocked cars. So few people yelled at him he almost forgot he was in Los Angeles.

Amid a clot of uniformed men on the sidewalk he spotted a

major's gold oak leaves. He jostled closer through a riptide of gawking pedestrians, and was three yards from enlightenment when the building wall folded down to bury them all.

His knees hit the sidewalk and he banged his forehead against a payphone carrel. Then a falling brick skinned his skull and severed his tielines with the real world.

. . . and his dog, Spot!

This time, Seward's eyes opened and did not deny the hospital room or the car commercial gibbering from the TV set. In an adjacent bed was the mummy, plastered limbs hanging from wires and slings. One eye was unbandaged. It moved from the TV to check Seward's status, caught him awake at last, and widened.

"Christ on a fudgecicle stick, boy, it's about time!" It was the major. It was partly the dogface brassiness of the voice, partly the eye, which Seward recognized because his job had always necessitated attention to minute detail. He remembered the major's eyes, watching the building come down to meet them.

"You've been out colder than a nun's punky for two days!"

This was verified by an RN who stopped by to make Seward swallow pink pills. He promised to marry her if she would bring more water. She was stocky, pretty, obviously fatigued.

Seward watched the major's visible eye follow the nurse out, and wondered whether the soldier's body cast could accommodate an erection. Then the major's eye came back to him.

"You need an update, am I right? Course I am." He let loose a chuckle that was more a cough. "Jeezus. You're gonna *love* this."

As he spoke, another Cal Worthington commercial screamed at them from the TV, assaulting their senses.

* * *

At that moment David Seward had been hastily introduced to various airborne portions of the law firm of Pratt, Bancroft, Keanau and Hudson in West Hollywood, Cal Worthington—southern California's emperor of automobiles—was busy down in Long Beach taping new commercials on behalf of movie insomniacs and potential customers up and down the entire Pacific Coast. All night, every night, on nearly every station, the worst Z-movie dregs and awful sitcom reruns the affiliates could get away with were punctuated by an endless barrage of ads for Worthington Ford, Worthington Dodge, Worthington Suzuki . . .

Time had marched. What once was Ralph Williams and his dog Storm was presently Cal and Spot. Cal's dumb gimmick was to feature a different Spot for each spot, so to speak. An eagle, a rhino, a shark at Sea World. Almost nobody remembered Storm the German shepherd anymore—except for old Firesign Theatre fans—and as far as David Seward and millions of other co-Californians could recall, Cal had never stooped to using an actual dog. Something had been lost. Time had marched, and today Cal Worthington was Numero Uno.

His specialty was gang-buying leftover commercial airtime in the midnight-to-six leg, when the excitement of local TV slowed down a bit. If your set was on, you couldn't miss him, and cable had opened up whole new vistas for Cal to conquer.

The gangly car huckster had just hung a seven-foot boa constrictor around his neck when the Gorgosaurus rampaged in from frame left, flipping Hyundais and Daihatsus out of its path like cardboard boxes. Spot the boa panicked—maybe its reaction was racial—and slithered tight. Cal's eyes bugged. He took a header, clawing at the snake and hollering. The Gorgosaur flattened a Chevy Luv and spooned up its prey—cowboy hat, serpent, purple face and all. The audio track laid down the crunch of bones. Cal's final words were *keep shooting*. His cameraman, a UCLA film school grad, held bravely while his crew fled. Footage such as this could make him a star, he thought right up to the moment he died.

*   *   *

The mummified major was lecturing.

"Even smallfry artillery pulls their plugs, but what a friggin *mess*. Each one weighs *how* many tons? How much stinky, rotten goop all over the billboards and sidewalks if you blow them to hell? The sanitation crews threatened to strike right away. Yecch. You saw Fairfax Avenue."

Seward remembered.

He had watched a dreamy *banzai* wash along at strolling pace, its constituents nothing like the puppets of numberless Ray harryhausen dino-operas, or flaccid iguanas in cosmetic jazz, or the

96

honorable Godzilla. These monsters glistened and stank; bugs swarmed about them in clouds, riding the sour humidity of their advance. Thousands of beasts, walking north, massy and muscular, their shuffling strides emphasizing the sheer tonnage of living meat in locomotion, their metallic eyes afire with motility and hot, urgent life.

They were contrary to civilization. Their gigantism made them destructive quite apart from malice. Awkwardly they tipped over trucks and swept down streetlamps with their thick, switching tails. They blundered into each other, then backed into storefronts, demolishing them. Utterly unnoticed in the commotion, the odd screaming pedestrian got mashed into pate.

On the roof of his car, Seward had been transfixed by the shocking colors. The discordant clash of berserk pigmentation thoroughly contradicted the ho-hum deductions of decades of textbooks. The dinosaurs were vividly hued, bizarre, ultimately shocking.

The great industrial clockwork that was Los Angeles failed to command respect from these former tenants. The temblors of their footsteps pulverized the concrete; their basic hungers redefined highly-evolved citzenry as junkfood. The crowding turned violent when an Allosaurus was gored by a Styracosaur the size of a Patton tank. The shrieking carnivore rolled through the entrance to a supermarket, taking out girders like jackstraws and shattering tons of glass. Its insufficient claws pawing for the puncture in its belly, the Allosaur's every thrash took lives. Gawking shoppers were summarily dismembered or squashed. The Styracosaur rattled its fringe of horns, agitating the flies that had come for blood. The rhinoceros-like forward horn was obscenely red and jutting, an upthrust wet tusk. The east wall of the building was shrugged off by the thirty-ton Brachiasaurus walking through it. Its swanlike neck paid out like a vast orange ruler incremented in crimson hashmarks. The cutlass teeth of the Allosaur glinted off the supermarket fluorescents as it continued to die. In the parking lot, several tall, ostrich-looking reptiles nibbled at the tops of palm trees nurtured in this modern-day photochemical atmosphere, found the taste of the flowers brackish, and sent the trees plummeting down. Overhead, demonaic black shapes rode the thermals on wings of skin. An immense American flag tore loose from its mooring atop an insurance building and came drifting down, an undulating leaf of clashing colors, falling, falling.

In Seward's memory the descent of the football-field sized flag seemed the most terrible thing of all. The start flag for the apocalypse, perhaps. He saw billions of reptiles blacking out the concept of countries, casting entire continents into their shadow. This was no Army experiment gone haywire. This might be the end.

After being awakened by the comedy of the late Mr. Cal Worthington, Seward digested what the Major told him about the coming of the dinosaurs . . . and how they began to disappear as fast as they materialized.

"Tank crew zeroed in on a biggie," he said. "Poof—that dinosaur frizzed into static. They showed the tape on the news, slo-mo, instant replay and all that. You know when your cable service goes on the blink? Looked just like that. A monster the size of a concentration crane just zapped into a cloud of bluegreen vapor and swam away on the westerlies. And bam, bam, bam, there were dinosaurs appearing one second and disappearing a few minutes later, like they'd established some kinda beachead but couldn't hold, you know? Well, militarily speaking, our problem shrank like a gonad in formaldehyde. For a second there it looked like this was going to be a disaster for property values, and now and again somebody got chewed up or squished."

The major's drone blended with the TV, and Seward let the medication sweep him away for a bit. An ebony shape with hungry bronze eyes scudded past their eighth floor window. He fell into a natural sleep and dreamed again of Disneyland.

*   *   *

Aguilar had had himself a revelation up there on the Stirrup, or so he kept broadly hinting to Case. He squinted toward the valley of the 'dines, ciggie dangling from his sunburnt lips, an intense expression plastered across his face a hair too obviously. Aguilar rolled his own; the stench was similar to smoldering balsa wood.

"Nope. Just can't see him yet."

Case decided to humor him. "Moses, with a new, improved tablet?"

He frowned. "Brontosaurus, green mottles, black saddle, alternating red and green on the tail. Black tail tip. You talk to the Shack?"

98

"What for?" Case dropped into his overblown imitation of Shack Cocoberra's chili pepper accent: "Chak, he say, pardone señor, we don't go noplace today neether." Smoke and lees from the tepid tea in his thermos had congealed into an unlovely paste at the back of his palate. He coughed and spat uselessly. "I'm beginning to think he just wants to rack up overtime, is what I think."

"Naw. Shack's honest, at least."

"Overeducated, too." Case knew Shack's accent was mostly for atmosphere in the drive.

"Besides, it ain't worth it." Aguilar had made the argument before; this would not be the last time. "Easier to finish out, contract a new drive, get the sign-on fee upfront. When the drives move quicker he gets a faster turnaround on the fees."

"Yeah. Shack's honest." Mojos for authorized drives had to be licensed. In the beginning the licensing was akin to an emergency teaching credential, but the regs had been strengthened with the new administration. Taxes and prices always went up; wages chased but never caught them; with each preordained election came new rules. Always. These were the only facts of life with no ceiling. Today, mojos were just part of the paperwork.

"See Jack the Ripper?" Case said.

"What?"

"On the mountaintop. Playing cards. Who told you to look for the green and black bronto?" Neither man could get his mouth around calling such a creature an Apatosaurus, which seemed just too-too.

"I saw it in a vision." Aguilar had been chewing peyote again. Case realized he was smoking the fetid, creamtory hand-rolleds to deaden the smell of the buttons on his breath. Still dope-conscious but curious, Case had tried it with him once. It had tasted like turd-flavored Sen-Sen.

A dimetrodon snapped to, displacing air with a pop. Case thought of a flashgun in reverse. The paper lantern struts of its spine rattled and the webwork of translucent hide refracted the setting sun into an instant rainbow before the two startled drovers.

"Dammit," said Case. "I wish they wouldn't come in so goddamn *close.*"

The big dinosaur belched and tromped away on skinny, bent legs, defying gravity.

"That's why we be here, amigo," Aguilar grinned. "Keep 'em off the expressways." Dinosaur gridlock was still an occasional problem.

"What about the green and black one—the one your vision said you were supposed to look for?"

"Just supposed to *find* him; that's it."

"And all will be revealed unto us . . ."

"Don't make fun." Aguilar's face went dead serious so fast it was hilarious. He could get religion at the most bone-tickling times.

Case felt too centered to argue. "Whoa. Me friend," he said. And it *was* good—the view, the time of day, a smoke and a partner and breathing space and a dash of peace of mind. Wasn't that what all the Suits cried the blues for lacking?

In his lifetime Whitman Case had bailed out of a flaming bomber, survived seven serious auto accidents and three broken limbs, weathered eight muggings or robberies (two at gunpoint; another two during which he'd gotten the drop and walked away unrobbed), killed four men that he knew of in combat, missed catching a plane that subsequently crashed near Elkins Air Force Base due to pilot error, and nearly drowned once by getting his ankle tangled in a rope while white-water rafting down the Colorado. He had lowered his cholesterol and raised his fiber intake. He had lived through two surgeries—tonsils, and a detached cornea at forty-five. He had duly earned and spent several million American dollars, fathered no children, and married never although he had "seriously" cohabited with seven women, not counting Iris, who was as crazy as a dung beetle in a hubcap, and counting Pearl, whom he still thought of every single day. He had smoked maybe five zillion cigarettes and tipped back an oil freighter or so of coffee, black. He had lived drunk and sober, rational and pissed off beyond sanity, benevolently then selfishly, and did not believe in supernatural deities. Ever since he had first seen a dinosaur picture book as a child he had trusted in what the scientists had said.

To wit: DINOSAURS AND HUMAN BEINGS DID NOT LIVE AT THE SAME TIME. Despite all those great movies on Channel 11, the ones broken up by all the Cal Worthington commercials.

He recalled being saddened because it meant pore old humankind had missed the chance to know what thunder lizards *really* looked like.

And that had turned out to be wrong, too.

Case would never forget the day he had found differently. It was one of those calendar junctures people commonly stored, like the JFK shooting or the Apollo moon touchdown or that time the space shuttle blew all to hell.

He remembered, without a smile, and when he remembered there was no need to ask whether Whitman Case believed in God, friend.

* * *

"It took folks about twenty-four hours to learn how to stay out of their way," said the Major, meaning dinosaurs that materialized spontaneously. "Some say that the air ripples, just before. But once they got on the news, when they weren't knocking over buildings or eating people anymore, they were a huge hit. Some guy found out they'll eat dog food. He got corporate endorsements. They'll eat garbage, hell, they'll eat crap we wouldn't touch for landfill. They shit all over everything. If they have enough time before they wink out, they build nests and lay eggs. Sometimes they eat each other, which is pretty funny when your lunch vanishes into thin air right when you bite." The Major chuckled self-consciously. "Nobody *cares* where they came from. They're famous."

"They're ghosts," said Seward. He did not look over from his bed.

The quiet utterance made the Major's statistical monologue seem trivial. His unbandaged eye swivelled to. "Say again?"

"Ghosts." Seward watched the television, not seeing it ceaseless silliness.

He was reasonably sure the Major might ring for the nurse. "Boy's finally tipped over," he'd say. Concussion has scattered his dice.

"How do you figure that?" The Major was honestly curious, not placating.

"They're *actual* ghosts. Shades. They eminate from places of the dead. *Their* dead, their graveyards. Remember all the dinosaurs headed north, up Fairfax? They were coming out of Hancock Park. They were materializing at the La Brea Tar Pits."

"Ain't no dinosaurs in the La Brea Pits." The major was a local, and had toured the Paige Museum. "Just mammals. Mastodons. Sloths. Dire wolves. No dinosaurs."

"The fossil deposits and museum exhibits originated deep

within the alluvial layers we now plumb for fossil fuel. Not from the pits, my good Major; they're coming out of the tar itself, which means they're also coming out of the oil wells and petroleum refineries, which *also* means they're coming from the plastics factories and whiskey distilleries and any plant that presses vinyl." His voice hitched down to a murmur in the extremely clean room, while logic forged links. "Even the air is full of petrochemicals, hydrocarbons. Supernaturally, it makes good sense—spirits are literally coalescing out of thin air. Ghosts have been known to appear from thin air, you know."

Given that the dinosaurs were real, no foolin', then Seward's mind was magnetized toward the only sensible explanation . . . even though it was polarized against his life's calling.

And if they came out of plastic, that meant they were coming out of compact discs and cappucino makers and toy stores and Gucci shoppes, and even that machine at the Griffith Observatory that injection-molded you a souvenir rocketship for fifty cents.

"Real, live ghosts." The Major pretended to chew it over. His mind naturally sought a logistical panacea. "So . . . how many dinosaurs would that be, then? Total."

"How many centuries did the dinosaurs run the planet?" Seward asked back. "How long was the Mesozoic Era alone, ninety million years? Don't ask me what the lifespan of the average thunder lizard was, even given the bad living conditions and all. How many dinosaurs do you suppose could have been born in ninety million years? The human race has barely topped off its first millon, and just look at us. All those dead dinosaurs, all back at the same time. All our smog is just calling back to its roots. Just think what it must be like in the OPEC countries right now."

The Major grinned. Patriotically.

Seward tried to find sleep; his mind, rest. He had a dream, not a nightmare, of ghost dinosaurs randomly popping up in Disneyland, where there were mechanical dinosaurs. His dreaming mind wondered if they would fight, already knowing which side would win.

All those dinosaurs. Where would we put them?

More than the end of the world, Americans dislike inconvenience. Accommodations would have to be made. Seward slept on it.

*   *   *

102

SEDALIA

In the 1980s the theory was advanced that dinosaurs had demonstrated herding behavior, and a pile of paintings were done depicting that which had never been considered before. The paleontologist who had posited this theory was among the stampede of idea guys seeking the government's ear. Grants and endowments awaited those whose unsolicited assistance proved useful in a time of crisis. Once it was realized that the ghost dinosaurs were easily herded, and would follow each other straight out of whatever American metropolis they were clogging up, Whitman Case found himself a new job: Ramrodding herds of ghost dinosaurs out to the open desert. They couldn't starve there because they were already dead.

Case, Aguilar and their fellow drovers rapidly became the experts who observed all the twists first. If a 'dine laid down a mound of shit, it remained real after the ghost phased out, having eliminated the remnats of digested intake millions of years old at long last. Academics were eager to dive into the dinosaur poop and analyze. If the 'dines laid eggs while corporeal, and those eggs got fertilized by other corporeated 'dines, the hatchlings did *not* fade out, ever. That wrinkle didn't seem to worry the companies that budgeted the drives too much just yet. It had only happened once or twice. Case had seen baby carnivores try to attack ghosts. Plant eaters munched on ocatilla stalks and prickly pear. The dinosaur equivalent of hoof and mouth, or rabies, could not lumber ghosts. The drovers guided them out past the dunes, where they congregated in broad valleys.

Or would, Case thought, if Shack the mojo would undent his buns and give them the blessing to press on with the drive for two more days of travel time. Then they could dump this herd in with the other 'dines and buzz home for the usual kinds of relief, another thing that had not changed much for anyone of a droving bent.

It had been that Seward fella, way back when, who had come up with the idea of having psychics predict fair or foul for the drives, since ghosts were involved. To put it simply, these dinosaurs were part-timers, too. Since Seward had suggested the idea to the government, he was appointed to sift applicants and weed out the phonies, in accordance with his former profession. He remained an occult debunker until his death, but after the dinosaur thing his heart just was not in his work so deeply.

Another Camel kissed Case's bootheel; Aguilar declined his

offer of a smoke. Night was on in the desert and Jonas had a huge mesquite blaze crackling in a pit full of yesterday's embers. The drovers chowed down and tried to talk of things other than 'dines— lovers, the past, derring-do. Cars.

Ernesto Cocoberra trundled forth from his camper, a rotund, pasha-shaped man, small of stature, bright of eye, aware that his metaphysical dictates were preventing the drive from moving on, but good-natured enough that the drovers resented only the news, and not the Shack. He spoke their language without talking down or bullshitting them. It was inevitable that someone at dinner ask The Question, and tonight it looked like it was Case's turn.

Before Case could get whole words past his lips, though, Shack held up an oracle-like finger and said, "We're there already, Whit."

Aguilar made an arrgh noise, having none of this. "Aw, shit, Shack, we ain't moved nearly three weeks now. We ain't anywhere *already*. We're nowhere, is where we are."

You had to ask the question, Case knew. It was like a game. "Okay, Shack. But where are we?"

"Sedalia."

"Oh, great. What the fuck's *that* mean?"

"Quiet," Case said to Aguilar, who was pretty impatient for a guy who waxed so mystical a half hour previously. "What's Sedalia, Shack?"

"Crow, Whit—didn't you never watch no *Rawhide* on TV?"

Blank looks all around. Maybe the triple negative had them reeling.

"Oh, yeah." Jonas scraped his dish over the fire. "Clint Eastwood. Some other actor who died."

"Man versus cow," said Shack. "A whole series about a cattle drive."

Somebody sang *rollin' rollin' rollin'* sotto voce until Shack continued.

"Sedalia was the town they were driving the cattle to. Show was on the air seven years . . . and that goldanged cattle drive just went on and on, all seven years, and it *never* got to Sedalia." He folded his arms, a buddha in his certitude, making pronouncements in the firelight.

"That's TV for you," Jonas grumped. "Makes its own timeframe."

"Wait—are you saying we're never going to get clear of this drive?" It was Bridges, the one who had been singing a second before. He was the youngest guy on the drive, full of sperm and not the right age to hear absolutes. "You're not saying that, man." He pitched a crumpled cigarette pack over his shoulder and Jonas glared at him.

"Aguilar had himself a vision up there on the Stirrup today," said Shack. "Why don't you share it with us?"

Aguilar hemmed and hawed and scuffed and blushed and finally cut the crap and told what he knew.

"I suggest y'all keep an eye peeled for that green and black Brontosaurus," concluded Shack. "It has to be an omen. If one of us spots it, then perhaps I could make an intelligent forecast for the drive . . . since I don't enjoy warming my ass out here for days on end any more than you guys do. I want to get back to Reno so I can do some serious gambling, goddammit."

The air displacement of a materializing 'dine nearly blew down the campfire. It was a big guy, a full-grown Trachedon, mud-colored with bright orange speckles like dayglo paint and a smell that reminded Case of the blowback from a sewage treatment plant. Most of the drovers hit the deck. Bridges did not. Bridges had not been on the June drive, the one where a Stegosaurus had untethered a volcanic fart into the campfire and nearly flash-fried them all in a flaming cloud of primeval methane.

The Trachedon saw them and made distance.

"You're right," Aguilar said to Case, looking up with dirt in his teeth. "I wish they wouldn't come in so close, either."

*   *   *

All through the night the dinosaurs came and went. Incoming, they sizzled with the sound of ripping cloth or the tearing of dry jerky. They roared and hooted and keened in the darkness of the valley, as prowls begun eons ago were resumed in the residual heat that leached toward the stars from desert dirt. Then they de-rezzed with a carbonated, fizzy noise, blurring, breaking up and fading out.

Near dawn, just as the snaggletoothed horizon grew bloodshot, Case shucked his sleeping bag and ambled over to his terrain bike to catch a smoke and work the sleepy seeds out of his eyes. When it came to the reasons men and a few women chose to embark on dinosaur drives, you usually never winnowed talk down to details.

105

In that respect, the job was like Foreign Legion service. Case was able to keep most of his personal narrative tight to the vest. Each drover thought their reasons the most tragic or romantic—by god, it could be like one endless, overdumb country & western ballad—except that everyone was too chicken to actually match for best.

Case held the draughts of good gray smoke deep. It perked his nerves and glands, and gradually restored his definition of humanity.

The silhouetted dinosaur head interrupted the strips of horizon light, stalking, a gargoyle marionette. The outline read Tyrannosaurus, and that was enough for Case to kick-start his bike and investigate.

The beast was one big trainfucker indeed.

Its architecture and fluidity sustained no comparison to the lumpen elephants or whales of modern times. Its musculature was woven tight as the braids on a bullwhip, girder tendons and cable ligaments tauntly tuned beneath the stout mail of leather. Chatoyant eyes glinted in the predawn as it jerked its head around to fix the sound of Case's bike, speedy and alert, spoiling for trouble or some wet, carnivorous fun.

When something the size of a double decker bus sneezed, a drover might become dino toejam in an instant. Case did not hit it with the bike's hot spot and make it bolt, all those crookedly-meshed six-inch teeth rushing down to macerate him. He checked it out, as he had checked all of them out for two years now.

An oilslick smell hung about it, like the rich clots of grimy black that vehicles excreted onto parking lots and driveways. The Rex whiffed Case but did not seem peckish or feisty. Case imagined the thermal pits on its snout processing the air itself. What did its ancient brain tell it about the morning? Was it chilly, warm? Just right? Did it aspire to any goals beyond the prowl, and food for the day? Did it apply any sort of personal style to its killing technique? The fixed grin on the sardonic reptile mask was certainly the visage of a hunter, and most hunters, thought Case, were driven by pride.

Over the bike's phones, he picked up an Arizona radio station kicking off a weekend celebration of the Beatles. That was safe and innocuous enough, yeah; happiness was a warm gun. Case's saddlebags included a .457 packed with heavy-grain slugs, but he rarely used it on drives and had not even taken it out once this trip. What for?

In an emergency, in case a 'dine got uppity or just plain needed to die in a hurry, the drovers had customized ordinance, usually sleeved in a special holster to the right of the terrain biker's gas teardrop. They were commonly called asskickers—two feet of scaled-down bazooka pipe with a pistol grip that discharged a cannister of plastique similar to the powerheads used by divers against sharks. The idea was to provide an immediate one-shot stop in a crisis; the only effective way to prevent a contrary shark from gobbling you on the spot was to blow its jaw completely off. The concept had been handily adapted to land use against re-corporeated dinosaurs, and a balance of power had been swiftly inaugurated.

Case saw its violet eyes. I know you, oh yes I do.

He yanked the choke ring on the asskicker and flipped off the safety. Then he nailed the big Rex with his spotlight.

It was bright purple. One of its flanks was scorched and puckered from a burn—an earthly injury taken with it into the astral and brought back just now. In sum, that was enough for Case.

He shouted, and when the beast turned on him, he sighted through the red plastic grid.

Whitman Case's Corvette had been a thing of beauty to behold, a dream realized and a desire long coveted. It had been something in which he had invested the patience of a Russian consumer. Waiting for something gave you plenty of time to fantasize. Eleven coats of mirror-gloss canary yellow double-dipped in lacquer; chrome like the eye of a flame. A deadly serious 307 four-barrel carb and a police chaser block. A wheel sleeve of buttery leather that matched the buckets. A total boner of a driving machine, new radials not even *dusty* yet and it had become history . . . because some numbnuts Tyrannosaurus Rex had waited a couple million years and an epoch or two just to step on it.

The fireball born of Lloyd Larned's vaporizing Texaco station in Riverside had drawn Whitman Case to his front window just in time to see a purple dinosaur squash his 'Vette with no more effort than a hiccup required. Then the shockwave shattered the window and Case had other things to worry about.

He let out his breath; let the Rex eat a technological meteor. The explosion woke up the whole camp as thirty tons of Tyranno-casserole clouded the air with the reek of stale blood from another time, the dawn of time itself.

Two hours after breakfast, Aguilar spotted his own 'dine, the green and black one. The saddle markings on the brontosaurus, he

107

insisted, were unmistakable. It turned out to be a female.

Nobody spoke to Case. They figured him for drive jitters after he fragged the Rex. Shack got swamped once Aguilar reported the brontosaurus. *Pardone señor, we go noplace today neether.*

They watched the dinosaur all day. It got really boring really fast. By dinnertime most of the drovers had forgotten their noisy wake-up call and were mildly torqued at Aguilar.

"Big fuckin' deal!" snarled Bridges, throwing food and wasting it. He used fluorocarbon deodorant and owned a huge Jeep he used to modify the trails in national parks. Bridges had always been a litterbug; he didn't believe in much else. "Big revelation! Big mystical owlshit! Really pro, Aguilar, you asshole!"

Aguilar likened young Bridges to a behemoth phallus, and the other drovers had to wrestle them apart. The dust they'd kicked up hung around in the firelight, stubbornly. Shack shook his head sadly. Dumb mortals.

"You guys are so anxious the wrap the drive you can't hear the music for all the noise the orchestra is making," said Case. He'd been trying to use logic, like that Seward fella, whom he admired.

"See what?" Bridges was still aching for mayhem. He obviously hadn't had his butt kicked enough by living yet. "That fuckin' green and black 'dine? It's right over there, so what?"

"When did you spot it this morning?" Case said to Aguilar. It wouldn't do to tell Bridges to watch his language.

"About ten or so." Aguilar had coded a marker onto his digital watch to log the sighting. He was that bored.

"And our boy Bridges, with his keen eyesight, can still see it from here."

Jonas didn't get it. "And I hope it *stays* over there. Geez, don't you guys remember the farting Stego?"

Shack began to smile privately.

"Okay Bridges." Case focused on the boy. "Maybe you can tell the class what time it is right now. You *can* tell time, right?"

Bridges was about to aim and fire when he went rigid, his yap stalling in the open position. "Oh, Jeezus . . ."

Everybody looked at each other. It was poignant, in its way.

Case rather savored playing oracle. This must be how Shack felt when he channeled some blast of psychic insight. "That 'dine, gents, has been solid for over twelve hours. Somebody better call the Guinness Book, because this is a first, as far as my experience goes."

Top end before the average ghost dinosaur frazzed out was generally two hours. They came back, but they never lasted long; that was why the hazard factor had dwindled so quickly. This female brontosaurus showed no signs of going away, and it was an adult, not a newborn.

"A Maiasaur will be next," Shack said. "It will lay a full nest of eggs."

Case reviewed all. What had he accomplished? To cease the mad forward rush, the stampede of the simple day-to-day, that might actually be nice. He reconsidered all he had done, from losing his virginity to greasing the Rex that had wiped out his dream car, and realized right here, in the middle of nowhere, he had already found a valuable kind of peace. He had never thought in such terms before.

This really wasn't so bad, for a life.

The valley was full of milling dinosaurs. They were waiting and they had the patience of eons, because they had known—if only instinctually—that their time would again come 'round. Case wondered if he could be adaptable as that Seward fella had been.

"What do you reckon we oughta do?" Bridges asked Case. "Start shooting 'em? Is that why you bagged that one this morning?" The kid was actually worried.

Case grinned. Drovers never told all.

"Nope. I think we only need to do one thing, and that's find a way to welcome them home. No wars, no battles for dominance, all that useless military shit. You and I are the experts, Bridges. We oughta act like experts, and find out what the 'dines will need that we can provide, since they're coming home. Either we coexist, or *we* become the extinct ones. You get it?"

"What about civilization?" said Jonas. "No dinosaur could ever be a Magritte or a Blake or a Dali." His education was showing.

"Mm. More important, no dinosaur could ever invent Bic lighters or pop tops or bombs that suck away the whole atmosphere. Yes? That green and black brontosaurus is the first one that's not just going to disappear. It's back to stay." Home again, he thought. The former tenants were resuming residence.

He knew it would take awhile for them all to digest the potential of their new roles. Not everybody was going to like it, but Case wasn't worried. There was time, and time marched.

Right now it was time to fire up another cigarette.

110

Ardath Mayhar is, according to the button she wears, A MEAN LITTLE OLD LADY. But she seems pretty nice to me. She writes under several names, her own being the best known. She has written numerous novels and more short stories than a computer can count. An anthology of this nature wouldn't be complete without at least one story of the Weird Tales or E.C. Comic school, and this captures a bit of both. By the time you finish reading it, she will most likely be finishing a new book or story. She's always finishing a new book or story.

TRAPLINE

by Ardath Mayhar

Herzog tore a strip of jerky off the wolf haunch hanging behind the door and chewed it savagely. No chance to run the traps today. None yesterday, either, for the blizzards had come, trapping him in the cabin when his season should have been in full swing.

Even before the snow had piled deep, the catch had been scanty, sometimes nonexistent. He had seen few tracks as he made his rounds between snowstorms, and those had not been of the animals whose fur sold best.

There should be something moving soon, if the weather cleared, but he hadn't even heard a yowl or a screech, except for the wolves, for days. He needed wolverine, fox and lynx, mink and ermine to trade for cash and whiskey, when next he left the mountains.

And, dammit, a man oughtn't to have to eat wolf meat, anyway. He hated the critters, alive or dead, and particularly he hated them jerked. He hankered for deer or bear or at least a good tender rabbit. The traps weren't catching anything, and his sporadic hunts, when the snow lifted, had netted nothing.

111

Now he lifted his head and listened to the wind. There came a long howl down the gale, and he shivered. He and the wolves had been competing for the scarce supply of animals as this strange year went forward.

Instead of being able to make his three-day circle checking his traps, he had been trapped here, this time, for a week. The jerky was the last of his meat, and meal and coffee and beans would not give a man enough energy to survive in this bitter cold. If the blizzard didn't die down soon, he would be too weak to run the trapline.

He rolled another big chunk of wood onto the fire and settled onto the bearskin that served as his bed. Tomorrow, surely the wind would die down, allowing him to run the trapline!

*   *   *

When the shutters were outlined with pale light, he rose and poked up the coals, building a new fire from the remains of the old. He wanted to check the morning, but his routine, when cabin-bound, was inflexible. Only when he had drained the iron coffeepot and eaten his can of beans would he open the door to see what this new day had brought.

When the door swung inward, letting in a mound of new snow, the sparkle of sunlight on the burdened branches of the firs almost blinded him. He began to grin. Today, he would start off on the run. Tonight, at his first campsite, he would eat meat. He only hoped that he would also have wolverine pelts, for the miners in the lower ranges wanted those, in particular.

His snowshoes schuffled over the soft snow leaving deep prints behind him. The shadows pooled blue on the warm-lit drifts, and the depths of the forest were purple and blue-green, concealing his usual track beneath its carpet of white. But he knew that trapline the way his mother knew her kitchen. He went unerringly to his first trap.

It held, praise be, a fat porcupine, which would roast well and whose quills would be trade-goods, when he met with any of the Utes who sometimes traveled this way. He wrapped it well in burlap and stuffed it into his game-bag.

The next trap had held a fox, but only a stiff paw still remained between the steel jaws. Damn! Then he ran out of luck entirely. By the time he hit his campsite, he had found nothing but empty traps. But at least he had food. That would help him along his way.

*   *   *

The fat sputtered into the fire as he turned the spit on which he had skewered the porcupine. He heard the snuffle and snarl of wolves, beyond the circle of firelight. They hesitated, no matter how hungry they might be, to come near the blaze, but he knew that if he slept long enough to allow the flames to die down he would wake in the belly of one of the big gray beasts. Often, he thought that they had begun to trail him as he went about his rounds. Sometimes they came up to the cabin and marked it as if it were wolf territory. He was game for their eating, he sometimes thought, which was only fair. He had eaten more than his share of their kind!

Full of hot porcupine, he rolled into his blanket, propped against a fir tree in such a way that if he sagged he would fall over and wake. He dozed, rousing only when he needed to replenish the fire. The wolves gave up in the wee hours and went to hunt easier game, but he did not sleep fully, and when the sky lightened he was up, stirring the fire, heating the now frozen meat, opening a can of beans.

Still there were no wolverines in the traps. Damn! A silver fox, a small lynx, and a polecat were his morning's catch. His bait was not right, he decided, and he tried resetting the traps with meat from the fox, even though he knew that had failed before.

He should have been burdened with the weight of the pelts in his pack by now, but he plodded into camp two with a very light pack. One more day and he would be back at the cabin, his work gone for nothing. He could only hope that something with a valuable fur had stumbled into one of his waiting traps on this last leg of the run.

The tally began badly—one wolverine paw. But the next trap had been sprung and carried away into the brush. Had he caught a bear? His equipment was usually too light to hold one of the big beasts, but perhaps he had caught a young one or a small female. He moved along the furrowed snow-track until it disappeared into a frozen runnel filled with light snow.

He hung his pack on a branch, removed his snowshoes, and plunged down into the shifting layers. The catch had been buried, probably in the storm of the day before, for the track was only half filled behind it. He smoothed away the snow and stared into the blind eyes of the Frenchman from the other side of the mountain. This was the bastard who liked wolves! He'd had the nerve to jump Herzog for killing the beasts and letting them rot in their hides.

What in hell was he doing over here? In a blizzard? Getting into Herzog's trap? The man felt a hot surge of fury as he dragged the stiff body up the embankment and stretched it on the snow.

The other trapper had not been driven into the storm by starvation—he was still well fleshed. His buffalo-fur robe was new, and his double moccasins were little worn. Why had he risked everything in that blizzard? Had his cabin burned? Herzog had known men, suddenly without shelter, to freeze in these mountain storms. Probably that was it, but it made no difference. The puzzle was why the wolves hadn't eaten him as he lay in the snow, helpless for a while and dead for a lot longer.

Now a powerful notion was taking hold of Wilhelm Herzog. If nothing he tried for bait worked in this strange year, why not try something new, something strange, something that might attract wolf and wolverine alike? Why not use this damned Frenchman? Otherwise he would be wasted.

He skinned off the fur robe, the tanned deerhide shirt and leggings. Those were quilled, and he wondered what had happened to Villeneuve's Ute wife. Had she burned, too? Or had he beaten her once too often and found himself driven out of his cabin at knife-point? Herzog chuckled at the thought. He made it a point to take his Indian women first and kill them afterward. There was no risk, that way.

When he had the body naked, blue-chilled on the icy stream-bank, he tried his knife on the marble-like flesh. But it was hard as stone. He would have to be thawed before he could be cut properly for trap-bait.

It was not the time or the place to camp, but Herzog forced himself to build a fire, thawing out a circle to the bare needles of the forest floor. There he butchered his new-found animal with care, setting the chunks of meat carefully into the pack and putting the raw skeleton back into its former bed for the wolves to gnaw. That done, he covered the fire and set off again, baiting the empty traps with bits of Frenchman.

TRAPLINE

He came back to the cabin filled with satisfaction. Something told him that this was the turning point. His luck was about to change; he could feel it in his bones. He turned in, that night, warmed with more than his ritual slug of whiskey.

The blizzards set in again in the night. But in two days it cleared, and he was able to start out to run his traps.

There was an ermine in the first trap set with Villeneuve. A silver fox was in the second. Wolverines filled three, five, and seven. The rest ranged from rabbits to lynx, and a pair of wolves were still snarling and chewing on their paws in the last two. He dispatched them with his rifle and loaded up his bulging pack of pelts, grinning widely.

He had stashed the rest of the Frenchman in his cold-room at the cabin, and as long as the man lasted his catch was superb. He had stretchers of hides stacked against the walls, and he knew that his bales of furs would bring him all the supplies, all the whiskey, and all the women he could handle when he went back down the mountain in the spring.

Unfortunately, he ran out of Villeneuve all too soon. He'd been a big man, but there was only so much of him, after all. And once he returned to baiting with fox or wolf-meat, the catches dwindled abruptly. Wolverine, in particular, had loved the man-flesh, and he caught no more of the wily creatures.

So his spring selling trip netted him less by far than he had hoped. Yet as he wandered around the trading post he watched the other people there with new eyes. They were not men for the bragging with or women for the taking. They were not Indians who might turn into enemies or Frenchmen who were contemptible simply because they were French.

No. They were *bait!*

He left early, climbing into the summer forests and meadows, where hunting parties and prospectors ranged during the fine weather. He didn't go very far, and when he stopped he hid in the thickest of the woods and watched to see where men went, and how long they stayed.

Many approached the snowline, tapping at the rocks with little hammers or hunting the mountain goats. He considered their habits for some time. Then he set his traps.

By late fall he had nineteen bodies stashed safely in the snows on the heights, and when winter set in again, he brought them down, one by one, to be butchered for bait.

His fresh crop of furs was incredible, and he went out, late in January, to run his traps with his hopes running high. He already had about as many as he could carry to trade. He could save the rest of the bait, safe up there in the deep snows, for the next year.

He staggered under the weight of his pack as he came to the spot, no longer the site of a trap, from which he had tracked that providential Frenchman, whose bones, he was sure, had long since been gnawed to splinters by his friends the wolves. He sighed with satisfaction and went on, killing living catch and skinning out everything, until he came again to his cabin. When he shoved his snowshoes off on the porch and stepped to the door, he paused, listening. Something was inside. A bear, wakened unseasonably from his winter sleep? A wolverine, seeking shelter?

He slipped off his pack and pulled his rifle from its wrappings, working the bolt to make sure it was not too cold to move. Then he shoved the door open with his foot and stepped inside.

Something was there. He could feel it. He could see a vague movement in the darkness, as something came toward him.

He fired convulsively, but the rifle ball did not slow the approach of Villeneuve, the Frenchman. He was a rack of bones with strips of flesh hanging like fringe, dried and useless. The bones were pale, now, and hard. His grin was broad and humorless, the long teeth wolflike in the dimness.

Behind him came the partially stripped body of the Cree who had been brought down from the heights most recently. Other shapes moved there, as well, and he didn't want to see what they might be, though he caught the click of toenails on the rough wood of the floor. The wolves he had eaten—were they there, too?

Herzog stepped backward, dropping the empty rifle. His hands went up to cover his eyes. He could not believe that this was happening. Dead men did not rise up and walk!

Something fastened into his calf from behind, and he went down on his back on the porch, landing hard. As he gasped for breath, he moved his arm to see what new enemy threatened him.

The muzzle of a skeletal wolf, grinning as broadly as the Frenchman had done, loomed over his face. Hot saliva dripped from the lolling tongue onto his cheek.

"No!" There was no breath to propel the word. It came out as a gasp, but it brought a reply.

"Yesss . . ." came the hissing reply between those alarming teeth in Villeneuve's skull.

And then both sets of fangs descended upon his cringing body. And Herzog knew, at last, what it was to fear and to suffer and to die.

Al Sarrantonio has gone from short story writer to novelist in a short time. His work has been mostly in the horror vein, with an occasional foray into S.F. and fantasy. He has a clean, crisp style and two books of mine he borrowed and hasn't returned. Other than that, he's making his mark as both novelist and short story writer these days, and his is a name we'll be seeing a lot more of, and I don't mean on wanted posters.

TRAIL OF THE CHROMIUM BANDITS

by Al Sarrantonio

Ride the Wild West.

Ride the Wild West with the hiss of falling spaceships splitting the sky like comet trails.

Ride the Wild West with justice in your heart and the remembered kiss of a woman on your lips.

Ride the Wild West in a Toyota.

*   *   *

Mitch Hilligan hooded his eyes to squint into the lowering sunset of West Texas. Something itched at his fingers, then burned; he looked down to see the raw red end of a cigarette gouging into the flesh of his thumb and forefinger. He dropped the cigarette into the dust and ground it out with the toe of his boot.

"What do you think, Sparky—game's gonna start soon?" he said. He tried to bite his words before they came out, knowing how useless they were now, but still not quite used to the way things were. "Come on, Sparky, speak to me." The dog at his feet wagged its tail, its tongue lolling out expectantly. Hilligan cursed shortly and drew a dog biscuit out of the deep pocket of his poncho. He tossed it to the ground and the dog was upon it instantly, making crunching sounds that annoyed Hilligan. He tried to ignore the sound, then suddenly drew his foot back to kick the dog. He hesitated, his anger draining.

"You're a useless weapon, old pal," he said, reaching to pet the dog on the ruined head that had once held Sparky's intact brain. "Not your fault."

Hilligan straightened, and brought his binoculars up to his eyes. He scanned the horizon below, searching for the telltale signs of a campfire, but found nothing. He cursed and lowered the binoculars. Waiting for night to fall before trying again.

They were stupid, in most ways, but incredibly crafty. Here they were, a band of four, leaving their droppings—candy wrappers, empty food cans, milk cartons, beer cans, liquor bottles, pissmarks, piles of shit—and still, Hilligan had barely had a glimpse of them for three days. One silhouette glinting in the sunset two nights ago, a hint of horizon movement the day before. He knew he was close but still they were all but invisible, leaving a trail of crap but it was the Invisible Man's refuse.

"Yep, game's gonna start soon," Hilligan repeated, to himself.

Hilligan made camp twenty minutes later. The sunlight had dropped; the Moon was a weak sickle just cutting up the East. Stars burned into the purple of twilight; burned brighter into the blackness of night.

Sparky tried to piss, seemed to forget how, mewled as the wetness ran ineffectively down his leg followed by a runnule of tepid shit.

Hilligan cleaned the dog, settled him under the rusting rear of the Toyota Corolla and lit another cigarette. The dog, under his blanket, gave a large sigh and then slept.

Hilligan watched the stars, passing his cold gaze from Betelguess through Orion's belt and down to Sirius. The Milky Way stretched gauzily through the ecliptic, a pointillistic band of millions of tiny, distinct flaming suns.

"Games . . ." he said to himself, and then rolled into his blanket and lightly slept.

120

TRAIL OF THE CHROMIUM BANDITS

He slept heavily. The heat of day, not the light, awakened him. Sparky was still under the Toyota, awake, tongue lolling, dehydrated but not realizing it. He opened his mouth when Hilligan's eyes met his, and for a moment Hilligan had hope; an aching sense of loss, combined with an overwhelming wish—and need—for the dog the way he had been, washed over him. But only a weak rumbling sound came out. Sparky put his head down on a front paw, still panting.

Hilligan poured water into a bowl and gave it to the dog. By the sun, it was already nine o'clock. It had been stupid to sleep so long; by now the band would be miles ahead.

Hilligan ate a can of beans, washing it down with a warm can of Coors, and then packed the car. The engine resisted, coughing toward death and then suddenly roaring into its bad muffler like a lion. On the seat next to him, Sparky slept. The radio was on, hissing nothingness, the occasional snatch of Country-Western music from a faraway station.

The day, the miles, rolled on.

He found their trail at four. A telltale pile of refuse and body wastes broadcast their direction loudly: West toward Lawrence. He thought fleetingly of Anne; he had left her in Lawrence not four days before, and the salt-taste of her first kiss still lingered on his lips. He saw her amusement at his blush—"Why, *Marshall,* one would think you'd never been kissed before," and her deepening amusement and interest when he asked, "This love thing's sort of a game, isn't it?" and he remembered the look on her face that said, "Come back, come back soon . . ."

Hilligan turned his attention back to the bandit's camp. If anything, they were even less concerned with his pursuit. They had been reading; he found a pile of *Mad* and *Playboy* magazines in with the chili and tuna cans; on closer inspection, the magazines were smeared with shit, had been used as toilet paper.

Once again, he stood on a ridge and studied the darkening sky with binoculars.

A movement among a group of liveoaks.

Them.

A chill crawled up Hilligan's back. He knew they had stopped for him. *The game was about to begin.* The images he had been able to push aside the last three days flashed into his mind, stark and terrible. The town that had been Davidson, Texas, roasted to the ground, the huge trough of their ship nosed into what had been the library; the smell of broiled human flesh left in its wake; black human bodies with open mouths and empty charcoal eyes, smoking ruins that had been buildings, a McDonalds, a 5 and dime; what they'd done to Sparky, half his head roasted off . . .

He remembered the way the people of Davidson had looked up to him when they made him Marshall not three weeks before, after he came walking out of the desert with his dog like a movie hero, tall, sure of himself, unnaturally handsome, what a Marshall should be. They sensed trouble; he said he'd take care of it. "Thanks, Marshall," they'd said, giving him his Toyota to use. He'd believed he could protect them. And now their eyes were burned sockets, their mouths silenced even from screams . . .

Thanks, Marshall. He'd been on the way back from Lawrence when they'd needed him, seeing the black smoke from the desert through the windshield of the Toyota, roaring back into town just as the bandits were leaving, loading Jud Stern's Plymouth Voyager with tennis rackets and golf clubs and guns from STERN'S SPORTING GOODS, laughing as they did so, turning to regard him with their perfect mirrorchrome faces as he'd screamed, perfect human beings covered in chrome, running after them, one of them raising a lazy hand, turning the palm flat toward him but another standing next to the Voyager, smiling lazily, saying, "No, let's make a game of it."

The other shrugged, and lowered the hand to Sparky. The hand glowed metallically, and the dog buckled, then rose unsteadily again and pissed on himself, the look of the dead, the lost, in his eyes.

"Not that you have any choices, but we'll make it a real game," the first one said, lifting a rifle from a pile of guns in the back of the Voyager and tossing it to Hilligan. His metallic head, a perfect replica of a human's head in chrome, smiled. "We'll only use these." He turned his palm toward Hilligan, the threat of death held in check. "Agreed?"

Biting back useless rage and frustration, Hilligan nodded curtly.

The others had laughed, and they loaded into the vehicle and were gone, leaving their laughter behind, the laughter of tourists on holiday, having sport, packing picnic lunches from the ruins of

Davidson, taking clothes and guns and food, leaving behind Hilligan screaming and the silent screams of a dead town.

*   *   *

And now it was time for the game to really begin.

They were getting tired and bored. He knew because their toys had begun to be abandoned: the tennis rackets, the golf clubs broken in two. Soon their minds would turn to bigger larks. The town of Lawrence was only five miles to the East. They would head there next. Where Anne was . . . and continue their fun from town to town, from city to city, until there was nothing left.

Something spat past Hilligan's ear, pinged into the door of the Toyota.

"Shit," Hilligan said.

Crouched behind the fender of the Corolla, he waited for another shot. Raising his head tentatively, he searched the desert with his binoculars. No shot came, and then he saw them: a retreating band of silver glints in the distance, just disappearing behind an outcropping of rock. A careful look at their wake showed the half-buried wreckage of the Plymouth Voyager, half-merged with the side of the rock wall.

For the first time in days, Hilligan smiled.

"Shit, we're gonna win," he said.

*   *   *

He spent the next hour packing and camouflaging the Toyota in a stand of liveoaks. The only burden was Sparky's food, an oversize box of dog biscuits, the only thing the dog recognized now and would eat, but he gladly strapped it to the top of his knapsack, cursing not the weight but the bulk. One somber, lost look from the dog made him bite the curses.

"Come on, pal."

He set off at a brisk walk, the dog hesitating, then following mechanically behind, the sight of the dog biscuit box firing some barely connecting relay in his ruined brain.

After two hours, he badly missed the stuttering air conditioning

123

of the Corolla. Salt sweat had nearly blinded him, but he kept on. The sun was like a sieve, arrowing heat down at him. Paradoxically, Sparky didn't seem to mind; as long as the bright blue box with the hungry looking German Shepherd on it was in his eyesight, he marched resolutely in tow.

They passed the ruined Voyager at noon. It had been plowed deliberately into the side of the bluff and trashed; whatever hadn't been taken was broken. The van was haloed in broken flashlights, dart games, ripped clothing, crushed miniature televisions, portable cassette decks. Nearby, carefully placed to seemingly view the wreckage, was a severed human head, which on closer inspection turned out to be that of Stern, the sporting goods store owner. He had been placed to view the destruction of his own robbed goods.

Hilligan kept walking.

At one o'clock he had to stop. He ate a sparse lunch, sipping at the water canteen instead of gulping, until his thirst was slacked. Sparky ate a dog biscuit, fighting the blurred mechanism of his mouth to work on it.

As Hilligan watched the dog slap his tongue tentatively at a shallow bowl of water, he heard the unmistakable crack of a rifle shot.

The dog tensed momentarily, then resumed drinking as if nothing had happened, completely ignoring the round hole in its left eye.

The dog drank, liquid dripping down its ruined face into its water bowl, and drank its own fluids until its body suddenly collapsed.

The dog shivered and lay still.

Hilligan was already half way up the side of the outcropping. He hoisted himself between two peaked rocks as another shot rang out below him. "Just had to make sure, *Marshall*," a voice shouted, laughing. This time he saw where it came from.

He took aim at the spot and there, in his sights, was a blinding chromium head.

He pulled the trigger and the head flared in a shower of metal and flesh fragments as the soft pink fleshy head exploded.

The rifle shot echoed, then the tranquility of the desert returned.

Cautiously, Hilligan returned to his pack and removed his binoculars. He climbed the hillock and scouted.

A mere mile ahead was the remainder of the band. They had stopped in the bare shade of a stunted stand of cottonwoods, waiting for their compatriot.

He hoped they had seen what had happened to their scout; and then knew they did because the three of them abruptly walked out into the sunlight, blinding him with the metallic brilliance of their heads.

When his eyes had adjusted, he saw that between them they had two weapons, one of which looked like an automatic rifle. The third carried an inappropriately small red pack, the kind children carry schoolbooks in, stuffed to overflowing; as Hilligan watched the other two tried to load it further until the one bearing the pack suddenly lashed out, knocking the other to the ground.

Hilligan put the high power binoculars down and tried to sight through the rifle, but they were too far away.

He returned to the desert floor, mounted his own pack, and moved on.

*   *   *

When he got to the cottonwoods, the bandits were long gone. A scatter of Ritz Crackers and empty juice cartons attested to their stupidity. He hoped the juice had gone down burning hot.

He went on.

He spotted them forty-five minutes later, as they moved into the low hills. On the other side of those hills was the town of Lawrence. They were moving fast, spread out, twenty or thirty yards between them.

Hilligan sprinted to the nearest rock outcropping, balancing his rifle carefully on the lip of the overhang, and caught the nearest in his finder. It was the weaponless one with the pack, standing at the limits of range. Carefully, using the rock to steady him, he pulled off a single shot, watching the bright metallic head shatter, scattering the sandy ground with cookies, plastic jars of peanut butter, and soft flesh.

The other two glanced around, then broke into a run.

Night was coming, and they had made it to the hills.

*   *   *

The stars were up. The Milky Way rose like a glowing band. The night was Moonless, but Hilligan could see his way by the blue glow of the Milky Way alone.

He saw with his ears as much as with his eyes. He thought of a novel he had been given by Anne after taking the job of Marshall in Davidson. It was one of the Leatherstocking Tales by Cooper. With the book, Anne had also given him a book by Mark Twain with an essay marked out in it about how lousy a storyteller Cooper was. According to Twain, most of the suspense in a Cooper novel developed when someone made noise by stepping on something while sneaking around. Someone was always stepping on something and giving themselves away.

Up ahead of Hilligan, someone stepped on something.

"Sorry, Twain, Cooper was right," Hilligan muttered.

There was a line of jutting rocks ahead, threaded by a stony path. Hilligan crept to the first outcropping, avoiding any stepped-on somethings of his own.

He waited, and then there was another sound, very close.

Suddenly one of them appeared, the silvery luminescence of his head turning a mere yard from Hilligan.

It was the one with the automatic weapon.

Hilligan was quicker, and as a spatter of lead lined the rock wall to his right he pulled a shot out of his rifle and hit the other square in the chest.

The night flared and Hilligan briefly covered his eyes at the hissing explosion as the thing dropped its rifle, uttering a tiny cry as it was blown apart.

Beyond it, in the night, Hilligan heard the other one running. Fast.

Hilligan followed. They had entered a desert forest of cactus, up the side of a small hill. The cactus looked like they had been planted, lined up in neat rows up the side of the hillock, each giving the next just enough room to catch any available water.

Hilligan caught a brief glimpse of his prey, heard a scraped tumble of rocks which splashed down past him to the foot of the hill below.

"I'm coming for you, you bastard!" Hilligan shouted up into the darkness.

Only silence greeted him.

In the dark, with the night over him, Hilligan moved upward,

126

from cactus to cactus. Cursing his boots, he knew that he was the one making noise this time as he kicked a scuff of shale that slid down the mountainside.

He stopped, leaned into the curve of a prickly pear without touching it, and waited.

Still nothing.

The night breathed silence.

He felt presence; heard the faintest of sounds—

A silver-white hand appeared from behind the cactus and was on him before he could react.

He was knocked to the ground. A chrome head loomed over him. He heard his rifle slide away down the hill in the darkness. His attacker raised a Colt .45, then tossed it contemputuously away and held his palm downward over Hilligan.

"This game's over," the bandit hissed at him. "Tomorrow I'll play games in Lawrence. And then everywhere else on this miserable planet . . ."

The palm began to glow with silver light.

Something flashed in the darkness, hovered overhead, dropped on the alien's back.

The alien cried out and fell off into the night.

Hilligan pushed himself up to see the bandit clutching at his ripped-out throat, see it thrash helplessly before lying still.

"That would have been you in another second," Hilligan heard in his head, weakly. There was familiar laughter behind the words.

"Sparky," he said.

The dog lay panting a few feet from the imploded corpse of the desperado. His head looked like a scooped-out bowl, the top completely collapsed, wires and bio-tubes hanging uselessly. But there was the old look of unmistakably intelligent though weakening fire in one of his eyes.

"Should always check to make sure your sidekick has really stopped playing," the dog's thoughts said to him. "That bullet they hit me with fused a couple of the right circuits back together. It was like waking up from a bad dream. And you were gone." There was more humor than blame in the voice.

"Sparky—"

"Don't apologize, Mitch. I had just enough left in me to save your ass and this planet . . ." The voice trailed off tepidly.

As Hilligan watched, the weak light began to fade in the dog's eye.

"So long, pal . . ." the dog said in a dying whisper.

Hilligan stood in the darkness for a long time. The Milky Way, a blue glowing ribbon cutting the night, passed overhead toward the West and morning.

*　　*　　*

Finally, as the Milky Way faded, Hilligan picked Sparky up in his arms and headed back to the Toyota. He pulled off the camouflage, lay the dog gently in the back, and headed out.

The morning colored the east purple and yellow. Hilligan smoked a cigarette and thought about his own spaceship hidden out in the desert. He thought about the four bandits he had been sent to catch who had terrorized and destroyed so many other worlds, and about how his race's addiction to games had probably saved himself and this planet. And he thought about Sparky, his only weapon, and how he'd been constructed to look like any Earth dog. Hilligan thought about the thin plastic flesh that covered his own chromium skin.

Hilligan thought about what he would do now. He could go home, but somehow, the remembered kiss of a woman named Anne made him want to stay for awhile.

He had a feeling that love was a good game to play.

There was a tool kit out in that spaceship buried in the desert; perhaps he could spend his spare time trying to fix Sparky up. A good sidekick was hard to find.

Perhaps the town of Lawrence needed a Marshall.

Hilligan rode the Wild West in a Toyota.

Richard Laymon writes brutal, graphic stories with a sense of humor. His most famous works are THE CELLAR, and the recent FLESH. The following is in the tradition of the Western tall tale, with the special Laymon touch.

DINKER'S POND

by Richard Laymon

The prospector's yarn went like this. I just kept mum and listened him out.

*   *   *

From the start, she wouldn't have nothing to do with me. She was Jim's gal from head to toe—and all the goodies in between.

I told him, "Jim, we don't wanta bring her along."

"I sure do," he allowed.

"She ain't good for nothing but spawning trouble and ruination."

Jim said, "She's right pretty."

Well, I knew that, but it was off the point. "She only just wants to fall in with us 'cause of the strike. She's after our gold, that's all. Why, she likely don't even *like* you."

Jim got this drifty look in his eyes, and I could see his mind was back on last night when he'd sampled Lucy's wares. She'd met up

129

with us yesterday afternoon when we come strutting out of the assay office, which made me suspicious right away. I guess she kept herself stationed there, just waiting for a couple of prospectors to come out grinning.

Right off the bat, she latched onto Jim.

He's the gullible one. That's how come she sidled up to him, not me. Jim's got less sense than mule flop, and it shows all over his face.

You might say to yourself I'm peddling sour grapes when I tell you that's why she went for him, but it's not so. Jim's no younger than me. He wasn't any more sprucy, and he didn't smell any better, and I'm just as fine a specimen of manhood as him. In addition, we were equal partners, though Lucy couldn't of known that at the start.

Nope. Jim's just a stride short of idiot, whereas I've got a fair parcel of brains and common sense.

I'm not one to be led around by the pecker, but you can't say that for Jim, and Lucy knew it.

Next thing you know, I'm all by my lonesome in the saloon and he's got himself a fine room in the Jamestown Hotel getting convinced he's in love.

Which brings me back to that drifty look in his eyes while we're putting away steak and eggs the morning after.

"I reckon she likes me just fine," he said. "She's not real keen on you, though, George."

"Now, there's a fine state of affairs. How long have you and me been partners?" I asked.

He scrunched up his brow, giving it a shot. "I reckon it's been a spell."

"It's been a right *long* spell, and now you're all set to ruin us. A woman at the digs is the worst kind of bad luck, you know that just as well as me. You recall what happened to Placer Bill and Mike Murphy over on the Kern."

Jim puzzled over that, looking for the answer on the spikes of his fork.

"Let me refresh your memory, then. Why, Bill and Mike, they was thick. They was buddies more years than you got teeth."

"I got most my teeth," Jim allowed.

"Well, that's the point. It was a lot of years. You couldn't find better buddies than Bob and Mike . . ."

"Thought you said he was Bill."

130

"Robert William, that was his name. Some called him Bob, some Bill. Thing is, Bob and Mike was like brothers till the black day a woman showed up at their digs. She took to Mike, right off, and treated Bob so bad you'd think he had the scabbies. Poor Bob, he was left out cold and lonesome. But did he complain and carry on? No, sir. He was too big a man for that. He bore his troubles in silence. And you recall what happened then?"

"What was the gal's name?" Jim asked.

"Greta."

"I recall a Greta Gurney in Bible school. A redhead. Was this Greta that took up with Mike a redhead?"

"I don't believe she was."

"Didn't you never see her?"

"Let me tell the story, will you? You're enough to drive the patience out of a hospital for the blind and crippled."

"Well, I just . . ."

"This weren't your Greta. This was some other Greta. Now, the point I'm trying to stick you with is this—when she went strolling into the digs, she brought disaster and tragedy down on the luckless heads of Bill and Mike. It wasn't bad enough she spurned Bill and made a shambles of two fast pals. No, sir. That was bad, but it weren't bad enough.

"The way it turns out, she'd run off from her spouse. She didn't let on about that, however. No, she kept mum on the subject of her spouse. He was Lem Jaspers, a one-eyed smuggler from Frisco. And he went looking for her. And he found her out there on the Kern with Bill and Mike, and massacred the three of them."

"Killed 'em?"

"He killed 'em mean and slow. I'd tell you all about it, but I don't want to spoil your breakfast. Let me just say it weren't pretty. He put out Mike's eyes with a burning stick to make him suffer for look-ing at Greta. And he cut off Mike's pecker with a Bowie knife and shoved it up Greta's whatsis. He told her, 'You wanted it so bad, now you got it.'"

Jim was starting to look a little gray around the lips.

"After they was dead," I went on, "he took the skin right off Greta. Peeled her raw. He tossed her face in the campfire. The rest of the skin, he tanned it. I won't tell you about the tobacco pouch. But Lem used some of Greta's hide to fashion himself a new pair of moccasins so he could have the pleasure of walking around on her all the time."

"Mighty lowdown of him," Jim allowed.

"That wasn't the lowest of the low, either. Lem didn't let it go with taking out his vengeance on Greta and Mike. He took poor Bill and gutted him like a trout. Here, Bill was just as innocent as a baby, never put a hand to Greta, but Lem slaughtered him just the same."

"That weren't right."

"Right or not, Bill met himself a grisly end, and it was all because his buddy turned traitor on him and took up with a gal. Like I said, a woman at the digs is the worst kind of luck."

"What happend to Lem?"

"Well, I don't know. For all I know, maybe he got tired of being a widower and hitched up with your Lucy."

Jim spent a long time pondering that, scowling down at his plate and wiping his hand around on it to get up the last of the egg yellow. After he was done licking his hand, he raised his eyes to me. I could see he was grateful for the warning. But what he said was, "We'll keep our eyes sharp. If this Lem comes along, you and me we'll shoot him dead."

A man only has so much breath to spare in his life, and I'd just wasted a good parcel of it. I might as well of told my story to the butt end of a mule.

Later on in the morning, just before the three of us headed out, Jim took me aside. "I had a talk with Lucy," he whispered. "She don't know any Lem Jaspers, but she knew a Jasper Wiggens once. She claims she never married him."

*　　*　　*

I figured Lucy was bound to warm up to me, once she got to know me better. She got to know me a whole sight better on our travels back to the Stanislaus where we'd made our strike, but she didn't warm up like I hoped.

The way she looked at me, one would think I had nasty stuff hanging out my nose.

The trip took longer than it should've. Every now and again, they'd leave me on the trail so I could keep the mules company, and Lucy'd take Jim off into the woods. She did it mostly just to torment me. Half the time, she'd come back half unfastened to give me a look at regions she never planned to let me scout around in.

132

Lucy was as cruel and cold-hearted as any woman that ever crossed my path.

Still, I tried to be friends with her. I wanted to get into her good graces, even if not her drawers. And who knows but that the former might not lead up to the trail to the latter?

No matter what I did, though, she spurned me.

She even spurned my stories. Jim liked to listen to them pretty near as much as I liked the telling. On the first night, she sat there by the cookfire sighing and rolling her eyes around while I told my best rip-snorter about the squaw with the two-headed baby. One head was partial to one of her tits, and the other hankered all the time for the other. Trouble was, the heads didn't match up with the tits they favored, so the squaw had to hold the child upside down at chow time. The little scamp liked that just fine. Only thing was, he got so fond of being upside down he never learned the use of his legs. He grew up walking on his hands with his feet in the air, and drowned himself one day when he tried to wade a stream that weren't even waist deep.

Well, Jim just nearly split his sides while I told that one. Lucy, she just sat there acting like she wished I'd either shut up or die.

Before I could start in with a new story, she said to me, "George Sawyer, you're about as crude as the day is long. I'd rather be snake-bit than listen to another one of your vile whoppers."

"Why, that was a true story," Jim said, sticking up for me.

She turned her eyes on him. They were pretty eyes that glimmered in the firelight, but there didn't seem to be much warmth inside them. "If you believe that was true, Jimmy dear, why you've got dust in your brain pan."

Jimmy dear looked at me, scowling from the effort of trying to piece a thought together. "You been telling fibs?"

"A false word has never passed these lips. Why, I was there when the boy drowned, both heads down in the creek and his feet kicking like a hanged man."

Jim turned to Lucy, raised his eyebrows and said, "See?"

"All I see," she offered, "is one lying fool and one idiot. Makes me wonder why I ever took up with you in the first place, James Bixby."

That let the air out of his sails something horrible to witness. He sat there, slumped over and speechless, while Lucy flounced her way into the shadows and crawled into her blankets.

I tried to cheer him up. "How'd you like to hear about the time I got pulled under the quicksand and . . ."

"Never happened at all," he muttered, looking as if he'd caught me with a fifth ace in my hand. "You'd of gone down in the quicksand, you'd be dead, George."

"Well, I *would've* been dead, but there was such a heap of skeletons down there at the bottom that I was able to fashion myself a ladder and . . ."

I could see by his eyes that he was just starting to believe me again. I could see his doubts just melting away. But all of a sudden, Ludy called to him.

"Come on away from that lying, foul-mouthed nogood. Right this minute. I'm cold over here. Come on over and heat me up."

Jim was mighty quick on his feet after he heard that.

I was left all by my lonesome, listening to the lively crackle and snap of the fire, the wind in the trees, and Lucy grunting and squealing like a sow getting stuck by a hot poker.

My own poker got mighty hot while I heard her carrying on that way.

Lucy weren't a sow, even if she did sound like one.

Sitting there on my rock, I felt like the two-headed boy. One of my heads thought it'd be a nice idea to poke her. The other would just as soon put a bullet in her noggin.

Neither one of my heads done a thing about it.

After that first night on the trail, I didn't tell no more stories. A couple of times, I made the offer. The offer caused Jim to shake his head sadly, and caused Lucy to spit in the fire.

*   *   *

Finally, we got to our digs on the Stanislaus. We got there just after dark. Lucy didn't express any great fondness for our shack. I allowed as how she might rather sleep under the stars, but she asked me to shut my yap.

She spent a good portion of the night bellyaching about how she couldn't properly breathe in such close quarters, and how a woman requires some privacy, and how this was the one and only night she would ever spend beneath the same roof as George Sawyer, a lying man of such vile habits and temperament that he

134

was no better than a plague of worms.

Lucy not only gnashed her teeth and bitterly complained about our "hovel," but she refused Jim her favors. "My modesty won't allow it," she protested. "Not with *him* breathing down our necks."

I considered her remark about modesty to be a joke, but neither Jim or me was happy with her decision, which come as a letdown to both of us. On the trail, I'd grown partial to the sounds she made. I'd started looking forward to the three of us in the shack. She was right about close quarters. If she and Jim went at it in the shack, I was sure to hear more than her wild grunts and groans. I was likely to see more, too. The way I had it figured, that would suit Lucy just fine. The more she could torment me, the better she'd like it.

But maybe she reckoned it'd push me too far and I might join in.

Maybe she was right.

At any rate, she didn't risk it. She just left Jim alone that night.

While I tried to get asleep, I figured up a few of the wrongs she'd done to me and Jim.

She'd stolen my pal. She'd cheated me and Jim out of the pleasure we took in my stories. Finally, she was holding out, robbing Jim out of the reason he'd brung her along in the first place and keeping me from the pleasures of being a witness when she got herself poked.

Like I said before, I never met a crueler, colder-hearted woman.

Come the next morning, Jim set out with an axe figuring to knock down some forest and put up a mansion for his lady. I figured I'd let him handle that on his own. I was here to dig gold. His lady could sleep in the dirt, for what I cared.

I took my pick out to the mine and set to work. However, I couldn't get the blamed woman out of my head. I kept pondering on her, wondering what she might be up to now that she was all by her lonesome. Pretty soon, I come to figure this'd be a fine chance to visit with her. Without Jim around to muddle up the works, maybe I could set things right with her. Or at least give her my angle on matters.

Well, I went looking for her. Lucy weren't in the shack, and she weren't at the river. I scouted some more, and pretty soon I come upon her.

The gal was down by the shore of Dinker's Pond, slipping off her duds. I ducked behind the big old tree at the top of the slope, and give my eyes a treat. I'd gotten looks at bits and pieces of her along the trail, but now I got to see the whole woman and it weren't any wonder Jim felt obliged to bring her along. She could knock the breath out of a dead man.

Me, I got caught up in looking, and she was up to her knees in the pond before I sung out.

"Get on outa there!" I yelled.

She jumped like I'd jabbed her with a stick. I reckon she forgot to be modest, for she turned herself around and rammed her fists into her hips without even trying to cover nothing. "George Sawyer!" she railed. "You son-of-a-bitch! You dirty, rotten, lowdown, leprous, claim-jumpin' son-of-a-whore!"

"I ain't no claim-jumper," I informed the woman, and started on my way down the slope.

She aimed an arm at me and shook a finger. The finger weren't all the shook. "Don't you come any closer! Get outa here! You bastard, don't you dare come down here!"

I kept coming, and she started backing up till the water crawled around her waist. About that time, she remembered her modesty and so she hunkered down till she was covered to the neck.

"Wouldn't do that, were I you," I said. I sat myself down on a stump by the shore. Her clothes were heaped in front of me, but I kept my boots off them. "You'd better listen to me, gal, and step outa that water pretty lively."

"I most surely won't."

"Should've gone over in the river, if you wanted to get yourself wet. Shouldn't of come here."

"I go where I like. Sides, the river's so cold I'd freeze up solid."

"You're in Dinker's Pond," I informed her.

"Well, it's a good pond. It *were* a good pond till you showed up. Go on and get."

"Used to be a good fishing hole," I allowed. "Up till around a year ago. Just ask Jim if you don't believe me. But the fishes, they all petered out after we strung up Clem Dinker."

Lucy, she squinted her eyes at me. Then her hand come up with a rock. She kind of unsquatted there for a second and let fly. I got distracted, admiring her, or I could've dodged. The rock give me a good clip on the shoulder.

I jumped up, rubbing my hurt.

"Don't you come in here!" Lucy yelled, and fetched up another rock.

136

"Not me. I ain't a fool like some."

"I'm a fool, am I?" She pitched the rock, but I ducked it.

"You're a fool for sure, you don't come outa there."

"Jim, he's gonna shoot you dead."

"Jim'll be mighty grateful I happened to come on down here and warn you off."

"You just come here fixing to doodle me." All of a sudden, she lost her mean glare and found a smile. "You're scared of the water, George Sawyer. Ha!"

"I'm scared of *that* water. You'd be scared of it, too, if you knew what I know."

"Oh, dear me, yes. I'd be thrown into such a fright I'd hop right out and be ever so grateful. Oh, George, you're just pitiful." She eased herself back and started floating, all sprawled out pale and shiny on the water, grinning up at the sky. "You're just the most pitiful thing."

"I'm half inclined to leave you to your fate," I called.

She picked up her head, and the rest of her sank out of sight. "Did you say something, poor George?"

"Maybe I'll just go off and leave you."

"You can't leave, George." She must've found the bottom, for she come up a little. The water was almost up to her shoulders. It was too murky to let me see anything worthwhile, unless you count her smile. That wasn't under water, but I wouldn't count it. It was too smirky and mean. "Why, you haven't scared me witless yet," she said. "I spect, once I've heard your whopper, I'll just come out screaming and hurl myself into your manly arms."

She reckoned I *couldn't* scare her out of the pond.

I took it for a challenge.

So I set myself down on the rock. "Did you ever hear of a fella named Clem Dinker?"

"Why, no, George. Do tell me all about him."

"Clem, he was a crazy man that used to live in a tree over across the river. He was so skinny, looked like he never ate nothing. But that weren't so. Clem used to eat everything he could get his teeth on.

"When it come to food, he was just about the most patient, sneaky fella you ever seen. He'd sit so quiet, up in his tree, that birds'd come along and settle on him. When they done that, he'd grab 'em quick and pop 'em right into his mouth. Munched the tweeters up, wings, beaks, eyes and all. We used to hear him off in the distance, coughing up feathers."

Lucy shook her head and rolled her eyes up at the sky. "Well, George," she said, "I just got goosebumps running all up and down my body. You keep scaring me like this, I might just swoon dead away."

"If you swoon, you're on your own. Now, do you want to keep on mocking me, or you want to hear about Clem?"

"Oh, I beg your pardon. Please, go on."

"Clem, he'd eat just about anything. He just weren't particular. If he could get his teeth on it, he'd chow it down. Did I tell you had pointed teeth?"

Lucy laughed.

"Yes, ma'am. You may not care to believe it, but Clem filed all his front teeth so they come to points. They was so sharp, he couldn't talk much without ruining his lips. You'd be talking to the fella, and he'd no sooner answer back than the blood'd start flying at you. He'd act like he didn't even notice, and you'd be standing there getting rained on. It was enough to make you lose your train of thought."

"If your mama's had a lick of sense," Lucy said, "she would've strangled you at birth."

"I'm only just telling you how it was. I ain't making up any of this. You don't believe me, ask Jim. He'll tell you same as me. Why, I laid down for a snooze one day after chatting a spell with that man, and Jim come upon me and I was so bloody he took me for dead and had a grave half dug before I woke up."

"But that's off the point," I said before Lucy could start in again. "Thing is, Clem Dinker was crazy mad, and he'd eat anything he could get his pointy teeth into. Not just birds. We seen him eat a beaver, once. And there was a trapper over yonder had a hound till Clem got hold of it. He gobbled up squirrels, coons, coyotes, butter-flies, spiders, slugs and worms."

Lucy wasn't smiling any more. She was giving me a hateful look, and her upper lip had crawled up above her gums. I could see she was ready to start yelling, and I might never have a chance to finish my story. So I got to the point quick.

"Clem finally ate one of our mules. Her name was Jane, and we come upon Clem with his face buried in her innards. So we strung him up." I twisted around and pointed up the slope at the same tree

I'd hidden behind to watch Lucy strip off her duds. "See that branch there? The one sticks out this way? That's where we hung him from."

"You didn't hang nobody," Lucy said. She didn't say it spunky, though. Seemed like she'd lost some of her starch.

"I put the noose around his scrawny little neck, myself. We stood Clem smack on the edge, up there under the tree. The plan was, we'd give Clem a push, and he'd swing out over the bank and strangulate.

"But he was our first hanging. The mistake was, we should've made the rope tight between Clem's neck and the branch. Way it turned out, it had a mite too much slack in it. So when we nudged him off the edge, he didn't swing so much as he dropped. Plucked his noggin right off his shoulders.

"Well, we carted Clem's body off into the woods and planted it. All but his head. Being round like it was, it rolled on downhill and plopped into the pond here. We never could find hide nor hair of it. That's how come we call this place Dinker's Pond. His head's still in there, far as we know."

Lucy, she just sort of stared at me.

"After a spell, the fish in there started to peter out. Pretty soon, there wasn't none to be caught at all. Oh, you'd get nibbles pretty quick. Bring up your hook, and your bait'd be gone. But you never had a fish for your troubles. Me and Jim went through a whole parcel of worms before we give up on our old fishing hole."

Lucy, standing real still, slanted her eyes down at the water. Then she jerked them up at me real quick. I could see she was riled that I'd caught her looking at the water. "Weren't a breath of truth in that yarn, George Sawyer. It didn't tell me nothing I didn't already know—just that you're vile trash that ain't fit for human civilization."

"I ain't no liar," I said.

I caught her eyes checking around some more.

Then they darn near popped out and Lucy threw a hollar that made my hair stand up. She commenced to thrash around considerable. The water around her churned and bubbled and got kind of red.

I give some thought to splashing in to try and save her. Would've been mighty heroic.

139

*　　*　　*

That was the end of George's yarn, and the end of the whisky bottle sitting between us on the saloon table.

"And you didn't even lift a finger to save her?" I asked.

"She didn't amount to much, anyhow," George said.

"Now you want *me* going out to the digs with you?"

"Gets mighty lonesome out there. It surely does. I reckon I'd risk some bad luck for the company of a sweet thing like you."

"You've got Jim, don't you?"

"Well, he come at me with his axe when he saw what happened to Lucy. Couldn't talk him outa it. He got it into his head it was me killed Lucy and chewed her up that way. So I had to shoot him."

"Did you do her that way, George? Was it you?"

"Why, Mable, bite your tongue. I ain't that kinda man. And you ain't lowdown like Lucy was. That gal was pure poison. She was such poison I run across Dinker's head next morning in the pond there, afloating face up with his lips turned black."

Melissa Mia Hall is noted for her quiet, elegant stories. This one is a little less quiet, but still very much the kind of story she's noted for. Her work appears in both genre and literary publications. The following is of the literary publication type, and I mean that as a compliment.

STAMPEDE

by Melissa Mia Hall

Mama slumped down behind the steering wheel and stared out through the windshield at Mac's Corral. Mama stared real hard. Lots of assholes at Mac's this afternoon and it wasn't even five o'clock yet. Larry was there, all right. And her car was there, that dumb red Mustang she probably got off her last victim.

"Can't we listen to the radio?"

"It runs down the battery," Mama said.

"Just for a little while?"

"No, now shut up."

"Why?" her daughter whined.

"I said, shut up; I'm thinking."

"What're you gonna do to him?" her son said.

"I'd kill 'em," the little girl said.

"I'd beat the shit out of him," the boy said.

"I'd go on in there and spit on him," Kayley giggled.

"You kids shut up."

"I wish we could get cable. I just love MTV."

"You know what, Kayley—?" J.D. said.

"What?"

"I think life should be like that, music with everything."

"I know."

The sound of bubble gum popping made Mama wince.

"Don't you pinch me—"

Mama shut her eyes for a minute. "I said you kids shut up."

"He ain't gonna come out of there, Mama—he's gonna stay there all night making over that girl."

"She's really neat. She's 23 and already been married twice."

"That's not neat, Kayley." Mama turned on the radio to drown out their voices, hoping it wouldn't wear down the battery too much. Kayley punched J.D. and hung over the seat, trying to change the channel. "I'll do it, Kayley."

"Y-95, put it on Y-95."

Mama watched them in the rear-view mirror, watched them bounce on the seat. Mama could smell their young sweat and she loved them for a moment so passionately her red fingernails punched through the cheap car covers, ripping through the threads hungrily. "My kids," she whispered. "I can take care of 'em." Her body vibrated like a tuning fork or a lightning rod that had just been hit. What if she was an unfit mother, what if she couldn't take care of them. The music thundered. She blinked away sudden tears.

"See, this is like major neat. See—when we're bopping down the road with the radio on, it's like I'm in a video."

"Don't you wish life was like that all the time?" J.D. said.

"Yeah."

"It makes you important. Like you're gonna do it," J.D. said.

"Gonna do what?" Mama said, turning the radio off with a brutal twist of her thin wrist. The silence burst the air, a dart piercing a big fat balloon.

J.D. looked at Kayley, embarrassed. "Well, It, you know—"

"What?"

"It. Well—" J.D. said, blushing.

"What, sex?" Mama spat out, ready to burn him alive. Ready to jump over the seat and strangle her own son before he could get some girl pregnant and God knows what else. Too bad they had to grow up and get complicated. Her head pounded. Some boys are precocious at twelve. Not J.D.—not yet, please. She looked at him. He stared at his lap. His hands were small and seemed so helpless, twisting themselves in a loose knot.

Kayley watched the parking lot. She jerked at the sight of something, someone. Mama snapped her head around to catch a glimpse
of a man going into the bar. Kayley sighed. "Mama, Larry's meaner
than mean. We don't need him. We really don't. I wish Daddy
weren't in jail no more. I wish we was going to Disneyworld. I wish I
could be Tiffany or Debbie Gibson. Mama, can't I sing good? I
think I can—"

Mama stared at the small B-B hole in the lower lefthand corner
of the windshield. "Sure, baby, you sing real good."

J.D. snorted, "In your dreams—"

Randy hadn't meant to shoot it. He'd just been mad about losing the payroll. He'd just gambled the wrong thing at the wrong
time and now, he was paying for it. And they were paying for it, too.

"You could get a job here, maybe and see him everyday, just like
that there Maxine," J.D. laughed. She wanted to slap his smart-aleck
face but she couldn't reach him. "Shut up, J.D."

"I hear she swings her tits—not that she has any and he puts
twenty dollar bills in her g-string."

"Oh, God, J.D."

"You're nasty, J.D., a nasty old butthole stopped up and stinky."

"I'm not having that kind of language in my car."

"Daddy's car."

"Okay, Daddy's car." Mama missed Randy but this Larry had
been helping her out with the bills after she lost her job at K-Mart
and he wasn't such a bad guy till he got hooked on Mac's Corral and
the Heavenly Heifers, specifically Maxine, the star dancer and her
ruby red g-string. He'd gotten to spending more and more money
here and Mama was beginning to believe she'd have to give up on
old Larry. He was never obligated, of course; they weren't married.
She was being punished more than likely, for living in sin before the
eyes of the children; that's what was happening. But she'd miss
Larry's contribution to the family fund. They'd have to get another
apartment, a smaller one. She'd have to get another job immediately,
But jobs were scarce in Texas circa '87, especially if you didn't want
to work. And Mama had to be honest with herself, she didn't want
to get another job. She wanted to stay home and pretend she was
Donna Reed. And that was pure-d impossible. She just didn't want
to stand on her feet all day. She wished she'd gone to junior college.
She wished she knew computers. She wished she hadn't gotten
married in high school. She wished she'd gotten her GED. She
wished she wasn't so damn lazy.

"I think you oughta go on in. I think you oughta tell him to kiss off—"

"Mama, you really going in there?"

"Yeah."

"Don't forget to apply for a job—" J.D. pointed at the sign "Dancers wanted."

Mama laughed. "That'd be rich." She patted her ample thighs. "I'd knock 'em dead with these—"

"Kayley don't you think Mama's titties are big enough?"

"Shut up, J.D."

Mama opened the car door. She was going in there. She was going to go right on in, damn it all to hell and tell that Larry he was a son of a bitch and his services were no longer needed, stud or financial. Mama was going to go to work. She didn't want to be Donna Reed. Why not that woman on "Who's the Boss?" or hell, even Roseanne or better still, Barbara Walters. Nobody jacked around with Barbara. She didn't need no man, like her own grannie had told her all of her life, like even Randy told her as he went off to prison—"Honey, you can take care of yourself, and the kids, honey, I sure 'nough believe you can take care of 'em."

Yes, she could do it. She could become a success. Suck-cess. "J.D., watch your sister. Lock the doors. I'll be right back."

"What are you going to do?"

"Are you taking Daddy's gun?" J.D. hung over the front seat and tried to get a better look. "Hey, let me go—let me go."

"You're underage."

"I'll kill him for you," J.D. said, all excited.

"You shut up and be good."

"Damn—kill him good, okay?"

"I'm not going to kill anybody."

"I just wish you would. I never did like him, Mama. We don't need him, 'sides, Daddy's gonna get out in ten years."

"I can't wait," Mama whispered.

"Hot damn."

"There she goes—" Kayley said, "Turn on the radio."

"Is that loud enough?"

"Louder. Did she leave any of those cigarettes? You wanta smoke one?"

Their voices receded as Mama moved forward. Soon she couldn't hear anything but a pulse beating wild at her temples, in

146

her throat, in her breasts. Her thighs pumped. Her body swayed with a terrible music, a magical rhythm full of purpose and direction. She was a fine looking woman, full figured, in her early thirties, her brown hair curly and wild, a horse's mane. She threw her head back and pushed past a little man with an ill-fitting black toupee. "Excuse me—" she said. Mama was there on business. She entered the bar. It was dark and smoky. The dancers weren't officially on duty yet but a couple of topless waitresses weaved through the club, taking drink orders and staring blindly at a couple of leering patrons already three sheets to the wind and then some. Mama gazed around for Larry. She saw him with a group of men studying a racing sheet. The table was filled with longnecks and Larry didn't see her. The bartender asked her if she needed anything. She said no, not yet. There were a couple of women patrons, one was a jaded date and the other, a flame-haired possible prostitute. Mama sat down behind a pillar that obscured her face from Larry's view.

The man with the toupee came over and sat down. "Hey, babe, anything you want?"

"White wine."

"Sure, if they got it. Anything else?" He dared to touch her hand lightly. His sweaty fingers trembled. "You dance?"

"Sure, I dance." Mama smelled him. It was a frightened smell mixed with English Leather. She felt sorry for him.

"Here?"

"Nope." She freed her hand.

"Oh." The man stared at the stage and clucked his tongue. "They'll be on soon." It was plain he wasn't used to small talk.

"Swell." She thought most of the people that frequented Mac's were losers. But she suspected some of them might have money and decent reputations. She could do worse than hang out here. A lot worse. Mama pinched herself. It wouldn't do to think like that.

Suddenly the stage lights came on and the dancers began their show. Maxine of the red Mustang, came on, whirling outwards in red lizard cowboy boots she took off after an Alabama song. Then she slid into a Bob Seger song about turning pages. Her body was slender and boyish, her breasts high up and small, like skinned pears. Her white blonde hair was cut close to her head and her eyes were blue, large and expressionless. The earlier routine had been done at a frenetic pace, now she moved with fluid elegance and deadly nonchalance. Mama was reluctantly impressed. The men

147

watching her drew closer and closer. They surrounded the dancer with a cocoon of aching approval and desire. Mama left her table and followed.

Maxine danced slowly, undulating to Seger's hungry voice. A saxophone cried out and Maxine spread like molasses across the stage. A blue light fanned out across her body, then a pink spot and finally a red-orange bled across her vacant face. She was almost nude. She bent forward and the tips of her little breasts lightly whispered across Larry's face. Hands rushed forward. Money ringed her g-string like green and white flowers. So much money. Mama thought about how many bills she could pay with that money. Her hand fingered the gun in her jacket pocket. She was torn between the choice of victims. She was close enough to hear Maxine say to Larry—"Come on back now, sugar; you come back. You know what I do with it—"

Mama turned away. Maxine left the stage after picking up her boots and some pink carnations someone had brought. The men clustered around the stage, waiting for the next Heifer. Mama felt silly. The next dancer wore a white cowboy hat and waved a toy pistol around to the strains of "One More For the Road." Her tits bounced up and down furiously. Mama wanted to laugh. She decided she needed to talk to Maxine. She went around to the back. No one seemed to mind. Everyone thought she belonged. She was just some broad.

The dressing room was a cramped hole smelling of cosmetics, sweat, stale perfume and old tampons. Mama found Maxine sitting in front of a mirror studying the black tassles on her small nipples. "Like 'em? I don't. I wish I didn't ever have to wear anything ever at all. I'm too cute, you know, a nudist at heart." She laughed. "What you want? Mac's got no openings. 'Sides, you're a little broad in the beam and, let's face it, a little too old."

"May I talk to you for a moment?"

"I ain't been doing your husband or your man. I don't do that shit. I ain't no whore. I'm a professional so if you're hear to bawl me out I want you to know I ain't having it. I got principles. I'm a dancer, just like Bar-ish-no-cough. Got it?" Maxine ripped the pasties off, squealed and laughed again. "Look at them nipples. Ain't they something?"

Bimbo, idiot. Fruitcake dipped in anti-freeze. Mama felt foolish. This was the woman Larry worshipped. He came to this joint three days (at least) a week, just to see her. And yep, she could dance, but not good enough to warrant—Mama watched Maxine spread her legs. She watched her examine her supple thighs free of cellulite. Maxine oiled her legs happily.

"If I was taller I'd go to Vegas."

"How old are you?"

"Who are you, my mom? 21."

"Not 23?"

"No, I'm young—" Maxine lifted her chin defensively and the blank eyes suddenly burned. "I'm young, beautiful and rich."

"If that's true, how come you're working in this dive?"

"How come you're asking me that—you Barbara Walters or something? No, I've got it—you're a writer doing research—you doing a TV movie?"

Another dancer came in, a coffee colored black who was very tall. She put on a pair of horn-rimmed glasses and glared at Mama. "You're nothing but trouble coming here and bothering us. You a policeman or what? Some bitch getting off looking at us?"

"Can it, Yolanda—she's here to see me. That's right, ain't it?"

"Just call me Mama," Mama said softly.

"You don't look all that old," Maxine said charitably, pulling on a flowery pink kimono.

"Thanks."

"So you came here for something. I bet it's about some man."

"Maybe."

"He's been spending the rent money down here, I bet."

"Maybe."

"I'm sorry, sweetie, but that's the breaks. I don't make him come here," she shrugged her shoulders. "Hate to say it, but obviously you just don't supply him with what he needs—"

Mama felt cold. She did what she could. "But how can you do it?" she blurted out. "How can you do what you do? It's so stupid. You just dish it out and take it away—taking our money for shaking your ass. You're making it so nasty, so pointless." Mama crossed her arms and hid her hands in her armpits. "And when they come home what they've got is never good enough."

"It never is," Yolanda said before she left and the cowgirl returned, her boobs now flat and listless. "I'm so hungry," she told Maxine—"I gotta get me a hamburger."

Maxine stared at Mama. Her hands cupped her own breasts.

149

She wagged one up, one down. "I don't care. I don't care. Git it?"

Mama nodded and left. Maxine jumped up and followed her. "Wait."

Mama paused. She couldn't look at her.

"You got kids?"

Mama nodded.

Maxine said, "Me, too." She stuffed a couple of twenties into Maxine's jean pocket. "Hey, it's on the house. I'm not a heartless bitch. I can't help what men do, you know?"

*   *   *

The apartment complex rose up against the horizon like a vast network of old Army barracks. They'd only been built about five years and already seemed hopelessly outdated, the pseudo Spanish/country modern trim grating on anyone with the slightest artistic sensibilities. Mama passed a loaded dumpster and a cluster of teen-agers admiring a Harley. The bearded man who worked on it sported a double snake tattoo and a gold front tooth. He kept gesturing for more room, shooing them off like flies.

"What're we going to eat tonight?"

"I don't know."

"Do you think Larry will ever come back?" Kayley said.

It had been three days since her encounter with Maxine. Larry had seen her, afterall. He'd cussed her out and cleaned out the closet, simultaneously. She had no idea where he was staying. Maybe some motel but hopefully, not at Maxine's.

Someone had parked in her place. "I hate this—why do they do it?" She swore under breath and parked a row over in someone else's place. Fair's fair.

Mama didn't want Larry to come back. She had absolutely no feelings for him. He'd been meal ticket, that's all. He'd used her and she'd used him. Disgust filled her up like a thick chocolate milk shake. A piece of paper fluttered on her door. Behind on her rent. "Damnit, damnit, double dog damn it."

"Mama, you yell at me when I cuss."

"I know."

They entered the ground floor apartment, place of too temporary refuge. Kayley flipped on the TV and J.D. headed for the

150

refrigerator. "Don't you eat those hot dogs; that's for dinner."

"Chili and cheese?"

"Yeah."

"We still got some fritos—" J.D. announced brightly.

"So don't eat 'em up right now."

"Can I have a Coke?" Kayley asked. J.D. had already popped a top without asking.

"J.D., share that with your sister."

"Aw, mom—"

"I mean it." Mama took off her shoes and sat on the lumpy sofa. Her grandmother's rainbow patterned afghan fell into her lap. Mama held a corner to her cheek and felt like Linus.

Kayley had begun watching "Head of the Class". "I'm going to be smart someday," she said.

"Me, too," Mama said. "J.D., check the mail—" He left and came back with more bills and a letter from Randy. "Can I read it, mom?"

"Let me, let me—" Kayley piped up anxiously. Mama shook her head, "No, I'll read it." Kayley turned back to the TV. J.D. sat down beside Mama. She opened the letter carefully, like she was afraid her nails might set off a bomb. Her eyes scanned the first page. "Personal, J.D.—I'll read you the part for ya'll later, okay?" J.D. acted like he didn't care. "I'll start dinner," he said. It was obvious he was starving, but then, J.D. was always starving. Mama glanced at his thin, lanky frame with unadulterated admiration. Just like Randy. Her eyes returned to a slow perusal of the affectionate letter. She felt rotten and sleazy. He didn't know a thing about Larry and how she'd been shacking up with him like white trash just to make things easier. It made her feel like such a shithead. But it was pretty damn easy for a guy to be faithful in the pen. Unless a guy was gay, maybe. She slid the paper back into its envelope and stared at the TV screen. At least that was paid for. Suddenly, almost as if the TV had heard her, the vertical hold went haywire.

Kayley gasped. "Fix it, Bubba, fix it quick, Bubba." Mama and Kayley both held their breaths and let them out softly as J.D. turned the chili down and came over to see if he could fix it. Luckily, he could. J.D. was really handy with mechanical things.

"You know what," Mama said, after the TV was working again properly, "you kids are going to be proud of your mama. I'm going to get a good job."

"How?" J.D. snorted, stirring the chili. He'd heard it all before.

"I'll just keep looking till I find one. And I'll start going to the library and study for that GED. You'll see."

Her life hadn't been quite what she'd expected. One time, going down the highway, heading down for a visit with Randy, Mama had an awful experience. The kids had been playing in the backseat with one of those pac-man lap games and she listened, or tried to, to the radio news. It was hard. She forced herself to concentrate on the steady center lines, the occasional road signs, traffic around her but overhead the overcast sky pressed down. Spring air whispered through the window cracks and the outside air vents. Cool moist air, free air. Mama's temple throbbed with a headache, nothing bad, just a nagging presence of needle tips.

Randy had been in prison for about a year and they'd still had a little money in the bank. She had lost her first job. She had been working for a friend who had grown progressively cooler after Randy's conviction, to the point of not wanting her around as a friend or clerk in her trendy boutique on the Northside. Which was fine by Mama, since back then they still lived in Southwest Fort Worth in a comfortable middle class house. But after they returned from this visit, there would be no house. Mama remembered how that incident on the highway frightened her. It was like a disconnection to reality.

The highway had been real as were the nosily children in the backseat. The motion propelling the car forward was also real. But for a moment Mama—Mama was *not*. Her hands on the steering wheel continued to work. She didn't wreck the car. But her eyes widened into two cartoon circles and her mouth dropped into a small hesitant "o" as the change occurred, or rather, the disconnection began or at least, became a possibility.

She remembered how her arms were so pale. She hadn't been in the sun much all that past winter. She saw the hairs on her forearms with childlike wonder. Her nails shone a pretty seashell pink. Her hair hung down in a thick braid down her back, heavy and long. The radio hummed. Mama took the car off the road. It would be too easy to just let go and let some four-wheeler slam into them, crushing the children and that stupid little game they loved so much.

The car hissed as it stopped. The children kept on playing. Mama put the window down and looked into the tall grass. Cows grazing nearby stopped and looked at her. One of them, especially near, gazed right into Mama's eyes, brown, large, lonely. The cow chewed its cud and a steer came up behind her. Mama shivered. What was it doing to her?

"You cheated!" J.D.'s voice was shrill. Mama shook her head and looked at the herd again. She started counting them, hoping that the disconnection would progress no further, that she could hold on. The seat cushion beneath seemed to disintegrate. She felt as light as a feather. This might be a nervous breakdown. A horrible thrill shook her slightly but sharply. What would the kids do without her? Life held too much responsibility.

"Lookit that!" J.D. hung out the window, pointing. "Lookit that, Mama; what's wrong with them cows?"

"Lookee, lookee—" Kayley joined her brother. Mama followed their eyes. The herd was stampeding. They heard horrible, animal cries and the air filled with dust.

"They're going thataway, so we're safe," J.D. said. "I seen it on TV—we could get creamed. But don't worry Mama, we're safe—"

The disconection had continued. Mama had just kept watching the herd run over a ridge and disappear. Disappear.

Suddenly, all around them, silence descended like twilight.

"Where'd they go, Mama?" Kayley had said, her tiny voice tinkling like a wobbly piano key.

Where had they gone? Over the ridge into nothingness.

"What made 'em do that, Mama?"

"I don't know; something happened I guess." The disconnection had stopped. The car seat beneath her was once again substantial. The braid down her back doubled in weight. She started the car again.

"I seen it—"

"Saw it," Mama corrected.

"I saw that longhorn take his horns and stick it to that cow and she got mad—"

"Shut up, J.D." she'd told him. And they went back out on the highway. And now, after a succession of jobs—video store clerk, waitress, K-Mart clerk, Mama had lost her house, had taken up with Larry, a heavy equipment operator she met at a bar by TCU—he'd been a part-time student for a while—she had moved into an apartment complex in Euless to make life easier on Larry whose job was in the H-E-B area. He specialized in levelling lots and made pretty good money. And now Larry had gone to the dogs.

She wanted to do some levelling of her own, remember her manners and how she used to be when she first married Randy. Or back further still, when she lived with Grannie because her parents had died in a car crash when she was six. Grannie had sheltered her and told her she was smart and pretty. Then she met Randy. Her high school sweetheart. The babies had come, in their own good time, after a few blissful years with Randy so right the memories still made her chest hurt. Kids playing house. House of cards. It was the cards that started him to gambling. Started with Crazy Eights and ran right into Poker and then to other more darker games that included games with her head. But she still loved him. Loved him so much her heart hurt.

"Mama, mama—time to eat!" J.D.'s voice jolted Mama from her ruminations. The aroma of chili filled the apartment. She could go back to that highway anytime, go back to the herd and over the ridge. Into nothingness.

The kids plopped down in front of the TV to eat. Mama ate hers on the sofa, staring at a photo collage of happier times which hung over the TV next to a collection of fading woven baskets bought at Pier One about three years earlier. She'd forgotten that Christmas job. The hot dog was good. All beef. Later she would wolf down some Maalox.

Mama crunched a frito and heard J.D. tell Kayley that one day he was going to build a computer that saved time. Kayley asked him "What for?" and J.D. laughed, "So you'd have time to spend it when you really needed it."

A sudden whistling in her ears, a forward rushing. Mama held her plate and listened. It could happen here, the disconnection. She could just let go and J.D. and Kayley might end up with Social Services. A phone dead in her hand. How she hated for a phone to ring and ring and then to pick it up and say hello into silence.

"Does it taste okay? I checked the date on the hot dogs and they're supposed to be still good," J.D. said.

Mama jumped.

"You want me to heat it up in the microwave?"

She was fine, just fine. "It's okay. You got any homework?"

"Nope." Mama didn't know if she believed him but she didn't feel like pressing it. She didn't feel like pressing anything except maybe Randy—with a hot iron set on cotton and not permanent press. She was still angry with him, afterall this time, for bringing

154

them into prison with him. And then there was Larry and Maxine.

"You going to eat it or not?"

"I'm just not hungry."

"Can I have it?" J.D. asked.

"Sure."

"Mama, can I call Debbie?" Kayley asked. Her favorite programs were over and next to TV, Kayley loved talking on the phone more than anything. "I won't talk long."

"Sure," Mama grinned. That would be a first.

"I promise."

"Okay, baby."

Kayley ran to the phone. It had a long extension cord. Kayley carried it from the breakfast bar to the recliner in the corner, Larry's recliner. He hadn't come back for that yet.

Kayley held the receiver to her ear and frowned. She shook it like a rag doll. "It's not working, Mama."

Nothing. Her daughter held nothing to her ear and listened.

J.D. snorted. "We forgot to pay the bill, Mama. Don't worry, Kayley, we'll go down to the phone company tomorrow and straighten everything out, right, Mama?"

Mama thought about her checking account and her billfold. It still had one of Maxine's twenties. "Maybe."

"Mama, we have to have a phone—Mama—*really.*"

A new job any day now. Mama rubbed her arms. Larry might help out one more time. Was it laziness or just fear?

J.D. stacked dishes in the sink and coughed. "Can I go over to Ben's? I'll be back by ten."

"Sure."

Kayley turned back to the TV. She switched channels with lightning speed. "I think we ought to buy a VCR. Don't you, mama?"

"Sure."

"Really?" Kayley sparkled. She believed Mama was going to run out and get one—for a moment. Then her face darkened. "I'm going to go play," she said, before running to her bedroom. She slammed the door shut. The "Dirty Dancing" poster fluttered wildly.

"Sure," Mama said.

*   *   *

The burger joint was a safe neutral meeting place. Larry sat in a booth smoking a cigarette. Mama slid into the booth and met his gaze fearlessly. He smiled crookedly, revealing yellow teeth. "Hi, Josephine."

"Hi, Larry."

"You doing okay?"

"You still hanging out at Mac's?" Mama bit her lip. She hadn't intended to say that. He glared at her. Bingo. "No harm intended—you're seeing her, aren't you, the dancer, what's her name?"

"Maxine."

"Right. I hope you're happy."

"I am happy, happy as all get-out. At least she'd not holding onto some jailbird not worth a hill of beans."

Mama flushed hotly. This was going to be even more difficult than she had expected. She checked his eyes, without flinching. Angry, hurt and something else, contempt for Mama—or for himself for having anything to do with her? "I'm sorry about us, Larry. I didn't mean to abuse our relationship."

"Cut the crap. How much do you want?"

"I didn't come here to ask you for money."

"Well, what do you want?"

"Can't we be friends?" Mama sighed.

Warily, Larry looked over at the menu over the take-out counter. "I'm hungry. You want some fries or something?"

"No."

"Well, I do. Stay right here—I'll be right back." He stood and headed for the counter. A young waitress beamed. "Can I take your order?" she said. Mama looked over at the keys Larry had left on the table. She chose the ones she needed and slipped them into her purse. Then she arranged the rest back carefully so he wouldn't notice what was missing right away.

He came back loaded down with enough food for both of them.

"Thanks," Mama said.

"How are the kids?"

"Okay."

"Good. Listen—" he smiled shyly. "I really like you alot. I didn't mean to light out so quick-like. Maybe we could go out sometime. Maxine doesn't have a lot upstairs and I think we won't work out. She's a good dancer, though. I like dancers."

"I could dance."

"I know." Larry munched on his cheesburger and shook his head slightly. "But you don't love me, you love that jailbird."

"Maxine doesn't love you."

"Maxine don't love nobody but herself," he laughed.

"Maybe that's the best way to go," Mama said. She sat up straighter and held on to the table for support. "Listen, I'm glad to see you. I wanted to thank you for helping out for so long. I appreciated it. Me and the kids are doing fine. I've got a line on a new job. Bank trainee—you know, one of those clerks."

"Sounds good—taking other people's money. You better be careful though—" He was going to mention Randy. Mama wanted to strangle him. He sensed her disapproval. "They know about your husband?"

"No."

"Well, good luck."

"Thanks."

"Need a twenty—something—?" He reached for his billfold.

Mama's fingers twitched. She had lied about the job. It'd be okay to take just a little. She held out her hand. He gave her fifty dollars. She put it in her purse and nodded. "Thanks."

"Keep in touch."

"I will," she said and left the burger joing. She touched the keys in her pocket, talismans. Tomorrow was Sunday. God's day.

*　　*　　*

The security guard was in hog heaven. That woman had made him so happy. The Cokes they'd shared had been classic and sweet. He sat back against the wall and giggled when the tranquilizers hit at full force. So sweet. He hadn't thought an older woman would be interested in a kid like him. With tits like that—and hair like one of them L.A. women. But something had been in the coke and it wasn't just rum. He wondered why she wanted to drug him, had hoped for a moment that she was going to seduce him. Crazy woman. But a good crazy. He tried to get up to call someone. Then he fumbled at his belt for something he couldn't remember. And before he could figure out what to do next, he passed out, just as Mama came out of the fence with the dozer.

That highway she'd been on, what was it—I-35? Exactly so. No highways today. Mama steered the dozer with foot pedals, one right, one left. Larry had showed her how once, when he was still in love with her. Mama had never forgotten. Mama had always been a good driver. Randy had taught her to drive a stick shift, his old Chevy, when she was just sixteen. Randy had taught her so many things. Then he had to go bad on her by being stupid. Gambling. "All life's a gamble" he'd kept saying when the police came for him with a warrant.

"You don't gamble with other people's money—" she had shouted.

"But stockbrokers do it all the time—" he had laughed.

"You should've been a stockbroker—" Mama had said, tears running down her face.

"Maybe in my next life," he'd said.

Sorry son of a bitch. Stock-broker. Made her think of branding a steer. Break that stock. Cows mooing at the moon? Mama looked around from her perch. The expensive piece of equipment gave her enormous power. She moved down the street fearlessly. No one seemed to notice her. In such an obvious piece of mechanical perfection she was invisible. Cars parted the way for her. People accommodated power. No one seemed to care where she was going. Even a police car sailed past. She had concealed her hair under the hard hat she found in the seat of the dozer.

A savings and loan under new management loomed up ahead. She considered knocking it down. It was that previous savings and loan that had carried the second mortgage on their old house. The one they had lost. It had a wonderful built-in pantry in the kitchen, an all electric kitchen painted French Country Blue with imported tile. Grannie's Delft plates used to hang there in the dining nook. J.D. was looking after Kayley. They thought she was at the store getting groceries—tuna fish, potato chips and ding-dongs. Mama laughed. Foster homes. Maybe she'd turn around before she got any farther down this road.

Then Mama saw it, like the Emerald City of Oz, Mac's Corral. The parking lot was empty. She entered it and stopped. They weren't open on Sunday.

Looking at them cows on that highway—she'd felt like a puppet. Life hadn't made sense because it wasn't alive. She had believed, or rather, her body had given way to the notion something else controlled everything, that there was no such thing as control and the herd had proved it.

158

Prison. It would certainly land her in prison.

The dozer advanced upon the building. Her mind on the highway promised her the world around her was real. There had been a re-connection. Someone had answered the phone. The cow had looked into her eyes, recognizing her.

It would feel so good to hear the first biting crunch. She fixed her goggles and hunkered down. "Lever on either side to raise and lower your blade—" she whispered.

The door to the bar flung open. Maxine gaped at the dozer. She was dressed in gold spandex pants and a red halter top. "Hey you! What in the hell do you think you're doing? Hey—I'm talking to you!" She shouted over the roar.

Larry must have dropped her off to rehearse. Too bad. The Corral would've been enough.

Maxine waved frantically. "Stop that thing!" Too stupid to get out of the way. She gave the phrase "blonde bimbo" a whole new dimension. Mama laughed and kept advancing. Maxine's neon mouth kept working and her hands flashed foreign signals. Mama shook her head. Her hand gripped the lever too tightly. In her head she heard J.D. shout "You're cheating!" The dozer took over. It just kept going and that woman kept waving and screaming. Mama looked into her eyes. And went over the ridge.

Robert Petitt is from Louisiana, and, according to him, makes good barbecue. He writes a pretty good story too. The following is odd and raw and delicious as any good barbecue. Wonder if Robert makes rattlesnake chili.

RAZORED SADDLES

by Robert Petitt

(title and razored saddle idea stolen from Joe R. Lansdale)

Pike idly scratched at a loose flap of skin on the back of his left hand, cursed when it tore loose, the sticky flow of blood rousing him from the trance-like state that held him in its sway. He couldn't see yet—it was still a few hours from sunrise—and the darkness, which moments ago had been friendly, had now betrayed him. He tried to replace the patch of skin, found the surface slippery and too damn difficult to locate in the dark, and gave it up as being too much of a chore, too early in the day.

Couldn't keep a Bleeder from doing what he does best anyway, he thought. Why fight it, the bleeding would stop on its own accord, as it always did. And, if it didn't . . . who gave a shit? He went back to what he had been doing: thinking while waiting on the sun.

It was a night of heavy shadows and harsher stars. A light breeze, still tainted with an overlap of winter chill, tugged at the kerchief around his neck, like a playful strangler. Pike pulled the

161

sheepskin collar of his weathered jacket higher, tugged the brim of the tattered Stetson lower, then hunkered his body further down into the cavity formed by an outcropping of rock.

No sense taking unnecessary chances. If he passed out, as he had done on occasion, he might as well be comfortable.

He would have liked to have had a fire, but there were reasons against that. Chiefly, because the grass was still winter-dry and brittle, much too susceptible to an errant spark; and an ensuing brushfire could cause the herd to stampede, taking days to round them up again, at best.

At worst . . . well, he didn't care to dwell on that. Heat attracted other things as well, and though three hundred and six head of cattle didn't go far to counting as a big herd, that was exactly how many there were in the Greater San Antonio Area. Or more precisely, what was left of the G.S.A.A.

He found his eyes being drawn to the east, toward the Alamo City. Oh, it was still there, allright, intact, as he expected it to be; the nukes never got this far south. Sure, they had taken out New York and Washington, and a few others—no great loss there—but Star Wars had been a success, as far as the nukes went.

The Other Side had gone down—Pike had heard all that back before the Government had moved in and quarrantined the G.S.A.A. It had been a Big Win for the Good Guys, and the loss of a few cities wasn't much of a price to pay, considering. But . . .

But it seems like some things got overlooked during the celebrations. Namely, that all the folks on the Other Side weren't there when their homes ceased to exist. Quite a few were here, and they had retaliated in kind. Not with bombs and bullets, but with nightmares of the worst degree.

Like bacteriological warfare.

Several lakes and rivers were contaminated before the last group, operating out of Mexico, had been tracked down and eliminated. But by then, it was too late for some cities, San Antonio included.

The San Antonio River was now a thin blue vein, meandering through the downtown area, highlighting the buildings surrounding the River Walk in an amorphous blue mist: a poisonous shroud of shimmering blue, glowing like the color of death; a deadly shade that had choked the life from The Yellow Rose of Texas, leaving behind only corpses, mutations and the inevitable groups of scientists to puzzle out what it all meant.

Pike knew what it all meant, didn't need no degree to figure that one out. Meant there were no more Saturday nights in town dancing, drinking and listening to the laments of a country singer whose woman had run off, leaving him with nothing but the bottom of a bottle for company. Meant no more tight jeans to admire on the cowgirls struttin' their stuff to the strains of the Cotton-Eye Joe; no more waitresses in too-short skirts and legs that went plumb up to there; no more bullshittin' with the boys over a tall cool one; no more . . . nothing.

Not like it had been, anyway.

Pike tore his eyes from the river—he didn't like where his train of thought was taking him—found them settling in on the Loop, which was lighted year-round.

Loop 410 formed a non-concentric circle around the innermost part of the city; further out was Highway 1604, which created an even greater loop, but was at this time of year dark. Later, when the Season began, it would be lighted, along with the Loop and various intersecting streets and highways, so the overall effect—from the air—lent it the appearance of a gigantic rose.

Of course, all the lights were yellow—the media hype wouldn't allow it to be otherwise—and for three days in April, The Yellow Rose of Texas was site for the greatest sporting event on the face of the planet: THE RODEO. All in capital letters, because, after this rodeo, none of the others came close.

Pike had seen the tapes of the night shots last year, taken from the World Sports Television Network dirigible, and they were mighty impressive. Special filters had been used to downplay the bright blue of the river though, for whatever reason, they had elected to include a panoramic view of Lake Medina in the background, and it was every bit as blue and toxic as the river. Artistic license, Pike supposed, and it had been pretty . . . poisonous but pretty. Maybe it helped keep the women tuned in—who knew? As if they weren't as bloodthirsty as the men . . . again, who knew?

Pike felt the bite of the wind as dawn drew closer, wished again for a fire, but kept his eyes on the Loop, following it all the way around. No action tonight, he mused, must be too cold for the guards to come out and shoot the mutie rats that infested the city. Big rats, too, bigger'n dogs, but not at all like their smaller brethren. Nope, nothing at all like 'em. Good target practice for the guards, though; hard to miss anything that size.

Pike leaned back on his heels and roared his laughter at the thought that struck him then. Oh yeah, he laughed, oh yeah. Bigger and better in Texas—everything is bigger and better in Texas! Oh yeah!

He was still laughing when the first tinge of red touched the eastern sky.

*　　*　　*

Patterson stepped from the front door of the main house, mug of steaming coffee in hand, walked across the wide expanse of porch and eased his considerable bulk into a comfortable position on the steps. From there he had an unobstructed view of the valley where the cattle were just rousing for their morning feed, and though the sun wouldn't warm the air for some hours yet, he seemed not to notice the chill.

He took a slow sip of the lightly colored liquid, enjoying the burning sensation on his tongue and the warmth as it trickled down his throat. Real coffee it wasn't—purified water had been filtered through the same grounds for too long now—but if he concentrated hard he could almost taste the rich, savory taste of Colombian coffee on his palate. Almost. He sighed.

Well, it wouldn't be long now; the Hueys would be coming in, their cargo holds chock full of contraband supplies. All supplies were contraband nowadays—but the WSTN guys had the pull to make the deals and—this year, at least—he and Pike had gone all out to make the best package deal they could with the World Sports Television Network.

If you had something the WSTN guys wanted you could write your own contract—and Patterson and Pike had THE RODEO. In essence, they had the control of the greatest sporting event since the Romans packed the Coliseum for the annual Lions vs. Christians spectacle.

Patterson grunted at the comparison, then let his gaze roam to the main gate where a huge oak limb arched high over the stucco columns; the sun was directly beneath the arch and he couldn't read the sign suspended under the limb, but he didn't need to. It simply read: The Flying Triple P Ranch.

Triple P: Lucius Pike, George Patterson and Herb Phillips.

164

Phillips had gone Sidewinder three years ago, had his brains splattered all over the arena for his efforts; though he had had the good sense to do it in front of the WSTN cameras, so the ratings had gone ass-over-tea-kettle, and they must've shown the replay a million times since.

Phillips' widow had freaked for a while, but she had been a good lookin' filly and had ended up marrying a WSTN producer, who had pulled some hellacious strings to get her out of a quarrantine area.

So, that had left only Pike and himself to handle the ranch and the Rodeo, though Sabrina Phillips still retained one-third interest. Still, she didn't interfere, and she had kept her mouth shut; which meant that all was as it should be.

Until last Season, that is, when Pike screwed-up royally and let that sonofabitch fang him in the shoulder. Anybody with any sense could see Pike did it on purpose. Nobody moved that slow, let alone an ace rodeo clown, but Pike did. Thank God the few WSTN boys who saw it were easily convinced it was part of the act, or Pike could have bent over and kissed his ass goodbye.

As it was, Patterson had all he could do to hide Pike until the bleeding stopped and he was sure his friend would survive. Now, that was a laugh. Survive, shit!—the fool was immune, and he had known it the whole time. Though Patterson had heard of such people, and it had been years since he had, Pike was the only one he knew personally. Bleeders they were called . . . self-healers.

The sound of the screen opening interrupted his thoughts, and he turned to see Louisa standing in the doorway, wringing her hands and looking distraught. Even so, she was still a fine looking woman.

"Que pasa, Louisa? What is it?"

"It's senor Pike. He is not in his room. Nor is the young senor. He, too, is gone."

"Shit! Never mind, Louisa. You ring the bell when breakfast is ready. The men have a lot of work to do today and they will need to eat well. I'll find Pike and the boy."

Patterson stood and handed Louisa the cup, gave her a reassuring smile, which in no way removed the look of worry on her face, then strode off in the direction of the corral. He wasn't concerned with Pike, though he felt Pike was going Sidewinder fast, but the boy was a major problem, and he had promised Mrs. Phillips that he would take care of him, as there was no way that he could leave a quarantine area. Even a honcho for WSTN didn't have that kind of stroke.

The boy hadn't taken a horse—both of them were in the corral —which was a good sign. Patterson knew how the boy loved to ride, so he was thankful he didn't have to track him down on horseback, as horseflesh was as scarce as hen's teeth, and the risk of a broken leg in this rough terrain was an odds-on favorite to happen eventually, but that also meant the kid had gone on foot and finding him that way was going to be rough sledding. Of course, it had to be done. The first part of the Season was upon them, and it damn sure wasn't the time to be alone and unarmed in the GSAA. Especially if you were a retarded kid who thought everything in the world was your friend.

An involuntary shudder coursed through his body and, ignoring the horses nuzzling at him for some tidbit, Patterson headed for the bunkhouse.

The men were sleeping—the days of up before sunrise and hard at it were gone—another part of the cowboy legend run its course. With only two horses and three hundred and six head of cattle, there was little that thirteen men could do, even on a ranch the size of the Flying Triple P. There were only so many fences to mend, so many coats of paint to be applied, so many wells to be dug, until pure and utter bordeom set in.

Until the Season. Then the world turned upside down and there were not enough hours in the day to do all that needed to be done. And, with the boy missing, Patterson knew the Season began today.

"Rise and shine, girls. Rise and shine. We got us some chores that need to be taken care of first thing. Get dressed and get some food into you; Louisa should have your beans ready by now. Then we best be hittin' the trail; we got us a boy to find—and Pike, too, in case we run across him and he's in the mood to come on back to the ranch. Hell, he might have gone into town to see if they opened up a whorehouse since the last time we looked."

Laughter greeted the last statement, but the men moved quickly. It was only a few minutes until they were ready, but it was then the bell rang out and the hands cheered. The ranch foreman, Dils, eased by Patterson and clapped him on the shoulder.

"Perfect timing, boss man. And don't fret none about the kid; we'll find him soon enough."

"Thanks, Dils, I appreciate that. And while you're feeding your belly, I'll be cuttin' loose some firepower for you. If it warms up soon, we might be needing it."

"Yeah, I know where the boy likes to go. Want to cut out a few of the older cows, just in case?"

"Good idea, you do that. No time like the present to be prepared."

As it turned out, there was no reason to go looking for either the boy or Pike. A shout from outside brought Patterson and Dils to the door, and from there they could witness the arrival of the nocturnal wanderers.

Though Pike was short by anyone's standards, and his slight build was considered skinny by some, he was still one of the toughest hands that had ever put ass to saddle, and the way he handled the boy gave proof to the pudding. The Phillips' retarded son stood a shade over seven feet tall and packed some four hundred odd pounds on a mighty impressive frame, but Pike led him along like a docile puppy.

Dils and Patterson knew the grip Pike employed; they had been forced to use it on the boy themselves. When he got stubborn he made a mule seem pleasant; just plopped down on the ground and dared anyone to try to heft him from his chosen spot. So the men had learned a few holds to bring the boy along peacefully, like the one Pike was using.

Louisa thrust herself from the crowd of men at the eating tables and ran to take the boy from Pike. Louisa used a different hold; she simply grabbed him by the ear and jerked him down to her height, where she promptly began to curse him in a crude string of Tex-mex. The boy looked sheepish and didn't protest when she led him to the table. The men cleared aside and let the two of them have all the room they needed.

Pike noticed Patterson and Dils at the bunkhouse and sauntered on over to join them.

"Where'd you find him?"

"Hell, George, where do you suppose? Mornin' Dils. Looks to be a scorcher, don't it?"

Dils nodded and Patterson spit into the dirt.

"He was down at the silos again?"

"That he was, and he had built a fire, too. Good thing I saw the smoke or it would have been all over for him by now. Three of 'em crawled out as I was taking him away. He wasn't none too pleased about leaving either—seems to think they're his friends. What're we gonna do about him?"

"Don't get me to lying this early in the morning. We'll think of something later. Right now, Dils, you get some of the boys and take that string of cows down to the silos—you heard what Pike said. And take some guns with you, but don't shoot nothing unless you have too. We gonna need all we can get for The Rodeo. Join me in some breakfast, Pike?"

"Can't say as it'd hurt my feelings none. I done worked up a right powerful appetite this morning."

*   *   *

"Lucius, would it offend your sensibilities if I were to ask you a rather personal question?"

Breakfast was finished, the men were helping Louisa clean up and doing whatever other chores they had been assigned, and Patterson and Pike had retired outside the barn to split one of the last cigars on the premises. Pike knew when Patterson called him by his Christian name that something was up, but he was going to savor the encounter in his own way, and his own time.

"Sure, George, go ahead. But I want to ask you one first. Are you sleeping with Louisa?"

"Now, you hold on there a second, Lucius. We been friends a long time, and friends have no call asking things like that."

"Then I won't ask. Though, you got to be a bigger fool than I thought if you ain't. And I'm gonna answer your question, but I got something I want to show you, a favor I want to ask and a lot of things on my chest I want to unload. Let's go inside and take a look-see at what I made for you."

The interior of the barn was enormous, but even that vast expanse was filled with bridles, reins, saddles and mechanical contraptions of every sort, most of which defied description. Pike stopped in front of a blanket-covered shapeless mass; a grin etched across his leather-like features. He lifted a corner of the blanket slowly, letting the mood of the moment build, then with a flourish, like a magician performing some incredible feat, he jerked it aside to reveal the most beautiful, handcrafted Mexican-silver saddle that Patterson had ever seen.

168

RAZORED SADDLES

It was affixed to an array of highly polished steel tubing some ten feet in length, two tubes each side running horizontally, two feet apart and joined every two feet by welded vertical bracing. The saddle was attached to the top runner by a continuous run of ball bearings and anchored to both by an intricate series of stitches and bolts. Six-inch wide and one-half inch thick nylon surcingles were also attached at each vertical bracing on the left side of the bottom tube. On the opposite side were large locking clasps to hold the belts when they were properly tightened. A complex arrangement of pulleys and guide wires ran from the superstructure to the pommel of the saddle, where they disappeared beneath the horn.

Neither man broke the silence for several long minutes, each admiring the intricity of the work involved in creating such a piece of art. For art it was. The saddle especially: hand tooled and hand rubbed leather, soft as a baby's ass; the ornate hand-crafted silver gleaming like a pirate's treasure, even in the twilight of the barn. But the saddle would, in itself, be useless—the tracking system was what made the whole thing work.

How else could you ride a forty-foot rattlesnake in a rodeo?

"Well, I'll be goddamned," Patterson's awed whisper echoed about the cavernous room.

"I'd give you my thanks for them admiring words, but I'd really appreciate it a whole lot more if you'd git on up there and try it. There's more to it than meets the eye." Pike gave his old friend a lewd wink. "Com'on cowboy, show me what you know."

Patterson grinned, stepped into the stirrup and hefted his large bulk into the saddle. Pike stepped up and pointed at the horn.

"Push it forward and you travel up his neck—back and you go to his tail. High enough up on his neck and he can't get you with his fangs, low down on his back and he can't brain you with his rattle, like Old Bull did Phillips. Back and forth real fast and you stay in constant motion. Ride him good and you'll live, a mite slow and you won't leave the arena. Whatta you think?"

"I think it's all fine and dandy, but what is it I'm supposed to do to get him riled up enough to strike at me. You know them things is as peaceful as cows once they been fed for the Season. Hell, they are getting so tame that pointed spurs can't upset 'em, hardly."

"I got that figured too. When Phillips went Sidewinder on us, he used razor blades under his saddle. Pissed Old Bull off so bad he busted Phillips' skull. I went Phillips' one better. Push that horn to the left."

169

Patterson did and he jumped when the blades snapped free at the bottom of the saddle with a loud click. They were double rowed; one set pointing up; the other pointed down.

Pike laughed. "That ought to do it. I made them from the rotor blade off the chopper—good steel, that. And sharp. Let me tell you that they will cut through them snake scales like a hot knife through Louisa's butter. Ought to piss Old Bull off even worse than them cheap razor blades did."

"Old Bull? If you think I'm riding him you're crazier than a bed-bug in a whorehouse. Ain't nobody rode him since Phil pulled off his little stunt, in living Technicolor, and in front of the whole goddamned world. Now, give me one good reason why I would do anything that stupid for."

"For me. Push that horn to the right and let's do some talking."

The blades retracted, Patterson climbed down and the two men walked to the back of the barn where the chopper sat, broken down and neglected for the past twenty years.

"I flew one just like that, back in 'Nam in '70," Pike remarked, "seems like a lifetime ago. Then, when we started this ranch, I bought two of 'em at an army surplus sale, and we became the first ranchers in these parts to start herding cattle from the air. My, weren't we the pioneers, though."

He grew silent again, lost in memories, but Patterson didn't try to elicit more from him. When Pike wanted to talk—as he evidently did not—he would get around to it in his own time. It was but a few moments before he continued.

"As far as your question goes; no, I ain't getting Sidewinder. I know I'm a bit loco, but I ain't as yet gone suicidal. Though, I don't think I'd be too far from it if I have to continue on as I have been doing. There's where the favor comes in.

"Them scientist boys—down there in the city—they've had a lot of years to study mutations and big insects and rats, and I get the feeling it won't be long until they get the urge to spread out and start studying and dissecting things up this way. And they gonna find out that them rattlers are just as tame as those big rats; come right up to you and eat right out of your hands. Regular rats would eat your fingers, but the big ones won't; the bacteria has changed them, made 'em docile, same as the snakes. Same as the boy, who was born after the plague.

"Hell, if we didn't have them grain silos for the snakes to winter

170

up in, they'd freeze; and if we didn't stake out cows for them when the Season starts, they'd starve. The only danger that boy was in this morning is the snakes would've thought we had put him out there for food, and they would have ate him, because he's too slow in the head and wouldn't move. After they eat a cow or two, the boy could crawl up in the silos and sleep with them, and they wouldn't hurt him none, unless one of 'em rolled over on him. Then, he's so damn strong he could probably roll it back off.

"I guess what I'm trying to say is: you have this ranch, The Rodeo and Louisa. She has you and the boy—and the feeling of being needed she gets from feeding and caring for the hands. The hands have the ranch, The Rodeo, their chores and each other. It seems everybody here has a purpose, except me.

"The only time I was free was when I was flying that crippled bird right there, or riding a horse. Now, we're down to two horses; they're old and ain't got much longer, and even the WSTN can't get you no more because of the quarantine. They can fly in all the contraband, but they can't bring nothing living in here. Government's pretty adamant on that sort of thing.

"And I can't fly no more, because the Government put a restriction on all that, too. Besides, they took all my spare parts and busted up everything else, just to be on the safe side. So, I'm pretty loco, but I ain't Sidewinder yet. What I am is a Bleeder; I pulled a big patch of hide off my hand this morning; it bled for a while, and now it's already healed, like nothing ever happened to me in the first place.

"You and I both know I let that snake bite me last year. Hell, it was all I could do to make him bite me. Had enough poison in me to kill a hundred men, and it didn't even make me sick. You know what that means. If them scientists ever get a hold of me, I'll spend the rest of my life playing guinea pig in some underground laboratory. Then I would go Sidewinder. But what would I kill myself with? What?

"And that's why I need you to help me escape. I hear Wyoming is full of horses and good men who know how to keep their mouths shut. I need a diversion during The Rodeo, so I can steal a chopper and get the hell out of here. Will you do it—will you help me?"

*   *   *

Pike sat in the depression from which he had a clear view of San Antonio, as he had every night since his talk with George Patterson. But, this night was different than the other nights, for this was the last night in Texas that Pike would spend. The Yellow Rose of Texas was resplendent in lights: each petal shaped by the glowing highway lamps; her stem, the torches burning on each side of the San Antonio River.

The cameras in the WSTN dirigible were drinking in the sight; on the morrow that view would be seen in millions of households across the world. Pre-event hype for the spectacle to follow: THE RODEO.

Pike and Patterson had resolved all the problems they had foreseen. It wasn't going to be a great calving year, but a fair one, so the problem of feeding the rattlers wasn't as yet critical. Besides, there were plenty of rats that could be trapped and tied out for bait. Also, Pike had seen jackrabbits the size of buffalo, and they could be utilized as food. Louisa had agreed to lock herself up with the boy at the start of each Season, so he would stay away from the silos.

And four more of the riders had elected for the razored saddles this year. With that much blood flowing, the television ratings would soar and thus ensure the longevity of The Rodeo. And, in a few hours, Pike would know what life had in store for him. He nodded, and dozed.

*   *   *

It was time.

The loudspeaker blared out: "Next up, on Old Bull, is co-founder of The Flying Triple P Ranch and co-producer of THE RODEO, Mr. George Patterson. As you know Old Bull was the rattler last ridden three years ago by . . ."

Patterson forced the announcer's voice from his head; that wasn't the sound he was waiting for. His entire mental self was attuned for the drone of copter blades. A sound that never came. And suddenly, the chute opened in front of him, and reflex drove the pointed spurs into the side of Old Bull. The next instant he was in the arena, his spurs working furiously. At the same time he levered the horn up and down.

Faces in the crowd became a blur, focused, blurred. He had

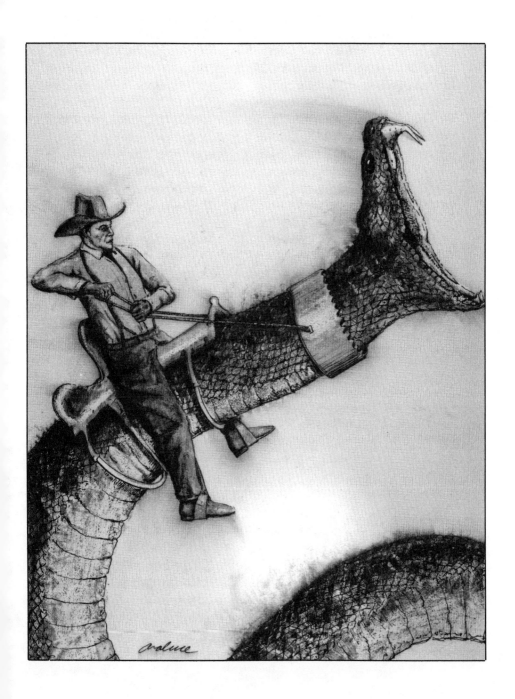

never seen such a gathering. Scientists had come up from the city to witness the event, along with the rich and famous who had enough pull to get into and out of a quarrantine area. He had time to recognize a great many familiar faces, but still no sign from Pike. He drove his legs faster, more furiously into Old Bull, but he refused to use the razors until he had seen what he had to see.

The audience seemed bored, distracted; they had witnessed three rides already, and only Dils had given them some action. He had zigged when he should have zagged, and the stone-hard rattle of his mount had caved in his side, busting up six ribs. The clowns had got him to safety before the snake could crush him—much to the chagrin of the spectators—and since then they hadn't had much to cheer about.

He could feel Old Bull slowing down, tired of expending so much energy. He was going to have to kick in the razors, or there wasn't going to be a Rodeo next year. No more Tennessee whiskey, no Havana cigars, no Swiss chocolate, no . . .

And then he saw it. Pike's signal.

Louisa sat in the lowest tier of seats, her large brown eyes full of concern, the boy next to her. And the boy was wearing Pike's best bandana, the one with the white Lone Star riding proud on a blue background. Patterson let out a Rebel yell that would have froze an Apache in his tracks, wrenched the saddle horn straight up and, at the apex, jerked it back down and to the left in the same motion.

He came down fast, in a gusher of blood. Old Bull went crazy. The crowd went wild. All eyes were riveted on the scenario being enacted in the middle of the arena. Only Patterson saw the chopper rise above the rim of the stadium, its rotor noise nonexistent over the frenzied roar of the spectators. The copter dipped once to the right, in a farewell salute, then it straightened out and disappeared to the northwest, flying low, under radar.

Tears stung Patterson's eyes, but he didn't have the time to wipe them away. He was too busy staying alive. He flipped the horn to the left, heard the click as the blades retracted, and he was back up on the neck, then coming down hard. He shoved the horn to the left. Blood splattered across his face. Old Bull did things no rattler had ever done before. Patterson grinned.

Oh yeah! Ride 'em cowboy!

And, together, man and snake rode into history . . . and legend.

Gary Raisor is generally noted for writing snap-ending, humorous horror stories. Recently he's been turning in other directions. In THE NEW FRONTIER, an anthology I edited for DOUBLEDAY, he wrote an old fashioned Weird Tales type story for me, and it was on the nasty side. This one is not horror, and it's on the gentle side. It's also strange and haunting and very clever.

EMPTY PLACES

by Gary L. Raisor

Me and Jake Summers, was hiding in the weeds outside a whistle stop in Lawrence, Kansas waiting to hop the next freight that come by when we seen the spaceship. It wasn't no big deal. They been coming in pretty regular for the last five or six years now. It's getting to where most folks don't pay 'em no more mind than if they was a busload of Japanese tourists here to take a picture of The Statue of Liberty.

I'm not sure what the spaceship was doing here, but I got a few ideas about it. Most folks would say I was just guessing and maybe they'd be right. All I know is what I saw. Yesterday I bought a notebook so I could write everything down before it got all foggy in my head. Whenever I think about that night I start to feeling sad.

This is the way I remember what happened.

Jake claimed that ship was like all the rest, just come back for a visit, and he didn't see no harm in what they did out there that night.

Maybe that's true. And maybe it ain't.

175

RAZORED SADDLES

There's some people that don't think their ships should be allowed to land at all. They say it ain't natural for animals that used to walk around here on earth to be coming back from space and gawking at us humans like *we* were the animals. Well, natural or not, they're here and I don't think there's much we could do about it even if we wanted to. They're a lot smarter than us.

It seems there's a race that sends around a giant collector ship from galaxy to galaxy, picking up species they think might be interesting. This race doesn't interfere. They just collect. After they make all their pickups, they head back out into space. But here's where the tricky part comes in, time ain't the same up there as it is here, especially when you're traveling faster than light and you detour through a black hole or two.

By our time, it's been several million years since they left earth and that's why they're so far ahead of us when it comes to smarts.

I don't know about all that, but one thing's for certain, it doesn't matter how far you travel from home or how many years you been gone—you still like to get back for a visit now and then. And that's what they been doing. Coming back home. In droves. They look a little different than us, depending on what species they were to start with. It's gotten to be quite a fad to see if you can guess which one.

Their visits have been pleasant, but what happened out in that Kansas wheat field wasn't so pleasant. It was kind of scary and kind of sad, all mixed up together. I think about it a lot. Especially late at night. I guess it was just our bad luck that me and Jake happened to be in the wrong place at the wrong time and saw that spaceship.

We ended up there cause I was trying to get Jake out of Chicago and back to Texas.

I remember the day all the trouble started. It was winter, and we'd just heard the news about an old friend of ours, Ernie Robbins, who'd been found frozen to death huddled under the steps to some bar over on Rush Street. The owner of the place was real pissed off that Ernie had picked his place to die. He told the cops he wanted Ernie out from under there before opening time or he was going to sue the shit out of somebody. The cops couldn't get the steps dismantled in time to get him out—so they broke off his legs instead.

We were out by the lake when we got the news, and Jake took it hard. He wouldn't say anything, just kept looking out toward the horizon. He wouldn't ever admit it, but I knew he was hoping for a

176

sailboat to come skimming along. Whenever something was eating at him, that's what he'd do, go out to the lake and watch the sailboats.

One time I asked him how come he liked sailboats so much. He just kept on staring out at the lake and I didn't think he was going to answer. But he did, he gave me a half-sad smile and said there wasn't much in the way of kindness anymore. He said a man needed something to fill up the empty places in his heart.

I asked him what the hell that meant.

He just kept on smiling and said it wasn't something you could explain.

There wasn't likely to be a sailboat along this late in the year. I felt sorry for him because it was his birthday and all he wanted was to see a sailboat. It didn't seem like a whole lot to wish for.

We finally gave up and went on back to an underground parking garage where we were spending the nights. That was when Jake started talking about his home back in Texas. Every year about this time, he pulled out a tattered picture of his family you can't even make out and tells me he's going back. I guess we been going through this routine for close to twenty years, the both of us knowing it was just talk, that he wasn't ever really going back. There was no reason to think anything would ever change.

No reason to think he was dying.

Our talk usually went like this; he'd give me a bunch of reasons why he thought he should go there. I'd give him a bunch of reasons why he shouldn't. He'd keep on talking until he had me convinced Crowder Flats, Texas was 'bout as close to heaven as you could get on this earth. Finally I'd agree to go and then he'd tell me he didn't want to. I'd get so mad I couldn't talk at all.

Only this time his heart wasn't in it. He just fell asleep with that picture of his family in his hands. I leaned over to check on him like I always did. Every time before, no matter how quiet I was, he'd open those colorless eyes of his and ask if I was going to tuck him in. We'd laugh since neither of us can remember the last time we slept in a bed. This time, he went on sleeping.

Later in the night I heard him talking. Something about a sailboat. At first I thought he was having a bad dream, but when I laid a hand on him, I felt the heat rolling off in waves. He was bad sick. When I tried to pull away to get him some water, he grabbed hold of my arm and wouldn't let go.

The only sound was the wind scratching around for a way to get at us. After a bit, he started up again and even though it was me he was looking at, I wasn't sure it was me he was talking to. I remember most of what he said, though. He spoke about working in migrant camps when he was a boy, traveling round from place to place, picking crops for strangers, and how he used to stand by his mama's tent when the work was all done and stare up at the lights in the big houses and wonder what it would be like to live there. His voice drifted in and out and once he called me by someone else's name. A woman's name. He kept asking her to forgive him. Over and over. Listening to him got to be more than I could bear. It wasn't right listening in on a man's private hell, so I pulled him into a sitting position and made him take a drink of water. Most of it spilled down his chin, but he seemed to come back to himself. The last thing he said that night was he didn't want to die someplace where nobody knew him. After that he was quiet.

The next morning I tried to take him to a doctor. He said it was too late for that, so I did the only other thing I could. I got us onto a fast moving freight headed for Texas.

We got as far as Kansas City before railroad security caught us and threw us off. I asked Jake if he wanted to see if we could bum enough money to buy a couple of bus tickets. He got kinda mad and said he might be sick but he still had some pride. So we thumbed our way to the other side of Lawrence where we knew we could catch a ride on a cattle-hauler. Jake was in a bad mood. He might be from Texas but he sure hated the smell of cowshit.

We were hiding in the weeds waiting for the train to come along, and that's how come we seen the spaceship.

When we first seen it, we couldn't tell much about what was going on. All we could see was a bright silver disk skimming in low over the wheat field, popping off and on like a Christmas tree light with a short in it. There wasn't nothing you could hear, but I could feel something vibrating way down deep in my bones and Jake got himself a real good nosebleed. Although we didn't notice that til later on. We weren't exactly afraid to get closer, but we figured it'd be better if we just laid low and watched. When you been on the streets a long time, that's the way you operate.

Pretty soon the ship settled about three feet from the ground and just sort of hovered there. It put off a silver glow that hurt your eyes if you looked too long. From so far away we couldn't tell the exact size of the thing, only that it was big. We didn't know how big until it opened up and what was inside began pouring out. They just kept on coming. And coming. There didn't seem to be any end to them. They were tall, thick-bodied, and at first I thought they had brown skin, but as a few moved closer, I saw it was fur. Shiny brown fur. I couldn't rightly tell what sex they were, but for some reason I got the impression they were female. Something about the way they moved.

Within an hour or so that wheat field was covered with tens of thousands of whatever was on that ship. They looked like some kind of giant shadow that could move by itself. A few got almost close enough to touch and that was when I seen something that turned the wine in my stomach sour. They looked sort of human, except on their foreheads . . . they had . . . horns. They weren't much in the way of horns, maybe about an inch or so, but Jake on account of being raised Baptist, began praying like he'd seen demons from Hell. I guess he must've figured they'd finally come for him. But I don't think they were demons or that they were even interested in us at all. I think they had more important things on their minds.

I wish I had the words to describe what they did. But I don't. All I can do is tell you the best I can.

A cold wind was blowing that night and there was frost on the wheat out in that field. Everything looked clean, untouched, just as it must have looked back at the beginning of time. Some of the creatures got down on the ground and rolled around. This went on for a while, until finally one of them raised a horn to its mouth. The sound cut through the night and it was clear as crystal, full of aching lonliness, and it made me understand what Jake meant when he talked about empty places in the heart.

The horn was a signal for them to begin.

They gathered in a circle that was miles and miles across, linking hands, and then they began to move, all of them together, as though they were somehow controlled by a single mind. I know this is going to sound crazy, but I think I knew right off they were performing some kind of ritual dance. One that was never meant for human eyes. It was as if they had gathered to say a last goodbye to something they loved. I can't think of any other words to describe what they were doing, it was a strange rhythmic stamping of their feet that shook the very earth with its force. Imagine what it must have sounded like, all those feet striking the ground at the same time.

179

Their movements were slow thunder, graceful, and full of sadness, though at the time I couldn't say for what.

The ritual went on for what seemed like hours, powerful, hypnotic, with their ship hanging low in the night sky shedding a silver light that pulsed in time with their movements. There was a time or two when me and Jake thought about sneaking away, but we were unable to tear ourselves away from what was going on out there.

Finally they just stopped and stood silent for awhile, as though all of them had turned to stone. Once again I was struck by the feeling of overwhelming anguish, of some loss too great to bear. It hung in the chilly air heavier than the dust they had stirred up. Jake passed me over the bottle and I took a long hard pull, but the liquor couldn't melt the lump that had lodged itself in my throat. I could see Jake was affected too. He kept wiping something out of his eye.

After a bit, they broke their circle and filed back onto their ship. Then they were gone. As though they had never been here. If it wasn't for the crushed wheat and Jake standing beside me telling me what'd we had seen, I would have put it down as some kind of dream. We didn't talk much about what happened until after we caught that cattle-hauler a few hours later. And even then we didn't say much because we didn't know what to make of it. Jake said it was about the damndest thing he'd ever seen or ever hoped to see. I kept trying to place what species had come out of that ship. They weren't like any kind I'd ever heard tell of.

We hopped a few more locals and I could tell the trip was taking what little strength Jake had left. On the last one we'd had to run some and he'd bled from the nose afterward. We needed some luck if we were going to make Texas.

It came. The next night we hooked up with a cross-state flyer that hugged the Arkansas-Oklahoma line and looked like it might have some legs on it. As the miles unrolled, what we'd seen back in Kansas became more and more like a dream. I could almost believe it was a dream, until I looked into Jake's eyes. They looked haunted. I wondered what mine looked like.

The train snaked through the night and the clatter of the rails kept us company.

On the third day we were riding along in an open boxcar, killing time watching traffic over on the interstate. Jake smiled and pointed at something through the open door. He said he didn't think he was going to get to see another sailboat this late in the year.

I looked to see what he was pointing at. It wasn't nothing, just an old white station wagon dragging along a u-haul trailer that swayed in the wind. When I turned back, I saw he had fallen over sideways. For an instant I thought he was asleep, only his eyes were still open and there was blood in the corner of his mouth.

He was dead, I knew he was dead, but still I kept waiting for him to look up and make some stupid joke, maybe ask me if I was going to tuck him in. He didn't, he just lay there in the straw where he'd fallen. His hat had come off and the wind grabbed hold of it and took it out the open door. It fluttered and danced in the air for a few seconds before settling down on the tracks like some kind of clumsy bird coming to roost.

I curled myself up in the corner of that old boxcar, closed my eyes, and tried not to think about anything at all. Once, during the night, I woke to the sound of a horn and I thought those creatures in the wheatfield had come back. It was only the horn from the train sounding.

The next morning I seen a sign welcoming us to Texas.

I made Jake as presentable as I could before we reached his home town. I washed his pants where he pissed himself and gave him my coat, which was a little cleaner than his. There wasn't a lot I could do. I wished I could have done more. I stayed on in town for a while, washing dishes at one of the diners until I got enough money to get him a stone. It wouldn't have felt right to let him lie out there with nobody knowing who he was.

One thing about washing dishes, it gives a man a chance to think. I'd been doing a lot of thinking lately. Too much, maybe, cause I don't sleep worth a damn anymore. Things keep running through my head. Sad things. Mostly I keep remembering what me and Jake seen out there in that Kansas wheatfield. I'm not sure I'll ever know exactly what it was. I got some ideas though. When I brought Jake home, I guess that helped me to understand a part of what happened.

What I'm about to say is mostly guesswork and there's no way I can prove any of it. I'm convinced the creatures who left on that spaceship weren't here just for a visit. I think something happened to their world and they had to come here.

And I think they came to ask us to take them in.

Only they found out a little bit about us. Hell, all they had to do was listen in for a while and they'd know what we're capable of. That's why they couldn't stay.

For a long time I couldn't figure what species they were descended from. The horns were what finally tipped me off. That and the shiny brown fur. They were descended from the buffalo. What they were doing out there last night on the plain was saying goodbye, not just to their ancestors who we had killed off by the millions, but to the earth itself. They knew there would be no welcome for them here.

In my heart, I want to believe they were wrong.

But I can't.

Home ain't always what you expect.

Jake's home wasn't what he thought it would be neither. That old tattered photograph he carried around in his pocket was a lie. You see, his family had been dead nearly thirty years, burned up when their house caught fire. So he was lucky in a way, he died with his dreams intact. If he had lived, it all would have been diffeent.

He would've seen it was nothing but a lie.

The visitors out there in the wheatfield weren't as lucky as Jake. They saw their dreams of home was a lie. Only they have to live with that lie.

Sometimes late at night when I'm all by myself, I look up at the stars and I wonder where they are. A snatch of an old song floats into my head. *Buffalo gals won't you come out tonight, come out tonight, and dance by the light of the moon?* Their strange sad dance in the moonlight haunts my dreams. I know it meant goodbye, and yet whenever I picture it in my mind, I try to see some hope in it, I want to believe their dance was a prayer before they set out in search of a new home. I want to believe they found that home. That's the dream I want to hold on to.

Well, the sun is coming up and I've got to get over to the diner before the breakfast rush starts. I've finished writing everything down in my journal. I haven't told anyone about what I saw that night and I probably never will. As for the rest of my life, I'm not sure what I'll do with it. All I know for sure is spring will be here soon and I've been thinking about Chicago. I've been wanting to take a walk down by the lake where me and Jake spent so much time. I guess now I understand what he meant when he talked about empty places in a man's heart. Whenever I picture Jake in my mind, I see him gazing out at the horizon. Always hopeful . . .

That maybe a sailboat will come by.

I hope they have sailboats where that spaceship went, too.

Neal Barrett, Jr. is in my opinion one of the best writers working today —in any field. Besides, how can you decide what field Barrett is in? His stories are so original he fails to fit comfortably into any box. This one continues that tradition.

TONY RED DOG

by Neal Barrett, Jr.

Tony learns purely by accident the Scozarri brothers have taken out a girl he liked a lot then dumped her at a pet food plant. The brothers work for the Tranalone family which is heavy into stuff like dog food and packing plants and anything that has to do with meat, so the guys who do legwork for Dominic Tranalone can drop off a stiff without driving out of town. Everybody on the street knows this is what they do, and anybody in the know buys their sausage and salami out of state. Tony figures what the brothers probably did was use the girl real bad before that. Leo and Lenny have warped ideas about social situations. Leo is mean, but Lenny's flat crazy in the head.

So Tony is mad as hell and out for blood. Nothing has pissed him off this much since the last re-make of *Geronimo*. That girl was real fine and she treated Tony nice. She didn't ever tell an Indian joke or call him chief. She had a smile on her face and her hair smelled good all the time. She didn't have to end up like that.

*　　*　　*

183

Tony thinks about the girl all day. He can't keep his mind on the job. It isn't right. A thing like that is all wrong and he's got to set it straight. What he ought to do is drop everything and do it now. Find those assholes and get it off his mind. If he does, though, Sal will flat shit because it isn't authorized, and Mickey Ric will come down on Tony like a safe, and Tony doesn't need that. So he'll have to see Sal and Sal will have to go to Ric and Ric will have to ask the old man. Which he won't, because Mickey Ric wouldn't help Tony on a bet. If Tony Red Dog was on fire, Mickey Ricca wouldn't piss and put him out. Besides that, Bennie Fischetti's sent the word down he doesn't want any trouble with the Tranalone family right now, he don't want to rock the boat.

Which leaves Tony right where he is which is nowhere at all, and the Scozarri brothers are laughing up their sleeves. Tony gets so wound up in all this he boosts a sky-blue Caddy instead of the black he's supposed to get, which fucks up his orders for the day.

*   *   *

Tony finds Sal where nobody can, which is at the back table of the Donut Shoppe where Sal presides twenty-two hours every day. Sal doesn't do without sleep, but at three-hundred-sixty-two pounds it is easier to nap where his is than go to bed, and there's donuts and coffee close by.

Vinnie D. and Bobby Gallo are there, and Tony says hello. Bobby and Vinnie are never real far from Sal, and Tony see's they're getting fat too. All you got to do is look at Sal, you put on maybe two or three pounds.

"I got to talk to you, Sal," Tony says. "Something's happened."

"I heard," Sal says.

"I want to do 'em," Tony says, getting right to the point. "Those bastards got it coming."

"Don't take everything personal," Sal says.

This is what Tony figured that he'd say. "Sal, I got a right. The Scozarri brothers knew I was seeing that girl. This is an embarrassment to me."

Sal blinks like an owl and licks sugar off his lips. "That's it right there," he tells Tony. "It's an embarrassment to you. It ain't business. It's a personal thing with you. You got the word same as me. No trouble. No hassle with the Tranalones."

"You could ask," Tony says, knowing how much good this will do. "It isn't just me. It's a reflection on the family. Tell Mickey Ricca that."

Sal pretends he's thinking this over, like he's making some real big decision in his head. He knows that's what a *capo* ought to do, that it lets the soldiers see he's on the ball. Sal "Hippo" Galiano is a *capo* without a lot of clout, since boosting cars and hijacking trucks now and then isn't all that big a family deal. It's not like he's Nick Cannatella who's the *caporegime* for dope, a guy even Mickey Ricca respects.

So Sal finally blinks and says, "Okay I'll make a call. I'll check it out with Ric. I ain't making no promises, you understand."

"Right," Tony says, "I appreciate it, Sal." He knows what he did before he walked in the shop. That even if Sal gets the nerve to make the call, Mickey Ricca's going to turn him down flat, that right here's as far as it's going to go. That if something gets done, Tony's got to do it on his own.

Sal is watching Tony close and he knows what's in his head. "Don't do anything stupid," he says. "You got a good job. Don't go and fuck it up. Find another broad. Take the day off. Have a little fun."

"Sure," Tony says, and even Vinnie D. can see that Tony doesn't mean that at all.

Sal looks Tony up and down. Takes in the alligator boots and the jeans, the black hair down to Tony's shoulders and the bandanna wrapped around his head. His mouth curls up like he's tasted something bad.

"Tony, listen," he says, "no fucking offense, okay? You got to dress like that? I mean, it's okay you're out in the sticks. You're attackin' the fucking wagontrain, fine. You're walking down the street here, nobody dresses like that, they got a suit. Vinnie and Bobby here, they got a suit. Anyone you see they got a suit."

Tony looks at Sal. "I'm not Vinnie D., I'm me, Sal. I got my blood. I got native ethnic pride."

"Shit, I'm an ethnic too," Sal says. "You don't see me wearing no toga and a sword, I got a suit. Everybody's got a suit." He digs in his vest and finds a bill and drops it on the table. "Here's a C, okay? Get a suit. Get a nice suit. See Harry down at Gold's and do something with the hair. Tell him that the hair's on me."

185

Tony picks up the bill, and Sal knows he's just tossed money down the drain, that Tony's not about to get a suit.

"Thanks," Tony says. "Ask Ric. Just ask him, okay?"

"I ain't promising a thing," Sal says.

*   *   *

Tony's wrong about Sal. Sal calls Ric because he knows Tony's got a short fuse. He knows if Tony does something dumb that it's Sal Galiano that Ricca's going to see. So the call is to cover Sal's ass, and this tells Rick what he already knew, which is Sal can't cut it anymore. He's got to call and check, he can't handle it himself. Sal's a stand-up guy; he's got a lot of friends who moved up while Sal stayed where he was, and Ricca's got to think about that. He makes a note fo find a club where Sal can put his name outside and some-one else can do the work.

Tony's wrong about Mickey Ricca too. Ricca gives a lot of thought to what Tony wants to do. He knows he isn't going to let Tony make a hit. Not while the boss is trying to work this scam with the Tranalone family, which is mostly Mickey Ricca's idea. What Bennie Fischetti's telling Dominic Tranalone is they ought to squeeze the South Side blacks and split the territory up. That the black guys are getting too big and cutting into everybody's take, and not working through the families like they should. Dominic Tran-alone hates blacks, so he's willing to talk to Bennie about that. What Tranalone doesn't know is that Bennie's been talking to the blacks on the side. He's going to use the blacks to squeeze the Tranalones out, and when he gets that done he'll put the black guys out of business too. So this is no time to start knocking off Tranalone guys, when everybody's supposed to be friends.

What Mickey Ricca's thinking is there ought to be a way to put Tony in the scam and also get the Indian off his back. He's got to be smart about this because it's Mickey Ricca's fault in a way that Tony Red Dog's where he is. Tony worked for Jackie Pinelli out in Phoe-nix, and did a favor Mickey couldn't overlook. What happened is, Charlie Franzone, who is Mickey Ricca's asshole brother-in-law, steals a car one night and rides around buck naked blowing coke. There's maybe three naked broads in the car which doesn't help. When the cops run him down, it turns out this car belongs to some

186

big cheese up in vice. They throw the book at Charlie, and Mickey Ricca's wife is like crying all night and driving Mickey Ricca nuts. So Ricca calls Jackie Pinelli and Jackie talks to Tony Red Dog. Tony flies out to L.A. and boosts a bottle-green Jag and gets the papers and the numbers all straight, and drives it back to Phoenix the next day. The Jag goes to a guy in the D.A.'s office Jackie knows and the case against Charlie kind of falls in a hole and disappears. Ricca's wife stops crying and Ricca sends Charlie off to Texas somewhere and buys him a car wash place, which he figures even Charlie Franzone can't possibly fuck up a whole lot. He sends Jackie five grand and asks Tony what he wants. Tony wants to come back east, he's tired of working in the sticks, and Ricca says fine, come ahead.

When he sees this guy he nearly shits, but he knows he can't send the guy back. Ricca owes Tony one and a debt is a debt. Which is partly why he hates Tony's guts and wants him out. Besides that, it's embarrassing to have a fucking Apache Indian working for the family. It don't look right. Ricca sees some guy, he goes to eat, this guy makes a fucking war whoop, or sticks a couple of fingers up for feathers on his head. It's a flat humilation is what it is, and Ricca wants to put an end to that.

So he thinks about this then he thinks a little more, and then something starts working in his head. Thinking's what got him where his is—thinking sideways and inside out until he's got every angle covered right. Now he thinks he's got something worthwhile. Something he can use. The old man doesn't like to talk a whole lot, but Ricca thinks he'll want to talk about this.

*   *   *

Tony spends the morning boosting cars then takes the day off. With Sal's hundred bucks he buys a white leather jacket with a six-inch fringe. There's even fringe on the sleeves and some beadwork on the chest. The beadwork's Jersey Navajo but what the fuck. The jacket's worth five bills if you bought it in a store.

The rest of the day he drives around, hitting all the spots he knows where the sleezeball Scozarris might be. He drives real slow past the meat packing plants and the dives that the Tranalones own. He hits the porno shops and a string of strip joints because he knows the Scozarris have a little piece of that.

It comes to him then that he's wasting all his time. It just hits

187

him like that and he nearly rams a cab. What a fucking dope! He's driving all over sucking gas and these guys are somewhere in the sack. There's daytime business and there's stuff you do at night. Leo and Lenny are into night, and that's when Tony's going to find them on the street. What he needs to do now is go home and sleep himself. Get a drink and a steak and go to bed. Start out again about ten.

Before he goes home he makes one more pass along the streets. He doesn't see the Scozarris but he sees something else. At a place where the Tranalone family likes to eat, he sees a black stretch limo at the curb. Tinted glass and guys in black suits, and stepping out is Tommy "Horse" Calise himself. Tony's impressed. Calise is *consigliere* to Dominic Tranalone, and one of the smartest guys around. You don't have to like a guy to admire the way he works.

Tony only gets a quick look and then Calise's inside, but he knows he's seen the Horse. You could go to a game there's maybe sixty thousand guys, you'd see the Horse right away. About six-foot-four, maybe one-forty-five soaking wet, and these eyes jammed up around his nose. Jesus, what a nose—it's a nose that could edge out any fucking nag at the track. Tony gets a look at a cute little number trailing right after Horse and he's got to laugh at that, because the nose isn't the only part that gave the Horse his name.

*   *   *

Bennie Fischetti is sitting in the dark. The room looks like a museum, the way Ricca figures that a museum ought to look. It's maybe ninety-six inside and the old man's got a sweater and a shawl. Ricca wonders what'll happen when he dies. Bennie's son Joey is the underboss now but he don't know shit about the business. The title makes Joey feel good. What Joey knows about is girls maybe twelve or thirteen. He's forty-three he wears a suit and tennis shoes. So what's Bennie Fischetti going to do? Who's going to run the family when he's gone? Ricca knows it's got to be him, but he can't read the old man's mind. There isn't nobody on earth can do that.

"Don Fischetti, I don't wish to take your time," Ricca says, "but I feel this is something you ought to know. We've got this *soldato* works for Sal, his name's Tony Red Dog. You seen the guy once, he's got hair down to here."

TONY RED DOG

The old man looks like he's awake, but Ricca isn't sure. He tells Fischetti how the Scozarris offed the girl and what Tony wants to do.

"The thing is," Ricca says, "this bimbo isn't really Tony's girl except maybe in his head. Tony sees a broad on the street he falls in love, that's his girl. What she was is a waitress turns tricks on the side out at Fatso DiCarlo's place, which is run by the Tranalone family. So the Scozarris, they were where they ought to be, and Tony's got no business in the place. What he's doing in there is sniffing after this broad. There's maybe two, three hundred places he could be, he's hanging out in a Tranalone dive. The guy's nuts."

The old man looks at Ric. He doesn't move, he just looks. "So why you bring this to me," he wants to know. "You are *consigliere*. I need to hear about an Indian? I don't need to hear about an Indian and a whore."

"Right," Ricca says quickly, "this ain't about that but it is. What I got's an idea, and that's the thing you got to hear. It's a business idea is what it is."

The old man seems to pay attention now. "Maybe I will listen," he says. "Maybe I will hear this business thing."

*   *   *

Tony drives around all night. He wonders if Leo and Lenny are laying low. Tony doesn't think they got the sense to do that. He asks a few questions, but he can't do a whole lot of that. The guys who got answers are the guys he can't ask. He drives by the strip joints and doesn't see a thing. He tries the packing plants again. He drives by diners and cafés, and it's light when he gets into bed. Okay fine, he'll try again. There's no big rush. They got to turn up, and he'll be there when they do.

*   *   *

It's after noon when he drops by again to see Sal. Sal doesn't ask why he isn't on the job. He sees the white jacket with the beads and he doesn't say a thing about that. He doesn't want to work Tony up, he wants to keep Tony cool.

"Hey, Tony," Sal says, "you're looking sharp. You had anything to eat? Vinnie, get Tony a couple of glazed."

"I'm fine," Tony says, and shakes his head no to Vinnie D. "So you call Ric or what?"

"I said I'd call, right?" Sal says. "So I called. Ricca says he fully understands. He says he knows how you feel."

"So it's okay or not?"

Sal forgets he's trying to be nice. Fuck it, you can't be nice to this prick. "Just listen, okay? You got no fucking manners. You got to talk, you don't listen to nobody else. Ric says he's going to get back. He says he knows you understand this ain't a good time. He says he don't like to see the Scozarris get away with this shit. He says he'll see what he can do."

"When?" Tony says.

"When what?"

"When's he going to get back?"

This burns Sal up. He doesn't like Tony's attitude at all. "Mickey Ricca gets back to you, pal, when Mickey Ricca wants to get back," he tells Tony. "That is fucking good enough for you. In the meantime, you keep your nose clean. You boost some cars for me like you're supposed to be doing right now. You don't do nothing else but that. You got that, Tony?"

"I got it, Sal?"

"Fine. You got it. I'm glad to hear you got it. I'm glad I'm getting through."

"Maybe you should ought to try a smoke signal, Sal," grins Vinnie D.

"Maybe I got a signal for you," Tony says. He looks right at Vinnie D., and Vinnie doesn't smile anymore.

"Both of you, just shut the fuck up," Sal says. He flips Tony a white envelope. "From Ric. He wants you to have it."

"What is it?"

"It's a Easter card," Sal says. "What you think it is? Go on, get some work done. You got a whole half a day."

Sal watches Tony leave. He doesn't like what's going on at all. He wishes Indians would stay on the tube. He likes to watch them on the tube. They can't cause him any grief in there, they got their hands full with the Duke. What Mickey Ricca said to Sal was, "Sal, you keep that crazy Indian on ice. Give him five bills from me. Make godamn sure he don't do something me and the old man don't want to hear. I'll be in touch. You stay where I can get you on the phone."

Sal wonders where Ricca thinks he'll go. He never goes anywhere at all. So maybe Ricca thinks that's funny, it's a joke. So go fuck yourself, Sal thinks, but he doesn't think it aloud.

What Sal doesn't like about this is he knows who Ric is going to call if Tony gets out of line, and he figures that's exactly what Tony's going to do. So what's Sal going to do about that? Chase him down the street? The truth is, Tony Red Dog scares the shit out of Sal, and he figures maybe Tony knows it too.

*   *   *

Tony doesn't go back to work. He goes to a movie instead then walks down to Otto's for a steak. The envelope he's got has three-hundred bucks from Mickey Ric. Which means Mickey Ric told Sal to give him five. Tony knows what it's for. Mickey Ricca's tossing him a bone. He's not going to do shit. He's going to tell him that he can't make the hit.

On one side of the coin, he sees maybe Mickey Ricca's right. Tony keeps his eyes open all the time. He knows more about the family business than a guy like Vinnie D. Sal sent him on a hijack deal once or twice with Daddy Jones, who's pretty high in the South Side blacks. Tony got along fine with Daddy Jones, who said he'd never seen a greaseball Indian before and even bought Tony a beer. So Tony knows the family's getting friendly with the blacks, and he knows there's got to be a reason why. Whatever that is, Tony figures the old man will end up on the top, and everyone else under that.

Tony understands all this and maybe Ricca's got a point, but it doesn't get Tony what he wants. He can't get the girl off his mind. That was an awful thing to do. About as bad as you can get. He can't let guys say the Indian's a real easy touch. You want to grind up his girl it's okay, he won't do a damn thing. Guys are talking like that, you can't show your face on the street. And if he waits for Mickey Ric, that's the way it's going to be.

While Tony is finishing off his steak, he looks up and spots a great looking broad across the room. He likes what he sees because the broad is looking right at him, too. He raises up his glasses like he's seen in the movies and the girl seems to like that a lot. She likes

191

it so much she leaves the bar and starts her way across the room. Tony likes the way she moves. She's built just right but she doesn't look cheap. She's taller than he thought and her dress is all black with no jewelry at all, like a girl in a fashion magazine. Her hair is classy too, real light blond and flipping up kind of cute on the ends.

She walks right up to his table. Just stands there and smiles. Doesn't say a thing. It hits Tony then and he stands up quick and gets her chair.

"I'm Jill," the girl says.

"Right, I'm Tony," Tony says. "What do you like to drink?"

"White wine will be fine."

Class, Tony thinks, and says, "Hey, I'll have one of those too."

She's got a little black purse like the dress. The purse is so little it couldn't hold a quarter and a dime.

"You're an Indian, right?" Jill says, this coming right out of left field. The way she says it, though, it doesn't turn him off.

"Yeah, I guess I am," Tony says.

"What kind?"

"Mescalero Apache."

"No kidding."

"Hey, I ever lie to you before?"

The girl laughs. She's got kind of blue eyes, and one side of her mouth turns up like she's telling some joke to herself.

"I'm nuts about the jacket," Jill says.

"It's nothin'," Tony says. "I got better stuff than this. I go somewhere nice, I got a closet full of stuff. I bet I got a hundred shirts."

"So you do that a lot?"

"Do what?"

"Go somewhere nice."

Tony's getting the message straight. This doll is saying let's make a deal.

"Yeah," Tony says. "I been known to go out. I'm a fun kinda guy."

"So what do you do?" Jill says.

"I'm in cars."

"Buying or selling?"

"Just selling. No buying. And what about you?"

"I'm an actress," Jill says.

"Oh, yeah?" This is maybe going to cost a little more, Tony thinks. A girls says 'actress' she isn't some hooker walks the street, she's got a place somewhere and the price is going to go through the roof.

"So look," Tony says, "you want to take off now, you want another drink, what?"

The little smile around her mouth disappears. "Sorry," she says, "I guess I made a big mistake."

"What? How come?" Tony doesn't get this at all.

"I shouldn't ever ought to do it," Jill says. "I mean you see a guy you like and say hello, that isn't going to work. You do that, the guy's for sure going to get the wrong idea. A girl can't do that 'cause the guy's going to think something else which is just what you're thinking right now."

She reaches in her purse and gets a little gold pen and writes something on the napkin by her drink.

"Listen, I think you're a real nice guy," she tells Tony with a smile. "You change your mind, you want to think about me like you're not thinking now, you got my number there to call."

She gets up and plants a kiss on his cheek, and Tony feels her hair brush his nose. He gets a little whiff of perfume then she's gone before he knows what to do.

Jesus, what kind of broad is this? Tony follows her out the door with his eyes. The most terrific looking girl he's ever seen and now she's gone. He feels kind of dizzy and he knows he didn't drink enough for that, he knows how to hold his booze. That's a crock about an Indian can't hold his booze, he can drink as good as anyone around. So he knows what it is, he doesn't have to think about it twice. It isn't just her bod, there's that too, but it's something more than that. He loves this girl is what it is. He doesn't even know her last name, but he knows he's got it bad.

*   *   *

First thing in the morning, Mickey Ricca's in the old man's Caddy, wishing he was still at home in bed. Don Fischetti doesn't hardly every sleep, so when he's got to go out which is maybe twice a year, he's up and out at six. He's got a meet at noon he doesn't care. Drive around, he tells Danny, and Danny drives around.

The Caddy's all green outside and in. The old man likes green. Fischetti and Ric are in the back. Danny Fusco drives, and Bennie's

193

son Joey's next to him. Joey's got egg on the back of his shirt. Egg, and a little crumb of toast. How did the dummy do that? Ricca thinks. How the fuck can a guy get breakfast on his back?

"The thing with Tranalone," Bennie says, "the thing with him, he likes to talk. Dominic likes to talk. Listen, let him say what he's got to say. It don't mean a thing, you got to listen all the same."

"That's the way he is," Ric agrees. "I seen him do it all the time. He'll start on something, he's off on something else. He gets done, you don't know what he said."

"Horse," Bennie says. "Horse is the guy you want to watch. What Horse Calise says, Dominic is thinking in his head. Tranalone talks an hour and a half. Horse says maybe two words. Two words, that's all you got to know."

"The Horse is smart," Ricca says. "You got to give him that. I wouldn't put the guy down."

"You do, and you make a big mistake," Bennie says. "Anyone sees through the scam that's Horse. Dominic, he isn't going to see. You talk, you don't have the time to think."

The old man leans back and takes a nap. Danny drives around. The Caddy gets six, maybe seven miles a gallon, so Ric figures he's got to stop for gas. Joey likes to ride; he sees some grade-school girl on a bike, and watches till she gets out of sight.

"The thing with the Indian," Bennie says.

"It's okay," Ricca says.

"I don't need a problem," Bennie says. "You got a guy he's black or maybe red. Maybe he's a Chink. You got a problem's what you got."

"You got my word, Don Fischetti," Ricca says.

"That Joey," Bennie says, giving Ric a nudge. "Always got his nose in a book. He don't read no junk he's reading high class stuff. He's reading something all the time."

Ricca's seen Joey read. Joey's got a stack of *Classic Comics* on the seat.

"Hey, you gotta be proud," Ricca says.

*   *   *

Tony doesn't sleep at all. He knows he ought to look for the Scozarris but he sits around the room. He can't watch the TV. He

194

doesn't want to eat. What he wants to do is call up the girl but it's the middle of the night. He wants to call her up now and tell her how he knows he's been a jerk. They can go somewhere and talk. Eat anywhere she wants. He won't try nothing funny, he won't even touch her till they know each other for a week. Jesus, he hopes she won't hold him to that.

He gets out early on the job. If he's working, he won't have to think about calling up the girl. He's afraid if he does she'll turn him down. She said he could call, but that doesn't mean she won't turn him down.

He's got a special order he's got to fill—Porsches, and they got to be showroom new. This kind of car's not as common as your Chevys or your Fords, but Tony gets the job done quick. Cars are like people, Tony knows; they like to hang around their own kind. So he hits some classy tennis courts and a couple of country clubs, and by noon he's got five stashed in Dio's garage, ready for the guys to go to work. Even Dio's impressed, but Tony doesn't care about that. What he cares about is calling up the girl.

*   *   *

Jill doesn't say no she says yes. Tony can't believe his luck. She says fine, she'll go out tonight if Tony wants, if Tony's got his act together and intends to treat her right. Tony says great, that's the way it's going to be. Jill tells him that she'll meet him at eight and tells him where.

Tony thinks about an hour what to wear. He wants to wear the white jacket with the beads but she's seen that before. He wears that, she'll think he don't have nothing else. He goes through everything he's got and ends up in his blue ostrich boots and a western-cut suit. The suit's kind of off-yellow white and there's a rattlesnake stitched on the back. The snake's got a genuine rattle sewn on with simulated ruby eyes. He looks in the mirror and he figures this will knock her on her ass.

The place where Jill says to meet her is a bar called 'A Streetcar Named Michelle.' Tony doesn't care much for bars with funny names. They usually got funny-looking people inside. Fags in tight pants and broads with purple hair. So he's glad to see this isn't that kind of place at all. There are people here in jeans and running

195

shoes, and people in businessman suits. A girl in a waitress outfit and a guy in greasy coveralls, like the guys down at Dio's garage. There's maybe a couple of fags but not a lot of funny hair.

Jill spots him and makes her way through the crowd, and Tony goes weak in the knees. Christ, she looks great. A white woolly sweater and a skirt and nice heels. She's got something sparkly in her hair and her eyes are bright as Christmas tree lights.

"Hi," Jills says, "say I *love* those boots. Tony, you look *out-standing.*"

"Hey, so do you," Tony says. "Listen, you ain't seen the back of the suit." Tony turns around and Jill lets out a kind of shriek and says she's never seen anything like that before, and Tony's glad he has the sense to dress right.

Jill puts him through the crowd and introduces him to everyone she knows, which includes some terrific looking broads. Everyone there is an actor or an actress, Jill says, only mostly they're doing something else. Tony has a few drinks, and starts to like everyone he meets. They don't talk like real people do but he likes them all the same.

And later on when they're out in the car trying to figure where to eat, Jill scoots in close and leans her head on his arm and Tony figures this is going to work. The girl's high class but she's got to come around. A nice dinner and that wine she likes to drink he's going to have her in the sack.

"So tell me about yourself," Jill says.

"There isn't anything to tell," Tony says.

"Come on, sure there is." She gives him a little toy hit that warms his heart. "Like, where'd you grow up?"

Tony doesn't like to talk about this but he does. "Arizona. On the Fort Apache Indian Reservation."

"Not good, huh?" She can tell that easy by his voice.

"It was okay, I guess."

"I don't think it was."

"Yeah, well you're right."

"So you got out of that."

"When I was fourteen, maybe fifteen. Something like that. Worked on a couple of ranches and other stuff."

"Then you got into cars."

"Right. Tucson and Phoenix. All over."

"And then you came here."

"Yeah. And then up here." Tony figures maybe that's about enough. "Look, what do you like to eat? Steak, seafood. You name it."

"Seafood's fine," Jill says.

"Terrific," Tony says, glad to talk on something that's not about him. "There's a place over on the east side, they got lobster they ship in fresh. They got 'em swimming in a tank."

"Hey, great," Jill says, "I haven't had a—*Jesus*, Tony!"

Jill has to slam her hands on the dash because Tony's suddenly turned the car around in the middle of the street. Guys are honking and yelling but Tony don't hear anyone at all. He just pulls up and stops because right there's the cream-colored Buick Lenny drives, parked at a Rodeway Inn. Christ, what's he going to do? He's got Jill in the car and everything's going real fine. If he dumps her off now he isn't going to get her back. If he waits and comes back, the Scozarris are going to maybe be gone.

"Look," he tells Jill, "I'll be right back. Sit tight, it's okay."

"What's going on?" Jill says. "What're you going to do?" She maybe looks a little scared.

Tony puts on an easy smile. "I seen a car back there. A guy owes me for the car. The guy's a deadbeat. You got to get these guys when you can."

"Yeah, right," Jill says, and doesn't look like she's buying this at all.

Tony gives her a wink and gets out and shuts the door. He stops for a minute at the trunk and gets a sawed-off pump and an old potato sack and puts the gun in the sack and walks back to the Rodeway Inn.

He doesn't know if they parked the car right before their door but his luck is running good. Leo opens up the door when Tony knocks and Tony jams the shotgun in his face.

Leo looks sick, like he might throw up.

"Inside," Tony says, and looks around fast to find Lenny. He can hear the shower going and that's another lucky break.

"It's about that fuckin' girl," Leo says.

"Sit down," Tony says, and Leo sits.

"So let's talk," Leo says.

"Let's not," Tony says. He picks up a cushion from the couch and tosses it in Leo's lap. Leo grabs the cusion and looks surprised and Tony jams the shotgun up against the cushion and there isn't

197

hardly any noise at all. Tony pockets the empty shell and peeks in the bathroom door and the room is full of steam. He goes in and opens up the shower door. Lenny is all lathered up. He's hairy as a dog. There's a little more noise this time but not much because Lenny's pretty fat. Tony turns off the water and makes sure he's got both empties in his pocket. He wipes down the gun with a towel and leaves it in the sink and takes a look at his watch. Three, maybe four minutes. He's sorry Lenny didn't get to see who it was but Tony can't complain. One more thing to do and he's gone. Hey, the night's turning out great.

*   *   *

It's not hardly morning when the phone wakes him up. He grabs it without even looking and Sal says, "Listen, I got a message from Ric you're going to like. Ric says it ain't a good time but he thinks you got a right. This is a personal favor from Mickey Ric is what it is."

Tony sees Jill's kicked off the covers and the sun's making stripes across her back, but Sal's got his full attention now.

"You're saying Ric don't mind," Tony says. "It's okay."

"What the fuck you think," Sal says. "I gotta say it twice? A couple of the guys, they seen the car. It's at a Rodeway Inn past the loop. You get off your ass you'll catch 'em cold."

It's warm in the room, but Tony feels a chill. "Right," he says, trying to keep what he's thinking to himself. "That's great, Sal. I appreciate the call."

"So get it done," Sal says. "Do it now. I don't want to hear you complaining no more. Get it done. And hey, I want to see you here at three-forty-five."

"Why three-forty-five?" Tony says.

"Why the fuck not?" Sal says, and hangs up.

Tony sits on the bed and looks at the phone. Like maybe Sal will say something else. Something that will stop the empty feeling in his gut.

Jill sits up and stretches and looks at her watch. "My God, I got to get to work," she says. "Who was that on the phone?"

"Get up," Tony says. "Get dressed." He's still looking at the phone.

198

"Huh? What's with you?"

"Just do it. Hurry up." Tony's pulling on his pants and looking for his boots. Jill is standing there naked still looking half asleep. She looks great. Tony wonders why you got to do stuff that you don't want to do when you'd rather be doing something else.

"You mind telling me what?" Jill says. She looks even better with her hands on her hips.

"Let's go," Tony says. "Get somethin' on."

"Last night it was get something off."

"Last night ain't today," Tony says, and starts picking up her clothes off the floor.

*   *   *

Tony's slamming gears and Jill is still complaining. She's got the mirror down, and trying to get her lipstick straight and Tony's taking corners like he might make the Indy this year.

"I don't care for your lousy driving style," Jill says.

"I'm driving just fine," Tony says.

"I lose my job I am moving in with you," Jill says. "I got to have some breakfast, Tony. I'm no good I don't eat. Just let me out here. Let me out I'll get a cab."

"Listen, I got a problem," Tony says. "What I got is deep shit. I got to think. I don't got the time to eat."

"Okay, fine. That's fine," Jill says. The way Tony looks, the way he talks, says now is a real good time to keep quiet and hope Tony doesn't run into a truck.

In a minute Tony stops and makes a call. Twenty minutes after that he pulls up behind the South Side Bowl-O-Lot and stops. There's another car there, a red Caddy with a lot of extra chrome. Tony doesn't say a thing to Jill. He takes the keys and gets out and walks across to the other car.

Daddy Jones is standing by the Caddy. He looks like a spider in a Panama suit. Big shades, and a lot of white teeth.

"Listen, I got trouble," Tony says.

"I expect you do," says Daddy Jones. "Going to happen, you working for the white-eyes, man. Them treaties don't mean shit."

"You want to hear this or not?" Tony says. Daddy Jones is too cool. Nothing bothers Daddy Jones and that irritates Tony a lot.

199

"My meter running, babe," says Daddy Jones.

Tony talks. Daddy Jones listens. After a while, Daddy Jones listens real good. When Tony's through, Daddy Jones thinks a long time.

"Keemo-sahby, this real heavy shit," says Daddy Jones.

"Tell me about it," Tony says.

"Got to talk to my man. Won't tell you a thing before I do."

"I know that. I know you got to do that."

Daddy Jones takes off his shades and looks Tony in the eye. "Man, you best be hittin' me straight. This better not be no jive."

"I am in enough shit without messing around with you," Tony says.

"I hear that," says Daddy Jones. He gives Tony a card with a number on the back. Tony goes back to his car.

Jill doesn't say a thing. She smokes and takes turns crossing one leg over the next. Tony drives a few blocks and then finds another phone. He calls Bennie Fischetti at his home. He knows Bennie doesn't take any calls, but some guy will give the old man his name.

Tony gets back in the car. He doesn't drive and he doesn't look at Jill.

"Okay, look," Tony says. "Who you doing this for? Who you supposed to call?"

For a minute Jill doesn't say a thing. Then she looks at Tony real surprised. "Tony, what are you talking about? You lost me there, hon."

Tony reaches over and holds her chin straight, not hard or anything, just enough so she doesn't turn away. "Listen," he says, "I'm not a bad guy, and maybe you'd have come on to me anyway, okay? Maybe not. But too much funny shit is happening to me, and I figure it's got to be you. I like you a lot. I'm not going to do nothing to you, all right? I ain't even mad. But you're going to have to tell me how it is."

"Oh, Jesus, Tony." Jill looks like she's going to cry. Tony lets her go.

"Sal or Mickey Ricca?" Tony says.

"Sal," Jill says. Her eyes are getting wet and she reaches up with a finger and wipes her cheek. "I hate this shit, you know? I had to. He didn't give me any choice."

"I know that," Tony says. "So what are you supposed to do?"

"Sal said it was a joke."

"Yeah it is. It's on me."

"Sal, he—all I know is he's supposed to call you this morning and tell you something to do. I don't know what. I don't know a thing about that. I guess that was him on the phone."

"He knew you'd be at my place."

Jill looks at her hands. "I wanted to be there anyway, Tony. You don't have to believe that but it's true."

"So what else?"

"He's going to call me at home. About noon. I'm supposed to tell him what I think you're going to do, anything I heard you say, which is nothing, by the way." She looks at Tony now. She's glad this is over, and Tony doesn't have to prompt her anymore. "Tomorrow night Sal says I hit these clubs and bars and like I'm supposed to be all swacked out, you know? Boozed up. And I let on as how I was with you today and I saw you—do something. I don't even know what. Sal's supposed to tell me that."

"Jesus . . ." Tony lets out a breath. It's about like he figured only worse. That godamn Ricca's thought the whole thing out. Even down to Jill spreading the word at some Tranalone bar that he's hit the Scozarris. Just a little extra insurance which is Ric all the way. Whatever, the guy is going to nail it down and you got to give him that. And then Jill sort of drops out of sight like forever, only Jill doesn't know about that, which is something Sal sort of left out. Everything's falling into place and he knows why Sal said 3:45, and this burns Tony up, because this is the time Mickey Ricca gets a shave and a shine every day down at Gold's, which is close to the donut shop. The son of a bitch wants to watch. He wants to sit in his barber chair and watch Tony go, he wants the fun of doing that.

Tony thinks for a minute but he knows this is what he's got to do, that he's got to trust the girl, and he's not too worried once he tells her how Ricca don't exactly plan to keep her around.

"Okay, look," Tony says, "I'm going to lay this out on the line. Don't ask a bunch of dumb questions, just listen."

Tony tells her how he works for Sal and Ric and the Bennie Fischetti family, which he figures that she already knows, and how he had this beef with the Scozarris only Ric wouldn't let him work it out.

"So when Sal calls this morning and says fine, go ahead," Tony says, "I know right off I been fucked. If Ric says fine and I'm set up and I know what Ric's going to do. I hit the Scozarris then Ric hits me. See, this makes the old man look good. The hit ain't business, so Bennie makes it up to the Tranalones and they figure how Bennie's getting old and ain't strong anymore and really wants to make peace. So the Tranalone family gets sucked in good and goes to sleep while Bennie makes a deal with the blacks. What you gotta understand is I ain't even a big player in this. What I am is a little extra angle for Mickey Ric. He looks good with the boss and he gets me out of his hair. Which is what he's been wanting all along because he don't want an Indian working for the family. This is no big news to me. This I already know."

"Oh, my God." Jill bites her lip and looks as if she might cry again. "So what are you going to do? I mean, there's got to be—" Her face brightens up like she's just had a great idea. "Tony. Tony, look— if you *don't* do anything to these Scozarri people, Ricca's plan won't work! Don't you see?" She reaches out and holds his hand tight. "I mean, you get out of town right now, Tony we could do that together, we do that and nothing's going to happen at all. Tony, I'd really like that. Honest. I really would."

"Yeah, well we got a little problem there," Tony says. He tells her how this is maybe not such a good idea since he's already done the Scozarris only nobody knows about that so it's going to be hard to back out.

"You what?" Jill looks kind of white. "When—when did you do that?"

Tony tells her when and she looks like she might get sick, either that or maybe hit him in the face.

"My God, what the hell kind of thing is that to do you got a date," she wants to know. "You take a girl out, the very first date you do that. I cannot be*lieve* this."

"Listen, it kind of came up," Tony says. "Something comes up that's what you got to do."

Jill doesn't want to talk. She turns away and looks out the front and does things with her lips, and Tony knows a broad does that there's no use trying to make her talk.

*   *   *

Tony gets her calmed down and then stops at a drive-in spot and gets her a breakfast to go. Jill feels better after that, so he tells her what it is they've got to do. Jill listens and it's clear she doesn't like this at all. What she'd really like to do pack a bag and leave town. Catch a plane to L.A. or Mexico and dye her hair. Change her name to Mary Smith. She knows that's not how it's going to be. If she goes along with Sal which she doesn't want to do she's got a real short weekend ahead. With Tony Red Dog she's got a chance. Not a whole lot because Tony's full of crazy ideas that won't work but it's too late to think about that.

Tony lets her off at her apartment and makes sure he's got her phone number right.

"Take it easy," he says. "Do what you got to do you'll be fine. You're going to be just fine."

Jill gives him a look. "Don't you tell me I'll be fine. Don't you say that to me."

"Okay I won't."

Tony starts to drive off, and Jill leans in the window and plants a nice kiss on his mouth. "You're going to be just fine," Jill says.

"Yeah, right," Tony says.

He leaves her there and goes half a mile and stops at a booth to call Bennie Fischetti again. The old man won't talk, but the word will get through that he called. Now he's got to wait. It isn't even noon he's got to wait. Drive around and get back to Jill and check in with Daddy Jones and then drive around some more. He thinks about Sal and Mickey Ric and how this is going to go down, but mostly he thinks about Jill. She's got a smile that won't quit and she's great in the sack but he isn't much in love anymore. Some but not a lot. She really set him up good and he can understand that, but this kind of takes the shine off of things. Like they maybe can't really hit it off. This really brings him down and he doesn't want to think about that, he's got a lot of shit to do.

*　　*　　*

Tony pulls up at the donut shop right at 3:45. Everything looks fine. It looks like an ordinary day. Inside, Sal is sitting in the back. He's got donut powder on his mouth, he's got coffee down his shirt. Bobby Gallo and Vinnie are there too. Bobby Gallo gives Tony a grin. Vinnie D. tries to look like there's nothing going down, but Vinnie's not smart enough for that.

"Hey, Tony," Sal says, and even Sal's got a smile. "Have a seat, you want a glazed?"

Tony sits. He knows he's okay, it's not going to happen here.

"So listen," Sal says, and leans as close to the table as he can. "How'd it go, you get it done?"

"Right after breakfast," Tony says.

Sal gets a kick out of this. He's shaking all over which is something else to see.

"Jesus. Right after breakfast," Sal says. He's spitting donut powder on his shirt. "Leo and Lenny. Like brushing your teeth, huh, Tony? Huh? Huh?"

Sal laughs and looks at Bobby and Vinnie D., and they think this is the funniest thing they ever heard. Boy, everyone's having a lot of fun, Tony thinks, and he sees how Bobby and Vinnie D. are kind of edging past Sal, Vinnie pretending he's got to sneeze, and Bobby going back for more glazed, which puts them both right behind Tony's chair. These guys are smooth, Tony thinks. These guys are slick as Goofy and Donald Duck.

Now Sal's not laughing anymore. Nothing's funny now that Vinnie and Bobby Gallo are where they ought to be.

"Tony, we got to talk," Sal says.

"Fine," Tony says. "You told me to be here, Sal, so here I am."

Sal shakes his head. "Not here."

"Not here what?"

"I mean this ain't where you and me got to talk."

Tony tries to look puzzled and surprised. "Sal, just what the fuck is this? You want to tell me what? I'm not any good at playing games."

Sal looks at Tony, serious and kind of sad, only Tony knows the sad isn't real.

"You carrying, Tony?" Sal wants to know.

"No I'm not carrying," Tony says. "Should I be?"

Sal looks at Bobby Gallo, and Bobby says, "Stand up, Tony, okay?" He says it real nice.

Tony stands and lets Bobby shake him down.

"Jesus Christ, Sal." Tony tries to look scared. "You're not gonna do me. Listen, what the hell for?"

"Nothing personal, Tony," Sal says. "It's business. It's just business is all."

"Fuck that," Tony says. "Hey. Whatever this is we can work something out."

"If I could do that, Tony, I would," Sal says. "There ain't nothing I can do."

And then Tony sees something that he's never seen before. He can't hardly believe what he sees which is Sal Galiano getting up. Jesus, it's worth getting hit to see that. There probably aren't four or five guys ever seen this before. This is not your plain everyday standing up. This is a major operation. This is a dumb Jap movie where the lips and the sound don't match; this thing's coming up from the mud, it's going to fuck up Tokyo good, it's going to dump a bunch of donuts on the Japs. Tony knows it wasn't Sal's idea, that Mickey Ric told Sal he had to handle this himself, but Tony feels pretty good. How many guys have got Sal Galiano on his feet?

*   *   *

When they get in Sal's car, Tony in back with Bobby Gallo, Sal up front with Vinnie D., Tony feels a little lump in his gut. He's felt okay until now. Now he don't feel right at all. He's thinking how he's screwed himself good. He's thinking maybe half a dozen things can go wrong, and he'll have to try to grab Bobby's piece, which Bobby's not about to let him do. He's thinking maybe Jill had the right idea: Get out of town and don't fuck with Mickey Ric. Instead here he is watching Sal take up the front seat and squeezing Vinnie out the door.

"Sal, listen," Tony says, "I got to make a call. You got to let me make a call."

This gets a laugh from up front. "You got to be kidding," Sal says.

"I'm kidding, a time like this? Sal, I got to make a call. I got to talk to Bennie Fischetti. That's who I gotta call."

"You're stalling," Sal says. "Shit, I'd do the same thing if I was you. I'd do the same thing. Tony, the old man ain't going to help. You got to learn to relax. That's what you want to do. Don't think about nothing at all. It won't take a minute, it's over like that."

"Relax," Tony says.

"That's the thing to do. That's the best thing to do."

Tony sees they're going up First, past the pawn shops and the bum hotels toward the Freeway east and out of town. He knows where they're going, he knows the way they got to take. He and

Bobby Gallo and Vinnie have been out there once before, when Eddie Pliers got greedy with the skim. The Tranalone family's got their meat packing plants; Bennie Fischetti's got a marsh. The Minellis had the marsh before that, which means there's stiffs out there from like 1922, and it's not a good place to stop and fish, you don't know what you'll maybe catch.

"You got to let me call," Tony says. "Fuck, it's not going to cost you a thing, I'm paying for the call. Sal, I got to talk to the old man. I got to do that."

"What for?" Sal wants to know. Or maybe he doesn't care, he's got nothing else to do.

"I can't say what for."

"So don't."

Tony seems to think about that. "Okay. It's about Mickey Ricca. That's what it's about." They're passing Eighth. They're passing through a neighborhood's going to the dogs, half the buildings empty, a few sleazy bars, stores going out of business every day.

Sal turns his neck around as far as it will go, which is maybe half an inch. "What you want to do back there is relax," Sal says. "You don't want to be thinking up shit because it isn't going to do you no good. Okay? Just shut the fuck up. Think about a broad. Something. Don't talk."

"You hear what I gotta say," Tony says, "you're not going to say don't talk. You're going to thank me is what you're going to do. You're going to say, hey, thanks, Tony. This is what you're going to do."

"Shut the fuck up," Sal says.

"Yeah, right."

"So what about Ric?"

"Forget it. It's got to be the old man."

"Fuck you," Sal says. "We'll do a seance thing. Bobby knows a gypsy broad. You can talk to the old man then."

Vinnie thinks this is a riot, and Bobby does too. They're coming up on Seventeenth and the Freeway's six, maybe seven blocks away, and Tony's thinking, shit, this is it, it isn't coming down and I'm feeding the fish. I been set up twice, and both times by the same fucking broad. And then they pass Nineteenth and here's a Caddy pulled up by a cigar store with a window patched up with silver tape, and coming out of this store is Daddy Jones. Daddy Jones and Tommy "Horse" Calise. Daddy Jones, the Horse, and Mickey Ric.

"Holy shit, look at that!" Vinnie says, and slows the car and stares at what he sees.

"Jesus," Sal says, "keep driving. Don't stop the fucking car." Sal looks at Mickey Ric and Mickey Ric looks back, and it's hard to say who's staring harder at who. Daddy Jones ducks his head. Horse tries to turn away, tries to get back in the store, but there's no mistaking Horse. Now the car's past and there's nothing else to see and nobody says a thing. There isn't anything to say except the two *consiglieres* of the two biggest families in town are standing back there together with the number two South Side black. Standing there like asshole buddies which is not the kind of thing you want to see.

"I'm talking, you don't listen," Tony says. "I got to make a call, you say, Tony, you ain't making any call."

"Call," Sal says. "Vinnie, find a phone. The guy's got to make a call."

*　　*　　*

Mickey Ricca tells the old man this is all a bunch of crap. It wasn't Horse at all it was some other guy, and anyway the colored had a piece in his hand all the time. He had a piece in his hand and Ricca couldn't do a thing. The fuckers pick him up, he's on the way to get a shine, he can't do a damn thing, and this Indian's behind all this is who it is.

Bennie Fischetti's old, he's not dumb. It could happen just the way Ricca says and it looks kind of fishy, hell it stinks is what it does, Sal and these guys they're passing by and there's Calise and the black and Mickey Ric, they just happen to walk out of this store, and who's going to buy something like that?

Only Bennie can't see how the Indian could be that stupid, he sets up a deal like this any kid could see through. An Indian's smart, he's got cunning in his blood. A deer shits somewhere he can follow it for miles. An Indian can sneak up on a fort. You don't even know he's there. And the Indian tried to call. He tried to call him all day. Bennie knows about that. And Sal Galiano, he saw the whole thing, Sal swears it was the Horse, how's a guy mistake the Horse?

And of course that's the thing, Bennie can't check it out with the Horse, he can't ask. The Horse wouldn't give Bennie the time of day. Anything's wrong in the Fischetti family, fine. That's fine with Horse Calise and Dominic Tranalone. And he can't ask the colored. What a colored's going to do he's going to lie. That's what your colored's got to do.

So Bennie don't know, he's got no way to get to the truth. What he knows is if Ric's talking straight he's let the Indian set him up. A guy fucks up once he can maybe do it twice and Bennie doesn't like to wait for that. A guy gets careless, he can bring you down quick. So maybe Ric's clean this time, he's maybe not. He's clean today so tomorrow's something else. Mickey Ric's a good man and Mickey's smart, but a guy that smart doesn't like to stay down he likes to move, and the way he likes to move is up. Besides, Bennie's thinking how Ric hasn't ever treated Joey good at all. Benny knows the kid's not bright, but Ric could show him some respect. Ric laughs at Joey and this is something Ric shouldn't ought to do.

Bennie calls in Nick Cannatella who's the *caporegime* for dope. He gives Nick a glass of wine and has a talk; when Nick leaves, he's the Fischetti family's new *consigliere*. Nick's a guy who's always treated Joey nice and he's got the whole family's respect.

Bennie sends Sal to Minnesota, where the family's getting heavy into cheese, a job where Sal won't have a whole lot to do and if he does he's got Bobby and Vinnie D. to help. Tony Red Dog gets Sal's old job, and now he's *caporegime* for hijacking trucks and heisting cars. Bennie gives Tony five Gs because he likes Tony's style, and Tony gives two of this to Jill who finds a sudden need for Caribbean sun. Tony gives a grand to the actor guy Jill dug up to play the Horse, which he did real fine, considering Horse isn't the easiest guy to do.

Bennie feels kind of bad when he's got to tell Ric the bad news; hey, a guy's got his faults, he's been around a long time he's done a job. Bennie tells Ric it's nothing personal, it's business is what it is, he wants Ric to see it that way. Bennie tells Danny Fusco to use the green Caddy, the one Bennie likes best, he wants Ric to know how he feels.

*　　*　　*

The first day on his new job, Tony spots a girl named Cecile, she works in a club down the street. Cecile's got a bod that won't quit and black eyes, and Tony knows he hasn't really ever been in love before. In spite of Cecile's great shape she cashiers in the club and don't take nothing off, and Tony's got to respect her for that.

He's been the new *capo* for two, maybe three or four days, he makes sure the guys on the street know Tony Red Dog pays his debts, this is something he feels he's got to do. He's got an idea what, because something's smelling ripe in the trunk and he remembers what it is. So he takes the potato sack out and finds a box and gets some real nice paper to wrap it up, and mails the scalps he took from the Scozarris to Dominic Tranalone. Of course he checks this out with Don Fischetti first, and Bennie, who don't think a whole lot is funny, gets a real laugh out of this, and thinks the Indian guy is okay. Listen, for a red colored guy he's okay.

Howard Waldrop has developed a cult following, and if the little fella will do more novels, he just might spread beyond that. His work is unique in the field of sciene fiction and fantasy. Sort of Cyril Kornbluth meets Philip Jose Farmer, but it still somehow manages to be its own thing. The following tells us about a once popular series of films and how they were made and what happened to the old cast. Sort of.

THE PASSING
OF THE WESTERN

by Howard Waldrop

From FILM REVIEW WORLD, April 1972:

A few months ago, we sensed something in the national psyche, a time for revaluation, and began to put together this special issue of *Film Review World* devoted to that interesting, almost forgotten art form, the American western movie.

The genre flourished between 1910 and the late 1930s, went into its decline in the 1940s (while the country was recovering from The Big Recession, and due perhaps more to actual physical problems such as the trouble of finding suitable locations, and to the sudden popularity of costume dramas, religious spectacles and operettas.) There was some renewed interest in the late 1940s, then virtually nothing for the next twenty years.

Now that some Europeans (and some far less likely people) have discovered something vital in the form, and have made a few examples of the genre (along with their usual output of historical epics and heavy dramas), we felt it was time for a retrospective of what

211

was for a while a uniquely American art form, dealing as they did with national westward expansion and the taming of a whole continent.

We were originally going to concentrate on the masters of the form, but no sooner we assigned articles and began the search for stills to illustrate them than we ran across (in the course of reviewing books in the field *and* because we occasionally house-sit with our twelve-year-old nephew) no less than *three* articles dealing in part with a little-known (but well-remembered by those who saw them) series of Westerns made between 1935 and 1938 by the Metropolitan-Goldfish-Mayer Studios. Admittedly, the last article appeared in a magazine aimed specifically at teen-agers with no knowledge of American film industry history (or anything *else* for that matter) edited by a man with an encyclopedic knowledge of film and an absolutely abominable writing style—who has nevertheless delved into movie arcana in his attempt to fill the voracious editorial maw of the six magazines he edits (from his still-and-poster-laden Boise garage) for a not-so-nice guy in Richmond.

That we could almost dismiss, but the other two we couldn't—two works by film scholars noted for their ability to find people, hunt up lost screenplays and production notes and to dig at the facts, both books to be published within a week of each other next month.

We've obtained permission to reprint the relevant portions of the two books, and the whole of that magazine article (including the stills) by way of introduction to this special issue dedicated to the Passing of the Western Movie from the American cinema—taken together, they seemed to strike exactly the right note about the film form we seem to have lost.

Join us, then, in a trip backwards in time—twice, as it were—to both the real events that inspired the films, and to the movies made about them fifty years later.

And, as they used to say on the Chisolm Road, "always keep to the high ground and have your slicker handy!"

—John Thomas Johns

THE PASSING OF THE WESTERN

From: THE BOISE SYSTEM: Interviews With 15 Directors Who Survived Life in the Studios, by Frederick T. Yawts, Ungar (Film Book 3) 1972.
(from the interview with James Selvors)

Selvors: . . . the problems of doing Westerns of course in those days was finding suitable locations—that's why they set up operations in Boise in the first place. See, no matter what steps people had taken, they'd never really gotten any good constant rainfall in the Idaho part of the basin—oh, they could make it rain occasionally, but never like everywhere else—it was the mountains to the west. They call it orographic uplift, an orographic plain. There used to be one on the west coast of Peru, but they fixed that back in the Nineteen-teens by fooling with the ocean currents down there. They tried that up here, too, in Washington State and Oregon, messed with the ocean currents; instead of raining in Idaho all they got was more rain on the Pacific slope, which they *did not need.*

Anyway, Griffith and Laemmle came out to Boise in '09, 1910, something like that, because they could be out in what was left of the Plains in a few hours and they could almost guarantee 150 good-weather days a year.

First thing the early filmmakers had to do was build a bunch of western towns, since there weren't any out there (nobody with any sense ever stopped and put down roots in the Idaho Plains when Oregon was just a few days away.) What few towns there had been had all rotted away (there still wasn't much rain but it was a hell of a lot more than there had been 60 years before.) The place actually used to be a desert—imagine that, with nothing growing but scrub; by the time the pioneer moviemakers got there it was looking like old pictures of Kansas and Nebraska from the 1850s—flat grasslands, a few small trees; really Western-looking. (God help anyone who wanted to make a movie set in one of the Old Deserts—you've got farms all up and down the Mojave River and Death Valley Reservoir and Great Utah Lake now that get 50 bales to the acre in cotton.) There was the story everybody's heard about making the Western in one of the new *nunatak* areas in Antarctica—the snow'd melted off some 3000 square miles taking fake catus and sagebrush down there in the late 40s. I mean, it *looked* like a desert, flat bare rock everywhere; everybody had to strip down to just shirt, pants and hats and put on fake sweat—we heard it froze; the snow's melted in

Antarctica a whole lot, but don't let anyone tell you it's not still *cold* there—it has something with not getting as cold by a couple of degrees a year—like the mean temperature's only risen like four degrees since the 1880s. (Filming icebergs is another thing—you either have to do miniatures in a tank, which never work, use old stock footage, ditto; or got to Antarctica and blast the tops off all jaggedy with explosives—the ones in Antarctica are flat, they're land ice; what everybody thinks of as northern icebergs were sea ice.) Somebody's gonna have to do an article sometime on how the weather's kept special effects people in business . . .

Int: What was it about the *Cloudbusters* series that made them so popular?

Selvors: Lots of people saw them. (laughs)

Int: No, seriously. They were started as short subjects, then went to steady B-westerns. Only Shadow Smith dying stopped production of them . . .

Selvors: I've talked to lots of people over the years about that. Those things resonate. They're about exactly what they're about, if you know what I mean. Remember *Raining Cats and Dogs? The Second Johnaon Flood?* Those were A pictures, big budgets, big stars? Well, they all came later, after the last *Cloudbusters* movie was made. I mean, we set out to make a film about the real taming of the West—how it was done, in fact. All these small independent outfits, going from place to place, making it rain, fixing up things, turning the West into a garden and a lush pastureland. That was the real West, not a bunch of people killing off Indians and shooting each other over rights to a mudhole. That stuff happened early on, just after the Civil War. By 1880 all that was changing.

We wanted just to make a short, you know, a three-reeler, about thirty minutes—there was a hot documentary and a two-reel color cartoon going out with the A picture *Up and Down the Front*, about Canadians in the Big 1920 Push during the Great World War (that being the closest the U.S. got to it)—this was late '34, early '35 ((release date April 23, 1935-Int.)) So that package was too much stuff for even a 55 minute B-picture. Goldfish and Thalberg came to me and George Mayhew and asked us if we had a three-reeler ready to go—we didn't but we told them we did, and sat up all night working. Mayhew'd wanted to do a movie about the rainmakers and pluvicultists for a long time. There'd been an early silent about it, but it had been a real stinker ((*Dam Burst at Sun Dog Gap,* Universal

214

1911—Int.)), so Mayhew thought up the plot, and the mood, and we knew Shadow Smith was available, and Mayhew'd written a couple of movies with "PDQ" Podmer in them so he thought up the "Doodad" character for him, and we went back to Thalberg next day and shook hands on it and took off for Boise the next morning.

Int: It was a beautiful little film—most people remember it being a feature.

Selvors: Mayhew kicked butt with that script—lots of stuff in it, background and things, lots of action, but nothing seemed jammed in sideways or hurried. You remember that one was self-contained; I mean, it ended with the rain and everybody jumping up and down in mudpuddles, and the Cloudbusters rolling out for the next place. I think if we'd never have made another one, people would still remember *The Cloudbusters*.

Int: It was the first one to show the consequences, too—it ended with the Cloudbusters sitting in the Thunder Wagon bogged up to the wheelhubs and having to be pulled out by two teams of oxen.

Selvors: That's right. A beautiful touch. But it wasn't called the Thunder Wagon yet. Most people remember it that way but it wasn't, not in that one. That all came later.

Int: Really?

Selvors: Really. Wasn't until the second one their wagon was referred to as the Thunder Wagon. And it wasn't painted on the side until the third one.

Int: How did the features, and the rest of the series come about?

Selvors: Thalberg liked it. So did the preview audiences, better than anything but the cartoon. It even got bookings outside the package and the chains.

Int: I didn't know that. That was highly unusual.

Selvors: So much so they didn't know what to do. But by then we were into the second, maybe the third. All I know is they set up a points system for us.

Int: Even though you were on salary?

Selvors: Me and Mayhew were in pig heaven. Smith got part of it, but the brightest man of all was Podmer. He wasn't on contract—he was, like, a loose cannon; sometimes him and Andy Devine or Eric Blore would work on two or three movies on different lots a day. Anyway, he sure cut some sweet deal with M.G.M. over the series. Podmer talked like a hick and walked like a hick—it was what we wanted in the character of "Doodad" and he was brilliant at it—but he could tear a pheasant with the best of them . . .

Int: So if you and Mayhew set out to tell a realistic story, about the rainmakers and the real business of winning the West . . .

Selvors: I know what you're going to ask next. (laughs)

Int: What?

Selvors: You're going to ask about The Windmill Trust.

Int: What about The Windmill Trust?

Selvors: That part, we made up.

From: *The Sidekick: Doppelgangers of the Plains* by Marvin Ermstien UCLA Press, 1972

(This interview with Elmer "PDQ" Podmer took place in 1968, a few months before his death at the age of 94. It was recorded at the Boise Basin Yacht Club.)

ME: Let's talk about the most popular series you did at M.G.M.

Podmer: You mean *The Cloudbusters?*

ME: You've been in, what, more than 300 movies . . .?

Podmer: 374, and I got another one shooting next month, where I play Burt Mustin's father.

ME: I'm still surprised that people remember you best as "Doodad" Jones. Three of the films were shorts, five were B-movies, and I don't think any of them have been on television for a while . . .

Podmer: Izzat a fact? Well, I know last time I saw one was mebbe ten year ago when I was over to my great grandniece's house. I remember when Bill Boyd was goin' on and on about television, way back in 1936 or so. He told all us it was the wave o' the future and to put all our money in Philco. He was buying up the rights to all his Roman Empire movies, that series he made, Hoplite Cassius. We all thought he was crazy as a bedbug at the time. He made quite a bundle, I know that.

ME: About the *Cloudbusters* . . .

Podmer: Well, it was a good character part. It was just like me, and the director and writer had some pretty good idea what to do with him. Also, you remember, I was the star of the last one . . .

ME: *The Thunder Wagon*. That was the one being made when Shadow Smith died.

Podmer: That was it. Well, originally of course it had pretty much another script—they'd filmed some of it—in fact they'd filmed the scene that was used in the movie where Shadow talks to me and then rides off to do some damn thing or other. Next day we got the news about Shadow drowning in the Snake River while he was hauling in a 14 pound rainbow trout. They found his rod and reel two mile downriver and the trout was still hooked . . .

ME: There were lots of ironic overtones in the death notices at the time.

Podmer: You mean about him being in *The Cloudbusters* and then dying that way? Yeah, I remember. He was a damn fine actor, a gentleman, just like his screen character. We was sure down for awhile.

ME: So the script was rewritten?

Podmer: Yep. Mayhew wanted to make it a tribute to Smith, and also do some things he hadn't been able to do before, so he turned out a hum-dinger! I got top billing for the first and only time in my life. In the cutting on the new version, they had Smith say whatever it is, then as he turns to ride away they had this guy who could do Smith's voice tell me where to take the Thunder Wagon, which sets up the plot. That puts me and Chancy Raines (that was Bobby Hornmann, a real piss-ass momma's boy, nothing like the character he played) smack dab up against Dryden and the Windmill Trust on our own. Course the real star of that last picture was the wagon itself. Mayhew's screenplay really put that thing through some paces . . .

ME: Tell me about the Wagon.

Podmer: You seen the movies, ain't you?

ME: Three or four times each.

Podmer: Then why ask me?

ME: Well, it looked like *you* firing off the Lightning Rockets and the Nimbus Mortars . . .

Podmer: It was me. I didn't use no stuntman! I wisht I had a nickel for every powder burn I got on that series. Some days I'd be workin' at M.G.M. mornings and hightailing it all the way across

Boise to the First National lot, and runnin' on the set sayin' my lines, and the makeup men would be bitching because I'd burnt half my real beard off, or had powder burns on my arms, or something. One of those other films I ain't got no eyebrows in a couple of scenes.

ME: What about the Sferics Box? I know some critics complained there was nothing like it in use among the rainmakers in the real Old West.

Podmer: Do I look like a goddamn engineer? I'm a thespian! Ask Mayhew or Selvors about that stuff. I do know I once got a letter from a guy what used to be a rainmaker back then—hell, he must have been older when he wrote that letter than I am *now*—who said he used something like that there Sferics Box—they'd listen for disturbances in the ether with them. Had something to do with sunspots, I think.

ME: That was twenty years before deForest sent the first messages . . .

Podmer: They wasn't interested in talkin' to each other, they was interested in makin' a gullywasher! That's what the guy wrote, anyway.

ME: In all those films, Shadow Smith never used a gun, right?

Podmer: Well, just that once. People talked about that stuff for a long time. It was the next to the last one ((*The Watershed Wars*, 1937—ME)) and they was that shootist for the Windmill Trust that called Shadow out to a street duel—Shadow'd just gone into the saloon to find him after all those people were killed when the Windmill Trust tried to make Utah Great Lake salty again, and Shadow's so mad he picks up a couple of guns from the bar and goes out, then you cut out onto the street, bad guy's standing in it, and Shadow comes out the saloon doors a quarter-mile away and starts shooting, just blasting away and walking up the boardwalk, bullets hitting all over the streets around the shootist, and he just takes off and runs, hightails it away. When Shadow realizes what he's done, that he's used gun-violence, he gets all upset and chagrined. People still talk about that. What few Westerns were made later, even the ones they started filming a few years ago in what was left of the Sahara Plains, they'd never done that—always romanticized it, one-to-one, always used violence. Never like in *The Cloudbusters*, where we used brains and science . . .

ME: It wasn't just Shadow Smith's death that finished the series, then?

THE PASSING OF THE WESTERN

Podmer: It wuz everything. Smith died. Thalberg had been dead a year by then, and Goldfish wanted to move Selvors up to the A-Pictures; he never could leave well-enough alone. The next one we knew was gonna be directed by just someone with a ticket to punch. Selvors tried to stay, but they told him their way or the highway. That was the middle of '38, just when the European market fell apart, and people was nervous over here—they didn't have to wait but till August before our market started The Long Fall, and people started the Back-to-the-Land movement; they ate allright but there wasn't any *real* money around. Anyway, that's about the time Mayhew had the garish-headline divorce and we'd be damned if we let other people write *and* direct *The Cloudbusters*. Also they took Bill Menzies away from us, too—he'd designed the Thunder Wagon, and most of the props and did the sets, and about half the effects on the movies—remember the credits, with that big thunderhead rolling in on you and suddenly spelling out *The Cloudbusters?*—that was Menzies' doing all along.

So we all got together, just after we wrapped *The Thunder Wagon* and we made a gentleman's agreement that there wouldn't be any more Cloudbusters films—it was hard to do, we'd been a real family except for that shitty Hornmann kid, I hope he's burning in hell—((Robert Hornmann was killed in a fight in a West Boise nightclub in 1946—ME)) and for me it was walking away from a goldmine, and my only chance to get top billing again. But it was easiest for me, too, since I had a picture-to-picture deal and all I did was line up enough work to stay busy for the solid next year. I also put out the word to all the other comic relief types not to go signin' anything with the name Cloudbusters on it . . .

ME: Have you seen Sergio Leone's A *Faceful of Rainwater?*

Podmer: Was that that wop western about the Two Forks Wars?

ME: Yes. It's supposedly an homage to the Cloudbusters, much grittier but not as good, I don't think.

Podmer: Nope. Ain't seen it.

From: BLAZING SCREENS! The Magazine of Celluloid Thrills, June 1972.

SOUNDTRACK THUNDER AND NITRATE LIGHTNING!
by Formalhaut J. Amkermackum

Imagine a time when most of the American continent was a vast dry desert from the Mississippi to the Pacific Coast!

Imagine when there were no lush farmlands from sea to sea, when coffee, rubber and tea had to be imported into this country!

Imagine that once men died crossing huge sandy wastes & when the only water for a hundred miles might turn out to be poison, when the Great Utah Lake was so salty it supported no aquatic life!

Imagine when the Midwest was only sparse grasslands, suitable for crops only like wheat & oats, or an economy based on the herding of cattle & sheep!

Imagine a time when rainfall was so scarce the only precipitation was snow on the high mountains in the winter & when that was melted there was no snow til next year!

These things were neither a nightmare nor the fevered dreams of some fantasy writer—this was the American West—where our forefathers actually tried to make a living—*less than one hundred years ago!*

YOU CAN TAKE A PLUVICULTURE BUT YOU CAN'T MAKE IT DRINK.

Then came the men & women who not only talked (as Mark Twain once said) about the weather but they did something about it! They called themselves storm wizards, rainmakers and even pluviculturalists (which is the fancy word for rainmaker!) & their theories were many & varied but what they did & how they did it & how they changed our lives & the destiny of the world was the stuff of legend. But at first everybody just talked about them & nobody did anything about them.

Until 1935 that is!!!

TWO THUNDERHEADS ARE BETTER THAN ONE.

That year George Mayhew (the screenwriter of *Little Lost Dinosaur* & *Wild Bill Barnacle*) teamed up with James Selvors (director of such great movies as *The Claw-Man Escapes, His Head Came C.O.D.* and the fantastic musical war movie *Blue Skies & Tailwinds*) to bring to the screen a series of films dealing with the life & times of the men who broke the weather & transformed the American West to a second Garden of Eatin'—*The Cloudbusters!*

THE GUN THAT DROWNED THE WEST

Aided by the marvellous & mysterious Thunder Wagon (in which they kept all their superscientific paraphernalia & their downpour-making equipment) they roamed the west through five feature films & three shorts that will never be forgotten by those who've seen them.

SHADOWS OF THINGS TO COME

For the lead in the films (except for the last one where he had only a brief appearance due to his untimely & tragic death) they chose Shadow Smith, the big (6'5½") actor who'd starred in such films as *Warden, Let Me Out!, My Friend Frankenstein* & lots more. Before the Cloudbusters films, his best-known role was as Biff Bamm in *Spooks in the Ring, Singing Gloves* and *Biff Bamm Meets Jawbreaker* all for Warner Bros. Shadow was born in 1908 in Flatonia, Texas & had worked in films from 1928 on, after a stint as an egg-candler & then college in Oklahoma City.

He fit the role perfectly (his character name was Shadow Smith also) & according to people who knew him was just like his screen character—softspoken, shy and a great lover of the outdoors. It is interesting that the Shadow Smith character in the Cloudbusters *never* used a firearm to settle a score—sometimes resorting to scientific wrestling holds & fisticuffs, but most usually depending on his quick wits, brain and powers of logic.

WHO DAT WHO SAY "DOODAD"?

As comic relief & sidekick "Doodad" Jones was played by Elmer "PDQ" Podmer—(the "PDQ" in the name of this old-time character actor stuck with him for the alacrity with which he learned & assayed his many roles, and the speed with which he went from one acting job to another, sometimes working on as many as three different films at three different studios in one day!) The character of "Doodad" was one of the most interesting he ever had. Many characteristics were the usual—he used malapropisms like other sidekicks ("aspersions to greatness", "some hick yokelramus" & he once used "matutinal absolution" for "morning bath") but was deferred to by Shadow Smith for his practical knowledge & mechanical abilities, especially when something went wrong with the "consarned idjit contraptions" in the Thunder Wagon.

221

Their young assistant, Chancy Raines (played by Bobby Horn-mann, who died tragically young before he could fulfill his great talents as an actor) was added in the second film as an orphan picked up by Smith and "Doodad" after a drought & sudden flash flood killed his mother & father & little sister.

Together they roamed the West, in three short (3-reel or 28 minute) films and five full-length features made between 1935 and 1938. They went from small towns and settlements to the roaring hellcamps of Central City and Sherman, Colorado to what used to be the Mojave Desert in California, and as far north as the Canadian border, bringing with them storms & lifegiving rains which made the prairies bloom—always in their magnificent Thunder Wagon!

SKYWARD HO!

The Thunder Wagon! A beautiful & sleek yellow and blue (we were told) wagon pulled by a team of three pure white horses (Cirrus, Stratus and Cumulus) and one pure black horse (Nimbus)!

Designed by director/cameraman/set designer/special effects man Bill C. Menzies (who had come from Germany via England to the M.G.M. studios in Boise in 1931) the Thunder Wagon seemed both swift & a solid platform from which Shadow, "Doodad" and Chancy made war on the elements with their powerful Lightning Rockets, Nimbus Mortars (& the black horse neighed every time that weapon was fired) and the Hailstone Cannons, which they fired into the earth's atmosphere & caused black clouds & thunderstorms (& in one case a blizzard) to form & dump their precipitation on the hopeful thirsty farmers and ranchers who'd hired them.

DON QUIXOTES OF THE PLAINS!

But the weather wasn't the only thing the Cloudbusters fought in the course of their movies. For they also had to battle the deadly Windmill Trust!

The Windmill Trust! A group of desperate Eastern investors, led by the powerful Mr. Dryden, dedicated to keeping the status quo of low rainfall & limited water resources in the Western territories! Their tentacles were everywhere—they owned the majority of the railroads & all the well-drilling & windmill manufacturing firms in the United States & they kept in their employ many shootists & desperadoes whom they hired to thwart the efforts of all the rainmakers & pluviculturalists to bring moisture to the parched plains. These men resorted to sabotage, missending of equipment, wrongful processes of law, and in many cases outright murder and

222

violence to retain their stranglehold on the American West and its thirsty inhabitants!

DESSICATED TO THE ONE I LOVE

Through these eight films, with their eye-popping special effects (even the credits were an effects matte shot of a giant cloud forming & coming toward you & suddenly spelling out the series' name!) their uncharacteristic themes & their vision of a changing America (brought on by the very rainmakers these films were about!) there were thrills & images people would never forget.

If you ever get to see these (& someone should really put the first three shorts together in one package & release it to TV) you'll see:

A race to the death between raging flood waters, the Thunder Wagon, & the formerly-unbelieving Doc Geezler & a wagonload of orphans!

"Doodad" Jones using the Nimbus Mortars to cause a huge electrical storm & demolish the Giant Windmill (30 stories high!) sucking the water from & drying up the South Platte River & threatening the town of Denver with drought!

The henchmen of the Windmill Trust (led by Joe Sawyer) dressed as ghosts in a *silent* (no sound of hoofbeats, only the snap of quirts and jingle of spurs heard in an eerie scene) raid on the town of Central City, Colorado!

The climactic fight on the salt-drilling platform above Utah Great Lake in the hailstorm between Shadow Smith and Dryden & three others seemingly plunging to their deaths far below!

The great blizzard forming over the heated floor of the (once) Great Mojave Desert, with its magical scenes of cacti in the snow & icicles on the sagebrush!

ACTION! THRILLS! WET SOCKS!

You can see all this and more, if you travel back via the silver screen & your TV set to a time not so long ago, when the Cloud-busters rode the Wild American West in their eight films:

The Cloudbusters (1935—a short, introducing Shadow Smith, "Doodad" & the Thunder Wagon!)

44 Inches or Bust! (1935—the second short—the title refers to the rainfall they promise a parched community—introducing Chancy Raines & the Windmill Trust!)

Storms Along the Mojave (1936—the last short)

The Desert Breakers (1936—the first feature, introducing Dryden as head of The Windmill Trust!)

223

The Dust Tamers (1936—with the giant windmill that threatens Denver!)

The Watershed Wars (1937—Dryden and Shadow Smith in hand-to-hand combat above Utah Great Lake!)

The Thunder Wagon (1938—the best film tho not most representative due to the death of Shadow Smith ((who appears only in an early scene & to whom the picture is dedicated)) but the Thunder Wagon is the star along with "Doodad" & Chancy—they have to cause rain in three widely-separated places & use the Hailstone Cannons to freeze an underground stream!)

So through these films you can ride (or saddle up again if you were lucky enough to see them the first time) with Shadow Smith, "Doodad" Jones & Chancy Raines, fighting the Windmill Trust & bringing the West the rain it so sorely needs & experience a true part of American history & thrill to the science & adventures of *The Cloudbusters!*

Lenore Carroll is much published these days, with a second novel and a number of short stories forthcoming. She lives in Kansas, doesn't know Dorothy or Toto, but she knows how to write a good story. This is one of the real ones. You might say it's a story about faith, something a lot of us could use more of. You might also say it's a story about guilt. Guess there's plenty of that to go around.

ELDON'S PENITENTE

by Lenore Carroll

When Eldon retired early and bought a house in Sante Fe, Tranquilino came with the garden. The owners recommended him and Eldon kept him on when he saw that the man was good. Eldon didn't care much about the garden, but he knew the value of a well-maintained property. He liked the idea of somebody living in the little adobe house behind the wall of the big house when he was gone.

Eldon adapted to Santa Fe. He bought a big silver belt buckle and a western hat and a down jacket for that first winter. He missed their grown kids, but Millie was dead, and the thought of that always made a place inside his chest go tight, so there was no point keeping the company going. He sold his business, sold the house and all of Millie's furniture with it and moved away.

He acclimated well, acquired a high altitude tan that set off his silver hair, found like-minded men—some married, some not—to drink with and hunt with and drive up into the mountains for trout fishing. He joined the historical society and the usual clubs. He found a few comfortable saloons where there were friendly faces, no pastel country club tourists, and a greeting from behind the bar.

But that's what led to his trouble. One night this little girl got into a fight with her boyfriend, a big guy, not handsome, but lean-hipped in a way that Eldon would never be. And when the dumb cowboy hit her, Eldon pulled her out of reach and said, "That's enough." His voice carried the authority of years of making decisions and giving orders and the cowboy backed off, saying, "This ain't the end of it, you whore. You'll come back, Kim. I know you." The cowboy stomped out, slammed the door behind him and spewed gravel as he gunned his pick-up out of the parking lot.

Kim was crying and hiccoughing and Eldon waited till she was quiet, then bought her a drink and listened to her story. She went off to the ladies' room and did something to her face and came back and had another drink. Then Eldon drove her home, since she needed a ride. And he resisted her invitation to come inside the old building, although it was difficult.

The next day he phoned, but got no answer until after five when Kim answered and said, "Sure, I'd like to see you again."

So then they started, first dinners, then drives out to country bars, then after a few weeks, he followed her into her cheerful apartment with its big, soft bed.

When he pulled into his garage after a late night with Kim and he noticed Tranquilino's light was still on after three a.m. He walked, a little unsteady from the wine, down the path to Tranquilino's door and knocked. He heard a soft cry from inside, not exactly alarm, almost of an animal in pain. Then Tranquilino said, "Who's there?"

"It's me. Eldon. Are you OK? I saw your light on."

"I'm fine, Mr. Hardacre," came the voice. "Do you wish to see me?"

Why was the gardener being coy? Eldon realized he had never looked inside Tranquilino's house and he was filled with a mighty curiosity, but had no reason to persist.

"No, no. Didn't mean to disturb you. I thought something might be wrong."

"Nothing is wrong," came Tranquilino's voice, a bit strained.

Eldon made his way to the big house, wondering what he had disturbed.

* * *

ELDON'S PENITENTE

The next day, Eldon came out onto the patio as Tranquilino raked the grass. Tranquilino worked for several nearby families and this was his day for Eldon's garden. It was meticulously neat. Eldon could see no weed marring the flower beds or the small patch of watered grass. The roses were fed and trimmed for the winter, the gravel paths bore rake marks, the junipers stood like stage props in their places. Eldon looked forward to the beer they would drink and the talk when the gardener finished.

"Looks good, amigo," said Eldon.

Tranquilino smiled, then bent to sweep some debris into a dust pan for the plastic trash bag. Eldon noticed something on his back and when he walked closer, saw red streaks soaking through the faded cotton.

"You hurt yourself, amigo," said Eldon.

"What?"

"Your back. It's bleeding."

Tranquilino quickly straightened and turned. "No, sir. It's nothing, just scratches."

"If you want me to put something on it, be glad to," said Eldon. "It's hard to reach those places by yourself." And he remembered Millie rubbing suntan lotion on his back that last trip to Miami and his chest clenched. He took a deep breath and waited for it to go away. One of these days, he'd have a heart attack and not even know it. He'd just think it was Millie. Why didn't I tell you I loved you when you were alive to hear it? Why didn't we enjoy things more? It doesn't mean as much without you.

"No, it will be all right," said Tranquilino.

*　　*　　*

Kim went to Laramie to visit her folks and Eldon wandered around the big house, lonesome for her. She wasn't as young as he had first thought, but at least she was older than his daughters. She'd been a secretary, then a data processor, in one city or another, all over the west. She liked cowboys, big sunsets and Scotch. Right now, she liked Eldon. He tried but couldn't imagine anything beyond their current relationship—friendly fucking, but not much real intimacy. Aside from telling her he was a widower, Eldon had never mentioned Millie. He craved touching, warm flesh and moist

227

places, as much as sex itself. He read that pets help people lower their blood pressure and he was tempted to buy a hunting dog, just for the pleasure of stroking it, but he hadn't the patience to train one. Millie had always trained the dogs, made them decent to live with, not just housebroken.

He returned from a solitary dinner wishing Kim were back and wandered around the empty house. He liked the terra cotta tile floors and handwoven rugs, the Indian pots and the baskets. But he missed something. Except for his toiletries, the house smelled unused. Maybe I'll get a cook, to put some good smells in this house. He selected a tape and dropped it in the deck, adjusted the sound. Mozart was always peaceful. He pulled off his boots and walked outside on the biting gravel, the moist grass plot, until his feet got cold. He looked around the wall at Tranquilino's house, but all was dark.

*   *   *

Then Kim returned and they resumed their evenings together. He didn't see her every night, but Fridays and Saturdays they had a standing date. Sometimes he would pick her up for a new gallery show or a movie before dinner and drinks and the trip back to her apartment. He bought her silver and turquoise—a necklace and earrings, a big ring, then a concho belt that cost more then he expected, but not more than he could afford. She stroked the aged, smooth silver medallions and beamed at him. Millie had never cared much for jewelry, got out of the habit when they were young and broke. Millie always said, "I don't need that stuff. I just want you," and he had gone off to make money and they hadn't spent enough time together.

"What's the matter, honey?" asked Kim. "You sick?"

"No, just remembering something."

"If it makes you stop like that, you best let it go. I thought you took sick all of a sudden." Kim put one arm around his broad back and sat with him on her couch, then jumped up to admire the concho belt again in the wavery glass on the bedroom door.

Now Tranquilino's light was on each night when he came home late. He saw shadows moving behind the shades, and sometimes faint noises. He never heard the cry again.

It was deep winter now, with spectacular sunsets spread out

228

over the Rio Grande valley. Each evening he nursed a drink in front of the big window and watched, tried not to think how much Millie would have enjoyed this quiet time, this beautiful country.

Tranquilino had found a woman who cooked three evenings a week and Eldon looked forward to her chile and posole and enchiladas.

                     *   *   *

Then one March evening, he and Kim went to the same bar where they had met. He should have known better. The glow of the beer signs was the same as they stepped into the stale beer-and-disinfectant smell of saloons everywhere. The TV up over the varnished wooden bar flickered with the sound turned down. They ordered, then Eldon fed the jukebox quarters and pushed numbers for slow dancing and led Kim out to the scarred parquet dance floor.

She had colored her hair a reddish-brown and done something with her make-up. He only saw wrinkles when she smiled. He placed one hand on her back, feeling the bulge where the flesh escaped the bra elastic. She didn't talk, but hummed a few notes now and then and smiled lazily when they separated at the end of a song. It was going to be a nice evening.

Along about eleven the cowboy appeared. He spotted them at a booth and was there before Eldon could stand.

"You ready to come back?" he asked Kim. It was more a demand than a question.

"Not now and not ever," she said.

"You're coming back sooner or later. Might as well be tonight."

"Leave the lady alone," said Eldon.

"I bet she don't leave you alone," the cowboy shot back. "I bet she does all kinds of things. And you pay for them."

"I've heard enough," said Eldon. It was hard to slide out of the booth and maintain dignity.

"What're you gonna do about it, old man?" sneered the cowboy.

"I'm going to ask you to leave one more time." Eldon was standing now. He straightened and felt his face go hard.

"And if I don't?"

Eldon swung and missed, then ducked. The youngster drew

back, then buried his piledriver fist in Eldon's middle. Eldon folded like a jackknife and the evening's Scotch tried to come back.

"Don't hurt him!" screamed Kim.

The cowboy reached across the table and dragged her out of the booth. He slapped her face and her head snapped. Eldon staggered toward them, but he couldn't straighten up. He never had to fight for Millie. He was ashamed of trying to fight the younger, stronger man and he was embarrassed that he'd done so badly.

The cowboy lifted one booted foot and pushed Eldon until he fell sideways, hands scrabbling at the floor tile.

"Let's go," said the cowboy and Kim grabbed her purse as he led her out the door.

"He wasn't that good in bed, anyway," she said.

Eldon felt the cold air from the open door for a moment, then rolled to his hands and knees and slowly, little by little, got himself up.

"Sorry, mister," said the barkeep. "He's mean and before I could get going, it was over."

Eldon waved a hand and shook his head. He couldn't speak.

"Hey, you going to be all right?" asked the bartender.

Eldon nodded and tried to take a deep breath. When he thought he could walk, he put bills on the table and left. The big Mercury rumbled and the heater defrosted the window, then Eldon drove slowly home.

Tranquilino's light was on and Eldon wanted company. He didn't want to talk about what happened, but he wanted to talk to someone. He knocked.

"Who is it?"

"Eldon, amigo."

"Is something wrong?" Tranquilino sounded worried.

"Yes." Weakness flowed up his legs and Eldon grabbed for the smooth door.

Then Tranquilino was half-carrying him to a bed and he sank clumsily. Then a glass of water. Then he tried to sit up and after three tries, made it.

"What happened?" asked the gardener.

"Fight. I lost." Eldon shuddered with cold and realized he must have left his down jacket at the bar.

"Let me help you. Man, you look bad."

"Thanks. I'm too old for such foolishness. Give me a minute."

Eldon stared across the room. There was a kitchen table with two plastic-upholstered chairs, an altar with a crucifix, a madonna and half-dozen candles in little glasses. It seemed warmer there. A TV on a table with peeling veneer, a sagging couch, covered with a handsome Indian blanket, and this bed. The kitchen and bathroom must be behind him. Then he noticed something on the table. Leather thongs hung down over the side and the wooden handle rested on top. It was a whip.

Tranquilino followed Eldon's eyes. He quickly picked up the whip and disappeared with it into another room.

"Penitente?" asked Eldon when the man returned.

"Of course not," said Tranquilino and looked away.

Eldon knew Tranquilino was lying, that he'd never admit it. Didn't the Catholic church outlaw that stuff? What do those people get out of it?

"Of course not," said Eldon, "but still there are men who suffer for the sins of others. Did I get that right?"

"Partly."

Eldon waited and when Tranquilino was silent, he asked, "Why do you do it?"

Tranquilino realized this was no idle Anglo question, so he searched for the words. In English, it sounded strained. "By suffering we unite everyone in God's eye, the sinner and the sufferer alike."

"And when I see the light on here late at night? Are you suffering for my sins, amigo?"

Tranquilino was silent.

"My own penitente!" said Eldon. "All the time I've been screwing Kim, you've been taking care of the punishment for me."

"No, no. It's not that way," Tranquilino protested.

"Close enough. I don't understand it and you can't tell me. I can drink and whore and you'll be here, cleaning up all the . . . guilt? No, the penance, the repayment."

Tranquilino as silent.

"I bet I could gamble and lie and cheat, even murder and when I die, I'll go straight to heaven because my penitente took care of it for me." Eldon laughed, but there was no joy in it.

"Let me help you to the big house," said Tranquilino.

He pulled Eldon to his feet and wrapped an arm around his waist. Eldon did likewise, because he was still unsteady. And he heard Tranquilino gasp and flinch. He pulled his arm away, then lifted the tail of the man's shirt.

The skinny brown back was cut with a hundred leather-thong crosshatchings. Random stripes seeped watery blood. Old white scars and brown, scabbed-over places were covered with fresh, new welts.

Tranquilino released Eldon and stood straight and silent, looking at Eldon with blank eyes. He was neither embarrassed nor ashamed nor proud.

"My apologies, amigo," said Eldon. "I didn't know you took this seriously."

"Very seriously."

"We must have a talk about this, but not now. Just follow me up the path. I'll be OK once I get to my bed."

And the two men walked slowly up the gravel path.

"Good night," said Tranquilino. "I'll wait until I see your light go on."

*　　*　　*

Eldon stopped going to bars, stopped meeting friends for dinner, stopped doing anything except sitting and brooding. He didn't feel particularly guilty about Kim, but the weight of mourning he'd avoided since Millie's death settled on his shoulders. Nobody would think he'd been a great sinner, but he felt he needed to do penance for his whole life—a life of small wins and unimportant losses, of compromises that diminished him. He thought of treasures unappreciated—Millie, and his kids who'd grown up before he noticed. I am an old fool, he thought. I never knew what Millie gave me until it was gone. I don't even know the words for it. Love, of course, and something more. As though she kept me afloat without my knowing it and when her hand was gone, I started sinking. I didn't love her enough when I had the chance, or tell her. I wish there were real, physical pain that would end instead of this hurting that seizes my heart.

On Tranquilino's day, he watched the gardener trim vines, sweep the cuttings, then go into the kitchen where he cleaned, since the winter garden didn't take a full day's work. Eldon followed the slim, brown man into the house, watched his slow, rhythmic movements with the mop, the scrub cloth.

"You seem contented, amigo," said Eldon. And I'm not, he thought.

"I have enough to satisfy me," the man replied.

"Instead of sinning, I should do as you do, try direct suffering for a while." Not this chest-squeezing Millie suffering. Eldon grabbed the door jamb for a moment.

"It isn't just suffering for its own sake," said Tranquilino mildly.

"It's not the sins of the world?"

"Not just that. It is hard to explain." He dipped the scrub cloth in the bucket, lifted it and wrung out the pungent cleaning solution, then he began wiping down the cabinets near the stove. "When I use the whip, I become one with every person in the world—good and bad. And with our Lord, who suffered for us."

"You make it sound simple and, well, right."

Tranquilino lowered his head, as if to agree.

That night, very reluctantly, Tranquilino admitted Eldon to his little house. In the shadows, the gardener's face was the color of the dark adobe. A weak light shone in the room. Eldon entered and looked around for the whip. It lay on the table and there were brown stains on it.

"Show me."

Tranquilino started to say no, then saw Eldon's misery. Tranquilino unbuttoned his shirt, removed it and picked up the whip. He began a prayer to Padre Nuestro qui estas en el cielo and with the same slow, rhythmic motions as his work, he flung the leather strips first over one shoulder, then the other. The prayers continued softly and the whip found his scarred back again and again.

Eldon watched in silence. At last Tranquilino stopped, crossed himself and lay the whip down.

Eldon slowly unbuttoned his shirt.

"No, no. You are not even a Catholic," Tranquilino protested.

"I am a Christian. I know some prayers." Eldon walked like a dreamer to the table and picked up the whip. The smooth wooden handle was still warm. He flicked the leather thongs. He stared at the Christ on Tranquilino's cross and whipped the leather over his shoulder. He gasped at the stinging pain. Then he did the other shoulder. Our father, which art in heaven. Hallowed be thy name. Thy kingdom come.

He heard Tranquilino pray with him. At the end of the prayer, he stopped. His heart raced and sweat beaded on his forehead. It wasn't the pain; it was the release. Breathing heavily, he carefully placed the whip on the table. Then he knelt before the image without knowing why. Tears came to his eyes. He hadn't cried since Millie died. Tonight the tears came peacefully, without the vise in his chest.

After a while, he stood and put his shirt on, shook hands and thanked Tranquilino and walked slowly back to the big house.

*   *   *

Spring came reluctantly to Santa Fe. Crocuses and daffodils blossomed and cactus flowers budded. Slowly Eldon's garden came alive. Each evening Eldon went to Tranquilino's adobe. Some nights he didn't remember how long he had flung the whip over his shoulders. Some nights the pain stopped him after a few blows. After a week, he found the door unlocked and Tranquilino gone, but he made his penance just the same.

When he began, all thought ceased. He didn't question why he did this or what it meant. He only knew that for the time he was doing it, he was at peace.

One night, when he must have stayed late, later than he realized, he met Tranquilino as he left. A woman giggled boozily on the Spaniard's arm. He could smell the beer from them both.

"Amigo," said Eldon in disbelief. "Not you!"

"Si, yes," said Tranquilino and Eldon couldn't read his face in the darkness.

The next morning Eldon heard the woman leave, then he went to Tranquilino's door.

"Why are you, the penitente, sinning?"

"I am only human," said the gardener with face blank as a raked path.

"And I am *your* penitente."

"There must be a balance," said Tranquilino. "For your redemption, you suffer. And for mine."

Eldon had been waiting for a chance to ask, and while this didn't seem to be the right occasion, time grew short.

"I want to go with you on Good Friday," he said flatly.

"No, no. You don't know what we do. You haven't learned all you must know. Never."

234

"Then tell me."

"I may not."

"But I've heard stories about men carrying crosses."

"Anyone may carry a cross," said Tranquilino. "There's no law against that."

"Then that's what I'll do," said Eldon. "I may not get it right, but that's what I want to do."

So Tranquilino took two stout pieces of 1"16" pine, rough finished, beads of sap still oozing from the grain, fitted them together crudely and left it for Eldon.

"I won't be back until Easter Sunday, in the afternoon," he said. "I'm going to my village."

"You won't help me do it right?" asked Eldon.

"There is no way to do it wrong," answered Tranquilino. "And you must do it alone."

*   *   *

At nine Good Friday morning, Eldon picked up the heavy cross. The short piece was more than six feet and the long piece at least twelve. It wasn't so heavy that Eldon couldn't lift it to his shoulder and drag it. He set out slowly, leaving a furrow in the gravel of his driveway. He walked down the street of his subdivision and saw neighbors come to the windows. I must be completely absurd. And I don't care. This is neither secret like the Penitentes, nor correct, nor a gringo joke. But this feels right.

The boards of the cross dug into his shoulder and he laid it flat across his back as he walked Camino del Monte Sol toward Canyon Road. He stopped to rest when he had trouble breathing. By nightfall, he had reached Christo Rey church at the top of Canyon Road. He accepted a drink from a silent woman.

His hands and feet blistered. It was years since he'd walked this far in the city. The muscles of his shoulders and back knotted and he had to put the cross down and work them until the spasms stopped. He sat at the top of the city and watched the sunset, then he continued. He could see the lights from around the distant plaza. He heard music and voices and the clash of china from the restaurants along Canyon Road. People at outdoor tables stared. The street was narrow and rutted. Cars honked, but he ignored them. He was walking downhill now and the cross seemed to urge him along. Don't push, I'll get you there, he told it. He could smell his own stale sweat. People stared from their houses. He could imagine them murmuring about the crazy Anglo. This will be my penance for everything. For all the things I've done and all the things I failed to do. For Millie, for my kids, for all the people I've known.

Tourists gawked out the windows of their dusty cars. No policeman stopped him. No one tried to hinder him. One time he stopped, in the dark of the night, dozed briefly on the curb, but when his head jerked forward, he rose and picked up his cross.

By morning he reached the bottom of Canyon. He trudged slowly down De Vargas, falling now and then. He saw the city awaken, as lights came on in houses and busboys opened restaurants to air and people swept their steps and watered their flowers. Workers going to the state office building and early tourists stared at him, the crazy penitente. He smiled.

Sometime before noon he reached the small, old chapel of San Miguel. He was fearfully thirsty and stumbling every few steps by now. His legs ached. His back was a focus of pain. His shoulders and arms had lost all feeling. His knees bled through his trousers from the falls. His hair was sweat plastered to his face.

His heart lifted at the sight of the cool shadow within the church. I tried to make up for everything, he thought. He couldn't tell if the pain grabbed his chest then because everything hurt now.

The Christian brother and tourists inside San Miguel stopped as he struggled painfully up the steps. They pulled aside, staring, and let him enter. He dragged himself the last few steps to the front of the church, carefully lowered the cross on the floor and lay face down beside it, arms outspread.

"I did it," he thought. "Amen."

Joe R. Lansdale lives and works in Nacogdoches, Texas, which is both Southern and Western in atmosphere. This story reflects this, as well as a negative aspect of the Western mentality. Where some might be so overwhelmed with their love of the West they would grow up to ride the rodeo, or ranch, or farm, or just drive pick-up trucks and wear cowboy duds and believe their word and their handshake is their bond, some are more obsessed by the darker side of our frontier past. They become the modern equivalent of such gunmen and desperados as Tom Horn and Billy The Kid. Only now, they may not wear Western garb, and instead of cowboys, their immediate heroes may be popular signing stars, and instead of range wars to fight or Indians or Settlers to hire out against, they have . . .Well, read and see. Also note that what we have here is the old story of the professional passing along his knowledge to the green kid.

THE JOB

by Joe R. Lansdale

Bower pulled the sun visor down and looked in the mirror there and said, "You know, hadn't been for the travel, I'd have done alright. I could even shake my ass like him. I tell you, it drove the women wild. You should have seen em."

"Don't shake it for me," Kelly said. "I don't want to see it. Things I got to do are tough enough without having to see that."

Bower pushed the visor back. The light turned green. Kelly put the gas to the car and they went up and over a hill and turned right on Melroy.

"Guess maybe you do look like him," Kelly said. "During his fatter days, when he was on the drugs and the peanut butter."

"Yeah, but these pocks on my cheeks messes it up some. When I was on stage I had makeup on em. I looked okay then."

They stopped at a stop sign and Kelly got out a cigarette and pushed in the lighter.

"A nigger nearly tailended me here once," Kelly said. "Just come barreling down on me." He took the lighter and lit his smoke.

"Scared piss out of me. I got him out of his car and popped him some. I bet he was one careful nigger from then on." He pulled away from the stop sign and cruised.

"You done one like this before? I know you've done it, but like this?"

"Not just like this. But I done some things might surprise you. You getting nervous on me?"

"I'm alright. You know, thing made me quit the Elvis imitating was travel, cause one night on the road I was staying in this cheap motel, and it wasn't heated too good. I'd had those kind of rooms before, and I always carried couple of space heaters in the trunk of the car with the rest of my junk, you know. I got them plugged in, and I was still cold, so I pulled the mattress on the floor by the heaters. I woke up and was on fire. I had been so worn out I'd gone to sleep in my Elvis outfit. That was the end of my best white jumpsuit, you know, like he wore with the gold glitter and all. I must have been funny on fire like that, hopping around the room beating it out. When I got that suit off I was burned like the way you get when you been out in the sun too long."

"You gonna be able to do this?"

"Did I say I couldn't?"

"You're nervous. I can tell way you talk."

"A little. I always get nervous before I go on stage too, but I always came through. Crowd came to see Elvis, by god, they got Elvis. I used to sign autographs with his name. People wanted it like that. They wanted to pretend, see."

"Women mostly?"

"Uh huh."

"What were they, say, fifty-five?"

"They were all ages. Some of them were pretty young."

"Ever fuck any of em?"

"Sure, I got plenty. Sing a little Love Me Tender to them in the bedroom and they'd do whatever I wanted."

"Was it the old ones you was fucking?"

"I didn't fuck no real old ones, no. Whose idea is it to do things this way anyhow?"

"Boss, of course. You think he lets me plan this stuff? He don't want them chinks muscling in on the shrimping and all."

"I don't know, we fought for these guys. It seems a little funny."

"Reason we lost the war over there is not being able to tell one chink from another and all of them being the way they are. I think we should have nuked the whole goddamned place. Went over there when it cooled down and stopped glowing, put in a fucking Disneyland or something."

They were moving out of the city now, picking up speed.

"I don't see why we don't just whack this guy outright and not do it this way," Bower said. "This seems kind of funny."

"No one's asking you. You come on a job, you do it. Boss wants the chink to suffer, so he's gonna suffer. Not like he didn't get some warnings or nothing. Boss wants him to take it hard."

"Maybe this isn't a smart thing on account of it may not bother chinks like it'd bother us. They're different about stuff like this, all the things they've seen."

"It'll bother him," Kelly said. "And if it don't, that ain't our problem. We got a job to do and we're gonna do it. Whatever comes after comes after. Boss wants us to do different next time, we do different. Whatever he wants we do it. He's the one paying."

They were out of the city now and to the left of the highway they could see the glint of the sea through a line of scrubby trees.

"How're we gonna know?" Bower says. "One chink looks like another."

"I got a photograph. This one's got a burn on the face. Everything's timed. Boss has been planning this. He had some of the guys watch and take notes. It's all set up."

"Why us?"

"Me because I've done some things before. You because he wants to see what you're made of. I'm kind of here as your nurse maid."

"I don't need anybody to see that I do what I'm supposed to do."

They drove past a lot of boats pulled up to a dock. They drove into a small town called Wilborn. They turned a corner at Catlow Street.

"It's down here a ways," Kelly said. "You got your knife? You left your knife and brought your comb, I'm gonna whack you."

Bower got the knife out of his pocket. "Things got a lot of blades, some utility stuff. Even a comb."

"Christ, you're gonna do it with a Boy Scout knife?"

"Utility knife. The blade I want is plenty sharp, you'll see. Why couldn't we use a gun? That wouldn't be as messy. A lot easier."

"Boss wants it messy. He wants the chink to think about it some.

He wants them to pack their stuff on their boats and sail back to chink land. Either that, or they can pay their percentages like everyone else. He lets the chinks get away with things, everyone'll want to get away with things."

They pulled over to the curb. Down the street was a school. Kelly looked at his watch.

"Maybe if it was a nigger," Bower said.

"Chink, nigger, what's the difference?"

They could hear a bell ringing. After five minutes they saw kids going out to the curb to get on the buses parked there. A few kids came down the sidewalk toward them. One of them was a Vietnamese girl about eight years old. The left side of her face was scarred.

"Won't they remember me?" Bower said.

"Kids? Naw. Nobody knows you around here. Get rid of that Elvis look and you'll be okay."

"It don't seem right. In front of these kids and all. I think we ought to whack her father."

"No one's paying you to think, Elvis. Do what you're supposed to do. I have to do it and you'll wish you had."

Bower opened the utility knife and got out of the car. He held the knife by his leg and walked around front, leaned on the hood just as the Vietnamese girl came up. He said, "Hey, kid, come here a minute." His voice got thick. "Elvis wants to show you something."

Richard Christian Matheson is best known for his film work and for his highly original short stories, most of which are brief and powerful and have appeared primarily in horror markets, and have recently been gathered in his short story collection SCARS. But he writes things other than horror, the following being an example, though you could say it has its horrific elements.

I'M ALWAYS HERE

by Richard Christian Matheson

"I'm always here,
please never cry.
You may refuse,
you might ask why.
One life as two, two lives as one.
I am your rose, you are my sun."

5:47 P.M.

Daddy is still. He stuck himself and he's sleeping bad. Blow-torching; fevered. His veins blister and rush. All the rust and suffering is going for his throat. He twists and moans, soaking in nightmares. It'll hit Baby soon. His dyed hair is black crepe on white casket skin.

I've been on the road with them for three days.

I picked-up the tour in L.A. as it slid slow and sensual across America, coming up that Gibson-neck heartland and making people feel again. Be alive again.

241

All the major venues, S.R.O. Critical raves. Brilliant this, brilliant that. "Wonderment . . . Perfection . . . Horror." I covered Elvis in '76 through his Australia, Japan tour for the STONE and it feels the same. Powerful. Out of control.

Sacred.

Nashville is close. Light quilts feed the ground; warm veins. I hit PLAY and walk over to sit beside Daddy and Baby.

"How you feelin', Baby? Can we talk a little more?"

We've already laid down five hours worth. Schooling. Family. Bones. We keep our voices low. Daddy talks in his sleep. She stares out the Lear's swim-mask window, cradles freckled fingers. Nods.

"Let's get a little more into some history. I've read you and Daddy met when you were thirteen . . ."

She fingers her 7-UP. Slips a delicate finger into a hollowed cube, watches it melt; a momentary ring.

"I was just a little girl."

Her blonde hair smells like apples. I tell her and she smiles. Her voice is soft. Gentle.

"I used to listen to Daddy sing when I was a kid. Had all his records. He was all that made me happy." Her accent is Kentucky; a calming sound. "My folks drank heavy, argued heavy. It was violent. Real violent." Her expression fell somehow to its knees and wept helplessly even though it barely changed. She looked at me, sad and happy. "Daddy sang like an angel. Sounded a little like Hank Williams. I wore out every album I had. Learned to sing harmony that was perfect with him," she whispered. "We're not talking too loud are we? He has to sleep."

Daddy moans a little. The coral bed inside his nervous system cuts him. Baby strokes his brow, kisses it.

"Okay, Daddy," she whispers. "I'm here. I'm always here."

I smile.

Baby nods, gently hums the melody to *I'm Always Here* and I remember hearing the haunting ballad when I was losing my marriage; drowning. It soared with mournful, aching confession and always made me cry.

"I loved that song, first time I heard Daddy sing it. That's when I knew for sure I'd do anything for him." She looks off. "Literally anything."

The Lear is slashing clouds and they bleed grey. We'll be landing in Nashville in ten minutes. Daddy and Baby go on at eight-thirty, right after the Oak Ridge Boys. I have orchestra pit, dead center. ROLLING STONE wants it all from up close. The faces. The music.

The poignant impossibility.

"After Daddy won the Grammy for best album in '81, it all started going bad. We've all heard about his marriage failing, money troubles. Why did he lose it all?" I'm already tinkering with the header for the piece. But it needs work. Something that plays with "seamless." I'm not happy with it.

Baby shades a palm over tired eyes; a priest closing the lids on a dead face. She thinks back, seeing the photo album that always hurts, the one that's always half-open; memories bound and trapped. A phrase occurs to me: "terrible questions, sad answers." From one of Daddy's early songs, "Being Left Ain't Right."

". . . drugs. All kinds. Daddy's still fighting it. It's hard for him. He's so sensitive. But . . ." she takes his sleeping hand as a nightmare wraps him in barbed wire. ". . . more than that, I guess you'd really have to call it loneliness. From the deepest part of himself. First time I managed to get backstage and talk to Daddy, I could see his eyes were like . . . wounds. It was more than being an addict. It was . . ." she licked lips, "I don't know, the despair, I suppose. Everybody he cared about was gone. His heroes. His family. They'd all left, abandoned him."

She sipped more of the 7-UP. Wiped her soft mouth with a "DADDY AND BABY '88 TOUR" napkin.

"I wanted to be there for him. So . . ."

"So, you followed him."

"Yes."

"Everywhere?"

"Yes."

"Like a groupie?"

"People said it. I never was that. I was his friend. His mother. Later, it's true . . . his lover."

I pulled out a cassette. Baby and Daddy's first album, MOTHER AND LOVER. Baby takes it, feels it in her curious, childlike hands.

"He dedicated all the songs to me. 'Course the biggest was . . ."

"*I'm Always Here* . . ."

"*I'm Always Here,* yes. It was our biggest seller until the new album. But you can never feel the same as the first one. The thrill."

We've gotten to the hard part. About the procedure.

243

I choose words carefully, watching her features for reaction as if staring at a radar screen, checking for impending collisions.

"This question is . . . very personal . . ."

"It's alright. Go ahead."

". . . did it hurt?"

She smiles the way some people do when they're in terrible pain. "Yes. It was extremely painful. After, that is. It hadn't been done before. But the doctor was reassuring . . . he'd been researching . . . in the same area of . . . procedure."

"Only in reverse."

"That's right."

"How long did it take?"

"Almost two days. Thirty-seven hours." She laughed a little. "You're probably wondering how I talked Daddy into it, right? Most folks wonder that."

She grew serious once again.

"When I met him, he told me he had nothing left and nowhere to go. He was sick. Owed money to agents, promoters, the government . . . it was awful."

"And he was ill."

"That's why he finally agreed. The doctors said he would die. He was weak. His whole body was like . . . a crumbling statue. It was just a matter of time." Her voice became loving, confessional. "I had to help. No one else cared like me."

I checked through my notes. Lawsuits. Divorce papers, bankruptcy bullshit. The guy's life hit the wall at a hundred and the windshield cut him into bloody, monthly payments that were impossible.

"He was dying. You have to understand. This giant talent laying in the hospital bed like some frail . . . child. The man I'd loved since I was a little girl. I gave blood, organs . . . whatever they needed."

"It wasn't enough." I was reading from an article in NEWS-WEEK; "Medical Breakthroughs" page. Couple years back.

She shook her head. No. It wasn't enough.

The Lear started down at a crash angle. I killed the tape recorder, returned to my seat, clicked my belt on. I glanced over and saw Baby talking softly into Daddy's ear, combing his hair with maternal fingers. She kissed his colorless hand and I could see he was speeding, sweating; tissues beyond repair.

I'M ALWAYS HERE

It started to hit Baby as the jet landed and she cried on Daddy's shoulder, like a little girl, a faint agony tearing her in half.

* * *

9:15 P.M.

Scalpers are getting rich. The guy behind me is standing and stomping. "Yeah! Baby we *luuvvv* you, hon!"

I turn when he whistles. He's some six-pack crammed into a fat Stetson and he's clapping and whooping it up along with the rest of the screaming Grand Ol' Opry House. My photographer is Green Beret, squat-crawling across the footlights like they were land mines. He's snapping Nikon slices of Daddy and Baby taking bows. They're dressed in sparkley, Country Western outfits that cost over ten thousand dollars. I asked at the Marriott penthouse when they were dressing for the show; a story I can't begin to tell.

But, by then, I will tell you, Baby was completely high. But it doesn't hit her as hard as Daddy. His system swallows most of it. She told me after the pain subsides, she feels numb and giddy. Sometimes paranoid. Daddy told her he was doing his best to cut the stuff off. Leave it. Drive past it like a hideous car accident you never wanted to see. But it'll take a few more months. Their doctors are furious. Everyone is trying to understand. Baby helps them when they see the love she has for Daddy.

Baby said it was worth it for her to wait.

A dozen rosy kleigs bouquet on the empty stage and as the two step into its calming circle, they thank the crowd; bow more. Baby smiles. Daddy looks serious, deeper; sadder.

Then, he softly touches the guitar strings at his waist and a radiant chord begins the trance. The audience feels it. I feel it. My photographer, changing film, stops moving, stares up at the stage.

Daddy starts to sing a low, suffering lullabye and Baby joins him, a foamy background harmony. He sings his half, looking into her eyes.

> "I need to tell you,
> I would've died,
> To say it outright
> should bruise my pride.

> But without your love
> to feed my life, without your heart
> at my side . . .
> Honey
> for nothing . . .

I look around and hear tears fill a thousand eyes as Baby twists her head to look at Daddy. They sing the chorus together, as if cutting themselves open and mixing their blood.

> "I'm always here,
> please never cry.
> You may refuse,
> you might ask why.
> One life as two, two lives as one.
> I am your rose, you are my sun."

*　　*　　*

The melody is slow, beautiful; feeling. The notes are inevitable and Baby's smile is a twenty-year-old Madonna looking at her perfect child. As they sing, their separate bodies now joined as one, which feeds Daddy, he is singing pure and strong like the old days. Like when he got up there with Hank Williams and Merle Haggard and Carl Perkins and knocked everybody dead.

How the surgeon was able to fuse their bodies, allowing Baby's younger, healthier fluids and strength to nurture Daddy's ailing flesh has been discussed on talk shows, analyzed on news shows, lampooned on comedy shows. It's shocking and touching to people. Repugnant and life-affirming. Everybody has a reaction.

I found it a hideous misuse of medical technique when I first heard about it. A grotesque immorality. Before I'd met Baby and Daddy. Until I saw the love she felt for him and the total dependency he couldn't hide, no matter how strong or renown he once was. Bathed in the warmth of her giving and her love, he had returned to being a child, carried not in her womb but outside it.

The lights have dimmed to a single spot and Daddy and Baby are singing A cappella, staring into one another's eyes; lovers, friends, mother and child.

246

I'M ALWAYS HERE

"I'm always here,
please never cry.
You may refuse,
you might ask why."

*   *   *

Throughout the house, couples are embracing, looking in silhouette like countless Daddy's and Baby's, joined for a moment in unguarded vulnerability. As I look around, I fight remembering how wonderful it was to be in love and hold my wife close when we were going strong.

I look up at Daddy and he's smiling for the first time all day. Baby whispers she loves him as the crowd screams for more and I suddenly notice how alone I feel.

"One life as two,
two lives as one.
I am your rose,
you are my sun."

*   *   *

The applause plunged and swirls around me; deafening rapids and I start to cry, wanting so bad to be close to someone again.

Chet Williamson is a nice quiet guy who writes some pretty mean things. I think with this story he's thrown his hat over the windmill. He's captured that old style of telling a story and melded it to the modern with surprising deftness. This one is like looking down the cold, dark interior of a rifle barrel. You'll see what I mean.

YORE SKIN'S JES'S SOFT 'N PURTY... HE SAID.
(Page 243)

by Chet Williamson

It was a land where a man could be himself, where none of the feebly voiced restrictions of society were to say him nay. The mountains, the winding trails, the arching blue sky alone were the only judges of a man's mettle. Here in the west a man could be a man, and a woman a woman. She knew that now, knew it with all the implacable truth of nature and of the west.

He turned his face toward her as his horse galloped into the dawn.

Eustace P. Saunders shut *The Desperado* with a delighted shudder, sat for a moment, his languid eyes closed, then opened the book again and looked at his illustrations, finding the smooth plates easily, sweet oases of images between the chunks of text. But dear God, what *wonderful* text. Here was romance, here was adventure, here was balm for the soul jaded by the tired and stolid fictions of society life. His gaze hung upon the frontispiece, wherein Jack Binns, the desperado, sat by the midnight campfire with Maria Prescott, the eastern heiress, touching her hand with wonder. Eustace didn't need to read the caption below—

"'Yore skin's jes's soft 'n purty . . .'" he said.

—and below, the page number on which the illustrated scene appeared.

Again he blessed Arthur Hampton at Harper's for giving him the assignment. Not that he had needed it from a financial standpoint, for he was far busier than he had ever been, regularly doing illustrations for *McClure's, Leslie's Weekly, The Century,* and *The Red Book,* as well as books. Indeed, even though pictures bearing the signature of E.P. Saunders had appeared in the popular magazines since 1883, these first few years of the new century had been more rewarding than ever, artistically as well as financially. The black and white washes he had done for last year's new Robert Chambers novel had been among his best, as was the gouache work he had done for the F. Marion Crawford short story collection. And then . . . *The Desperado!*

Arthur, God bless him, had seen something in Eustace's work that he felt might complement M. Taggart Westover's first book. It still amazed Eustace that Arthur had not gone after an artist who had already proven himself competent with western themes, like Keller, whose work for *The Virginian* had been so fine. Still, Arthur had thrown down the gauntlet, and Eustace, welcoming a change from the crinolines and frock coats of contemporary city novels, took it up, but with more than a touch of hesitancy.

Still, the final results were admirable. Arthur called them Eustace's best work ever, and Eustace had to agree. It was because he worked them in oils, he felt, and also because he gave them his soul.

He had originally intended to do them in gouache, but, upon reading the book and falling utterly in love with it, decided to work in oils instead, even though the reproductions would be monochromatic. There was more *color* in this book, he thought, than any other he had illustrated, indeed, than any other he had ever read. Then too, the fact that they were done in oils made them easier to repaint when they came back from Harper's.

For repaint them he did, placing his own face and form over that of one of the main characters. It was not Jack Binns, the desperado, whose visage vanished beneath layers of paint, but Maria Prescott, the heroine, for Eustace P. Saunders was a mental practitioner of what he considered a Secret Vice, referred to, when it was done so at all by people of breeding, as The Love That Dares Not Speak Its Name. Only in the case of Eustace P. Saunders, it was so secret that Eustace had never practiced it save in the darkened boudoirs of his imagination. It was not that he had never had the opportunity, for he suspected that a number of his colleagues shared the same predilection, and had even received a proposal of an illicit, illegal, and societally perverse nature from one of the younger illustrators who was as open with his brush as he seemed to be with his longings. Eustace, out of fear of exposure, had tactfully refused. Indeed, Eustace had been chaste with both sexes for all of his forty-three years, and had intended to remain thus until *The Desperado* seduced his mind and turned his fancies to outdoor love of a most healthful and manly nature.

He placed the book down upon his reading table with a sigh of regret that he had finished it once again, then brightened as he realized that its grand adventure could *begin* again as well. All he need do was turn to page one. Dear God, what a place—the west, where a man could act as he pleased without fear of polite society's repercussions, where his fancies could come to blazing, lusty life, a land where the pseudo-life of his paintings could exist in total reality.

Eustace stood, sipped another few drops of sherry, and climbed the steps to his studio, where he turned on the lights, illuminating a number of paintings and other works sitting neatly on easels or drawing tables. He walked to the closed door at the end of the long room, withdrew a key from the pocket of his lounging jacket, and unlocked the door. Inside was a small chamber ten feet by eight, with paintings and drawings both framed and unframed leaning against the walls. Eustace drew a white sheet from half a dozen large, unframed canvases, wrapped his spindly arms about them, and carried them into the studio, where he leaned them against a table, drew up a chair, and sat down.

The effort had made him a trifle breathless, but he grew more breathless still when he looked at the first painting. There he was, Eustace P. Saunders, seated next to Jack Binns, who was holding his hand and gazing lovingly into his eyes, which gleamed orange in the firelight. He could almost hear the words, spoken in a soft, gentle drawl—"Yore skin's jes's soft 'n purty . . ."

Eustace looked for a long time, until he could hear not only his lover's voice, but the crackle of logs burning in the fire, smell the biscuits and coffee he had cooked for Jack and himself, feel the soft wind blowing across the Badlands.

After a time, the vision faded, as it always did, and he turned to the next picture, and the next, and the next, until at length he arrived at the end of the book, in which Maria, at first held for ransom, eventually wins the love of the wild outlaw, reforms him, marries him, and stays with him in his vast and honest land. In the final illustration, she stands outside their modest cabin, built with their own toil, and waves to her husband and lover as he rides off to begin his day's work on the range—

"He turned his face toward her as his horse galloped into the dawn."

But now, instead of Maria, a plain white blouse, a long leather skirt, and a bandanna replacing her eastern finery, this painting, like all the others, bore the image of Eustace P. Saunders, dressed in western garb, waving goodbye to Jack.

"Why can't it be that way?" said Eustace, tears forming in his eyes for his lost love, his love never found. "Why?"

Then it came to him. It could. In the west, land of promise and dreams, anything was possible. He didn't have to go on painting his desires, for in the west he could live them. *The Desperado* had told him that, and he believed it as he had never believed the tales of the Christ he had learned at his mother's knees. With all his heart, he believed in this primitive kingdom where none would say him nay.

*　　*　　*

He did not go into the west, however, with the stated nor even the conscious intention of seeking love. He went, as he put it to Arthur Hampton and others, in order to breathe in the heart of the west, to immerse himself therein in the hopes that his art could faithfully portray the country's sights and sounds and spirit. To this end, Eustace took along a great many supplies: innumerable sketch books, rolls of canvas, oils, watercolors, and more. His baggage totalled a dozen large trunks, for, since he did not truly intend to return east, he thought it prudent to bring as many of his possessions as possible, all the fewer that would need to be sent for later.

His destination, chosen after only brief deliberation, was Deadwood, South Dakota, the same area in which *The Desperado* was set. Eustace travelled alone, beginning on a bright April day a series of train rides that brought him to Deadwood four days later than had been scheduled, an hiatus that, rather than discouraging him, only further whetted his appetite for his final destination. A transfer from the St. Paul Railway to the Northwestern in Rapid City proved to be the final stumbling block, but, after receiving assurances from the conductor that all his trunks were safely aboard the baggage car, Eustace P. Saunders arrived in Deadwood late on a Friday afternoon.

He had no time to drink in the aroma of the west, which, to his way of thinking, was rather soured by the smell of horse droppings which carpeted the dirt street next to the ramshackle railroad station, for he had to immediately attend to his trunks, which had been unceremoniously dumped onto the platform by the baggage car man, who, without a wave of regret, pulled the massive door closed as the train rattled out of the station toward its next stop. Eustace sought and obtained the attention of a noble young scion of the west, and gave him a quarter dollar to go to the hotel and inform the manager that Mister Saunders had arrived and needed a cab for his luggage. When a half hour passed and the loiterer did not return, Eustace asked the man at the ticket window for directions to the hotel, and if he would be kind enough to watch Eustace's trunks while he fetched a cabman.

The man replied through a mist of tobacco spittle that he was closing up and had no leisure to observe luggage, but that he would stop at the hotel and inform the proprietor that a guest was in need of teamster service.

After another half hour, a rickety wagon drawn by two horses dropped anchor in the Sargasso of horse dung. Painted in faded letters on two of the remaining side boards was the legend *Barkley Hotel, Deadwood*. The coachman, a living embodiment, Eustace thought, of the old west, jumped down from his box, entirely oblivious to the way his boots sank into the equestrian mire. "You Sanders?" he said through a broken picket fence of yellow teeth, making Eustace think that perhaps the art of dentistry had not penetrated this far west.

"That's Saunders," Eustace replied. "I have some trunks." And he gestured to the small mountain on the platform.

"Holy jacksh_t," the man expostulated. "Never seen so g_dd_m many in my f___in' life!"

Muttering vociferously, the rustic nonetheless carried them one at a time from platform to wagon, dropping only one in the reeking miasma. Eustace opened his mouth to protest, but a harsh glare from the man made him slap his mouth shut. When the trunks were loaded, the frontier coachman climbed onto his box and fixed Eustace with a withering stare. "You comin' or ain'tcha?"

Eustace glanced tremulously at the surface he had to cross to arrive at the coach, then said to himself, "I am, after all, in the west, where a man's character is not diminished by the presence of honest soil on his boots," and stepped boldly into the muck, wincing only once when part of the gelid mass crept over the edge of his shoe.

Despite the presence of horse manure in his heel, Deadwood struck Eustace P. Saunders as a veritable fairyland. This then was the west, and these bold men and women who lined the wooden sidewalks were the pioneers of their age. He felt a tingle of hormonal as well as intellectual excitement as he recalled the second plate of *The Desperado*:

"It was a new world to her, and one she feared to enter."

He wished he could open the trunk that contained the *Desperado* oils and gaze at it right now (they were the only finished works that he had brought with him, for how could he have his maid discover them when she prepared his other work for delivery to the west!). But he could see it in his mind's eye well enough—Eustace P. Saunders riding into the town in a stagecoach, looking out from its windows at the rough men lining the street in front of the saloon, leering at him with unnameable desires in their head beneath their ten-gallon hats.

And God, yes! there was a saloon now, and, glory of glories, on the other half of the building that housed it was the Barkley Hotel. It had been everything he had dreamed it would be, a rough-hewn, clapboard edifice of three stories, with loungers out front waiting no doubt for the sun to go down. But none of them, he noticed, wore a gunbelt. It was a bit of a disappointment.

As Eustace walked into the hotel, the imprecations of the teamster dying away behind him, the idlers eyed him, but Eustace felt that it was more out of curiosity than from any interest in a lasting bond of manly friendship. Ah well, he thought, Maria Prescott too had been looked on with mere curiosity upon her arrival in the west, as primitives are apt to gaze upon a rare and lovely flower without understanding its potential for pollination.

The manager of the hotel, Mr. Owen Barkley, was rather more solicitous than had been the grizzled coachman, and Eustace was relieved to find that he had indeed been expected, even though Barkley addressed him as Mr. Sanders, perpetuating the error the coachman had made. Barkley himself showed Eustace to his room on the second floor, a clean if Spartan chamber boasting the scant amenities that most third class eastern hotels would have offered.

"And what brings you to our little town?" asked Barkley, a fat and florid man in his early sixties.

"Art, really," Eustace replied.

"Art?"

Eustace then spoke of the magazines and books he had illustrated, and Barkley's eyes glowed. "I've got that Chambers book— my sister back east sent it to me last Christmas. And we've got lots of your magazines in the lobby—*Country Gentleman, Harper's,* lots of them—d_mn good pictures in them too. An artist, eh? My, that's really something."

They chatted all during the time it took for the coachman to bring up all twelve trunks, and it took only until trunk number three for Eustace to inquire about outlaws.

"Outlaws?" Barkley said, as though the word was foreign to him. "I'll tell you, Mr. Sanders, there sure aren't many outlaws these days. We're pretty d_mn civilized now out here. But when I was a youngster, well, things were mighty different then . . ."

It took until trunk number five for Eustace to persuade Barkley to end his reminiscences of gunfights past. "Please do try and think of some in the present day," Eustace pleaded. "You see, the reason I came out here was to sketch and paint some of the more, shall we say, adventuresome of your denizens, in order to add as much verisimilitude as possible to my work."

"Uh-huh." Barkley nodded. "Uh-huh. So you're lookin' for some bad men. Well, I'll tell you, anybody commits crimes nowadays our country sheriff—that's Zed Dorwart—arrests them pretty d_mn quick, so they're either behind bars or hung."

"But isn't there anyone," Eustace persevered as trunk number six arrived, "who has eluded the law, who is secreted in some hole-in-the-wall, as it were?"

Barkley thought for a moment. "Nope," he said.

Then the coachman *cum* teamster *cum* porter spoke up. "Them Brogger brothers are mean sonsab_tches." This uninvited comment earned the menial a glance from his employer sharp enough to send him out of the room with more haste than was his wont.

"The Brogger brothers?" Eustace repeated. "Now who are they?"

Barkley shook his head grimly. "You don't want to get mixed up with the Brogger boys," he cautioned. "They're not outlaws, they're just crazy."

It took until trunk number eleven for Eustace to wheedle the full story of Olaf and Frederick Brogger from Barkley. They were two brothers in their early thirties. Born of a Norwegian father and a Scotch-Irish mother, they were hated by the god-fearing Norwegians in the county because they gave Norwegians a bad name. Rejecting the farm life of their father, they had purchased a small spread where they raised enough stock to get by, though many said that it was not their skinny herd of cattle, but thievery around the Deadwood area that brought them the little money they had. Nothing had ever been proven, however, though it was felt that the Broggers had more luck than skill or intelligence.

"Mean as coyotes but a lot dumber," was Barkley's studied opinion. "Used to come to the saloon, bother people. Zed told 'em not to come back no more, so they went down to Terry, but even the women there won't have nothin' to do with them. Cause fights, sometimes people been found beaten, but they won't say who 'twas done it. One time a few years back Zed found a feller beat somethin' awful—died without comin' to. He'd been in an argument with Fred Brogger a few days before."

"Fred—is he the worse?" Eustace inquired.

"You could say. Olaf's quieter, but still waters run deep. Fred's the loud one, and Olaf does what he says."

The poor lad, thought Eustace. No doubt influenced by his evil older brother to follow a life of crime. And he thought of the illustration on page 362, of Jack Binns placing a protective left arm around Maria's (now Eustace's) shoulder, while his right hand pointed a pistol at his former partner in crime, Texas Bill Wyatt—

"So,' Wyatt sneered, 'throwin' over yer old pard fer a skirt!'"

"YORE SKIN'S JES'S SOFT 'N PURTY. . ." HE SAID.

Jack Binns had seen the light. Love had made him do so. And Eustace had read time and again that love was capable of a great many such things.

"I'd like to meet them," he told Barkley.

The hotelier's eyes grew wide, and his face even more pink than before. "No sir. You stay away from them two. Bad medicine, both of 'em. Some of the other things you hear said about them, why, I wouldn't even repeat to a Christian gentleman."

Through the door came box number twelve, and its bearer let it drop onto the straw mat floor with a weary sigh. "That's all of 'em," he said, extended his hand for the silver dollar that Eustace deposited therein, and left the room.

"Hope you have a good stay," said Barkley. "We got a fine restaurant downstairs, and the saloon is open till midnight. You need anything, just pull that cord on the wall."

"Now that you mention it," Eustace said, wiggling his toes, "do you have a bootblack in town?"

*   *   *

Rather than go through his trunks to find another pair of the several he had brought, he waited until his shoes came back, and in the meantime removed his soiled socks and washed his feet in the basin. Freshly shod, he descended to the restaurant, a surprisingly comfortable room that could have been uprooted from New York's west side, had it not been for the more rowdy clientele. Eustace ordered a steak with potatoes, and watched the people, some of them cowboys surely, finish their meals and pass through the swinging doors into the saloon side of the building, from whence came the strains of ragtime music and frequent hearty shouts.

His meal finished, Eustace joined the throng, sitting at a table well away from the bar, where the most active customers sat and from which the loudest yells (often good-natured curses) emanated. He suspected that the sherry he nursed had been sitting on some dusty under-shelf for many years, as it seemed to have turned to a syrupy vinegar.

He had just made up his mind to take a chance on the beer, when he heard a familiar voice behind him. "You're askin' about the Buggers."

Eustace turned and saw the wizened old gentleman who had carried his trunks. "I beg your pardon?"

"The *Buggers*. The ones you'se talkin' about with Barkley."

"Do you mean the Broggers?"

"I calls 'em as I sees 'em." Without being invited, the man sat across the small table from Eustace. His aroma, as before, told Eustace that he was less than fastidious in his toilet habits. "You wanta see 'em?"

A thrill ran through Eustace. "Olaf and Frederick?" he said breathlessly, and the man made a face. "Yes, I would like very much to meet them."

"I can take ya there. Fer a price."

"Where?"

"Terry Peak. They place is north o' there."

Eustace nodded sagely. "Yes, Mr. Barkley mentioned Terry."

The old man shook his head disgustedly. "Not Terry, not that little sh_thole in the wall. I'm talkin' Terry *Peak*. You wanta go there?"

"Yes. Yes, I do."

"How much it worth to ya?"

"Well, I, I—"

"Ten dollars?"

"Well, yes, of course, I'd be willing to pay ten dollars."

"All right then, you be in back of the hotel at five o'clock tomorrow morning."

"Five o'clock?" It was a bit early. Eustace seldom broke his fast before nine.

"It's near 'bout eight miles to there, and I start workin' for Barkley at seven. It's then or never."

"Well . . ." Eustace thought about the cold and darkness of five o'clock in the morning, then thought about a land "where none of the feebly voiced restrictions of society were to say him nay," of handsome young rogues living under a sky as blue as an outlaw's eyes, of high cheekbones sculpted by the western wind, of taut muscles roiling beneath skin bronzed by the western sun, of Olaf and Frederick.

Only they wouldn't be called that, would they? No, they would be Oley and Fred, the Brogger Boys, scourge of the west, with passions as fierce as the country that bred them—passion for the land, for adventure, and for other, more secret cravings that they might never have suspected, but that could be awakened . . .

"'Yore skin's jes's soft 'n purty—'"

"Whut?" The old man grimaced. "Whut you say?"

Eustace cleared his throat. "Five o'clock will be just fine."

* * *

He was unable to sleep at all that night, since he could not find the alarm clock that he was sure he had packed, and he did not want to inform the front desk that he was to be awakened so early, as that might have aroused Barkley's interest. Even had he been able to find the alarm clock, his excitement was too great to permit slumber. He was, however, able to uncover the clothing that he had purchased in New York especially for this occasion. The outfit consisted of a checkered shirt, a leather vest, a pair of hand-tooled boots (not overly ostentatious), and rugged dungarees, to be held up by a belt that matched the subtle pattern etched on the boots. He sponge-bathed thoroughly before dressing, and made certain to wear his softest underclothing.

Just before five o'clock he added the final touch—a large, white, soft-brimmed hat with a leather band. He tilted it on his head until he fancied the look was jaunty enough, then took a deep breath and walked down the back stairs and out into the biting morning cold.

He had expected to find the old man there with the hotel wagon, so was quite surprised to find instead his cicerone astride one horse and holding a second by the reins. "Whutcha starin' at?" the man asked. "Mount up 'n let's go."

"You want me to . . . ride that?"

The man stared at him for a moment. "Whut you *want* to do? F__k it?"

"But . . . what about the wagon?" said Eustace, stammering both from fear and the cold.

"Can't take a d_mn wagon where we're goin'. Now mount up and stop funnin' me."

"But I can't ride!" Eustace admitted.

The old man shook his head. "Sh_t," he muttered, and spat in the dust.

A brief lesson in equestrianism ensued, and in another five minutes Eustace was seated astride the horse, one white-knuckled hand gripping the saddlehorn, the other holding tightly to the reins. "Jes' hold on to the b_st_rd," the old man said, "and he'll follow me— and keep that d_mn foot in the stirrup!"

Once Eustace learned the folly of bouncing upward while the horse was sinking earthward, the comfort of the ride increased, and within a few miles he found that he was actually enjoying the motion, although the area of his anatomy that straddled the saddle was beginning to feel a marked tenderness. After five miles of riding, however, the tenderness became undeniable soreness as the old man turned off the main road onto a stony trail on which the speed of the mounts was not reduced to compensate for the increased irregularity of their route's surface. In short, Eustace ached unbearably in his manly parts, and it was only by keeping the beauties and glories of what lay before him in his mind that he was able to curb his whimpering as his horse's foot slipped once again, jostling him painfully.

After what seemed an interminable ride through spindly trees and over an infinity of boulders, they came out upon a small plain between the trees and what looked to Eustace like a tall mountain. "See 'at cabin up air?" the man called back to him.

Eustace squinted through the morning haze and was able to distinguish a small building nestled amidst the trees at the base of the mountain, which he rightly assumed was the aforementioned Terry Peak.

"'At's it," said the man, and turned his mount so that it came back to Eustace's. "Got my ten bucks?"

Eustace nodded, took ten dollars from the change purse in his vest pocket, and handed it to the man. "Aren't you going to take me up and introduce me?"

"Innerduce ya? Yer funnin' me agin."

"But you'll wait here, won't you?"

"Wait? Wait fer whut?"

"Why, for me, of course! How will I get back?"

"You *come*, didn't ya? You get back the way you *come*."

"But I . . . well, I really wasn't paying attention."

"Sweet J_s_s Chr_st in a g_dd_mn wh_rehouse!" his guide ejaculated. "F__kin' h_ll, ain't you got the f__kin' sense God give a f__kin' goat? Just follow the f__kin' *trail*, fer cr_ssakes! The horse'll getcha back. G_dd_mn dudes . . ."

The man dug his heels into his horse's sides and started to pick

260

his way back down the trail. Eustace watched him go, feeling suddenly lost and alone. What if the Brogger brothers were not at
home? He sincerely doubted that they would have a menial with
whom he could leave a card.

Still and all, it was rather early, and he wondered if they had
even risen yet. Perhaps it might be better, he considered, to wait for
a short time until he observed signs of stirring within the brothers'
humble home. Finding such a course sensible, he attempted to urge
his steed onward toward the cabin, but no matter how he tried to
persuade it, it refused to stir, and he decided his only recourse was
to dismount and walk the remaining distance.

The dismounting, however, was more easily said than done.
Unable to recall how he had come to be sitting on the horse in the
first place, Eustace was able to disentangle himself from the
Laocoon-like web of harness and stirrups by disengaging both feet
and pushing himself slowly backward until he slipped off the rear of
the mount. Reaching the earth, he attempted to keep his footing,
but was unable to, and the seat of his dungarees came into oblique
contact with the steaming pile of droppings the weary steed had
evacuated but a short time before. Wiping himself as clean as possible with leaves, Eustace took the bridle and led the horse to a nearby
tree, where he tied it with a square knot, and then started to walk
toward the cabin.

As he drew nearer the modest abode, the picture came strongly
to his memory of himself, dressed very similarly, walking toward the
hole-in-the-wall of Jack Binns, for, after having escaped the lustful
clutches of Texas Bill Wyatt, Maria, instead of returning to Deadwood to inform the law of all she has suffered, returns instead to
Jack's hideout:

"Her heart pounded as she neared the cabin, knowing that her
own true love, dangerous as he might be to the rest of the world,
was within." (Page 414)

And Eustace's heart pounded now, pounded with excited an-
ticipation as the cabin grew nearer. There was no smoke rising
from its stone chimney, and no noise from within. Though he was
tempted to look through one of the uncurtained windows, his
eastern gentility restrained him from doing so, so he merely sat on
the natural stone stoop that served this Romulus and Remus of the
range as a front porch, readjusted his trousers so that he ached only
mildly, and waited.

It was not until he sat down on an unmoving surface that he realized just how tired he was. A night without sleep and eight miles of hard riding had exhausted him, and he allowed his head to droop, his eyes to close, and he slept and dreamed.

He dreamed of a vast prairie, of Olaf Brogger or Jack Binns (they were of course identical) standing at his side, their arms around each other's waists, of looking into Olaf/Jack's clear, honest eyes, of Jack/Olaf's leathery but soft lips opening to speak, of the words coming out like the scent of wild roses on the free wind—

"Vat the h_ll is *this*?"

When Eustace opened his eyes he knew he must have slept for more than a few minutes, for the sky was far brighter and the sun further up in the sky. He blinked several times to adjust his eyes to the additional illumination, and realized that the voice he had heard had not been in his dream.

"Who're *you*?" The words were harsh and guttural, spoken with a hooting accent Eustace had never heard before. He looked up and saw, glaring down at him, a pale-bodied man wearing only a pair of red flannel drawers. A mop of tousled blond hair capped a stubbled face deeply fissured with pockmarks.

"Olaf?" came another voice from inside.

"Some stranger out here," Olaf called to the one inside, and examined Eustace quickly with his eyes. "No gun, though. Vat you here for?"

Eustace stumbled to his feet, stepped off the stoop, doffed his hat, and made a short bow with his head. "You're Olaf Brogger?"

"Who vants to know?" The man was shorter than Eustace had expected, but had a chest like a barrel.

"My name is Eustace P. Saunders. I'm an illustrator from New York City."

The door slammed open, and another man whom Eustace took to be Frederick Brogger came outside. His hair had a reddish tint, his face was as scarred as his brother's, and he wore a night shirt, from beneath whose hem could be glimpsed the end of his dangling member. Eustace glanced away quickly. "Who's this?" Frederick asked.

Eustace reintroduced himself, trying to keep his gaze only on the men's faces.

"Vat you mean an illusdrader?" asked Frederick.

"I draw pictures. For magazines and books."

262

"I saw a book vunce," Olaf said. "Our mother had a book."

"Shut up, Olaf," Frederick said, punctuating the command with a blow to the arm.

Eustace noticed that Olaf did not even wince. Oh noble and brave lad, Eustace thought, it is as I had thought—an artistic temperament restrained by a crude and unfeeling sibling. A rough Esau to your kindly Jacob.

"So vat you vant here?" asked Frederick.

"I thought I might . . . draw your pictures."

"Vhy?"

"I had heard . . . that is to say, in Deadwood . . . that you were, um, rather rustic and free individuals."

"They vould say anything about us in Deadwood," Frederick said, splitting a morning gobbet of phlegm into the dust. Then a look of shrewdness came into his cratered face. "You pay us to draw our pictures?"

"Well, yes, I'd be happy to."

"You haf money?" Olaf asked.

Eustace smiled tenderly at the lad. "Yes, of course."

"Who come out here vith you?"

Why let them think he had been guided? Much more romantic, after all, for him to have sought them on his own. Besides, he didn't even know his old guide's name. "No one," he prevaricated. "I came alone."

The two brothers nodded in unison. "So," said Frederick. "You vant to draw now?"

"Well, actually I haven't brought any materials along. I really wanted to meet you first, get acquainted. I think it's very important to know one's subject before beginning work. I mean to say, I do a great deal of research before I—"

"Research?" Olaf said, his bushy eyebrows furrowed.

"Yes, research, uh, gathering background information, um . . ." My, Eustace thought, this was not going smoothly at all. Then the image came to him, and he smiled. "Scouting the trail, so to speak."

"Scouting the trail," Frederick repeated, and nodded. "Come inside, Mister Illusdrader. Ve haf coffee."

Eustace followed the two brothers into the cabin, the furnishings of which consisted of a small table, two chairs, and, near the fireplace, a bed with a mattress of straw ticking on which blankets were tossed at random. Pegs on the wall held a modest assortment of clothing, as well as several rifles, and rough hewn shelves contained a few dishes and some cans of food. Piles of gear whose purpose Eustace could not guess lay in the corners. "Sit down," Frederick said, gesturing to the bed while he and Olaf each took a chair.

At first fearful that his smeared dungarees might stain their bed, Eustace hesitated, but when he observed the condition of the bed, he felt that the traces of horse dung remaining on his trousers could do no further harm, and sat. For a long time the men only looked at each other without speaking, and although Eustace was uncomfortable in the silence, it at least gave him leisure to observe the Brogger brothers.

Olaf was by far the more attractive of the pair, stout and well muscled, and although his face was pitted by smallpox scars, there was a regular handsomeness about his features, and the brightness of his hair, even in its uncombed and unwashed state, was stunning. The same blond shade was evident in the hair of his chest, particularly in the tufts about his nipples. Eustace glanced at Frederick, who was apparently oblivious to the nakedness of his nether parts, his legs spread in seeming unconcern of his lack of modesty.

"Olaf," Frederick said finally, "get us some coffee."

The lad obediently went to the fireplace, removed a blue enamel pot from a hook, and poured the steaming liquid into three chipped and cracked cups. The first he gave to Frederick, and the second he took to Eustace, who made sure to touch the dirty but strong fingers that gave him the cup. Whatever message of masculine friendship was sent was also received, as Olaf paused, and looked deeply into Eustace's eyes, a look that thrilled him to the marrow of his bones. Things seemed, he thought, to be going rather nicely after all.

Olaf sat down, and they drank their coffee and continued to look at one another. Finally Frederick spoke again. "Vat you looking at Olaf for?"

Eustace snapped his head around toward the older brother. "I beg your pardon?"

"You're looking at Olaf. You're looking at him as if he were a *vooman*."

"Oh . . . oh no. I'm sure you're mistaken."

But Eustace was wrong. Frederick was not mistaken. Frederick knew the look because he had felt it on his own countenance many

264

times before. Unbeknownst to Eustace, but hinted at among the denizens of Deadwood and Terry, Frederick and Olaf, unable to find solace of a romantic nature among the looser women of either town, had for a long time resorted to comforting each other by the very homoerotic means of which Eustace had only dreamed.

Frederick's eyes narrowed. "You know, Mister Illusdrader, maybe you're right. Maybe vith your pretty clothes and your pretty smell, it's *you* who vants to be the vooman."

There was a way to come to this, Eustace thought, but surely not so bluntly. It made it all seem so very cheap, so utterly sordid. "I'm awfully sorry, but I have no idea of what it is you're talking about."

"How much money you got, Mister Illusdrader?" Frederick asked.

Eustace looked to Olaf for help, but the lad's keen, brave eyes were fixed on the dirt floor. "I . . . well, perhaps fifty dollars or so. With me. Why?"

"Because I think ve maybe take it from you vithout you drawing our picture. And then maybe ve shoot you and put you in the voots for the bears to eat, yah?"

Ice seemed to surge through every one of Eustace's limbs, and his mouth was suddenly too dry to protest. Fear held every muscle as he watched Frederick stand and take a rifle from the wall.

"No, Frederick," came Olaf's voice. "Don't kill him."

Yes! Exhilaration shot through Eustace, melting the ice, replacing it with the fire of love. He had seen the young man's eyes when their fingers had touched, and now was the moment of truth, the moment when Jack Binns would save Maria from Texas Bill. In another second, Eustace was sure of it, Frederick would say the Norwegian equivalent of, "So! Throwin' over yer old pard fer a skirt!" and the battle would begin in earnest, a battle with only one possible ending—happiness, love, eternal devotion!

Olaf looked at him and smiled. "Don't kill him, Frederick." He stood up, walked to the bed, and sat next to Eustace, then took his hand. "Your skin is just as soft and pretty as a vooman's."

Oh yes! As if it was destined! All fear left Eustace's heart as he looked into Olaf's bright blue eyes, felt the warmth of his hand.

"You vant to *be* a vooman . . ."

Olaf, still holding Eustace's hand, began nodding, and the smile on his face twisted to something that terrified Eustace even more than had the prospect of death.

"Ve can *make* you a vooman . . ."

*　　*　　*

The old man arrived a half hour late for work that morning at the Barkley Hotel. Owen Barkley, having noticed that his new guest was absent from breakfast, and recalling his conversation of the day before concerning the Brogger brothers, was quick to formulate an hypothesis, and the old man was quick to ascertain it upon fear of losing his position.

Two hours later, Sheriff Zedediah Dorwart, the town doctor, and three deputies armed with Parker double-barreled shotguns and Winchester .30-30's rode into the clearing that housed the Brogger brothers' cabin. When the sheriff had been told by Owen Barkley that Wiley Andrews had taken an eastern guest out to the cabin on Terry Peak, he had left town immediately with his deputies, fearing for the easterner's welfare, and, with a premonition of violence, had asked the doctor to accompany them. The five horsemen tethered their mounts at the edge of the clearing near a horse they recognized as belonging to Owen Barkley, and the sheriff and deputies walked stealthily toward the cabin. Not until they were within a few yards of the front door did they hear the moans.

Sheriff Dorwart then pulled his Colt Army .45 from its holster, ran to the door, kicked it off its hinges, and followed it swiftly into the single room, where Frederick Brogger leapt from the bed, dashed to the opposite wall, and from it yanked a rifle which he attempted to turn upon the sheriff. The sheriff shot him directly in the chest, and the charge thrust him backward against the wall, down which he proceeded to slide like a sack of lime. He was quite dead when his bare posterior struck the floor.

Olaf Brogger, in the meantime, was trying to dislodge a Colt Dragoon pistol from somewhere within the folds of a red and heaving mass upon the bed, but stopped when two of the deputies pressed the muzzles of their shotguns against his head and upper back. It was not until he stood up, stark naked and smeared with blood, that the lawmen ascertained where it was the gun was lodged. Then two of the men, who had witnessed many gunshot wounds of various and violent types, turned pale, and the sheriff's arm went up to point his pistol directly into Olaf Brogger's face.

"Take it out of him and then drop it," the sheriff said. "And may g_d d_mn your soul, you be gentle."

Olaf did as he was directed, careful to keep his fingers on the grip alone, and not to allow them anywhere near the trigger. The barrel, which had refused to disengage before when forced now slid out smoothly, and Olaf, the shotguns still prodding his skin, dropped the weapon on the floor.

"Doc!" the sheriff called, then said, "Tie his hands." He coughed up and spat out the bile that had risen to his throat. "Chr_st," he said softly of the thing moaning on the bed. "Oh dear Chr_st."

Eustace P. Saunders's toothless mouth was horribly bruised; the flesh of his chest had been severed so that large flaps of skin hung down in a hideous parody of a woman's dugs, and his organs of regeneration had been detached from his body and lay on the dirt floor amid his scattered teeth. His heart's blood was everywhere.

"Is there any way he's gonna live?" one of the older deputies asked the doctor, who shook his craggy head.

"He's lost too much already. Best I can do is make him comfortable," and he drew from his bag a vial and a needle.

"He vanted to be a vooman," Olaf began to say, but the youngest deputy brought up the butt of his shotgun and broke the Norwegian's jaw, knocking him to the floor.

"Sorry, Sheriff, Doc, but d_mn it . . ."

"Never mind," said the sheriff. "Take him outside. And keep him naked."

"And get Mr. Sanders some water," said the doctor, who pulled a blanket over Eustace while the deputies conveyed Olaf outside, where two remained with him while the third got water from a bucket that stood next to the stone stoop. The doctor trickled water into Eustace's mouth until he regained enough consciousness to begin screaming.

"All right, son, all right," said the doctor, jabbing him with the needle. "This'll make you feel better." The doctor shook his head, looked at Olaf, then at the sheriff as the screaming subsided. "I can't believe you're gonna waste a trial on that son of a b_tch. I sure as h_ll don't want to testify about this."

Sheriff Dorwart nodded sagely and examined the lined and leathered face of his eldest deputy. "What do you think?"

"If the doc don't say nuthin', I never will."

The sheriff looked again at Eustace lying on the bed. "Any man does that to another doesn't deserve a trial. I can't be party to it, neither can the deputies, we took oaths. But nobody's to stop you, Doc, from swattin' a horse's _ss."

The doctor smiled grimly. "I'm game for it."

"What about Hippocrates?" the sheriff asked.

"Hippocrates would've cut the b_st_rd's throat himself and laughed about it," the doctor said.

The sheriff sat rapt in contemplation for a long time before he spoke. "Get him ready, Dan." The deputy left the cabin.

"Whe . . . where . . ." Eustace called from the bed. His eyes were open, and he was attempting to raise his head as if to look about the room.

"Just take it easy now," the doctor cautioned.

"Where . . ." said Eustace through his toothless gums. "Where . . . Olaf?"

"He's outside," said the doctor. "He won't hurt you again. He's going for a little ride in a minute."

"Take me," Eustace said through bloody froth. "Want to . . . see."

The doctor looked at the sheriff. "Why not?" Sheriff Dorwart said. "He deserves to see it if any man does." Then he whispered to the doctor. "Will he ever tell?" The doctor shook his head.

When the deputies hauled out the bed on which Eustace lay, Olaf Brogger was saddled naked upon his horse, and a rope trailed from around his neck over the branch of a large tree down to the trunk, where it was firmly tied. The deputies put their strong hands beneath Eustace's shoulders, raising him gently so that he might more easily see the tree, the rump of the horse, Olaf's bare back.

The doctor walked up to the horse and gave it a resounding blow upon the left flank. It whinnied, reared, and bolted, its involuntary rider remaining in the space it had just deserted, his legs jerking, shoulders twitching, the rope twisting so that his choking, swollen face turned toward Eustace, who remembered:

"He turned his face toward her as his horse galloped into the dawn."

Eustace found just enough strength to raise an arm, and, like Maria Prescott, like the Eustace of the painting, wave farewell to his handsome, western lover.

There is nothing that dies so hard as romance.